FRACTURE

Book Three of the RED MAGE Series
Written by XANDER BOYCE

TABLE OF CONTENTS

ACKNOWLEDGMENTS

Every book there are so many people to thank. It's sort of like that saying: It takes a village to raise a child. It takes a crowd to write a book.

Thanks to Ryan, Joe and Amber for making the last fight hit the notes I wanted it to. Thanks to Danielle, Dakota and Chandra for pushing me forward when I couldn't see the next steps. Most of all I want to thank my parents, I don't know where I would be without you.

PROLOGUE

After the tempering, came the storms. The people of before had been soft, and their mettle needed to be tested. Those that held to the old ways fought those who forged a new path. It was their willingness to fight against the powers that were that allowed the forces that would be to rise. Jason, The Destroyer, fought against the dark tides, but it was in the storm that we found our faith; it was there that the Gavel of the Lord was first raised. For it was he that showed us the new path, he that dared to fracture themselves for their fellow men.

This is a story from the time before the Greater Age, before the Hundred Heroes were made strong in the fires of the First Age's death. A tale of the first rebel, a tale for the bright day, for the shadows grow darker. This is the story of those who battered the storms to rise in defiance.

- Taryn Hollingshead, Seer of the First Gate

CHAPTER ONE – CONSOLIDATION

Drew was still covered in the blue goop that passed as manaborn blood. He slid into the chair at the center of the control room. The naga had fought hard for this node, but like the last few he had taken, their resistance had proven ineffective. He glanced over at Aevis and nodded. "Alright, copy control settings from Nat's Park node, allow temporary access to the class four individuals."

"Granting access now," Aevis said, and the room quickly filled with his closest friends. JP punched his shoulder as he passed, the former cop had taken to laying down in front of the monitors for all these meetings. Sarah and Katie were next in, the two women seeking the seats on either side of Drew. Daryl and Luke were last in, Daryl would lean against the back of the room, while Luke would stand behind him, ready to defend against any attacks even here.

"Alright, first thing, pull up the map," Drew instructed the AI, and a map of his territory sprung into view. At the center of the map was the Stadium. Appropriate since, as a Habitat, it was the beating heart of the reclaimed territory. To the west of it were the three nodes that once made up Fort McNair, now they were a Resource Concentrator, a Dungeon Training Center or DTC, and a Biological Growth Accelerator. The south held a single node on the other side of the river, another DTC at the DIA building, and the first node Drew had taken over.

To the east was the former DoT building that had been converted into a Healing Chamber. Northeast of that was the Marine Barracks, which was set up as a Forward Operating Post. The Marines kept themselves mostly separate from everyone else, but they had integrated a little over the last few weeks. Two other nodes were connected to those two. One directly southeast of the DoT building had been designated as a Housing Supplement Node, which was basically just a fancy way of saying it was actual housing, something the Habitat didn't have nearly enough of. East of that was Naval Reactor. Drew wasn't sure what it had been before Advent, but it was now a Xatherite Concentrator.

Sitting between the two Navy Yard nodes was their current location, which Drew had already renamed from the weird alphanumeric designation the system had given it. "So, what are we gonna do with this bad boy?"

Sea Command Purpose Designation Tool
1. Biological Growth Accelerator
2. Dungeon Training Center
3. Forward Operating Base
4. Healing Chamber
5. Mana Funnel
6. Resource Concentrator
7. Feeding Pit
8. Xatherite Concentrator

"No new options," Sarah said with a frown. They had been hoping that ten would be a lucky number. Nothing new had shown up since they took over the DoT building, raising the total connected nodes to seven. That had opened the Forward Operating Base, Habitat Node, and the Housing Supplement Node. They had only been able to assign one each of the Housing Supplement and Habitat nodes. The Sea Command node marked their tenth node, and everyone had been hoping it would unlock something special.

"There will not be any new options until twelve connected nodes." Luke, as a seraph sent from the human protectorate to guard Drew, was the most knowledgeable about the system. "That is when the command node and communications array will become available, as well as a number of other ancillary designators."

"Alright, that doesn't answer the current dilemma, though," JP said from his spot on the floor. "We still don't know what to do with this place."

Drew was slightly envious of the gun expert's prone position. The chair melded to his shape perfectly, but he wouldn't mind taking a nap. It had been almost a month since he had slept last, and he was beginning to miss it. That reminded him to cast energizing rain, bathing the entire room in the exhaustion-chasing warmth of one of his most potent spells.

Energizing rain and the skill it was linked to, Invigorate, were a force multiplier, allowing him nearly constant fully rested uptime to accomplish the work of dozens. Which was a good thing, because Drew and his team were doing the work of at least that many. The naga had been making constant assaults, and Drew's ability to keep their combatants running was turning the tide against their almost insurmountable numbers. Well, that and his ability to carpet bomb half a block in devastating magical spells.

Shifting slightly, Drew moved the sheath at his side so that it wasn't poking into him. The blood-red sword it contained was a constant reminder of the real losses the Advent had taken as its toll. The world was safer now, but they were on a ticking clock. Soon the world bosses were going to spawn, and they were smack dab in the middle of where the most powerful one would be calling home. Hence them clearing out the naga and expanding the safe zone around the stadium.

"Does anything else open up at twelve nodes, Luke?" Drew asked curiously. They didn't have to make a decision right now, the plan was to take over the last two nodes on the yard, finishing what was being called the Naga Campaign.

"No, but I recommend we wait until your next unlocks," Luke said. "The command node will give you much more granular control over the nodes, while the communications array allows us to coordinate our activities easier."

"Well, those both sound like things we're going to want to recess a little away from the front lines," Drew said with a frown, glancing at the map in front of him. "We'll keep this one idle for now, building the remote console, of course, and then convert it to the command node and the next into the comm array. The last one we'll turn into a FOB, I guess." The Forward Operating Base was the only defensive structure he could build. It provided quarters for troops and allowed him to construct stationary weapons and defenses. "Guess this place was meant to be a command center."

They took a few more minutes to rest and talk to Aevis. They had plenty of work to be done, but his people needed some time to decompress. His spells went a long way toward keeping everyone alert and physically ready to respond to danger, but the mental toll was real, even when the mission was as successful as the sea command node had been. The Marines and irregulars outside were taking their own break, the reserves taking over the immediate guard duties while those who had fought caught their breath.

"Alright, ladies and gents, time to make the rounds. We've got a red and two indigos to distribute. I want a nomination from each of you in an hour." Drew's team hadn't gotten any new xatherite since the stadium; they had been giving them to the rest of the combatants. His group would ask around, finding those who had distinguished themselves in the fighting, and the xatherite were then given to the best. Although he already knew where the red was going. Sarah had a red node connected to a green ability that linked all the members of the group, giving them a sense of where everyone was.

The red they had just gotten was a perfect match for that.

| Xatherite Crystal Name: Major Empathy |
| Xatherite Color: Red |

Xatherite Grade: Basic
Xatherite Rarity: Uncommon
Type: Magic
Effect: Enshrouds the target in an aura that reflects a portion of the damage they receive back to the attacker. Lasting for 10 seconds.
Mana recharge time: 57.4 seconds.

It was a perfect match for Sarah's usual role as the group's tactical shot-caller, allowing her to buff whoever was about to receive damage and hurting the attacker. Drew suspected that it would link with her mind connection and add a damage reflection ability to the group. Drew had harvested the red, as he had the other two they had found since they killed Gonzales in the passages under the stadium. Daryl had collected the indigos, they were both useful scouting abilities, but nothing that would drastically increase the effectiveness of Drew's group.

The first was called sharp sight, and it essentially allowed people to magically track things. Useful in the right hands, but Drew's group was far more likely to be busting heads than looking for heads to bust. The second was a variation on Daryl's telepathy ability. It allowed the user to receive messages from select individuals designated at the time of casting. It was useful but would be more valuable in the hands of someone like Colonel Hoeffecker, who was in charge of all military operations.

Drew did his own rounds. This was one of Drew's least favorite parts of these missions, not that he didn't like talking to the men. But there was inevitably someone who wanted to suck up to him by telling him how great he was. Katie rescued him from the overzealous irregular that was giving him a play by play of his own battle against the giant naga that was acting as the guardian of the node.

"Sir, I have an urgent message from command. If you could, please follow me." Katie kept a straight face as she rescued him.

Drew made a quick apology for leaving and then followed after the brunette. "Thank you!" Drew said, looking around, he frowned when he realized that there were too many people around to justify spending some alone time with his… girlfriend? They hadn't really defined their relationship at this point; they had been too busy to take more than a few minutes of stolen kisses since the dome went up.

"Sadly, it's true, the major sent a runner," Katie said, the careful smile she kept when they were in public slipping slightly. "Looks like the naga are getting ready to mount a counteroffensive."

Drew let out an exasperated sigh. There was just no winning with the naga. They had put down hundreds today, but it seemed like every time they killed one, two more took their place. A counteroffensive meant that Drew would probably have to do more chain storm casting. After they had made the housing expansion node, Drew had stupidly upgraded his storm spell to the next tier.

Xatherite Crystal Name: Squall
Xatherite Color: Red
Xatherite Grade: Advanced
Xatherite Rarity: Common
Type: Magic
Effect: Create a localized storm around a target. The storm will have a radius of 15m and will cause high amounts of wind, water, and lightning damage within its radius.
Complete Linked Skill bonus: Double benefit from your mana discharge stat.
Elemental Tempest Constellation: Elemental effects doubled.

> Total effect: Create a localized storm around a target. The storm will have a radius of 15m and will cause ample amounts of wind, water, and lightning damage within its radius.
> Mana recharge time: 1 minute, 17 seconds.

Stupidly, because it now did a ton more damage, and lasted longer, but he could only cast three or four squall variants before he went into mana fatigue. Which meant he had to be much more choosy about when and where he cast his big AoE spells. The limit was based on how many elements he put into them, the more links, the less he could do before he was tapped out, with one exception. He had avoided upgrading his holy shield, and since it was three tiers lower in grade that dragged the whole spell down a tier from all his other ones.

The major wanted him back at the housing annex. It was the tallest building in the area by a far shot and protected by the shield. Drew glanced back at the tired soldiers who were getting roused to fight against the swarm again and sighed.

"I hate having to run away like this," Drew murmured to Katie.

"It's not running away, it's taking a tactical position." Katie had been working on getting the fortifications ready while everyone else was resting, and he could tell she was worn out. Her primary ability was creating walls. Incredibly helpful in just about every aspect of battle, she could create short walls that made it nearly impossible to advance, or strong bulwarks to fight from. Like Drew, she was too valuable to risk unless they had to, which meant that unless there was a node to take, Drew was sitting in the safety of the shield, killing from a distance.

It didn't feel right to him. At this point, it was a well-trodden argument between the two coasties. Katie was more than happy to stay where it was safe. There was something in Drew's blood that craved the adrenaline of a fight. Reaching the top of the tower after five minutes of uncomfortable silence from

Katie, he looked around and then rolled up his sleeves, mostly to hide the fact that they had gotten shredded again; if Min Sun saw them, she'd give him another ear lashing. The former seamstress wasn't as scary as Katie when she was angry, but it was close.

CHAPTER TWO – PRICES

Finishing off the seals for a holy frostfire storm, Drew could feel the mana fatigue come over him. Invigorate would be off cooldown soon, so he slumped back against the wall and waited. Over the naga campaign, Drew had discovered that the holy variants of his spells caused less mana fatigue. Now that he was running into mana fatigue, Drew had uncovered many interesting things about how his linked spells worked. He had also gotten very good at determining how much mana fatigue a spell would give him.

Each spell had a mana cost attached to it. When Drew had channeled a certain amount of mana through his body, mana fatigue would happen. The base squall spell, for example, got him ten percent of the way to mana fatigue. Gravity squall as an advanced linked spell was his most expensive ability, and it took him fifteen percent of the way to mana fatigue. Holy frostfire storm, despite using four links, was still classified as an intermediate grade linked spell. It only cost him about seven percent of his mana fatigue, likely due to holy shield being such a lower tier.

Comparing that to his fireball spell, which only used up about half a percent of his fatigue, even when he combined three xatherite into holy frostfireball. The problem, of course, came any time he combined the master grade gravitas spell with… well, anything. Gravity point, the upgraded version of his gravity ball, had actually changed its name when he upgraded to greater fireball, and he hadn't noticed. It cost him a full two percent of his fatigue to cast despite only having two linked spells.

That was the main reason he hadn't upgraded any more of his xatherite, despite nearly all of them being ready to upgrade. Well, at least all of the normal rarity ones. Aeon, the singular rarity xatherite he got from Ares, still hadn't even become attuned. For that matter, stricto mentis clypeus—Ares' other gift—was limited in rarity and also hadn't become attuned. Minor mana tap, minor holy shield, major lightning bolt, major acid arrow, major mana sight, major blink step, greater fireball, and greater cone of frost were all still rare grade. They were all ready to be upgraded, but after the debacle that was his squall upgrade, he had been putting it off.

None of his advanced tier xatherite had even leveled up. With a frown, Drew turned to Luke, who was almost always near him these days. "Any idea why I haven't leveled any of my advanced tier xatherite yet?"

"Of course." Luke paused as he organized his thoughts. "Xatherite are usually broken down into three categories: low, mid, and high. Low and mid xatherite gain in levels by, well, just having them slotted and living life. They grow faster if you actively use them or are in combat situations, but you do not have to do anything, and they will still grow. High-grade xatherite, which are the advanced, master, and legendary grades, improve slightly differently.

"For example, the mark III full-body suit is required to absorb a certain amount of damage before it upgrades to master grade," Luke said, pointing to the chain chomp around his ankle. The ball and chain was the dormant form of the suit, which Luke couldn't regularly use because of the limited mana on Earth.

"So, you can only level it once a month here?" Drew asked, frowning down at the ball.

"No, it can take damage in the ball form, although I think it receives reduced credit for that," Luke said, shaking his head. "The problem is that all of my xatherite are… known. The seraphs have long figured out what they do, what it takes to upgrade them, and what xatherite link best with them. Your xatherite are new; the system's rarity setting is… a bit of a misnomer. I have never seen the exact versions of most of your spells, think of it more as how much mana it takes to use them than anything else."

"So, they won't go up until I figure out what the hidden requirements are, and I have no way of determining what those hidden requirements are," Drew summarized.

"For the most part, yes," Luke answered.

The cooldown on invigorate was up, so Drew cast that on himself and then leaned back. He wasn't sure if the headache was coming from the idea of how little he knew about his xatherite or the mana fatigue, but he was hoping it would die down soon. They had been up here for hours while the newly conquered node was fortified. Katie had set up a location in the rear of the node where Drew could cast invigorating deluge. Daryl, standing next to him, was keeping track of the naga movements. When they gathered to make another push, Drew would cast a storm.

Rinse and repeat. The process of creating the fortress-like city around the stadium was almost entirely on Katie's shoulders, her create wall spell had upgraded to fashion bulwark... five, maybe six days ago? Drew couldn't remember the exact date, everything had become a constant blur of activity. The naga looked like they were pulling back now that the walls were up, though. They would probably try to burrow through beyond, but that response would need to come from the fighters on the ground.

Drew, Luke, and Daryl stayed at their overwatch position for another twenty minutes before Colonel Hoeffecker found them. Drew saluted the other officer, but she waved it away. "Sit down, Drew. You look like you could use it."

Drew returned to the cement of the roof. "What can I do for you, colonel?" They were both so busy that he rarely saw the colonel unless he was invigorating her.

"Came to discuss the last two nodes on the yard," Hoeffecker said, looking out over what had essentially become a warzone. "Scouts that went into the next one said it was full of paper monsters."

"What?" Drew stared at her in confusion. "What is a paper monster?"

"I don't know, they just described it as a paper monster," Hoeffecker said. Turning to look at Drew, she studied him for a minute. "You need to sleep."

"I'm fine, ma'am. Invigorate has been keeping me running just fine," Drew said, even as Hoeffecker pulled a bag of jerky out of her pouch and threw it at him. Drew attempted to catch it, but it slipped through his hands, impacting his chest.

"No, it's not. You're the only one who hasn't gotten any sleep in the last month. You're awake and mentally present, but you're getting slower. Make a mistake like that in a dungeon, and it could cost your life. The naga aren't going anywhere, we've got a solid defensive structure in place. You will be getting some sleep, lieutenant, that is an order."

Drew opened his mouth to argue but then stopped and forced himself to do a mental check. Physically, he felt just fine; his muscles weren't sore. His reactions would be faster in the dungeon, he had let his guard down since they were safe behind the shield, but he'd been hogging all the invigorates for himself lately. Needing them to keep himself alert enough to be useful, and to deal with the mana fatigue.

"Drew, get some sleep," Luke urged. "Trust us to keep things moving while you recover."

Looking between the two for a moment, Drew let out a heavy sigh. "Alright, but we should plan the attack first."

"Nope, we can plan when you're not burned to the wick. Your ideas will be better then anyway. I'll tell the men to get into a holding pattern and to plan around not getting boosted while you're out," Hoeffecker said, giving him a soft smile to remove the bite from her words.

Drew got up with a grunt and waved goodbye. Luke and Daryl followed him. "I think I actually have a room here…" Drew trailed off, remembering that had been part of the node claim. When the housing annex had been created, he noticed a center column that housed the lift. Different from an elevator because you stood on a platform and thought of what floor you wanted to go to. You would then be moved to that location, without any delay or disorientation.

Most floors could be accessed by anyone, and the thought of where you wanted to go was somewhat nebulous. You could specify a level or your house. Or even someone you wanted to visit, which would take you to where they currently were. Drew thought of his own home, and suddenly the group was at the top of the building. A large penthouse had been set aside for him—as the owner of the node—Drew had only been there once before, not needing a place to sleep. He picked a door at random, waving the other two off as he closed the door behind him.

A large room, centered around a bed that was much larger than Drew was used to sleeping in, was next to a massive window that looked north, giving him a view of the Anacostia River. His eyes caught as they scanned the horizon. Just visible behind the curve of a hill was the Coast Guard Headquarters building. He couldn't see it, but knowing it was there reminded him of where all the madness started; he hadn't been back there in weeks. He wondered if the wereghast of his friend Rob was still there.

Thinking about Rob made him turn his attention further to the southwest. He could just barely see Reagan Airport, which was mostly unrecognizable at this point. Nature was working hard to reclaim everything, but the area where the sidhe seed ship had landed had already turned into a forest. The trees looked nothing like the ones on Earth, though, the green had just a bit too much purple in it for terrestrial flora. "What are you doing?" he mused aloud.

The actions of aliens aside, Drew pulled off his boots with pleasure, wriggling his toes as he stripped down. With a start, he realized that he had nothing to change into, so he headed to the bathroom and took a quick shower. Looking in the mirror, he wondered if it would be possible to get a haircut. His wavy hair was getting long enough now that the sides were flipping up, giving him wings. He hadn't had his hair this long since… middle school. The curls always made him cut it long before it got to that stage before joining the military and after it had been kept short by regulation.

Briefly, Drew considered at least trimming it with his knife, but decided it would look worse like that than it did currently, although not by much. The bed was calling to him, and he sunk into the sheets. The bed felt too large, and Zoey wasn't there to lean against him. He pulled the covers over his head to block out the light and closed his eyes. He could feel sleep beckoning him, but a part of him wondered if he would wake up in the presence of some ancient god if he fell asleep.

The military had ingrained the need to catch sleep whenever possible, though, and he went through some of the relaxation exercises he had learned. Slowly the tension drained from his body, and sleep claimed his mind.

* * *

It was his stomach that woke him up. Drew could smell food. Sitting up, he saw a tray next to him with a bowl of stew and some bread. The sky outside was light, but it was lashed by the rainbow-colored rain of a mana storm.

The bread had become a luxury that Drew was happy to eat, even after testing the stew and finding it was cold. Chewing on the crust, he watched the storm as he got dressed again. His gear was significantly worse for wear, the cockroach shells that made up his armor having numerous long scratches on them. The clothes were worn, with holes on the elbows and knees, mostly where he had fallen or rolled to avoid attacks. His mana rampart spell had a slowing effect on it that made dodging much easier, but that didn't make the ground impacts any more fun.

The last thing he put on was Robbi's blood sword. Drew had woken up with the blade after taking over the stadium. It no longer drank blood or changed shape like it had for Robbi, and Drew was by no means skilled in its use. He wore it more as a reminder than anything else, a reminder of the costs paid. He couldn't see any of Arlington through the storm, but he imagined the jungle was only going to get bigger. Reminding him that there were undoubtedly more bills coming.

CHAPTER THREE – FORWARD

Stepping out of his room, Drew almost tripped on Luke's slumbering form. The seraph was sleeping across the floor in front of his door. As he moved to step over him, the chain chomp rustled the painted on face, pointing itself at Drew. That was enough to wake Luke up, and he sat up before Drew was more than a few paces away.

"Morning, Luke," Drew said with a grin as Luke rubbed the crust from his eyes.

"What time is it?" Luke muttered blearily.

Drew cast an invigorate on him, the tired look in his eyes inspiring mercy. "No idea, mana storm going on outside so… sometime after dark, I would guess." Mana storms appeared every five days right before dusk and lasted a few hours. Which meant that it was relatively close to that point still.

"Mana storm?" Luke did the math in his head. "We must have been asleep for about a day and a half then." Arching his back in a stretch, he worked the muscles that had become stiff from disuse.

"I already had food, but we can get some for you if needed," Drew said, glancing around. There was no sign of Daryl, but he could have easily been in any of the closed doors off of the main suite.

At the mention of food, Luke's stomach grumbled. "Yeah, I could do with some food."

The two headed down to the main cafeteria. A couple of people were busy cleaning, but there was a pot kept with some of the stew from dinner. Grabbing a bowl each, they sat at one of the tables, Drew taking the time to watch the people around them as they ate. He didn't get a chance to interact much with the regular people of the stadium. A few of them gave him an odd glance like they sort of knew who he was but weren't quite sure, the rest treated them like any other late-night eaters.

By the time they were finished with their silent meal, Drew was ready to get away. The initial stares had multiplied as people discreetly pointed at him and told their neighbors who was eating with them. Drew hadn't had a chance to eat in the cafeterias often lately, and he had the feeling he wasn't going to do it again soon. The feeling of having people stare at him and whisper while he ate was a distinctly uncomfortable one.

"Alright, let's go find the major." Drew said, unable to handle the whispering from the crowd.

"You mean Colonel Hoeffecker?" Luke asked with a grin. Drew kept forgetting that she had been promoted.

"Oh, right. Let's go find the colonel," Drew said with a nod. Heading to the lift, he tried to jump to her, but she didn't appear to be in the building. With the mana storm going on, they couldn't leave, and Drew had no desire to wait where people could stare at him. So, he went back to his room to wake up Daryl. He was surprised to find Sarah and Daryl talking at the table while eating. Apparently, they had gotten food from somewhere better than the cafeteria, since they each had pieces of bread to go along with their stew.

"Hey, Drew!" Sarah said with a wave of her bread. "We were just going over the plan for the next node." A rough representation of the node had been created using various objects on the table. Drew took a moment to figure out what each object represented. He had been battling over this territory for so long that it didn't take him long. While he studied the node, Sarah and Daryl ate their food; Luke took a spot at the table by turning a chair around and leaning his shoulders against the back of it.

"So, this is the last neutral one?" Drew asked. While none of the nodes changed colors like the red ones he claimed or the two violet ones in Arlington, somehow the naga had taken over additional nodes and were using them to make more naga.

"As far as we can tell, the naga are down to one node, the one over in the parking lot there," Sarah said, pointing. "This last one they skipped, which probably means that the native monster spawns weren't something they wanted to fight."

"Why aren't we just skipping it too? Get rid of the naga first?" They didn't quite have a clear line of attack, but they could swing around from the northeast, bypassing the building.

"Hoeffecker doesn't want to leave an enemy behind our front lines. We're doing a clean sweep down the line so that there are no surprises," Sarah responded.

Nodding his head in thought, Drew considered the map. "Alright, so what is the plan? Coasties go in, take the node while the other teams cover defense?"

Sarah swallowed her food quickly and nodded. "Sort of, they want you to do another barrage, knock out these two snake totems." She pointed to two cups that were positioned to the south and east of the HR building. They had killed a few of them before; no one was exactly sure what they did, but the naga didn't like it when you destroyed them. "Then, we deal with the naga counter-attack. After that gets beaten back, we'll delve into the DTC and claim the node."

"Is it just us for this one?" Drew frowned; they'd been taking various groups with them on their delves to get them used to the process and get them some experience.

"Yeah, Hoeffecker wants to keep as many of the teams topside as she can, since she isn't sure how the naga will respond." Sarah hesitated for a minute before saying, "Instead, she's having us bring some of the kids." She was watching Drew's reaction carefully.

"The kids?" Drew frowned, they had made it a rule that anyone under eighteen couldn't join one of the squads, and were instead assigned duties inside the stadium. There ended up being a gap, with most of the kids over sixteen having xatherite but not being able to use them. "No, absolutely not."

"They've been through training, and they're just there to get some levels in their xatherite. We're only bringing ones with defensive and offensive powers, so they won't be helpless if they get separated," Sarah said, pulling out a few pieces of paper and handing them over to Drew. It contained a list of the kids they were bringing as well as their xatherite.

Drew clenched his jaw as he studied the list. It was clear why Hoeffecker wanted them to get some experience, most of these kids already had better powers than a lot of the active squad members. He even recognized some of them. One was the lightsaber kid he had rescued in the DIA building. He apparently also had a shielding ability that blocked ranged attacks; it was a low-grade ability that could be quite powerful if leveled up.

Studying the list told him that all of them had indeed been carefully selected. They all had abilities that would benefit drastically from the bonus experience given to everyone in the party when Drew claimed a node. "I don't like it," Drew said with a frown. "We banned the kids for a good reason. Their instincts were terrible, and even if their powers were good, they kept getting into trouble."

"We need them," Sarah said with a sigh. "It's getting worse out there, Drew. We've had to double our scavenger group sizes. And even then, they're bringing back less and less every day. We're mostly self-sufficient now, but we haven't found anyone to the north for a week. The naga are blocking the eastern routes… and from what we can tell about Arlington…" Sarah trailed off since Drew was well aware of the changes that were happening to the southwest.

"Still just two," Drew said with a sigh. A few days after he had woken up in the stadium, one of the nodes to the southwest where the sidhe seed ship had landed had turned violet, another followed a week later. It wasn't for sure that the sidhe had managed to take over those nodes, but the odds against it weren't good.

"Alright, so the fact of the matter is that we need the kids, we need as many people as we can get. And you are the best chance they have of upgrading their xatherite without dying, so these three kids are going to come with us as we take over the node," Sarah said with a sigh. Drew could tell that the ensign didn't want to bring them along any more than he did. But they were all picking between poisons at this point.

"Fine, but we're going to get them equipped with some proper equipment. I need to replace mine anyway, so we'll bring Min Sun all the stuff we've been hoarding and see if she can't upgrade us." Drew held up his arm, showing off the hole in the elbow of his uniform.

Sarah wrinkled her nose, and then nodded. "Probably a good idea, anyway. Once we're done with the node, Hoeffecker wants to head into the naga's den as soon as possible, unless we have run into a lot more trouble than you can handle."

He glanced at the table and made some mental calculations. "Can we secure it that quickly?" Drew asked. They had been playing a game of slowly advancing trench warfare for the last few weeks.

"We won't need to if we can take out the naga nest. They won't be able to mount a counter-attack anyway, so our forward push is all the fortification that we'll need," Sarah answered.

"Yay for being surrounded by angry snake men as we invade their homes," Drew remarked dryly.

"Well, it's better than the alternatives," Daryl said. Drew glanced over at the scout and quirked an eyebrow, Daryl shrugged. "We all know we're on a clock for whatever is happening in Arlington; we can't afford to let the sidhe dig in much more. So after we take out the last two nodes, Hoeffecker is going to send us there."

Drew frowned. Going to Arlington meant going to his… well, not home, since the amount of movement that the military required meant he didn't really have a true home, but going to Zoey. After a month, he wasn't sure what to expect, odds were both she and his roommate Lincoln were dead. But he couldn't pretend that the need to know what had happened to them didn't eat at him. "Yeah, I guess we need to go put a stop to what they're doing either way."

"If they can take over nodes, then we need to stop them," Luke said with a frown. "I was hoping that it was just a lower-ranking member of the Fae. But this means that it is one of the higher-order sidhe. They are like weeds, not too hard to root out at first, but if you give them enough time to dig in, they are nearly impossible to remove."

"We can't be sure that it's the sidhe taking over the nodes," Sarah said with a frown. "It could be that some of the humans have leveled up and can take them over now. I mean, the Pentagon is there. There are bound to be high-ranking officers there, any of them might have become capable of claiming a node."

It was an old argument they had been arguing back and forth ever since the first node had been claimed. Drew rubbed his forehead; he was sick of hearing it. "We've gone over this, and there is no way to know until we get to the other side," Drew said, meeting Sarah's eyes. "Until then, let's work on the things that we can handle. Where are the kids now?"

Sarah met his eyes, glaring back for a second before visibly letting it go. "They should be in the complex somewhere."

"Alright, let's go grab them so we can be ready to go when the storm lets up. I imagine Min Sun is back at the stadium proper?" Drew asked, and Sarah nodded her head. "Alright. Might as well grab everyone and see if she can refit us all. We're all looking a bit ragged at this point." Drew's group had been in the thickest fighting for the last two weeks, and it was beginning to show.

CHAPTER FOUR – UPGRADE

The new armor was awesome. Min Sun had dyed several pieces of thick crocodile hide a deep navy blue, then layered blackened snake scales over the chest and back, protecting the most vulnerable spots with an extra layer of armor. A strap system allowed him to loosen pieces up and vent air to cool down a little without having to take the entire thing off. Since Drew rarely actually slept, he kept his armor on most of the time and this would allow him to relax during those few moments when he took a break.

The leg armor was similar: large blackened scales across Drew's thighs and hips with a built-in place to store one of pappy's bags. Like the chest armor, there were additional straps to allow him to loosen and cool off. Thick boots with a heavy tread, gloves, vambraces, and a set of snake scale pauldrons in the same style completed the set, leaving him mobile while concealing the vast majority of his skin. A thick leather cap protected his skull, but it was far too hot to wear unless he was worried about an attack.

On each lapel was the single silver bar of his Lieutenant Junior Grade rank. It was still strange to him not to have his old chevrons on the uniform.

Everyone else was being equipped similarly, although it was clear that most of them were in the prototype versions of the gear that Drew now wore. Min Sun's tailoring xatherite was hard at work, making sure all the new armor fit the wearer. Drew enjoyed trying to figure out how the armor had evolved as he watched everyone else get equipped. A series of buckles would appear, go through a refinement or two and then disappear, only to be replaced by a different configuration repeated on three different sets. Drew cast invigorate on Min Sun, allowing her to make rapid-fire adjustments.

Sarah and Katie's armor took the longest. Min Sun had to rework a large portion of the sides of the chest piece to accommodate their frames. The three kids they were bringing along with them were off to one side; they were in a very basic set of armor that looked like it had been mass-produced to fit a wide variety of people. They had already been issued armor, probably while Drew was sleeping. The lightsaber kid was named Gary. His only weapon was the lightsaber at his hip. Drew couldn't help but be a little jealous of the fact that the kid got a laser sword.

Next to Gary was a thin Asian teenager that Drew assumed was Joe. Joe's weapon was a long rebar pole that he leaned against like a staff. He had a red xatherite called adderstrike, one of a dozen variants of skills that allowed his melee attacks to deal more damage once every few seconds. The kid also had an orange buff called fox's agility, which made him faster and more dexterous. London was the third kid; the taller girl had dreads tied into a clump behind her head. Taller than the two boys by half a head, she had no visible weapons, but Drew knew that the pouch at her side probably contained pebbles.

London's powers were a mix of Gambit and Jubilee. Her attack ability allowed her to charge a rock up, causing it to become like a grenade, exploding eight seconds later. Her defensive ability was called dazzle, and it shot off a bunch of bright lights in a cone from her hand. They didn't do any damage on their own but allowed her to blind and damage her foes when combined with her charge ability. Lastly, she had a violet that turned her sweat into some sort of neurotoxin that would numb anything biological that it got on. The notes on her powers had told him to avoid talking to her about it. Apparently, she was sensitive as it had caused some incidents.

Drew winced, realizing that she had a bit of Rogue in her as well. He thought about going over and talking to them, but he discovered that being randomly friendly with people ended up being even more awkward now than before the Advent.

Drew walked over to JP, who was practicing pulling guns out of various holsters that had been cleverly disguised by the snake scales. The armor made the former cop appear larger and more intimidating while only partially hiding the plethora of guns he kept about his person.

"Hey," Drew said with a nod. "What do you think of the kids?"

JP paused for a moment and then shrugged. "I'm sure they'll be fine; most of them won the xatherite lottery. Very few people have both attack and defensive abilities. I think they'll surprise everyone when things hit the fan."

Drew glanced back at the kids who were shooting the two of them edgy looks, clearly understanding that they were being talked about. "Huh, they don't have hearing upgrades do they?"

"I think the Jedi-kid has something that lets him know when others are paying attention to him," JP said with a shrug. "Kind of surprising really, how cohesive his xatherite move toward making him exactly like a Jedi."

"It happens if you have a clear enough ideal in your head," Luke said, having joined them when Drew wasn't looking, the seraph's near-constant presence not really a surprise at this point. "That is how we build units. We are taught a way of approaching the world and are given plenty of examples. That is how I got chomp, actually." He pointed to the ball and chain around his leg.

"One of the main parts of my training to come here was learning about your culture. That included playing your video games." Luke smiled slightly. "It is always interesting what the frontier planets create to replace some of the more advanced aspects of civilization."

"You don't have video games?" Drew asked with a frown. He obviously hadn't been playing many lately, but he had played a significant amount in his lifetime.

"Not like here; we would never do something so silly," Luke said with a frown. "The Protectorate's entertainment is all based around the war. People watch tournaments and wargames. I will admit that my own childhood was not normal, but even then… few people have the luxury of doing something purely for entertainment. We have very different problems than the ones you had before Advent."

The three men looked at each other awkwardly before Drew finally shrugged. "Well, I guess this is one of those instances where my mountain is your molehill and vice versa." Drew turned back to the kids. "What is your opinion on including the kids, Luke?"

"I am actually the one that suggested we bring them," the seraph said after a moment of consideration. "In the Protectorate, you are an adult as soon as you receive your map. This will be as safe a delve as they could hope for. Many would pay dearly to have a red mage escort their progeny through a dungeon. I think you worry yourself needlessly. You will be surprised at how well they do, and if they are not strong enough, we will have three fewer stomachs to fill."

Drew wasn't sure how to respond to the seraph. It was evident to him that Luke saw the world through a completely different lens than he did. "Right," he said after a few breaths, still not sure what to think of the blond man. The man had saved his life more than once over the past few weeks, risking his own body to protect Drew, and he couldn't fault his courage, but he had a feeling that he didn't value human life nearly as much as Drew had been taught to.

Standing in uncomfortable silence, the three men waited. Min Sun made short work of the uniforms, though, and the rest of the group was ready to go just a few minutes later. Sarah had the golden bar of rank on her lapels, while Katie had a chief's anchor, a rate awarded to her after the naga attack on the stadium. None of the others had any military ranks on their uniforms, although they all had a patch of the Coast Guard symbol's crossed anchors on their shoulder.

The colonel had been adamant that each of the new units needed their own individual unit patches to create cohesion. Drew's group had been unanimously called the coasties for so long that it had made sense to just use the already existing symbols. Drew wasn't sure how he felt about people who weren't actually members of the Coast Guard using the logo; Hoeffecker had said it would help. It was just strange to have a unit patch; coasties didn't do that. Hats or t-shirts with unit information were the only things you could wear with your uniform.

Just another part of the apocalypse, but then again, wearing giant crocodile and snake armor also wasn't a traditional part of his Coast Guard uniform. Life was weird. "Alright, let's head out," Drew said with a shrug.

Drew had been through some of the bunker systems in Europe from World War II on tour, and traveling to the front lines felt similar. Katie's distinctive walls had created a network of tunnels that burrowed through the once-open streets around the stadium. They regularly passed rooms full of dirty men and women who were sleeping or playing cards. The ready response teams that were never far from the front line of the war. Drew could feel their eyes on him as they walked past. The quiet whispers followed him everywhere he went these days.

It was unnerving. It was how Drew imagined movie stars were treated, and he could understand a little better when they would lash out at the fans and paparazzi that trailed them. Getting to the front line was almost a blessing. They were still a few hundred feet from the DTC entrance, but there were few nagas around. Already the noose was being tightened around them, and they had been pushed back on either side of the building they were going to be entering.

They waited in the shadow of a summoned wall while Daryl scouted ahead, his invisible bird making sure that nothing was going to ambush them when they made their way to the entrance. After a few minutes of searching, Daryl's telepathic voice told them it was safe, and Luke led the way out. The large seraph's eyes scanned the newly created courtyard before he allowed Drew to exit the safety of his concealed position.

Drew stepped out into the open air and walked toward the DTC's entrance; his new dark blue armor did nothing to conceal his approach across the concrete. He could feel the eyes on him again, who knew how many people on the front lines were watching him enter the DTC, watching him go forth to conquer their enemies. The weight of their expectations was an almost physical presence. It caused him to straighten his posture, and he walked forward, trying to project confidence.

There was no way to tell if it worked, but it calmed down Drew's nerves a little. He only relaxed when they opened the door, and he entered the DTC. Glancing behind him to make sure the door was closed, he let go for a moment, relaxing back into his usual self. He could feel the magic. The white lines under his feet from the leylines converging under the node were almost relaxing. He breathed in the air, which reminded him of a library. The smell of old paper seemed off, but he smiled.

"Let's go Fahrenheit 451, people," Drew said with a grin, and he gestured for Luke to take the main tunnel forward.

CHAPTER FIVE – O.C.F.C

The office building was enormous. The first area they entered had clearly once been a lobby. A reception desk was off to one side, and there were splatters of blue blood scattered around the entire room—evidence of the failed attempts by the naga to take over the node. They advanced carefully through the room, but nothing attacked them. When they had a good position, Drew nodded to London.

"Light her up," Drew commanded London, who looked around and then shot sparkling lights into the room to illuminate the dark corners.

"This place is crazy," the teen responded as she looked through the now-illuminated room.

Moving through the next hallway, they found more evidence of the naga invasion—blue blood was splattered across the wall—when they suddenly heard a loud rasping. To Drew, it had the distinct sound of dozens of people continually turning pages in a book. They waited as the sound got louder, everyone ducking back behind cover even as London launched more of her sparkling lights down the corridor, illuminating it in flashes of red, purple, and green.

What came around the corner of the big room they were looking at was a massive cloud of loose paper swirling in the shape of a dust storm. Drew immediately shot a fireball at it. The cloud tried to dodge with an angry rasping sound, but at least half of the swarm took the blast head-on and burst into flame. The fire quickly spread to the rest of the paper, and it went up in a flash of heat and light, burning for a few seconds before the entire creature had been consumed.

Everyone waited in silence, holding their breath while waiting to see if any additional monsters would appear. After almost a minute of near silence, broken only by the sharp inhalations of breath around them, everyone slowly got back to their feet.

"I think it is clear," Luke said, and he began leading the way down the corridor. It opened up into a large room with several cubicles set up. One side of the room was made up of windows that cast a strange light over the cubicles, leaving most of the room shrouded in darkness that was broken by the flashes of light as London's ability filled the room.

Drew could tell he would get a headache from the multicolored light, which seemed to come in every color that fireworks did. Each color lasted for a few seconds and then faded out, but there were almost always multiple colors going at any given point in time. It created strange shadows that would take some getting used to before they were really comfortable with them. Luke made his way into the room, walking through the cubicles, the chain chomp floating behind him, darting around like it had a mind of its own.

About halfway through the room, the cube farm opened up into a small alcove. Here a large copier and a few tables had been set up around a water cooler. It felt like an ambush to Drew, but he couldn't tell what it would be. That feeling was reinforced when Gary said, "I can feel something aggressive looking at us."

Halfway across the space, Luke paused, some noise alerting him to the necessity even as an explosion of black ink erupted out of the copier and blanketed the entire group. Several droplets caught on Drew's exposed flesh and started to burn. A barrage of attacks hit the copier, which had come to life and was charging at Luke. Drew launched a lightning bolt, which crackled around the copier, the stun on the bolt taking effect. JP shot several rounds into the machine, all of them loaded with his sonic bullets, and sent pieces of plastic, glass, and metal flying.

Luke's chain chomp smashed into the side even as the copier opened its top portion to try to bite the seraph. Joe's rebar pole hit the printer simultaneously from the other side, and the printer seemed to crumple. But it was Gary who ended up killing the beast, his lightsaber cleanly bisecting the machine in another explosion of ink. Drew immediately cast refreshing rain in an attempt to get the acidic ink off his skin and heal the minor wounds it had caused.

"Sound off, anyone injured?" Sarah called out, and a chorus responded in the affirmative even as Drew realized that Luke and Gary were bent over and clutching their eyes.

"It got in my eyes," Gary said. "It burns like crazy."

"Bend back, let the rain wash it out," Drew said while Sarah helped Luke and Joe helped Gary turn their heads up so that Drew's rain could wash the acid out. Meanwhile, Drew was on the lookout for any more monsters that would take advantage of their vulnerability to attack. It took a few minutes, and once they were clear, Sarah cast a heal on the two men.

As soon as Gary was feeling better, he took Joe's stick of rebar and began hitting the copier. "I. HATE. COPIERS!" he shouted, his words between each hit. Drew glanced at Katie and Sarah and raised an eyebrow, silently asking if he should step in. They both shook their heads.

Sarah mouthed, "Just let him work it out," to him, where the kid couldn't see them.

Drew nodded slightly, and they waited until the kid's breathing had become ragged. He stepped up next to him and put a hand on his shoulder. "You okay there, Office Space?"

The kid turned and looked at him in confusion. "Office Space?"

"Yeah, there was a… movie where a bunch of upset office workers steal their copier and beat it up with a bat." Drew pointed to the remains of the copier on the floor. "Sort of like that."

"Oh," Gary said, and there was a strange blankness to his voice. "I… guess I'll never get to watch another movie."

Drew awkwardly patted the kid on the back, unsure how to respond. He shot Katie a 'help me' glance. To his frustration, she just grinned and gave him a thumbs up. London and Joe came over to stand next to Gary. The three teenagers huddled close together, giving each other the emotional support of their presence.

"Alright, so… from now on, I'm just going to gravball any printers we see," Drew announced to awkward chuckles from the rest of the group. A couple more paper swarms attacked them, but given how much sound they made, the group always had plenty of time to get ready, and Drew's fireball burned them to ashes. So the rest of the room was crossed pretty uneventfully.

The next room looked like it had been initially a large cafeteria, but all the tables had been pushed to the side, and a large number of office chairs had gathered in the center. They were all clustered in a circle around two office chairs who were spinning around erratically.

Everyone stopped and stared. It took Drew a minute to realize they had walked in on an office chair fight club. The others got there eventually as one of the chairs managed to knock the other onto its side. The circled chairs all flapped their cushions in celebration. "Holy shit," JP said.

Drew thought that was the wrong thing to say because, aside from the sound of the two chairs fighting, the room had been almost deathly silent. JP's words sent a ripple through the chairs, and there were a few squeaks of metal on metal as the chairs all turned to look at them. Both sides sat there and stared for a moment, taking in the absurdity of the entire situation, and then the chairs charged.

Immediately, Drew launched a gravball in the middle of the group. Fireball and its other elemental variants exploded out in a fan at the same time, and he felt a slight hit as he channeled enough mana at once to be felt. The rain of destruction was enough to knock most of the chairs off course, except those in the center hit by gravball. Those crumpled together in a screech of metal and a puff of cushioning.

The closest part of the circle was devastated by Drew's attacks, but the second line advanced without concern. Drew could hear the report of shots as JP unloaded sonic rounds into the chairs. London shot more fireworks that caught the chairs on fire but did little to slow them down. Katie stopped the charge; a two-inch tall wall spread across the entire room, causing all the chairs to lurch forward and then land on their sides. Their momentum lost, they began struggling to get back on their wheels, but the melee fighters waded through the mass, smashing and cutting them to pieces.

It took a few minutes, but there wasn't a lot of danger left after they had rolled over Katie's wall. When all the chairs were smashed and motionless again, they grouped back up in the center of the room, near where the original group had been.

"So, I might be really off on this one... but was that an office chair fight club?" JP asked.

Sarah turned and put a finger to his mouth. "JP, what is the first rule of office chair fight club?"

Several people responded in unison. "We do not talk about office chair fight club." All the adults except Luke started laughing. Luke and the three kids looked at them all confused.

"How did you all know that was the first rule of office chair fight club?" Luke asked with a concerned look on his face, which set everyone into laughing again. "I do not get it. Was office chair fight club a thing before the Advent?"

The kids didn't know either, but Luke's innocent questions kept everyone laughing until Sarah actually had to sit down on the hard floor. Finally, Katie relented. "It's an Earth custom we keep from the children until they enter the workforce," she said, and Drew wasn't sure how she kept a straight face, but it set Sarah off laughing again.

"Alright," Drew said, wiping his face. "No more talking about office chair fight club."

Luke was happy to keep leading them deeper into the building. They ran into more office chairs and paper swarms, but it wasn't until they were on the second level that they met the real terror of the Human Resources building. A single chair was charging Luke, and he was swinging his leg to smash it with his ball and chain when the seraph cried out in pain and collapsed, the ball knocking the chair off course slightly but not destroying it.

The chair spun around, hitting Sarah in the thigh and causing her to cry out in pain as the top of the chair turned even faster, its arms gaining momentum, and it smashed into Joe's sternum, blasting his rebar aside and knocking him down. The chair zoomed past the group, getting ready for another charge.

Drew blasted it with a gravball, which took out the cubicle walls next to it. Luckily, that revealed a small ball of crumpled paper about the size of a cat that shrieked as it was exposed, sending the entire group except for Drew to their knees in pain. An acid arrow impacted the ball center mass and it immediately disintegrated into a ball of paper pulp.

As soon as the creature was down, Drew looked around. Over the shrieking of the chair's squeaky wheels, a paper swarm had approached them unnoticed. It was now too close to the group to hit with a fireball. Everyone else was still clutching their ears, so Drew launched a cone of frostfire at the swarm, causing most of the paper to crash to the ground as it was covered in heavy shards of burning ice that eradicated the swarm.

Standing in the sudden silence, Drew's eyes darted about the now mostly empty cubicle. Luke recovered first, standing looking around with an almost palpable aura of anger in his eyes. The rest weren't far behind the seraph.

"What the hell was that?" Katie asked, rubbing her head and wiping the trail of blood from her nose.

"A psychic attack of some kind," Luke said with a grunt. "And a particularly powerful one."

"It was… an endless series of questions," Sarah said. "My name, my phone number, my DoD ID number. Almost like… every question on every form the military ever had me fill out."

"Exactly," Daryl announced, having broken his invisibility during the attack. "I really hope there aren't many more of those things in here."

"I'm going to guess that's why the naga left this place alone. If Drew hadn't been able to kill that thing, we would have all been easy pickings." Sarah had sat down and was holding her water bottle to her forehead.

"One more thing to thank… the powers that be for, I guess," Drew said, not wanting to say Ares' name in front of the kids. "So, how are we going to handle those things in the future? If that swarm had been any closer, I wouldn't have been able to fight it off before someone got hurt."

"Now that I know what to look for, I think I should be able to see them, but we're gonna have to slow down a bunch if you want me to scout all the cubicles fully," Daryl said, glancing at the melted paper ball.

"I could just launch a storm into each room," Drew said. "It's far enough between rooms that I'd probably be fine on mana fatigue."

"Not exactly the most subtle approach, but I think that beats having to experience that attack again," Sarah said, standing up and looking at the others. "You guys, alright?" she asked the three kids who were still huddled together.

"Uh, yes," Gary said, glancing at the other two. "I think I can tell when they're getting near, actually. My sense intentions ability was going haywire before the attack, but…" He trailed off with a shrug.

"Do you think you can predict if there is one nearby?" Katie asked; the brunette had been closest to the attack and hit harder than the rest of them. She still seemed to be catching her breath.

"I…" Gary trailed off, looking at Joe and London for support. "I probably can. But I'll need to test it a few more times, first."

"Alright. Sarah, get everyone healed up while Daryl does a scouting run into the next room. If we can find another of these formballs, we'll test Gary's ability to see if he can sense the thing. If we don't find anything, we'll move forward until we can test it. If Gary can actually sense them, we'll go back to blitzing. Otherwise, we'll do this slow and steady. I don't want another ambush like that if we can help it," Drew said, and everyone nodded in agreement. Daryl blinked out of sight even as Drew cast energizing rain, and Sarah looked at those who had taken drive-by hits from the chair.

CHAPTER SIX – FORMBALLS

Two rooms later, they still hadn't found another formball, but neither had Gary's sense intent skill gone off. Which meant that they were still hopeful that it would work. Drew was just tired of waiting. He stood there, staring at the way forward, and fidgeted with the straps on his armor while he waited for Daryl to scout the area ahead.

Katie came up behind him and slipped her hand into his. "Penny for your thoughts?" she asked.

He flashed a tired smile at her before turning his attention back to the hallway. "I just..." Drew paused, trying to think of what he wanted to say. "I don't like the idea of letting people down. The longer we take in here, the more chance that the naga will counterattack and I won't be there to stop it."

"Drew, you can't do everything," Katie said after he paused for a moment. "You've been working yourself ragged ever since I met you. Going off on your own or charging into some monster's hive. You have to be more careful. Honestly, I don't know how you keep going."

Drew turned his full attention to Katie. "Are you alright?" She was looking down, so he brushed a strand of her hair away to get a better look at her face. Taking that moment to really see her, to his surprise, Katie looked... worn out. There was still a small crust of dried blood under her nose from the formball attack, but what was most concerning was that her eyes had lost most of the fire they had possessed when he first met her.

"I'm..." Katie trailed off, refusing to meet his eyes. "Surviving, Drew. That's what most of us are doing, just getting by." She looked up finally, her eyes meeting his and searching his face. "How do you do this?"

"Do what?" Drew pulled her in closer, circling his arms around. They were as alone as Drew ever was these days; Luke had taken a chance to have a quiet chat with Sarah, and JP was off to the side, showing the kids his guns.

"Just keep going. It seems like this isn't even hard for you. You've almost died half a dozen times, and you just keep going back for more. How do you do that?" Katie whispered into his shoulder. The brunette had buried her face into his neck.

"I… I don't know," Drew said softly. "I just know that there is work that needs doing, so I do it. I focus on one problem at a time, just solving the task at hand. I guess… if I think about everything I have to do, it would become… impossible. So I just focus on the next step, I take that step, and then I focus on the next. Just one step at a time, I can handle one step."

"I'm not sure I can anymore," Katie said almost too softly for him to hear. "I just want my old life back."

"Oh, that'd be nice. Maybe a vacation? Where would you go? The Bahamas or that Incan city in the mountain, uhm, Matsu Pica or something?"

"Hah, with our luck, the Bahamas are filled with… like, angry mermaids, and a dragon has taken roost in Machu Picchu. I think I just want a weekend at home on the couch watching garbage TV. Something where I don't have to do anything. I can just sit there and veg out."

"Woah now, I don't know if I can be friends with someone who watches reality TV," Drew said with a laugh.

Katie pulled back and looked at his face, the lines of worry evident. "Well, not like it matters anymore," she said softly.

"No, I guess it doesn't," Drew answered with a sigh. "I'll add it to the list of things we want back when we take over the world."

"Take over the world?" Katie managed a soft laugh. "Well, at least you don't dream small." They lapsed into a companionable silence for a few moments, Katie resting her head against his shoulder, only drawing away when Daryl came back.

"I found one," the scout announced, and Drew could feel Katie's body tense up at those words. "It's hiding in the back corner of the room. It should be easy enough to isolate it and attack it without anyone else getting hurt."

"Alright, Gary, you're with me. Everyone else stays here. Give a holler if anything big comes knocking," Drew said, releasing Katie, adjusting his armor for a moment while everyone else shifted position. Gary and he advanced. If they did draw the creature's ire, Drew was the only one immune to its psychic screams. He stepped over one of those floor bumps designed to hide cables as he walked through the cubicles. It was strange how depersonalized they all were. There weren't any pictures of family or motivational posters like he expected in a cubicle farm.

Drew reached into one of his side pockets and pulled a glowrock out, tossing it down the hallway, illuminating the dark room. It was needed now that they were far from the group and London's fireworks. "Stay behind me, Gary," Drew said even as he realized that Gary's lightsaber was far more likely to be useful than his own weak sword skills. They inched forward, past strangely empty cubicles. Drew watched his feet carefully, worried that he would step on something loud and tip off the formball.

Gary patted his shoulder to get his attention. When Drew looked back, he was pointing to a cubicle on their left. Drew nodded and launched a gravball into the middle of the cube. His fingers were ready to throw several other fireball variants at the target if the first didn't destroy it. The cubicles compacted together, the spell's force crushing them with the sound of crunching wood and twisted metal. Drew's eyes darted around, looking for the crumpled shape of a formball.

"Pretty sure that got it," Gary said behind him even as Daryl's telepathic voice confirmed it in his head.

The two headed back to the main group, and Drew smiled. "We're good. Gary felt it before we got there, so we should be able to pick up the pace a bit."

They cleared the next few rooms quickly enough. A few more printers were destroyed before anyone got near enough for the mimic-like creatures to attack again. They had clumped up a bit more so that everyone was close enough to Gary for his sense intent to apply to them, shifting from a line to a more diamond shape. The hallways were wide enough that they could easily walk down them side by side. As they turned around one blind corner, Gary called another halt. "Hold up. I can feel… something."

"Another formball?" Sarah said, as she did another scan of the area. Most of the monsters hid in the more open cubicle areas rather than in the hallways between them.

"No, this is different… it's a… well… a different kind of attention, angry like the formball, but… colder? I don't really know how to explain it," Gary whispered after a moment of thought.

"Daryl?" Drew asked, and the scout sent a mental note that he was already on it. They waited in tense silence for an update, their eyes darting around the hallway. Only the hushed sound of their breath broke the quiet. No one wanted to trigger another attack before they were ready.

"I couldn't find anything," Daryl said quietly, after several minutes of searching. Everyone turned to Gary.

"I, uh, it's still there." Gary closed his eyes and focused. "It's less… condensed though, like the intent is spread out over a larger area. I can't get a good read on it," the teen said, opening his eyes again and looking around helplessly. "I'm sorry," he announced.

"It's alright, Gary, we'll figure it out," JP said, patting the kid on the back.

"Okay, extra cautious until Gary gives us the okay," Sarah said, gesturing for the group to move forward. Almost immediately, she stepped closer to the wall to look back and was enveloped in a shroud of crinkling paper. The large sheet detached from the wall and was conforming to her like a second skin, especially around her neck and head. The next second, Sarah stepped through the paper, her defensive ability kicking in and allowing her to phase through the strangling paper.

Joe stepped in with his rebar, swinging wide and ripping a hole through the thin material. Gary swung his lightsaber, which activated with a buzz, burning a bisecting line through the beast, which filled the room with the smell of burnt paper. Drew was at a loss. He didn't think that lightning would do much against paper and everyone was way too close to use a fireball. Thankfully, it didn't seem like he would need to step in, as the two teens took turns swinging their weapons and decimating the creature, which seemed unable to figure out what had happened when Sarah slipped out of its trap.

Fifteen seconds of wild swinging later, and the two kids had mashed it into a pulp. "I think you can stop now," Sarah said, and they both looked up at her with wild eyes, breathing heavily.

"Well, that was terrifying," Sarah said, looking around. "If anyone else gets attacked by one of those, what are we going to do?"

"Ummm, we could rip it off?" JP asked.

"I could try to cut it off. I think the issue is going to be breathing, right? It looked like it was trying to strangle you," Gary said, looking down at his lightsaber.

"Shoving a lightsaber into someone's mouth sounds like a bad idea," Drew said, looking at Robbi's sword at his side.

"Especially in the heat of battle, or if whoever is being smothered struggles, which they will if they can't breathe."

"So…" Katie prompted, looking around the group to see if anyone has any better ideas. "What do we do?"

"I mean, I guess we can just trust in Sarah's ability to heal us after we slice each other up trying to cut our way out," Drew said with a frown. "I think that'll be a last resort, though. We had a good amount of warning that thing was around. I should be able to fireball it before anyone gets captured again."

"That's putting a lot of faith in Gary's ability to sense these things," JP pointed out, and everyone turned to look at Gary.

"It's okay. No, I can do it," Gary said as he had gained confidence over the last hour of dungeon delving. Gary looked up, meeting Sarah's eyes. "I really can."

"Alright, we'll mark that as plan A. Plan B is going to be to use *knives*," Sarah stressed the word, while also giving Gary's lightsaber a pointed look, "to cut the person out of the paper."

No one had a better idea, so Luke led the way deeper into the dungeon. Luckily there weren't any additional types of surprises. Using an ever more confident Gary to sense the ambushes, they managed to descend three floors in total before they came to the pyramid room. Daryl, who had been scouting ahead, came back to tell them what they would be facing.

"Looks like a bit of everything. We've got a formball the size of a beachball, a big office printer, two walls that look like they're covered in ambush paper. Last but not least, there are a few dozen each of chairs and pens," Daryl said from somewhere nearby. The scout hadn't made himself visible just yet, but they'd gotten used to his voice appearing out of nowhere. "The formball and printer are clearly the biggest threats. The rest are minions of some variety, probably no stronger than the ones we've already fought. There are just a lot of them. And there is plenty of space for the chairs to charge around."

"I can take care of the chairs," Katie said. "Not sure about the pens."

"Standard formation then?" Drew asked, glancing at the others. The standard formation was for Katie to barricade the entrance, leaving eye slits for the others to see inside and shoot spells. The opening salvo was Drew's four most damaging storm spells, which gave him plenty of time to cast an energizing rain on himself, getting rid of some of the mana fatigue. By the time the storms cleared, Drew was ready to launch a full volley of his fireball variants, while JP would unleash his own storms of bullets, while everyone else made sure the wall held.

That much firepower was usually more than enough to take out an entire boss room. It had worked so successfully that most guardian rooms were actually safer than getting to them. Exceptions came when there wasn't visibility into the room before seeing the guardian or when it was big enough to ignore Katie's walls, both of which had applied to the giant fire crocodile below the stadium. Thankfully, few dungeons deviated from the standard layout sufficiently for it to be a problem.

"No problems with standard formation here," Sarah said, and she looked around the group to see if anyone else did. "Alright. Katie, you're up. Let us know when you're ready."

"Give me a minute," Katie said as she touched the floor. A wall sprang up in front of them, three small viewing ports, just large enough for JP and Drew to shoot through while the third was there for the others to watch. Drew and JP's light shows were the best entertainment they got in the post-Advent world. The wall itself was almost five feet thick by the time Katie was done. They all waited for Katie to recover from some of the mana fatigue. She needed to be ready to seal the viewports if they needed to. "Okay, good to go," she said, giving Drew a thumbs up.

Drew had begun casting gravity squall as soon as Katie said, 'Okay.' With layered attack spells, he had discovered that the gravity ones usually kept things contained a lot better, so leading with them meant that he was more likely to have easy targets for the rest of his spells. Once gravity squall launched, he focused on holy frostfire storm, and then holy firestorm, and holy frost storm. Holy's radiant damage had proven remarkably capable of cutting through any damage resistance a monster might have against the more mundane elements.

The four spells together dropped him to a little over sixty percent of his fatigue allowance, but the speed at which it happened caused him to lose focus for a moment as it crashed over him like the tide. The wave of exhaustion faded, and he began casting invigorating rain. To his surprise, midway through his cast, JP started firing his gun, followed by dull thuds against the barrier. The bright flashes of light illuminated the moderately dark space as he used his elemental bullets. Drew almost lost his focus on the spell by the unexpected report but managed to fumble through to the end, looking up. In an aberration from norm, his viewport had been collapsed, as had the extra, leaving only JP's open still.

The former cop was busy unloading through the small area. Which shouldn't have been an issue yet since the storms were still going on. Drew moved slightly so he could see through the hole and blinked in surprise. Black lines of ink stained the small porthole, and JP's hands were speckled with more of the acidic material. The printer had barreled through the storms and was bashing its body against the wall. A gravball ripped half the creature off and caused a high squeal that sounded like a printer roller grinding against its other parts.

"Printer should be handled. Get ready for the formball," JP said even as he dropped one gun and drew another, this one's bullets spewing tracer rounds like red streaks, the telltale mark of JP's fireshot.

Drew couldn't help wishing for Trista's tracer bullets that left lines of burning fire in the air in a situation like this. The storms wouldn't end for a few seconds more, so Drew launched a lightning bolt at the printer.

"Opening your viewport again!" Katie shouted over the noise, and Drew shifted back to his original spot, giving Katie a nod. She reopened the port, only a narrow line of sight was visible, looking straight toward the back of the room where the formball had been. The storms were still raging, though, and all he could see were flashing lights and debris being thrown about in a chaotic cacophony. His eyes darted about, looking for the formball in the maelstrom.

The storms ended, one after the other, until there was a sudden silence, which almost felt like he had been deafened as Drew's eyes scanned through the room. The pressure in his head suddenly picked up even as everyone else cried out in pain. Forcing himself to keep his eyes open, he continued to scan the room. Katie collapsed into him, one hand clutching his arm while the other twisted through her hair. Movement at the edge of his vision caught Drew's attention, and he shifted his glance to the back corner of the room. There he saw the indistinct form of a lopsided balloon, and immediately he launched a holy frostfire ball at it. The orb exploded in red, white, and blue lights.

Half a second later, the pressure left Drew's mind. He kept an eye out for any more movement as the humans around him began to recover from the shock of the mental attack.

"I really hate those things," JP said as he wiped an arm across his upper lip where blood had crept down from his nose. Drew found the printer a few moments later, its form collapsed in on itself, the lid hanging off to a side with only one hinge still attached to the main body.

"I think we're clear," Drew said, reaching down to help Katie stand up again. The brunette had twin trails of red from her nose as she shook her head.

"Yeah, just imagine if we had to make an incident report after this," Katie muttered, and everyone but Drew gave halfhearted laughs.

"Best part of the apocalypse is no more paperwork," Sarah said. "Everyone gather up, I'll heal us."

Part of her xatherite leveling was that her heal now had a much larger area of effect, allowing her to heal multiple people at the same time as long as they were close together. Drew wasn't sure if it would work against the mental damage that the formball had inflicted on them.

Drew stepped back, allowing more of the others to take advantage of the healing. He was still fine, even after the assault, but he glanced through the arrow slit in the wall, looking for anything else still moving.

"Katie, could I get a door?" the red mage asked. "I'll go claim the node real quick." When there was no obvious response, he looked back and the rest of the team was on their knees dealing with the aftershock of the formball's attacks.

Katie waved him off when he stopped to check how she was doing, so Drew shifted his attention to the rest of the party. Luke, Sarah, and JP were in a similar state to Katie, but London and Joe were lying against a wall, their heads between their knees, near the back of their formation. The kids were following orders to guard their rear, and it looked like they hadn't seen any action other than residual damage from the formball. Gary stood over them, having recovered quicker than the rest. He stood with his back to the group, the unlit blade in his hands, watching the darkness.

"They alright?" Drew asked and Gary turned around in surprise, the buzz of his weapon deploying in fright.

"Sorry, Mr. Drew!" Gary shouted, the light from his saber disappearing as he disengaged the device. "They'll be okay, just got hit a bit harder than they expected."

"What about you?" Drew asked, looking the kid over.

"I'll be fine, Mr. Drew. I can sort of deflect it now that I know it's coming," Gary said, and Drew patted the kid on his shoulder.

"Alright, we're going to rest here a beat until everyone recovers. Shout if you see anything." Drew pulled out a bag of jerky and handed a piece to Gary before distributing some to the rest of the group. Hopefully the food would help settle them.

When everyone was back on their feet, Drew glanced over at Katie who nodded back at him. With a thought, she opened a door. The room reminded him of a scene from the first Ghostbusters movie. Paper and machine parts were strewn about in the wake of his storms. The only location that was clear was the pyramid near the back of the room. He could hear footsteps behind him, but he knew that it was Luke following him like always.

They got halfway to the pyramid when gunfire sounded out behind him. Glancing back, he saw JP looking over at the last of the printer remains, which was twitching in death throes, a rifle in his hands.

"I saw the printer tray moving. Figured it was trying to ambush you," JP said with a shrug.

"Oh. Thanks," Drew said a little sheepishly. He had already been so focused on claiming the node that he had forgotten rule one of Zombieland—double-tap. For good measure, he threw a shocking acid arrow at the thing. When it finally stopped moving, he continued forward to the pyramid. Glancing back at the unmoving printer, JP and the others began going through the bodies, looking for xatherite and making sure there weren't any other surprises. Drew tried to swallow, but his throat felt dry, and he pulled a water bottle out of his pouch of holding and finished half of it in one gulp.

There was a growing sense of fear in his mind that the pyramid would again reject him, saying that the guardian wasn't dead like it had back in the stadium after Robbi died. Drew put a comforting hand on the blood-red hilt at his side, letting his fingers bite into the wire wrapped grip. His other hand reached out, and he watched the red light fill up the space as the doorway appeared on the side of the pyramid. And then he was somewhere else. Drew let out a sigh of relief as he claimed the node.

CHAPTER SEVEN – BAD FEELING

Forty-five minutes later, they were already back at the entrance to the paper node which had been renamed to be Navy HR node. The well-oiled machinery of the node takeover took little time, mostly since it could be done through the remote administration console.

"You know, I would think that the Remote Admin Console would be just a standard install for the most part." Drew's attention returned to the group as he finally finished all the initialization steps required for a freshly conquered node.

"There are reasons to keep some nodes off the grid, but for the most part, you are correct." Luke had been guiding him, a gentle hand on his elbow as Drew was lost in menus only he could see.

"Fair enough. What is the plan now?" Drew said, turning to Sarah. The brunette was by far the most likely to know the next stage of the attack plan.

"We'll report back to Hoeffecker that we conquered the node. I imagine we'll have an hour or so while they rotate the reserves in. Once all the troops are in position, we'll move forward with the assault on the last naga node. I imagine we'll want to take out most of the other totems before we move on the node itself, so probably a few hours of Katie pushing the walls forward. We're not expecting much resistance until we get into the node itself.

"I think the major wanted to do a full unit for the actual assault process." Sarah finished as they breached the surface.

"She thinks it'll be that hard?" Drew asked after taking a deep breath of the fresh air.

"I think it's more a matter of wanting to give as many people as possible a chance at the bonus experience. Especially since we won't need as many people guarding against another attack," Sarah answered, looking around for a runner. "I'm going to go report. Meet you guys back at the forward command post," she called out as the rest of them spread out in the area around the node.

Drew saw a familiar form and walked toward Hargrave. The man now had a reptilian bent to his features resulting from the crocodile skin xatherite used to save his life. His skin had a distinctly green tint to it, as well as some crocodilian bumps. It wasn't the most abnormal shift visible in the courtyard. They all added together to make it so that a good chunk of their people no longer looked strictly human. Pausing, Drew glanced over at Luke and frowned. If anything, the seraph looked more idealized as a human, without any physical mutations.

"What do humans off Earth look like?" Drew asked after looking around to make sure that no one was near enough for them to hear.

Luke considered his words for a moment. "Well, it depends. Xatherite that change your physical appearance are both common and slightly stigmatized. Humans look much like you or me in the upper echelon or among the Iron Fleets. However, it is not uncommon for the human form to be a more distant memory on the frontier planets or among the lower levels of major planets. As a member of the Order, you will be expected to maintain a nearly flawless human appearance. There are rumors that some of the gods have some physical alterations, but they are kept well hidden."

"Seems rather limiting. We're not exactly in a position to give up xatherite if it doesn't fit some ideal we have of humanity," Drew said with a frown. The xatherite that had altered Hargrave's physical appearance had saved his life, after all.

"That is why you see it more among the poorer class of citizens. They trade an element of their humanity for power."

"I see." Drew scratched his chin even as he resumed his walk toward Hargrave. He hadn't actually gotten a chance to talk to the man since he had recovered.

"Good to see you up and about again."

"Thanks. I'm told it was pretty touch-and-go for a bit there."

"You're feeling up to speed then?"

"Yes, sir. I managed to stumble into some fights when the naga assaulted the stadium. Nothing on the front line, but we held back a couple of the big ones that managed to break in among the Numb." Hargrave shook his head slightly. "Nasty business. We ran out of ammo right before the shield went up. So I guess that's two lives I owe you."

Drew waved the thanks away. "Just doing what had to be done, same as everyone else," he said, nodding to a few of the other fighters who were listening in on their conversation. "Glad you made it through. I heard some bad things from people still up topside when it happened."

"Yeah, we're all mighty glad to have the shield up." Hargrave's words got a general assent from the other fighters near them. "We'll be even better when you finish off the last of these snakes."

"That's the idea. You hear anything from the other fronts?"

"Nah, the shield keeps everything out. Honestly, for the most part, we're stuck inside it as much as monsters are stuck outside. The north and east sides keep getting worse. Scavenging groups grab anything they can when there's a clear moment, but those are getting rare. Might be able to make some more headway when we clear up men along the river, but I wouldn't count on that too much. The snakes are bad, but the stuff coming in from the national mall… that's the stuff of nightmares."

Drew turned his mana sight on as he looked to the north. The mall was thick with ley lines, dozens of them intersecting each other and all feeding into two massive nodes that he assumed were the Capital Building and White House. "Yeah, there are a ton of nodes up there."

"Yeah, we figure any survivors will be further away from that mess, probably across the Potomac."

"Which has problems of its own," Drew said with a frown. With mana sight still active, he could see the violet-colored nodes in Arlington. "Well, one problem at a time," Drew said. They continued to make small talk with some of the other fighters. Almost all of them had been at the stadium longer than Drew, although two had been part of the DIA building rescue. Drew set up a rotating refreshing rain in the courtyard, and the troops filtered through it as he talked with Hargrave.

Colonel Hoeffecker arrived after about thirty minutes, beckoning toward Drew and Hargrave to join her as she set up near one of the back walls.

"Glad you're both here. We're going to go all-in on this attack. Drew, you'll have two Marine fireteams and then two more groups of four, made up of some people with xatherite we really want to level up, so that they can get some linked skills. The Marines will be responsible for keeping them alive while your unit does most of the clearing. I know it'll slow things down for you a little, but we need some more of those force multiplier links. I know you've asked permission to go south. If we get a few more high-end linked skills, we're pretty sure we'll be able to hold the base while your team tries to find more survivors in Arlington.

"Part of that mission is going to be trying to hook up with the Pentagon. At this point, we have to assume anything north of us is dead. This means the best chance of finding any VIPs is there. Dealing with whatever is claiming those nodes is also vital. Hopefully, it's friendly, but…" Hoeffecker trailed off.

"Well, you're the best bet of taking out anything that isn't friendly.

"Anyway, before you can go in, we're going to need to take out the last two totems the naga have set up." Hoeffecker gestured to a table and began pulling out objects from her pouch, creating a makeshift map of the area around them. Drew wasn't sure if she was pulling stuff directly from her pouch of holding or using her utility xatherite, which allowed her to pull out small objects to meet specific needs. It was one of the few xatherite that Drew actually coveted. It couldn't make anything larger than a hand, but there were a lot of things smaller than your hand that were useful, like deodorant, pens, or a razor.

The map she created showed them in between two small Eiffel tower miniatures, which Drew assumed were the naga control towers. Next to the blocks of wood and books, which represented streets and buildings, respectively, the parking garage that was the last node was represented by a plate.

"We're going to have you take out both control towers from a static position here." The colonel pointed to a large stack of books a block to their northwest. "Blanket the area in a storm, then hit it with as many fireballs as it takes to break the thing into pieces. We'll rest and then have you take out the other one as well."

"Why didn't we take them out before we went into this place?"

"We wanted them focused on defense while you were under. We've had them under a constant barrage for the last ten hours. The idea was to keep their spellcasters burning mana, trying to keep the totems safe while you were busy. While you're taking out the totems, we'll get the four fireteams that are going up with you into position."

"Up? You think the pyramid is above ground level?" Luke questioned.

"We know it is. The node is in the parking garage, and the walls are still open. Intel says it's on the level below the roof."

"Any chance we can just skip it all, take out the guardian, and claim the node?" Sarah questioned.

"We would still have to kill them sooner or later. They will not just disappear. When you kill the guardian, any remaining will probably go berserk," Luke answered.

"Right, so no skipping to the top," Drew said. "Which doesn't change because that is exactly how we do every dungeon. So we clear the whole thing, while the rest of the troops contain the naga and make sure they don't overflow the node."

They took a few more minutes to discuss troop placements before splitting off to allow everyone to get into position. Drew climbed up to the top of the building and then focused on the totems. The battle plan progressed precisely as expected.

"Something feels wrong," Drew said as he destroyed the last naga totem. "This is too easy."

"What could they be hiding?" Luke asked beside him, and Drew shook his head in response.

"I'm not sure. I suppose we could have finally broken their spirit, but something tells me that's not what's happening."

"What do you want to do?"

"Daryl? You around?" Drew raised his voice as he called out.

"Yeah, I'm here," the scout responded, fading back into view.

"I want you to do a wide sweep with the bird. Something about this feels wrong."

"I think you mean it feels fishy," Daryl answered even as he closed his eyes. "I'm sending the bird out wider now. Nothing around the totems."

"I'd give anything for a radio right now," Drew muttered. He stayed on the tower, waiting for the other shoe to drop while Daryl did his scan.

"Clear up to the barracks, doing a sweep along the Mall side of the shield," Daryl said and Drew tapped his fingers impatiently. The north side was the least likely route for an attack as it was the only portion of the shield wall facing land.

"I doubt they have anything that can get through the shield. If they did, they would have used it already," Luke opined between the two men.

"No one said anything about my fishy joke," Daryl mentioned from the other side of Luke. "I'm a little hurt."

"Yeah, it's a bad comparison. They're more like snakes than fish," Drew teased.

"They are amphibious. Neither fish nor snakes work very well," Luke responded.

"There are amphibious snakes," Drew said. "Stuff like the yellow thing in Florida. Crap, what was that called?"

"Water moccasins?" Daryl asked.

"Well, yes. Water moccasins are also water snakes, but there is… another one. That's named something yellow?" Drew almost had the urge to pull out his phone to Google it, and for a moment, the reality of everything that they had lost hit him. "Damn, I miss the internet."

"One of those things you sort of took for granted, right?" Daryl said. "Like I know I didn't grow up with the answer to every question in my pocket. But I sure got used to it over the last fifteen years."

"Yeah. Wonder if they even make encyclopedias anymore. We should probably try to save some of those. Are there any libraries near here? Well, aside from the Library of Congress, which I'm sure has some super annoying book monsters in it."

"Maybe as we get further away from the district, we'll be able to find more stuff intact. Hoeffecker wants us to go into Arlington, right? That's where you lived, isn't it? Any libraries near there?"

"I honestly don't know. I sort of stopped using libraries somewhere along the line. I switched to digital books when I joined the Coast Guard, so I didn't have to drag so much stuff between billets. I know where a few are in Boston, but I haven't wandered the streets in DC."

"Well, I'm sure someone will know where one is. We just have to hope they survived. Books would be a good way to give the non-combat classes something to do," Daryl answered, then switched back to official mode. "Alright, bird's on the west side of the stadium now. Nothing attacking west from Fort McNair."

"Is there something like the internet in the Protectorate?" Drew turned to Luke, who had remained suspiciously quiet throughout the conversation.

"Several of the Orders have their own proprietary information relay system, although that would be more akin to just email. I do not know much about your internet. We only learned about it as a cultural touchstone. The closest I know of are species that carry a hive mind. Earth had some very interesting and unique technological advances that I know some of the Orders would be very interested in learning about."

"Would be?" Drew said with a frown. "Does that mean they don't know about Earth currently?"

"You have to remember just how large the Protectorate is. We span almost a million inhabited worlds. Earth's formation was part of the military faction's efforts to create a more effective fighting force. It is entirely possible that several of the other factions have information on Earth, but details would be restricted. That information was locked down even more after the first split. The rise of new Red Mages will disrupt the balance of the factions for generations."

Drew took a moment to digest the idea that there were essentially tiers of Orders and political blocs of power within the Protectorate. "What other factions are there?"

"There are three major factions within the Protectorate. The Military faction is perhaps the strongest and is headed by the Order of Dragons. The Order of Felidae runs the Development faction, and the Order of Manticore heads the Exploration faction. There are a few dozen other factions aside from the big three, but they are significantly less powerful."

"Clear to Buzzard Point," Daryl announced.

Drew worried his lower lip as he considered. They could respond pretty quickly to anything east of Buzzard Point, which meant that it was unlikely whatever the naga were up to involved them. The growing fields of Fort McNair were the most vulnerable population center since it was outside of the shield. He doubted they'd be making an attack on any section within the shield. They had tried that a few times early on, and it had not gone well for them.

"I don't get it. Where could they be?" Drew said, glancing south.

"Found them," Daryl shouted in surprise. "There are signs of a significant passage across the river. Looks like they're heading deeper into Anacostia. Should I follow them?"

Drew cursed under his breath. "Are they heading east or south?"

"Let me send the bird higher, and I'll see," Daryl said.

Drew waited, considering their options. If they were heading toward Bolling, they could probably cross the bridge and try to root them out, but the orcs had been becoming more active to the east. It would take a significant force to bypass the Coast Guard Headquarters node where they originated from to track down the fleeing naga.

"Looks like they're going around the orc's territory. I see what looks like a couple of fights between the two groups, nothing serious, just a bunch of blue blood."

"Alright, sounds like our best bet is to clear the node. They'll all go berserk when we do that anyway, right Luke?"

"Unless they manage to claim another node, then yes."

"Well, let's do that while they're dealing with the orcs and hope there aren't many anywhere near more humans," Drew said with a vicious grin.

CHAPTER EIGHT – SNAKES

There was a certain catharsis in blowing stuff up. Drew could feel the power thrum through him as he lobbed fireballs at the naga in the parking garage. It almost made up for the fact that the entire delve was pissing him off to an unreasonable degree.

They had battled through the first and second floors already, and they were halfway through the third floor where the node guardian would be, and everyone was miserable. The reason for this misery was the water. The entire parking structure was flooded. Only about an inch of water, but because it all slanted downward, everything had a slight current to it. Their feet were cold and wet. And dodging, or any kind of fighting, caused water to get kicked up, so they were all soaked to the bone.

Not to mention that with the treacherous footing, all of them had fallen several times. The bruises were healed up quickly enough, but that didn't make the entire thing an enjoyable experience for anyone. The only respite they got from the relentless stream of water was when Katie would create a small lip around them, diverting the water away long enough for them to rest. Although that didn't save them from the continually dripping ceiling above them.

"Water dungeons are the worst," JP complained. The gunman had it the worst of any of them. He had already lost two of his pistols from falls where they seemed to disappear into the shallow water. He had just finished fishing out the third pistol. "I'm going to have to clean all of my guns when we get out of here."

"Don't you clean your guns after every dungeon?" Sarah said, poking the former cop in the shoulder.

"Well, yes," JP responded with a frown as he put that pistol away and pulled another out of his pouch. "This time, it's just going to take longer." Everyone managed a slight chuckle at the depressed tone in JP's voice. They hadn't been in the garage for anywhere near as long as most dungeons. But they were all more than ready to be done with the naga.

"Alright, nothing else until we get to the guardian. The boss chamber doesn't have a divider or anything. The pyramid is in a large open area with at least a dozen goliaths and casters," Daryl said. They had paused for the scout to go ahead and check out what was ahead. "Other problem is that they clearly know we're here, and it looks like they're prepared for a long siege.

"They're all behind cover with several killing funnels set up. The cover is mostly piles of cars that end a few feet from the ceiling. We could probably punch through them, but I counted five of their big snake guys that will probably converge on any hole we make. And we've got about a hundred feet of open space. Even worse is that they've managed to create water channels on the downward slope of the ramp. It's about twice as difficult to keep your footing there as we've been working with already. Lots of weird currents that move in opposite directions."

"Well, that sounds like a nightmare," Drew said, stretching his arms and back with a loud groan.

"Yeah, and it looks like more of their mages up there. So expect them to be able to do something with all that water," Daryl added.

"They are not technically mages," Luke argued. "They are water manipulators. It is a very different thing." Everyone ignored the seraph. This was the fourth time he had tried to correct them on what the naga should be called.

"Alright, so we've got a hundred feet of killing field before a fortified position. Sort of works in our favor. Katie, if you can make a wall, I'll take out the cover. They'll either have to charge down their own killing field, or we'll just zig-zag the wall up the ramp. We'll take it slow just in case those casters of theirs have something up their sleeves, but I don't think we need to worry too much about alternative tactics. Ideally, we can shunt the water off to a side somewhere so that we're not standing in it." Drew glanced around the group seeing if anyone had questions.

"That's a lot of walls," Katie said with a frown.

"We'll take it slow. Rushing it would just put us in more danger. As long as they're trapped up there, we don't need to worry about anything else. We'll play it safe, and no one gets hurt," Drew said, and no one seemed inclined to disagree.

They moved up the ramp until they got to the blind corner that Daryl said marked the killing field's beginning. Katie placed her hand on the wall, and they watched as it began extending out and up the area. With a loud crash, a portion of the wall bowed inward. Whatever had impacted it shook the mortar loose even as a brick fell out of the wall.

"Right… thicker," Katie muttered under her breath, and the section of the wall quickly repaired itself. Several more impacts could be heard as the wall crawled its slow way out. "Drew, could you give me a storm up there to distract them?"

Drew really wished that reflections counted as line of sight, a mirror around the corner would make this so much easier. He began forming the seals with his hands even as he shifted slightly to look out around the corner. Katie had left a small slit for him to look through. It took him a bit of moving his head around before he could figure out what he was looking at. After five seconds of casting, he placed his lowest level storm variant at the top of the ramp.

"Done," Drew announced even as he watched the crumpled up form of a car careen off one of the sidewalls and then roll down the hill. The storm and lack of targeting had thrown it off course, but a ton of metal, rubber, and plastic was still a ton of metal, rubber, and plastic rolling down a hill. Drew relayed what the impacts actually were, and Katie grunted as the wall grew thicker and longer. When they got near the other side of the slope, Katie created a small channel to direct the water away from the group along the edge of the wall and then began summoning a second angled wall. Dozens of cars littered the area behind them, evidence of the naga's attempt to bombard the barricade.

About halfway up the second side of the ramp, they paused. Katie was getting close to topped off on mana fatigue, and Drew's covering squall spells were burning through his own at a prodigious rate. Casting a refreshing rain, they both took a breather to recover. The warm shower washed away the fatigue.

Next to him, Katie shivered. Drew blinked. The rain was getting colder…

"The naga are attacking through the rain!" Drew said as he grabbed Katie's arm and ran down the ramp away from the spell. A burning sensation lit up his exposed hand as he was hit by a small piece of hail. Drew's shout roused the group, and they all fled down the ramp to behind the first wall. Which was when the cars the naga had been throwing down the ramp seemed to explode. Dozens of snakes the size of a hand burst out of each, surrounding them with hundreds of baby naga.

Drew was in front, and he launched cones to either side of their path. The tiny snake creatures died by the handful as they froze to the slick floor. Even more encountered the slippery surface of the ice and lost traction, sliding to the end of the path.

"Fuck!" Drew heard JP shout behind him. "Little fuckers are poisonous!" Glancing back, Drew saw JP shaking a snake off his boot.

"I think you mean venomous," Sarah grumbled even as she stepped on another snake. Her thicker pants and combat boots were mostly protecting her legs even as she used the spider leg spear to sweep more of the tiny creatures out of her path. Drew used his last cone spell, the gravity variant, to cover their retreat. Rounding the corner, he could see the concerned faces of the Marines preparing their defenses. He led the group toward them.

Luke's chain chomp was making low sweeps at high speed, keeping them from being overrun even as he was the last of the group to retreat. Needles flashed past him as naga burst out of the channel, running along the side. An outstretched hand from Drew launched a volley of fireballs at the wall, blanketing it in explosions and wrecking the small, unfortified channel. The shockwave from the blasts propelled them forward, causing most of them to lose their footing and scramble to get up from the damp floor.

"Everyone hold at the resting point." Drew pushed Katie forward as he turned. His cones were off cooldown, and he used them to help clear their retreat. The area was already filling back up with the shallow water, and he cast a lightning bolt into it. The bolt didn't do much damage before the charge diffused through the surrounding water, but it did manage to kill a snake or two each without requiring any real aiming. He followed Luke back to the resting point. Several of the Marines had joined them, throwing crayons with one hand while the others grasped their swords.

Drew began casting a storm, hoping to cut off the small critters and whatever other major offense the naga had prepared for this. Figuring that a holy firestorm would be the best bet, his fingers began the process of casting the spell even as the first of the goliath naga swept around the corner. Crouching low to avoid hitting its head on the ceiling, the twenty-foot long snake man sprang forward toward their group, and Luke roundhouse kicked it.

The chain chomp around his ankle slammed into the beast first. The impact hit its bulk up and toward the wall. The head of the creature smashed into the concrete next to them; its tail whipped out and smacked the seraph. Luke had deployed his wings, shedding a bright light around the previously dark area.

The tail smashed into them and sizzled even as Luke slammed into the opposite wall. Behind Drew, the report of gunfire opened up; either JP, the Marines, or both. He wasn't sure.

Flashes of color whizzed past him as crayons dug into the beast, penetrating the thick skin and leaving only a small portion exposed. Drew's storm went off, hopefully cutting off the approach of any more goliaths. This allowed Drew to rejoin the fight against the beast by launching a gravity point at its center mass. The gravity ball caused the scales around its midsection to explode outward, creating a web of shrapnel that skittered off the concrete walls and floor. Drew felt an impact against his shoulder but his mana shield kept him from being injured.

All four of his acid arrow variants shot toward the confined creature. Acid and lightning splashed across its face even as the spell's disruption aspect locked up its muscles while the rest of the group riddled its body with projectiles. Assuming the group could handle the goliath, Drew ran to the still-open slot at the base of the wall. More naga were building up, waiting for the holy firestorm to end. Drew began casting a gravity squall.

Already three more of the goliaths had gathered. The burned remains of a fourth was sitting half out of the Holy Firestorm, clearly having been trying to escape its ravages. The body was too heavy for the storm to move, but it had been enough to finish the beast off. Six of the tall naga casters were behind the goliaths. Drew's gravity storm hit them all.

The heavy thud of massive bodies hit the wall before the ever-shifting gravity wells within the storm pulled them back shook the world, even as Drew launched fireball variants into the storm, causing even more damage to the contained monsters. A holy frostfire storm followed his battery. A sudden wave of fatigue came over him as he ripped through his mana, his legs collapsing underneath him.

He skinned his face as it rubbed against the wall on his graceless way down. Without thinking, he cast invigorate on himself. As the fugue state faded, he could still hear the loud echoes of gunfire. He glanced down the passage; the Marines and civilians were battling against another wave of the normal naga from their rear. The bright light of muzzle flashes illuminated the room as they fought, but they seemed to be holding their own. Movement in the corner of his vision had him scrambling to his feet, a wave of the snakes was making their way toward him, and he launched a cone of frostfire to kill them. His team was still fighting against the little beasts, but they were now surrounded by a much taller wall.

The smell of burning flesh and wax filled his nose as he made his way over to the barricade. Jumping over it after launching a cone of frost along one side, he briefly considered using blink step, but he didn't want to burn through any more mana.

"Prepare for more incoming!" Drew shouted, unsure if his storms had caught enough to counteract the trap. Katie was on the floor, grasping her head, clearly deep in a mana-fatigue-induced migraine. Luke and the others seemed to be doing fine taking out the few tiny naga that managed to crest the wall. JP's rain of arrows and bullets were clearing large swaths of enemies. Drew launched acid arrows at the naga attacking the Marines, taking out six with the variants before he turned his attention back to the corner.

The storm spells only lasting for thirty seconds meant that if they were going to do a second thrust, it would be any time now. They were all soaked through and moving more slowly because of the extra weight, but the ground underneath was only damp. While they waited, Drew took the time to cast arsenal, the upgraded version of his dancing blades ability. That should be enough to take out any snakes near him so that he could focus on the naga casters that would undoubtedly be coming around the corner shortly.

Drew could feel that there was still about forty-five seconds until holy firestorm came off cooldown, which meant the way up the ramp was probably clear of the two storms he had left there. He held off, splitting his attention between the up and down slopes, waiting for the naga to make their entrance.

Gunshots rang out to either side of him, but they got less frequent. The number of snakes finally diminished to the point that they were no longer posing a threat to the barricades. Drew was doing his part by launching cones over the side whenever he saw a large enough grouping.

"What are they up to?" Drew asked with a frown, wiping sweat from his forehead.

"Want me to check?" Daryl was visible for once, trying to avoid being hit by the random fire that was spreading around the area.

"Give it a little bit, go invisible, and check through the crack," Drew said, frowning. "They clearly know what our abilities are and were ready for us. I don't want any more surprises. Anyone know where those snakes below came from? We cleared everything."

"They climbed down from the walls. Who knows where they were hiding." Sarah answered.

Drew looked at Daryl and shook his head, putting his hand together in the shape of a bird he mimed going around the wall. Daryl nodded his head. Drew wasn't sure if the naga could hear them, but at this point, he wasn't taking any chances. Holding his hands up so that he could use them to aim his fireballs if anything came around the wall, he waited for Daryl to report.

"Looks like they've retreated back up to the top of the ramp," Daryl said twenty seconds later.

"Okay, let's clear the snakes down here. I'll do another rain out of their sight, and hopefully, they won't be able to manipulate the water. Otherwise…" Drew shrugged. Invigorate would work, but it was slow. With a fifteen-minute cooldown, it would take them an hour or so to get to the top of the ramp using their old method.

CHAPTER NINE – OPTIONS

"Daryl, keep eyes out while we finish up down here." Katie was in the worst shape of all of them, having dipped heavily into her mana fatigue to build the emergency structures after already being low. A few of the secondary group had gotten injured, but it was nothing that a single heal from Sarah hadn't been able to fix. They had handled themselves well and even got a xatherite out of it.

It had been a dimly glowing red crystal that Drew had harvested.

Xatherite Crystal Name: Minor Hydraulic Push
Xatherite Color: Red
Xatherite Grade: Primitive
Xatherite Rarity: Widespread
Type: Magic
Effect: Creates a jet of water that pushes the target with a weak amount of force.

As far as attack spells went, it wasn't great, but there weren't many water-based attacks around, so it would be a great linked spell. Drew briefly considered adding it to his own map to open up another constellation but dismissed that idea as he thought there would be a chance for a better grade and rarity pretty easily. He also wanted to spread the xatherite they were getting among the defenders since Drew wasn't sure how easy it would be to shuttle xatherite back to the stadium from Arlington.

Drew traded the xatherite to the sergeant who was in charge of the Marine fireteams. Heading back to the crack, he cast gravity point at the top of the ramp. The spell quickly compacted the cars there until they had an open avenue to progress.

"Why are we just now doing that?" Katie asked with a frown.

"Because I just thought of it," Drew said with a slight shrug. A minute later, Drew had cleared the ramp's top, and Daryl scouted the garage's upper level.

"Just one last naga caster that looks about the size of a goliath, at least as far as I can tell. There are still a bunch of random car walls built up. Even then, this one looks mostly dead already. Burn marks and a bunch of cracks in its scales like something heavy hit it."

"Probably was in the two storms then. Maybe it tried to rescue some but couldn't?" JP was already pulling out his big .50 cal rifle as they talked. The sight of him taking the massive gun out of the pouch at his side was still a weird sensation for Drew.

"Or it's bait, and we're supposed to expect them to be mostly defeated and rush things." Sarah was leaning against her spear even as she was swapping her quickdraw magazines to replace the ones that had been emptied in the earlier sortie.

"Yeah, for having so much less firepower than we do, they set up a pretty good ambush." Drew cracked his neck, glancing up the ramp. "I still think we jump to the top of the ramp at this point. I'll do a storm up there, and then we can have Katie build one last wall, and we'll go in standard formation. Once we're up there, we'll take it slow and clear the area with gravity points from behind the wall. I doubt an hour or two, either way, is going to change the naga getting a new node."

Katie grunted. Even after a rain, she was still running low. But she nodded her head in agreement. "Let's get this over with," she said, pushing off the wall and cracking her neck.

Drew moved to the crack and began casting another holy firestorm through the cleared passage. The bright red and white flashes of light from the storm created strange, flickering shadows on the concrete. When it was mostly blocked by Katie's wall, they continued up the ramp to the new safe zone. They passed three bodies of goliath nagas, broken, burned, and torn into pieces. Additionally, several body parts from naga casters littered the ground around the side of the ramp, thrown there by the fury of the storms.

The entire group pulled face coverings down to block the smell that was already filling the enclosed space. Which were a disgusting combination of feces, the coppery tang of blood, and the sickly sweet smell of burning flesh.

"I feel like we could have done this in a better way," Katie muttered as she crouched next to the wall, one hand pressed against its surface while the other hand massaged her forehead, trying to fight back her headache.

"Sorry. Still kind of new to this whole magical superpowers thing. It would be nice to take a few weeks and get familiar with all the spells." Drew wondered if he would ever have a few weeks to just consolidate things ever again. Maybe after they defeated the world boss? That seemed like such a faraway thing, though. Katie's response was a non-committal snort; they were all doing their best despite the difficult circumstances, and she knew it.

Now that the wall was built, Katie probably wouldn't need to use much more mana. Drew stepped up to his opening as JP did, and the others did the same. All of them trained their long-range weaponry on the naga curled around the pyramid.

It was more sinewy than the regular goliaths, sharp frills adorning its stubby arms, and the sides of its head had a hood like a cobra. Like most of the naga, its lower half was more like a lower three quarters and resembled a snake's body. Its coloration was the real giveaway on it. All the naga types had distinctive coats. The casters had thick blue lines across their scales, where the pure melee monsters had orange stripes, and the spine throwers red.

There were a few combination variants, but for the most part they all fell into those three schemes. Drew glanced over at

JP, who had the .50 cal up and was staring down the sights. Drew looked around the room but didn't see any other monsters. After the intense fight the naga had put forth to this point, this all felt almost anticlimactic.

"So, this feels like a trap," Drew muttered, and JP grunted his assent. "But I honestly don't know how it could be. I feel like we're missing some important part of this."

"What do you want to do, then?" Luke's words had a tint of amusement in them. Drew had realized pretty quickly that unless Drew was in mortal danger, the seraph would let him make his own mistakes. Drew considered it for a moment and then shook his head.

"I'm going to try to talk to it. Get ready to shoot if things turn south," Drew muttered before stepping forward. Holding up his hands to show that he was unarmed didn't seem like it was going to be all that worthwhile, given that he had been casting spells from his unarmored hands for weeks. And given that the naga had planned this ambush, they were bound to know what he was capable of.

"I just want to know why," Drew called out and the naga hissed softly.

"Becausse we could." The naga's response was soft, even as it carried all the way to them. Drew wondered if it was xatherite empowered. "We thought we could." There was sorrow in the voice. "You are sstrong, sstronger than you sshould be." The naga reared up, its coils constricting around the pyramid.

"If only your nesst had been elssewhere, we would have ruled over thesse sspawning groundss. Sstill, it matterss not, our clutch will ssurvive." Drew frowned at the naga's words that meant that they were sure of their ability to take over one of the nodes on the far side of the river.

"I'm afraid I cannot allow that." Five of his fireball variants erupted from Drew's hands. The sixth, gravity point, appeared in the middle of the naga, compressing the already-broken scales. To his side, the report of gunfire echoed out as the rest of the team unleashed their own deadly projectiles. The snake reared, responding to the impacts of its flesh and then, with an ear-rending cry, fell to the ground and moved no more.

"That's it?" JP shifted the rifle around as he scanned the room for more threats. "All that work… for that?"

"Daryl, anything else in that room?" Drew was getting nervous. Everything about this last dungeon just felt wrong. They had prepared good counters to his team's abilities, only to just… stop trying at the end? Had they broken the naga's will to fight back by defeating the ambush?

"Don't see anything." Daryl interrupted Drew's musings.

"Alright, let's clear the room and get the secondary group up here," Drew said as he stepped through the opening Katie created in the wall. He could hear other footsteps behind him, but he tuned them out as he looked around the space. Broken cars littered the room, but there were other signs of habitation. A hand-drawn map was visible along one wall, but even from here, it was apparent the naga had defaced it to the point where it wouldn't help much. Black ink splattered across two-thirds of its surface area.

"Clear," JP called out from behind him. A quick glance back showed that he had replaced his .50 cal with a handgun. He was checking one of the various offshoot passages to the side, looking behind cars.

Drew didn't think there were any more of the large naga, but he was worried they might have more of the snakes inside vehicles like they had used to bombard their earlier barricade.

"Careful, they might have more of those snake bombs," Sarah called out a mirror of Drew's thoughts. Enough light streamed in through the sides of the parking garage that they could see but glowrocks were being thrown to illuminate any dark patches. Drew walked forward slowly, Luke's footsteps splashing into the shallow water behind him. His target was the pyramid in the back, the still form of the naga coiled around it. He could see a purple light start glowing from the back of its head, and Drew assumed at least one xatherite had grown out of the dead guardian.

Stepping around the body, he saw the large crystal. He sighed in relief in seeing that it was violet rather than indigo. "Big and bright violet here," Drew called out. This one was big enough that they were going to want to have one of the growers harvest it. Violets were their best chance at getting a sustainable food supply. Stepping over to the pyramid, he placed his hand on it, letting the red door appear, even as he kept turning his head, looking for more naga.

"Greetings, Sub-Lieutenant. Would you like me to begin your standard takeover procedures?" The disembodied voice of Aevis, Earth-3's assigned system AI spoke, the voice coming from nowhere and everywhere all at once.

"Not yet, Aevis. Hold off on the claim just yet." Drew teleported back out of the pyramid before the AI could respond. "Guardian confirmed dead," he called out.

"Sarah is already going to get the others," Luke told him from the side. "She left as soon as you disappeared." Drew glanced toward the opening. He had only spent a few seconds inside the pyramid, so Sarah must have taken off at a run to be out of sight already.

"Nothing else up here, and we haven't found any other xatherite." JP showed up a few seconds later, his guns already sheathed. "Daryl is notifying the colonel about the crystal. Should have someone up here to gather it in no time."

Drew somehow doubted that. It would probably be more like an hour before they managed to send someone to the growing area and then bring back one of the growers. Just getting an escort for them would probably be difficult.

Drew cast a refreshing rain over Katie; the brunette was still nursing her head like she was in mana fatigue, and he didn't want to waste too much of the cooldown while he was inside. He had a feeling this was going to be a significant node. So it was likely he was going to be spending some time inside.

Moving quickly, Sarah rejoined the group. She was slightly out of breath from having run the entire time. "They'll be right up. This new armor makes sprinting super hard," she huffed out. While they waited, Drew cast solar offering on the big naga's corpse, filling up his vitality pool. It took the others a full minute and a half to get caught up to them, the Marines clearly pacing themselves with the others. Seeing them, Drew turned back to the pyramid and began opening the door.

"Welcome back, Sub-Lieutenant. I assume we can begin now?" Aevis asked when he reappeared in the node's control room.

"Indeed, and of course, grant access to the tier four individuals as usual."

"Very well, this node is currently designated as PNSN-44. What would you like to change that to?"

Drew frowned. They hadn't even taken the time to rename the last few nodes. "Designate this as… Naga Bane." He moved forward and took his customary seat in the middle of the command center even as Luke and JP appeared behind him, the others following shortly after. Several chairs appeared, and a large table extended from his location. Everyone took the seat closest to them as they went to work, taking off their helmets and the more annoying armor pieces.

"Alright, Aevis. Show us the options."

Naga Bane Node Designation Tool
1. Biological Growth Accelerator (1)
2. Dungeon Training Center (5)
3. Forward Operating Base (1)

```
4. Healing Chamber (1)
5. Mana Funnel (0)
6. Feeding Pit (0)
7. Resource Concentrator (1)
8. Xatherite Concentrator (1)
9. Armory (0)
10. Foundry (0)
11. Command Post (0/1)
12. Communications Array (0/1)
13. Sensor Augment (0/1)
14. Transport Depot (0)
```

Drew's eyes went to the end of the list, and he whistled in appreciation. There were six new options: The armory, foundry, command post, communications array, sensor augment, and transportation depot. The communications array and sensor depot were grayed out as if to demonstrate that they were unusable. Their earlier plans had not accounted for most of the new additions.

"Holy shit," JP said to his left.

"Why are the communications array and sensor augment grayed out?" Sarah asked with a frown.

"They both require a connected Command Post to function," Aevis responded.

Drew looked at the map of their nodes. They currently had five nodes designated as DTCs. Two of those were supposed to be DTCs, being used as training and theoretically to get beef from the DIA node. With the bridge being moderately dangerous to cross, they hadn't really started using that to its fullest potential. The other three DTCs were waiting on more nodes to get their final assignments.

"Alright. Who can we contact with the communications array?" Drew ran his hand through his hair.

"The communications array will allow you to communicate instantly with any other array within the inner solar system," Aevis' disembodied voice said to the room.

"Does that include the other-dimensional slices?" Drew continued his line of thought.

"It does indeed."

"What do the armory and foundries do?" Drew asked.

"An armory has safe areas to store large stores of ammunition, weapons, emergency supplies, and acts as a dedicated catastrophe shelter for a small number of people, being fully capable of supporting one hundred humans for an extended period. A foundry is designed to assist in the creation of any object; additional modifiers can be purchased to amplify its use for specific crafting professions or more general usage." Aevis' response had everyone looking around the room.

"And the transport hub?" Drew asked, finally looking around the room and at the expressions, except for Luke, whose face was calm. The rest were clearly very excited by the prospects.

"Transport hubs facilitate the creation and utilization of various means of transportation based on specialization; common uses are vehicle creation, maintenance, or teleportation hubs."

"Alright. With the new node options, I don't feel comfortable using the earlier choices. I'm going to bring Hoeffecker and the council in on this. Install the remote admin console, Aevis." Drew stood up from the table, and the others followed.

CHAPTER TEN – PLANNING

The node at the housing addition was the easiest to get all the required people into but it had still taken almost an hour for everyone to gather. Drew sat at the central desk. Aevis wouldn't let anyone but him sit there. The AI would teleport anyone else who sat there out of the control room. Senator Gunn and Hoeffecker had both tried before they decided to just let Drew sit at the head of the table, so to speak. Gunn sat at the foot, while Hoeffecker sat to Drew's right.

Hall, the former detective and head of security, sat to Drew's left. Sarah sat between Gunn and Hoeffecker, the three representing the military group, including all the battle teams. Between Hall and Gunn was an unassuming man Drew had only met once before. His name was Brady, and he represented a faction within the stadium that had been gaining power of late. They called themselves the Sons of Liberty. This was the organization that Robbi had been a part of that initially wanted to separate from the stadium. They had changed their tune when the dome went up, openly allying themselves with Drew.

Standing around the room was Captain Snyder, who had survived being shot in the depths of the stadium. The stadium's conversion to a system recognized Habitat had removed most of the maintenance boss' responsibilities. Mostly he was relegated to food preparation and taking care of the Numb. Next to him was Miss White, who represented what most people called the Growers, the people responsible for growing the stadium's food. Dak had been invited but declined, saying he was too busy at the resource concentrator to come unless it directly impacted his work. Standing along the other side of the room were Pappy and Min Sun, both of whom had refused chairs when offered.

The map was already up and showing the list of options that were available to the group. White didn't really have much to say, as none of the buildings would directly affect her organization, but she was there to make sure her people were represented. The colonel had been briefing them on the situation. The short version was that any attempts to go close to the National Mall were rebuffed by stronger and stronger monsters.

"Is there any chance we could get another node?" Gunn asked, looking at the map again.

"There is a chance," Hoeffecker said after a moment. She pointed to a node to the northwest of them. "This is the only real option. We could also try for the eastern Market node, but I'd rather avoid provoking anything anywhere near Capitol Hill at the moment." She pointed to the CG HQ node. "This one has been taken over by the orcs. It's likely to be as hard a push as the naga campaign was. Doable, but I don't really want that many of our people on the other side of the river.

"Every time we cross the Frederick Douglass Bridge, it takes a beating from the aquatic creatures, and honestly, we're not sure how much longer it's going to last. We might switch over to the 11th Street bridges, but that forces us to move through the orc territory as well. Which would be fine if that was the push we were wanting to make. However, we need to get to the Pentagon. Someone or something over there is claiming nodes, and the Pentagon itself is our best bet of reconnecting with any more VIPs.

"We have thought about trying to make for the Woodrow Wilson Bridge further to the south. But that increases the distance we need to travel by eleven miles, almost four times as much as taking the 14th Street bridges. We think Mr. Michilak's people could sneak through the waterfront, take out the node here, and then continue through the tidal basin, taking over the Jefferson Memorial node before heading directly into the Pentagon."

"So we send the only person able to conquer nodes and a large portion of our firepower over the Potomac where they will most likely be cut off from us for who knows how long?" Gunn asked, glancing at the map. "I don't see how that is going to put us in a better position."

"With the shield up, this is one of the few chances we're going to have of finding more survivors," Hoeffecker said even as she pointed to the violet nodes. "What we do know is that aliens, most likely hostile, landed on the planet here. And we cannot allow them to dig in any more than they already have. We've all seen what is happening in Arlington. The airport is basically a jungle at this point. Whatever they are doing is big, and we need to handle it before it's too big for us to handle."

"None of us like it, but we clearly need to at least investigate these aliens. The Sons of Liberty don't have anyone that is a match for your current team," Brady said from his spot at the table, turning to talk to Drew. "But we can provide you with communication devices and a few other tools that will allay some concerns about your mission."

Drew could feel Hoeffecker's body tense next to him. The woman had been trying to get the Sons to work more closely with the defense forces since they had announced their presence. "Oh, now you want to help?" she started, but Gunn held up a hand to forestall what was bound to be a lengthy rebuke from the colonel.

"It's okay, Tracey, I think we all understand how valuable the Sons' assistance will be. I assume the expedition planning will be handled by the military as they see fit. What we've gathered here to discuss is what to do with the three nodes we have, now that we have additional options." Gunn drew everyone's attention back to the map. "I think the priorities here are the foundry, sensor augment, and communications array."

"If I may intrude," Aevis' voice spoke through the room. "As I have said before. Two of those, the sensor augment and communications array, are contingent upon having a command post installed in the linked node structure."

Gunn paused, looking at the map again. "What benefits does the command post give?" he asked, and Drew frowned.

"The command post allows for more coordinated control over nodes, unlocks additional options for development, and a finer degree of customization over all linked structures. It also comes with a warning system, internal communications system, and augments automatic defense construct's response."

"Right, so we want one of those regardless," Hoeffecker announced, and no one disagreed with her. "Do we convert one of the old ones into a command post, or do we use the Naval Sea History building? I think it's probably a building we want to keep centralized. We can't lose the housing addition or the Habitat. That leaves the Institute over on McNair, which is currently our main DTC, or the DoT building, which is our healing chamber."

"Aevis, how much mana does a command post require to create?" Drew asked with a frown.

"Command posts require twenty-thousand units of mana. At current levels, the DoT building will take three months to regenerate to that point, while the Institute node will only require one and a half," Aevis responded with her usual crisp intonation.

"Not worth it," Drew stated. "So, that leaves the Naval Sea History building as the command post." Looking around the table, no one disagreed with him. "Make it so, Aevis." A timer appeared underneath the Naval Sea History building, indicating that it would become a Command Post in eighteen hours.

"What do we do with the other two?" Drew looked around the room. "Honestly, as much as I would love a communications array, I have it on good authority that the only people we'll be able to talk to are from the earlier slices of Earth. Which might be helpful as far as gaining information about how the system is run, but I don't think that will play a pivotal role in anything at the current time."

"So we put the communications array on the shortlist for the next node?" Sarah asked, and everyone nodded in agreement. "Which leaves us with the sensor augment, armory, and foundry. I personally think we should put the foundry next to the command post in the HR building and the sensor augment in the..." She paused, clearly annoyed by the choice. "Naga Bane node."

"That would be too much distance between the nodes, especially the bones and stones," Pappy said, stroking his short beard. "But there is much lost mana from reconfiguring if we do that. An alternative: create a safe road between the two." Drew had noticed that the eccentric old man's speech pattern had shifted over the last few weeks. The bones and stones probably referenced the resource concentrator and DTC, which supplied most of the bones the crafter was using these days. "Better than other options. It should be a foundry."

"What exactly does the sensor augment do?" Hoeffecker asked, nodding to Pappy to indicate she understood his opinion.

"The command post has a limited ability to sense incoming threats to the connected nodes. The sensor augment improves the range and fidelity of that warning system by three times the original distance and resolution. With the augment, you would be able to track significant threats through most of Capitol Hill and the closer sections of Anacostia. The sensor's effectiveness is reduced by water, but should also be able to track threats in the Potomac and Anacostia rivers. However, its radius will not be sufficient to have any significant tracking on the other side of the Potomac, except around the node at the DIA building."

As Aevis spoke, the map was shaded in two different colors—a red one for the warning system's original strength and orange for the expanded section.

"So, four blocks with the augment and to the walls without it. Does the range increase if we manage to take over more connected nodes?" Hoeffecker looked at the map with a frown.

"Indeed, the radius is dependent on the distance from conquered nodes, with additional amplification of resolution based on overlapping zones of influence, which usually is not relevant, but due to the high concentration of nodes in this area will have an increased effect." Aevis shifted the map again to varying shades of red and orange spreading away from each node, with overlapping regions getting progressively darker.

"Alright, so sensor augment and foundry," Hoeffecker announced, glancing at Drew, who nodded his agreement she turned her attention to Gunn. "Senator?"

"I can't say I wouldn't appreciate the armory. Having a safe place to put our most vulnerable citizens would ease quite a few minds. But I agree, our focus needs to be on strengthening our position. Especially if we are going to be temporarily losing our most valuable defender." Gunn nodded to Drew. "Does anyone have any arguments against this course of action?" The senator glanced around the room, getting a head shake from Brady, Hall, and White. Snyder looked like he had eaten something sour but also shook his head.

"Alright. Let's do it," Hoeffecker said, then coughed as she remembered that Aevis only responded to Drew.

"Aevis, please turn the HR Dungeon into a foundry, and the Naga Bane node into a sensor augment," Drew repeated the colonel's request with a grin.

Hoeffecker shook her head slightly. "Drew, I think we're gonna need you to stick around long enough to set up permissions in the command post." She glanced at the map. "Which gives us just under eighteen hours to prepare. Well, that's all for now. I'm sure we all have things to do." Standing up, the rest of the people at the table followed her lead.

Drew found it odd that they ended all of these meetings by shaking each other's hands, but he shook everyone but Snyder's hand as they filed out of the room. The captain avoided it by looking at a piece of paper as he passed Drew. Hoeffecker gestured for Drew and Sarah to stay behind and kept Brady back as well. When they were alone in the control room again, she motioned for them to sit back down.

"So, Mr. Brady, what sort of help are the Sons willing to offer?"

"We'll be giving Mr. Michalik a communications device so that he can talk with us at any time. We also have a member that managed to create an improved version of the glow sticks that operates as a flashlight but does not need to be recharged. Aside from that, we'd be happy to send some of our people with him. I know you want to keep the group small and mobile, and we have a couple of people who have skills that would facilitate quicker movement."

"What crystals are we talking about?" Hoeffecker asked, her tone cold. Drew knew that a large portion of her efforts had been in cataloging abilities that would assist in defense of the stadium.

"We have a member that has expressed interest in going with Mr. Michalik that has an ability he calls a 'stealth field,' which reduces the distance friendly targets are detected by non-friendly targets." Brady either didn't care about the venom in Hoeffecker's words or did not detect it.

"And why is this the first time I'm hearing about this ability? An ability that would no doubt assist greatly in the rescue and salvage attempts we have going on throughout the area."

"Because quite frankly, colonel, you have no authority over our people. As citizens of the United States, we are not required to follow military edicts unless a state of martial law has been declared. Our militia is happy to work with the federal government and its military. Still, we are not beholden to abide by your laws except as required by the Constitution of the United States." Brady returned Hoeffecker's icy glare with one of his own. "We understand the good that you've done, colonel, and you have done everything in your power to protect helpless citizens. But the Sons of Liberty are not powerless, and while we remain on US soil, we will not bow to a military dictatorship.

"Mr. Michalik has, independent of his position in the military, done more to keep his fellow citizens safe than anyone else. We believe that he is acting with us and our best interests, so we are more than happy to work with *him* to save our people. Especially considering he is a member of a peacekeeping force with jurisdiction in US territory."

"Mr. Brady, I'm Army, not the CIA. I can legally operate on US soil. And whatever else you say, America has been invaded, and the military is doing everything we can to keep her citizens safe." The two glared daggers at each other.

"Mr. Brady, in times like this we need to have a clear command structure. Colonel Hoeffecker makes the most sense to have leading our defensive effort. And she has done an admirable job thus far," Drew interrupted into the quiet. "I understand you want to make sure your rights are not infringed upon, but turning on each other is not going to assist anyone."

"We need to discuss who all is going. This is a dangerous mission, and I'm not going to force anyone to come with me," Drew said, hoping to break the tension in the room. "I'd like to meet with your… man? Woman? Before we make any final decisions."

"His name is Clive, and I'll arrange a meeting…" Brady trailed off, and it took Drew a minute to figure out he was asking for a time.

"Let's do it tomorrow morning." It was almost nightfall and Drew decided that he would sleep again before heading into unknown territory.

Brady nodded. "I'll have him meet you at the west gates tomorrow at, say... eight? That way he'll be able to demonstrate his skills a bit."

"That should work. I'll hopefully know how many spots we want to fill with external volunteers by then." They all stood up, and Brady shook Drew's hand before turning and exiting the control room.

"I really hate that guy," Hoeffecker said from his side.

"Yeah... that ability sounds like the perfect way to kill someone," Drew said, sitting down with a frown. "Lead them somewhere dangerous and then drop the stealth field in the middle of it all."

The colonel sat down and sighed. "Welcome to my life. Ever since the Sons went public, they've been a thorn in my side. Unfortunately, they have enough power that they could really hurt us if they wanted to."

"That bad?" Drew had been on the frontlines and was never one for politics, so he had missed out on a lot of the politicking.

"You have no idea. The Sons are at least willing to work. They have too many secrets and don't play nice with others, but they get stuff done. There is a group of people who refuse to do anything at all until they have an election, then complain about us violating their civil rights when we don't give them food." Hoeffecker ran a hand through her hair. "DC was always a bit of a shit show, but somehow these people are still clinging to party politics even after the world went to hell in a handbasket. Especially since the shield went up and people felt safe again, they went right back to bickering."

Drew just shook his head. "Well, I'm glad you're dealing with them."

"Well, I don't imagine you'll have any better luck where you're going. The Pentagon is full of people looking to further their own agendas and willing to let others hang for a difference of opinion." Leaning back, she closed her eyes and massaged her temples. "Anyway. Let's talk about your battle plan for this trip."

CHAPTER ELEVEN – ADVICE

"First off, we need to talk about who is going. Unfortunately, your team represents a good chunk of our strategic assets, and quite frankly… we cannot afford to lose all of you." Hoeffecker opened her eyes and looked at Drew. "Namely, Officer White and Miss Sabin." Referencing JP and Katie, respectively.

"Until Mr. Kyle can recreate gunpowder, we are far too reliant on Officer White's ability to refill magazines. A full three-fourths of our fighting force use guns as their main source of damage. He also represents the second most potent supply of damage dealing we have." Drew couldn't help but nod his head at Hoeffecker's words. Dak Kyle had been working on gunpowder as an inferior replacement for smokeless powder in their bullets but still hadn't been able to come anywhere close to the kind of supply they would need.

"And Katie?" Drew asked, wanting to hear her reasoning.

"Well, Miss Sabin is a bit more tricky." Hoeffecker paused for a moment. "She personally requested to stay here. She's not as irreplaceable as JP, but…" She trailed off, and Drew could understand. Katie's wall ability was incredibly potent wherever she went.

"She asked to stay here?" Drew swallowed and thought back to their last few conversations. Katie had told him she didn't think she could keep doing this. But why would she have talked to Hoeffecker first? "Well, that makes things awkward."

"Drew, despite what I just told Brady… the government is basically in a state of dysfunction that I don't think it will ever recover from. We have a chance to rebuild the rules a little. Which is why I haven't said anything about that relationship until now. There is a reason the military discouraged romantic relationships in members of the same chain. It makes stuff like this… sticky." Hoeffecker sighed and looked at the map. "I don't know what this means for you personally, and I'm afraid I can't give you a lot of time to figure that out.

"Mr. Swaze will be going with you as a scout. I'm tempted to replace Ensign Rothschild with a different healer; she's the best we have. However, I have a feeling you're going to need the best, especially without Miss Sabin. I don't think anyone would be able to get Luke away from you, so he'll be your front line. How do you feel about the kids?"

"I'm not taking a couple of teenagers into a commando-style mission," Drew said with a frown.

"I don't think you should take all of them. But Gary Kramer, the Jedi kid? I think he'll be very helpful in avoiding dangerous situations, plus his lightsaber can cut through just about anything he puts it against, which makes for a very quiet way of making holes. That could be useful. He is young, but he'll follow orders and won't complain. Kid basically worships you. But, most importantly… we can spare him."

"Those last points don't comfort me at all," Drew said with a frown. Still, the sense threat skill Gary had displayed in the HR dungeon had been very valuable, especially if it had leveled up. "Alright, just Gary from the kids, though."

"The one thing I don't have to give you is someone that can make a safe redoubt anywhere near as well as Miss Sabin. We do have some that can create temporary barriers. And, of course, some could eventually become as potent as Sabin's xatherite, especially if they're fighting with you. I think that's going to be an important ability to have, and we'll probably start getting battlefield control members on as many teams as we can. Sadly, they aren't super common." Frowning for a minute, she considered. "How would you feel about Chief Mather?"

"Bill? Isn't he a healer?" The chief had been among the first group of survivors that Drew had found. The big man had healed him after being injured fighting squirrels on the highway.

"He is. But you'll probably need another healer if you find more survivors, or if Sarah gets hurt. I know Luke has some weak healing as well, but the real reason is that he has an orange ability that can make a safe space… as long as you bring a few blankets with you."

"Blankets?" Drew asked, confused. Bill's healing xatherite had also had the odd requirement that he hug you for it to work.

"Yeah, the chief's xatherite are all a little odd. This one is called 'Blanket Fort.' If you set up a blanket fort, you're safe from monster attacks inside."

Drew glanced down. Bill's healing ability had been called Daddy's Embrace, if he remembered correctly. "What happened to his family?" he asked quietly.

"No one knows for sure, but… they weren't among the survivors at the DIA building." Hoeffecker sighed. "He's taking it better than most, but he wants to stay busy and be of use. I think going with you will help him deal with it."

"Does he have any attacks?"

"No, he's mostly yellows and oranges. He has oranges to make him hit harder, and he carries around a metal club that he can use pretty well."

"Well, I guess we'll need some extra blankets."

"Good. We can send a few more damage dealers with you, but I think you're better off with a smaller, fast-moving group."

"Okay, maybe the Sons guy will be worthwhile. We'll have to adapt some new strategies." Drew frowned, his thoughts returning to Katie and why she wouldn't want to go with him. His glance drifted across the map before focusing on the nodes next to him. "Any information on this node?" he asked, pointing to the node on their way north to the bridge.

"None whatsoever. Without the map, I don't think we would have even realized there was one there. There are monsters out there, but no cohesive type of them, and there aren't any important buildings there. As far as anyone can tell, it's just a couple of restaurants and an apartment building there," Hoeffecker said with a frown. "Although we haven't gone that far north in a while. Groups tended to disappear, and it's still uncomfortably close to the Mall."

"Yeah, even if I take over that node, are we even going to be able to use it for anything?" Drew asked with a frown.

"Not really, no, but I'm more concerned with making a link to the nodes on the Arlington side. But…" Hoeffecker pointed to two other nodes. "You'd also have to take out the FCC building here, and the Jefferson Memorial. That gives us a direct link to the Pentagon node. They're probably all too dangerous to use for anything, but having them is important for continuity. Plus… with the sensor augment, we'd get a better idea of what the situation is on the Mall."

"Three node takeovers are going to slow down our progress a lot," Drew said as he chewed his lip, looking at the node map. "Is there a compelling reason not to do it on the way back?"

"Well, they'll probably be easier to take over now than then, but it'll also get your people some upgrades to their xatherite. The new members of your team don't have the advantage that the long-standing members have of being there when you've taken over a bunch of nodes. They'll see some pretty dramatic increases in strength. You'll also probably get a bunch more xatherite, which will increase your fighting capability." Hoeffecker shrugged. "I think a short detour will be valuable. A few days isn't going to change their situation much. Except for the aliens, and even then, you can think of this as a shakedown cruise. Get all the kinks out of the new group before you fight something intelligent."

"I talked to Miss Rothschild, and the naga had your number pretty good. If they had a bit more firepower to back up their attack, the battle could have easily gone the other way. I don't think we should underestimate these aliens. Give the new team time to grow together a bit rather than rushing to fight them. That way, you'll be better prepared for whatever they send your way."

"I have a feeling that will happen regardless of if we take over the nodes, but the experience gain for the new people would be... nice. That's another good point, though. Are we sure we want to give something like that to the Sons?" Brady gave Drew a bad feeling. He was a zealot for his cause, and Drew just didn't trust people like that.

"Depends entirely on who it is," Hoeffecker said. "I know Robbi was a member of their group, but he didn't have long to spend with them. A week at most before he got sent out on that long patrol that found you. My experiences with militias have all been... less than stellar. But if they have as much influence as they seem to..." She ran a hand through her hair in frustration.

"What about Snyder? He hasn't said a word to me since the shield went up." Drew wanted to direct the colonel's attention away from the powder keg called the Sons of Liberty.

"He's been unnaturally quiet. I think being injured shook him up more than he wants to admit. I don't know what his service record says, but that seems like the first time his life has ever been in direct danger, and he's handling it poorly."

Drew tried to think if any of the officers he knew had ever been put in a life-threatening situation. In the Coast Guard, officers didn't really go on boarding missions, a few here or there, but mostly it was the enlisted while the Os stayed on the ship. "Could be. I imagine that's relatively easy in the Navy, depending on where your ship is."

"Yeah, we don't exactly chat, but he's never talked about former posts." Hoeffecker frowned for a minute as she considered something and then shrugged it off. "Anyway, he's good enough at his job. I mean, he's pretty much only taking care of the Numb at this point. Which is a pretty thankless job. We've had a few of them 'wake up,' but I don't have a lot of hope for any great source of power there. Seems like anyone with a personality to fight didn't end up Numb in the first place."

"There's a method to that madness," Drew answered. "What are they doing now? These woken Numb?"

"Honestly? Not much," Hoeffecker said with a shrug. "A large chunk of the population does nothing. We've tried enticing people into workgroups by offering more food, and we get some… but sixty percent of our population just sits in the shield doing nothing."

"That's… not sustainable."

"We can't force them to do something, and now that we can pretty easily provide enough food for them…" Hoeffecker trailed off and shrugged. "Not really my problem. That's what the senator is for, and he's working on it."

"Well, I hope he figures it out soon. Is there anything I can do to help you before I leave?"

"I'm going to think about who I want to be able to access the command post. If we can set it up so that I'm the only one that can grant and remove access while you're gone, that will go a long way toward stabilizing some of the power struggle issues. Or maybe it will cause more. I don't really know. I'm not used to having to work this closely with so many civilians." The colonel shrugged in slight defeat.

"Well, if you can think of anything, let me know." Drew sat in silence with Hoeffecker as she stared at the map, deep in thought.

"Just stay alive. It's hard to find dependable help, and you solve far more problems than you create."

"I cause problems?"

"A few, like sleeping with one of your subordinates." Drew could sense that there was some real annoyance in that statement, but she wasn't overly judgmental. "But I understand it. I could use some stress relief myself." Drew coughed in surprise, and that made Hoeffecker laugh.

"Well, good luck with that, ma'am." Drew frowned as he realized that Hoeffecker didn't really have any peers in the stadium. Snyder was probably the closest, but he was an ass, which left Drew… Hall and maybe White were the only people she could confide in.

The colonel just snorted in response and stretched. "Well, it's nice to get a break, but I suppose it's time I get back to work." She put a hand on Drew's shoulder. Mana rampart slowed her hand down slightly but Drew let it land on his shoulder. "Damn, that's weird every time I feel it," Hoeffecker said before shaking her head. "If I can give you a suggestion, Drew? Talk to the rest of your team before you talk to Miss Sabin. I have a feeling you're not going to want to be super social after that."

Drew let out a heavy sigh and then nodded his head. "Yeah, I suppose you're probably right. I think getting told your girlfriend wants to break up with you from your CO is probably a new low for me."

"You don't know she wants to break up with you. She just doesn't want to be around when you kill monsters," Hoeffecker said with a shrug. "Although staying behind isn't any easier. My first husband decided it was too hard to think about me getting shot on my first deployment. Coming home to an empty house is never a fun thing, but… just listen to her reasons. Like I said with Chief Mather, we're all just barely scraping by here."

"I'm not," Drew said with a frown. "I mean. It's hard, right? I don't enjoy the idea of people dying or anything. But… this feels right? Like this is the world I was supposed to be born into. I always thought I would hate being an adventurer. Delving into dangerous monster lairs seems like a stupid idea. I was never really an adrenaline junkie, but I have never felt more alive." He looked into Hoeffecker's eyes. "Does that make me broken somehow?"

"No." Hoeffecker returned his gaze without hesitation. "It just means you've found your calling. And we're all damn lucky you did too. Because without you, none of us would be here." She held up a hand to forestall his argument.

"Oh, some of us might still be alive. But without you, there would be no dome. We'd all be slaves to that creche, or sacrificed by the trolls, or beaten down by the naga. I'm not sure what a red mage is, Drew." Drew blinked. Hoeffecker never used people's first names. "I'm not sure what makes you different from the rest of us, but it's clear that you are. And I'm damn sure glad you're on our side. Because any monster smart enough to know you're coming for them should be shaking in their boots."

Not able to help it, Drew flashed her a grim smile. "Thank you, ma'am. I think I needed to hear that."

Hoeffecker kept his gaze for a moment and then nodded her head. "Just remember that. We're guardians, not warmongers. They invaded our home first. And we've sworn an oath to protect it from enemies both foreign and domestic."

Hoeffecker patted him on the shoulder and then stepped out of the control room, leaving Drew alone with his thoughts.

CHAPTER TWELVE – DTR

Drew sat in the soft glow of the control room and thought about what Hoeffecker had said. He was learning to really appreciate these moments of quietness. There weren't many places he could be alone, and even fewer where he could be alone and not worry that monsters were going to attack him. Still, there was a sense of guilt in taking time for himself, and with a resigned sigh, he stood up and stretched.

Drew turned away from the map and exited the control room, appearing at the housing module's top. The pyramid here was on the second-highest floor of the building, which was mostly empty. A few benches littered the area, and large transparent walls gave a commanding view of southern DC. Drew would have thought more people would spend time up here, but most people avoided it. To his surprise, there were actually two people waiting for him.

Luke was the one that he had been expecting. The seraph's status as an alien was known to the council, and they had flat out refused to allow him to sit in on the meetings. That didn't stop him from hovering around the pyramid, waiting for Drew to leave.

The other person he had not been expecting. Katie stood off to the side, nervously rubbing a glowrock. The teleport out of the control room was silent, and neither of them had noticed him appearing. Drew cleared his throat, and they turned to look at him. Katie had a forced smile on her face, but her eyes looked worried. Drew felt a strange stab of pain. They had only known each other for a few weeks, but they had been wonderful, at least for him.

Now that the colonel had pointed it out to him, he could see that she was not handling the end of the world as well as he had thought she was. Her clothing looked just a little more rumpled than it should be, and there was a weariness around her eyes that he knew no invigorate was going to fix.

"Hey," Drew said, deciding to break the ice.

"Hey back." Katie was looking him up and down and seemed to realize something. "She told you?"

Drew nodded his head to the elevator. "Yeah, maybe we should go somewhere a little more private?"

"Your room? Sure." Katie said as she turned, walking forward slowly. Drew caught up, and they walked about an arm's length apart. It was strange how easily distance came. Earlier that day, they had cuddled and kissed, and now…

Drew felt a pit slowly forming in his stomach. He had always hated conversations like this. They didn't talk again until they got to Drew's suite. Luke appeared next to them.

"I will give you two some space," the seraph said before heading into his own room.

Drew gestured toward the main sitting area, and Katie paused long enough to pull off her boots before sitting in the corner of one of the long couches, her legs pulled up against her chest and a pillow held in her arms. The lounge area was nice. The sofas were well made and looked like they could have come from Earth.

"Are you angry?" Katie asked just as Drew had finished taking off his boots and was in the process of loosening his armor to its most comfortable configuration. He paused and looked up at Katie, who was watching him, and he shook his head.

"No. I'm not angry." Even as he said the words, Drew realized he wasn't. "Just… sad? Although that's not the right emotion either. I guess some part of me knew this was coming. I know you don't like the danger."

"I don't know how you do it. You walk into those dark dungeons with all those terrible monsters that want to kill you, and you just… fight them." Katie clutched the pillow tighter and closed her eyes. "Every time we do, I'm sure that it's going to be the last one. That this time it's gonna be my turn, and I'm gonna die just like Juan and Mitch. That something is going to eat me like Robbi." Swallowing hard, she looked up. "Those naga today? They almost killed us. All of us. If you hadn't seen the trap, we would have been dead. And I, I just…"

"Can't do it anymore," Drew finished for her, sitting down on the other end of the couch, far enough to give her the space she wanted but still within reach.

"Yeah." Katie's words were almost a sigh. An audible sense of the weight that had been building up on her.

"What will you do?"

"I'll be building walls. Gunn has some ideas for ways to make the whole compound more livable and safer, putting up a wall around the entire area."

Drew nodded. It was important work. The dome only covered about a third of the space they had claimed. The command post might extend that some, but probably not a ton, and they'd need to start building up the area outside of the shield. "And what about us?"

"I…" Katie started but paused, looking away from him and playing with the fringe on the pillow she was clutching. "I don't think I could stand waiting for you to come back. I remember talking to wives at my first unit. They put up a brave face, but you could see how hard not knowing was on them, you know? And I don't think I could handle that. That would make me crazier than I am now."

"You're not crazy," Drew said as an almost knee-jerk reaction. "If anything, that's probably a more normal response than wanting to dive into danger every chance I get."

"You could stay too. You know." Katie still didn't look up. "Let someone else handle it."

Drew considered her words for a moment and then shook his head. "No, I don't think I could. I don't buy into this whole… chosen one thing. But the fact is that I can do something, and I have a better chance than anyone else to make it work."

"I guess I know that," Katie said with another sigh. She looked back at Drew and brushed her hand out of her face. "I sort of wish I would have met you before the world went to shit."

"Nah. I wasn't nearly as impressive before I could throw fireballs around. I was just… a quiet nerd." Drew ran his hands through his hair. It was getting long enough that someone probably would have yelled at him for being out of regulation back in the old world.

"Maybe, but at least all your dungeon delves then were in video games," Katie said, and for the first time in a while, she had more of that fire that he had fallen for.

"Well, and tabletop games." When Katie looked at him confused, Drew laughed slightly. "It's not important. How long have you been… feeling like this?"

"I think since the dome went up. Hearing that you had almost died and then waiting for you to come out…" Katie suppressed an involuntary shiver. "I think that's when I realized that someday you might not make it through. That even as good as you are, eventually, there might be something strong enough to take you out."

"I'm sorry I kept forcing you to come in with me…" Drew said, and Katie glowered at him.

"You didn't force me, Drew." She paused, trying to think of how to phrase it. "You never ask more of anyone than you ask of yourself. I think that's what makes m—people love you." He could tell she had been about to say that was what made her love him but changed it at the last second. "You never ask for any credit. You never tell someone else to do something dangerous. You're always charging in first to make sure it's safe for everyone else. Honestly, you're the hero we need, but not the one we deserve? Did I say that quote right?"

"I think so?" Drew shrugged. "I always thought that movie was a little too... dark, to be honest. I only watched it once. But I'm not a hero. Batman managed to save the day without killing anyone. I can't save the day, and I've killed a lot of stuff."

Katie threw the pillow at him. "Don't you ever think that killing monsters is a bad thing, Drew Michalik. Everything you do is because they came here and killed people first."

Drew snorted. "Hoeffecker just told me the same thing."

"Well, you should start listening to the smart women in your life."

"I will just as soon as I meet some," Drew said, throwing the pillow back at Katie, and she caught it with a look of mock anger before tossing it back at him.

"I hate to say this because it's so cliche, but it really is me, not you. Honestly, Drew, you're dependable, smart, courageous, selfless. Everything I always thought I wanted in a man."

"But the reality falls short of expectations?"

"No, the reality is impossible to keep up with," Katie said with a shake of her head. "You're off to save everyone, and I just want to hide and never have to fight again. I don't think that's something I can realistically do, but I can't keep up." Katie reached out and laid a hand on his knee.

"Well, we never really said what this was," Drew said after a few moments of thought. "We've been going pretty hard. I'll go over to Arlington, and when I get back in a week or two, we can see how you feel then?"

Katie shook her head and looked down. "I don't want to be the girl waiting at home to know if her guy is going to make it back home or not. I couldn't take that."

"You know I'm going to do that either way, right?" Drew said, putting his hand on Katie's and curling his fingers through hers. "I'm not going to stop caring about you just because you don't want to help me fight monsters."

Katie sighed heavily and squeezed his hand. "I won't stop either. But I can join the rest of the people here and just… cheer you on from afar."

"You say that like I have a fan club or something."

"I mean, you do," Katie said, raising an eyebrow as she studied his face. "Wait, you didn't realize you have a fan club? Drew…" She paused, trying to come up with words. "You're such an idiot sometimes. Everyone here knows that without you, they're monster food. Do you know how many people you saved during the naga attack? How many people watched monsters melt in front of them after you put up the shield? How many people see you heading out only to come back and tell them that the world is now safer because of something you did? Hell, even the Marines worship you. And that's not mentioning all the people that saw you destroy an *army* of trolls on your own while the rest of us just watched.

"When I say that I can't keep up, that's the sort of stuff I mean. They know you've bled for them, and they love you for it. You're literally the only thing everyone agrees on. Well, everyone but Snyder, but no one cares about him."

"I guess I hadn't really… thought about that." Drew was surprised by the ferocity in Katie's tone. "I just did what needed to be done."

"You keep saying that like it's a normal thing to do. Like it's just taking out the trash at the end of the day." Katie sat back and shook her head. "I mean, I get that is your way of processing everything, but God, Drew…" She trailed off. "Like I said, you're the best man I've ever met, and that makes you infuriating."

"Sorry?" Drew leaned back and looked at the brunette. "You know that's a terrible reason to break up with someone?"

"I know." She let her voice get low. "I didn't say it was the smart choice. But I'm afraid, Drew, afraid if I let this keep going that someday you're not going to come back. And that would destroy me."

Katie leaned over and kissed him on the forehead. "Good luck." She stood up and walked to the elevator. Drew watched her leave, she turned back once to look at him, and he could see tears forming in her eyes. A final wave and she disappeared from sight.

Drew collapsed on the couch, staring up at the ceiling. "Hoeffecker was right. I don't feel social right now," he muttered to himself. He let the sadness roll over him, gave himself over to it, to feel it fully and completely. He wallowed in sorrow for several minutes. Then he sat up and wiped the tears from his eyes. There was work to be done still.

To his surprise, Luke stood at the elevator, waiting for him. "Shall we?"

Chapter Thirteen – Bill

Daryl had a room in his suite, but he didn't respond when Drew called out to him. It was hard to say with the invisible man, but Drew assumed he was getting food or something. The idea of food was actually a pretty good one. Drew had a quick bite after the battle, but after the conversation with Katie, he could use some comfort food. Finding his way to the cafeteria, Drew glanced around the room. There were two lines of people waiting for food.

The much shorter line was filled with people wearing armor and carrying weapons. There were more melee weapons these days, mostly spears and clubs, but rifles were still the weapon of choice. Drew still hadn't met whoever made the rifles, but someone clearly had a xatherite that summoned them. Drew wondered what sort of person got a xatherite that would allow them to summon a gun. Had they been an enthusiast before? An arms smuggler? A gun lobbyist?

Drew and Luke got into line with what in his mind was the adventurer group. The room had a low rumble, but around him, silence prevailed. Drew had gotten used to it, actually. A silent circle followed by a louder than usual ring as people around him were too nervous to talk while those further out felt free to whisper about him without fear of being overheard. Drew nodded to the group in front of him. They were all wearing an arm sash with bands of yellow.

That meant they were probably part of some sort of team. Looking around, he saw that most of the people in this line also carried armbands, although there were a large number of them that wore white bands with a single black X on them. Drew tapped on the shoulder of the nearest and pointed to the band.

"What team are y'all on?" he asked. The man whose shoulder he had tapped on just stared at him for a moment, his eyes blinking rapidly and his chest rising and falling. Luckily, one of the others volunteered the answer.

"We're the Bananas, sir." The girl that answered was young. All of the Bananas were. Drew guessed most of them were in their early twenties or late teens.

"Nice to meet you, I'm Drew Michalik." The guy whose shoulder he had tapped on still hadn't moved. "This guy gonna be alright?"

The girl slapped the kid's shoulder with an audible thump, which seemed to snap the guy out of whatever stupor he had been in. "I'm Banzi!" he shouted, causing everyone in the room to look at him and the kid locked up again, much to the amusement of the other Bananas. Banzi clapped a hand over his mouth, and his eyes went wide, clearly mortified.

"That's Bonanza, I'm Tuft." She pointed around the room and gave everyone's names. Drew was absolutely positive that none of them had been born with the names they gave him. Drew nodded his head in greeting.

"Nice to meet you all. When did the armband thing happen?" Drew decided to ignore the kid who had announced his own name incorrectly.

"Uh, a few days ago. The colonel wanted an easy way to distinguish between groups," Tuft answered.

"Fun." Drew didn't know what else to say to that. "What about the black Xs?" He nodded toward a group of three a few steps ahead of them.

"Oh, that means they're doing combat tasks but not officially part of a combat team yet. Sir." Tuft added the sir on almost as an afterthought, and Drew had to hide the shake of his head. It still felt weird to be called a sir, but at least they weren't saluting.

"Alright, so, yellow for the bananas. Green are the dragons, I think? And the pink panthers. What are the other groups?" Drew could see brown and black as well, but he wasn't sure what teams those colors designated.

"Oh, the black are for the cobras. And the brown are for the… uh…" She paused for a moment, clearly embarrassed, before saying a word under her breath that Drew couldn't hear.

"What was that last one? The brown furs?"

Tuft's ears were glowing bright red at this point, and she shook her head. Bonanza came to her rescue, shouting, "*Turds!*" Once again, everyone paused and looked at him, and the kid seemed to almost wilt as he realized he had shouted again. Drew looked over at the five people with brown armbands who were looking their way and laughing. They had an unpleasant air to them, which Drew assumed lent itself to calling themselves the Turds.

"I see." Drew did a quick count and saw that the bananas clearly had the most members, aside from the unaffiliated group, which made up at least half of the adventurers. There was another group of eight or so yellow bands already eating. The rest of them seemed to be in groups of four or five. "Why Bananas?"

"It's a bit of a joke, really," a third member of the group spoke up for the first time. "We tried to join the Red Dragons, and they said they'd have to be bananas to be willing to accept someone like us."

"Oh, right, there are two dragon groups," Drew said with a frown. "Well, congrats on forming your own team." They sat there for a few minutes as the Bananas all waited for Drew to say something else. Glancing over at Luke for a suggestion, the seraph just gave a slight shrug and went back to his typical stoic silence.

"There are also the Gray Knights, White Walkers, and Black Cobras," Tuft offered.

"Weird that they'd do gray and pink, and no one picked blue yet," Drew remarked after a moment of thought.

"Well, you're blue," Tuft corrected.

"Oh, yeah, that makes sense." Drew was covered head to toe in blue armor. "I guess I didn't realize we were considered one of the groups. Right. Well, I just wanted to ask about that. Where are you guys coming back from?"

"Uh, we were at the naga base... with you," Tuft said, glancing around, clearly a bit upset that he hadn't noticed them. Drew tried to remember if the group that had gone into the parking garage had worn any colors. He knew the Marines hadn't been, but had the other people? He didn't think so.

"Ahh, that ambush was pretty rough. Glad no one got hurt, right? Did you see where they came from?"

The Bananas exchanged a few more confused looks. "We weren't... in the naga base, they only allowed one from each team to enter. We were guarding the base camp?" Tuft explained, and Drew blushed slightly. He had just made like four social faux pas in as many minutes.

"Oh." The entire group fell silent after that. No one else joined the line behind Drew, so there was nothing to break the awkward silence until they got to the food. Drew and Luke took their bowls of stew and sat down at a table on their own. The groups on either side of him shuffled off pretty quick, and almost immediately after he got his food, two dozen more people got in line to get their food. "You know, I don't think I'm going to miss this place as much as I thought I was going to," Drew muttered into his stew. Luke just gave a slight laugh.

Sarah, Daryl, and JP showed up a few minutes later and joined him after getting their food.

"So, when are we heading out?" JP asked between quick bites. Drew blinked and glanced over at Sarah, who shrugged slightly.

"Well, the team is heading out as soon as we finish up the command post's set up tomorrow. But..." Drew trailed off, and all three of his teammates looked up at him. "Hoeffecker is splitting up some members of the team."

"That's bullshit," JP said with a frown. "Who isn't going to Arlington?"

"You and Katie. Too many of the people are still reliant on guns, and you're their only source of ammo. And they need to build up a better defense system, so Katie is gonna be making walls," Drew answered in a rush.

"Well… fuck," JP said, putting down his own spoon. The apparent annoyance on his face warring with the knowledge that his leaving would severely handicap the defense efforts. "Are they sending anyone else instead of us?"

"Chief Mather, Gary, and the Sons have a stealth specialist I'm going to vet tomorrow. Assuming Sarah and Daryl are okay with coming." Drew glanced at the other two and received an immediate confirmation.

"I'm sort of surprised they're sending Bill," Sarah said with a frown. "He's one of the better healers here. Even with the healing recovery center, that's going to hurt survival chances."

"I think the colonel is expecting a lot fewer attacks now that the naga have cleared out. We've recovered everyone nearby we're likely to, so I think the plan is to dig in here while we scout ahead," Drew said with a shrug. He hadn't really asked what the plan was, but that was what made the most sense.

"Well, at least I'll still be able to check in on you guys," JP groused. It took Drew a minute to realize he was talking about his ability to look through most of the group's eyes.

"Yeah, that's still really creepy," Sarah remarked. Their conversation fell into a comfortable banter after that. JP was clearly upset that he was getting left behind and unwilling to let the last few hours he had with them go to waste. Drew felt slightly guilty as he noticed that everyone gave the team a buffer, even as their conversation got louder.

Eventually, they all finished their meal and got up to clear the space for everyone else. "I need to find Bill and Gary. You guys happen to know where they are?" Drew asked.

"Bill is probably with the medics. Gary…" Sarah paused, thinking. "I have no idea where Gary would be. We can try the housing area? I'll come with you."

"You guys aren't gonna ditch me until tomorrow," JP announced, and Daryl just shrugged.

"Alright. Let's go find Bill," Drew announced, but Sarah was the one that knew the fastest way there, having spent the most time at the healing chamber.

The node had once been the Department of Transportation. Ten stories of glass walls with a massive skylight over an atrium had turned into a quarter-mile high mountain retreat. Bright globes of light bathed the area in perpetual daylight. Rock terraces with a babbling brook filled with pools of hot water and steam as it descended down a slope. Like most nodes, it held that weird larger inside than outside appearance.

Sarah led them through an idyllic mountain valley that was far more at home in a cultivation novel than inside the confines of a building. Crossing several small wooden bridges, they turned around a tree only to find a well-lit cave entrance that delved deeper into the mountain the healing chamber had been built from. A few steps past the tunnel entrance, they took a turn and were abruptly in what Drew could only describe as a lavish reception room.

Perfectly manicured bonsai trees sat atop beautifully shaped living wood tables, moss-covered benches. Veins of crystal covered the ceiling above and shed bright light throughout the area. The far end room was covered by a softly tinkling rock wall with thousands of mini waterfalls that disappeared into a hole at the bottom.

"Why don't we live here?" Drew asked, looking around in amazement.

"The more people in the healing chamber, the less effective the entire place is," Sarah said as she led them through another hallway that appeared out of nowhere as soon as they got close to it. "Most of the healers stay here since it helps us to recover from our mana fatigue. But we try to keep everyone else out unless they are in immediate need of healing."

"I'm pretty sure this is better than my penthouse," Drew said as she led them through a modern-looking hallway. The ever-present light illuminated the room perfectly without over-saturating it. They came across a small alcove, and Sarah knocked on the door.

"Bill, you in there?" she asked, even as the door opened and Bill stepped out. He looked ready to respond to whatever crisis had landed at his door. Drew caught a glimpse of a bed and some personal effects before the door closed behind him.

"Hey Sarah, what's wrong?" Bill looked at the four of them, confused. He gave each of them a quick scan.

"Nothing medical. Drew wanted to talk to you."

"Hey, Chief," Drew said, sticking out his hand to shake the other man's.

"Evening, sir." Bill took his hand.

"Got a minute to talk?" Drew glanced at his group and made a shooing motion as Bill nodded his head.

"Yeah, sure. We can use the exam room here." Bill pointed down the hallway away from where they came. Sarah pulled JP and Daryl down toward the reception area. Another few steps and a door became visible. Drew wasn't sure how the hallway managed to hide these doors until you were right on top of them, but he figured it was something to do with the magic of the node. Stepping into the room, there were several comfortable-looking chairs and a low padded table.

"What can I do for you, Mr. Michalik?"

"Well, I'm sure Colonel Hoeffecker will notify you of orders, but I feel like this is something everyone should have a decision on themselves. If you don't want to go, I'll talk to the colonel and we'll find someone else." Drew explained the situation, what they were going to do and when they were leaving.

"It would be an honor to join you," Bill said, standing up and shaking his hand again. "I'll be ready tomorrow, sir."

"Okay, talk to Min Sun about getting some gear. Tell her you'll be on my team. Apparently, we're the blue one."

Bill raised an eyebrow in confusion. "Everyone knows that." He headed to his room.

"Well, not everyone," Drew muttered to himself, still thinking of his earlier conversation with the Bananas.

CHAPTER FOURTEEN – CONVERSATIONS

Finding Gary took another hour or so; the teens had apparently claimed an entire floor of the housing area. Dozens of them were shouting and playing games. Stepping onto the floor was a bit of a culture shock to Drew. Everyone else was so morose, but here were a bunch of kids playing what looked like capture the flag with their powers. A large, central atrium had been turned into a maze of desks, chairs, and blankets.

"Hey, do you know where Gary is?" Drew shouted as a kid dashed past them, four white orbs hovering around him and seeming to make him run faster. The kid whizzed to a stop, the orbs shifting to arrest his momentum faster than normal, and he turned to look at Drew.

"Holy shit, it's the Blood Blade!" The kid didn't look to be much older than fifteen to Drew, but the shout seemed to bring the game to a standstill as dozens of heads popped up over the top of the maze to look toward him. "Gary! The Blood Blade wants you!"

Drew's hand went instinctively to the hilt at his side. Robbi's ruby sword was suddenly a heavy weight at his side. Gary himself poked his head up, saw Drew, and then popped back down behind the maze. By the time he came to the front where Drew was, dozens of teens were surrounding him. They were all looking at him, and he could feel the expectations in their eyes. Gary pushed through the crowd to the front. He was still wearing the blue armor Min Sun had given him.

There was clearly some sort of social significance since the others parted as soon as they realized who it was. A few of the older kids had the white armbands with Xs on them that meant they were fighters, not on a team.

"Hey Gary, got a place we can talk?" Drew asked, and Gary looked around.

"Sure, my room is this way." Gary gestured behind his back and along the corridor the maze was built from. He quickly turned and headed in that direction, and the kids all shifted to allow the four adults to move through. Drew nodded to them as he passed.

Gary's room was the second closest, and he pushed open the door. Inside, he could see half a dozen beds spread around the room haphazardly. Sarah pulled the others back, leaving Drew and Gary to enter the room alone.

Drew was a bit surprised by the lack of furniture. His own suite had been fully decorated, the decorations clearly a mix of things from the surrounding area. Drew had assumed that all of the rooms would have been furnished by the system, but maybe they had, and the kids had appropriated all the other furniture for their maze.

Gary plopped down on a bed and looked at Drew. He was curious but also still clearly nervous.

"So, how have you been?" Drew said awkwardly. It'd been a few days since they did the HR dungeon, and he wasn't sure what the three teens had been up to in the meantime.

"Good. We don't get a lot of work, so we mostly just play and practice. A few of us started up as runners." Drew quirked an eyebrow in confusion at the term. "It's sort of like a messenger and a cargo hauler all in one. Pappy's bags make trucks and stuff sort of worthless, so we just take stuff from one spot to another. Mostly for the crafters. Although some teams will hire you to run for them so they can stay at the DTC longer. We used to go on some of the scavenging runs, but there haven't been many of those lately."

"Yeah, I heard it was getting harder to do that," Drew said, scratching his neck.

"I'll do it," Gary said, and Drew blinked at him.

"I haven't asked you to do anything yet," Drew said with a frown.

"You're going to Arlington, and you want to take me." Gary just shrugged when Drew looked at him askance. "People don't pay attention to kids. They told me you were gonna take me an hour ago."

"Well, you should know what we're going into. We're heading north and crossing at the 14th Street bridges. Going to take out two nodes on this side of the river before getting into whatever is turning Arlington into a jungle. It's going to be a small team. You're replacing JP; obviously, you fill different roles, and you have different utility, but we're going to be relying heavily on your sense intent xatherite."

"Alright, when do we leave?" Gary looked almost excited at the idea.

"Gary… it's going to be dangerous. I'll do my best to protect you, but I can't guarantee you won't get hurt or killed."

"Nowhere is really safe now, though, is it? I had to fight naga in the stadium when they attacked. I was in the troll prison. The worst part is that they still keep dismissing me as a kid and telling me I can't do anything to help, even though people are dying." Gary's fists were clenched. "You are going out there and saving people. I want to be part of that. I've always wanted to be a Jedi like Mace Windu. The Jedi were protectors of the weak, and that's what you do. I want to help people so that no one else has to lose their family."

Drew laid a hand on Gary's shoulder. "We can't save everyone. Hell, I've had four people die trying to protect me. And dozens more in battles where I wasn't strong enough to save them. Those kids out there? They called me the Blood Blade. That name doesn't belong to me. This is Robbi's sword." Drew pulled the blood-red sword from its sheath at his side and looked at it. "Robbi, who died because I couldn't kill a giant fire breathing crocodile fast enough. I carry it as a reminder of all the people I failed to protect." He looked up at Gary. "I'll never be strong enough to protect everyone. I can't promise that. But I'll always give it all I have. I'll do my best. That's the only promise I can give you."

Gary looked at the sword, which caught the light and reflected it dozens of red-tinged flares across the room. "I was in a few of Robbi's classes on how to use a sword. He helped me a lot, even though my sword is… different."

"I had forgotten that he was doing those. Seems so long ago," Drew said after a minute, glancing at the sword. "I've never used it."

"So it's just me? Not Joe and London too?"

"Just you. Like I said, we're trying to do this quick and fast, might be one more, but probably just the six of us."

"It doesn't seem like enough," Gary said even as Drew stood up and sheathed the sword.

"It never does. The unofficial motto of the Coast Guard is, 'more with less.' Which I always hated, but it fits this situation just fine. We always get more tasks, more responsibilities, and less resources to handle them. I wish I could let you think about this or tell you not to come. But that's just not the reality we live in. Get everything you need and say your goodbyes tonight. We'll be leaving tomorrow around noon. Meet us… Shit, I guess we'll be setting out from the main gate."

Gary followed Drew out, where the rest of the team was surrounded by teens. Sarah was looking over some scrapes and bruises that the kids had acquired but hadn't gone to get healed. JP and Luke had a large group of older kids around them. All of them had some form of weapon, and Luke was correcting their stances. Daryl was nowhere to be seen. They had only been in Gary's room for a few minutes, so Drew was surprised to see them so involved in their tasks. They all shifted their attention to him, however.

"Alright, that's it for the evening. I'm heading up to my room to get some sleep. Luke, you can stay here if you want. I promise I won't be leaving my room." The seraph frowned for a moment but then nodded his head, giving Drew the space he needed.

The elevator took him to his suite, and he was surprised to see JP behind him. Drew wasn't really in the mood for conversation, but he also didn't really want to snub the guy as they left him behind. He shifted his path from his bedroom to walk over to the large panel windows on the southern wall. The darkness made it difficult, but the moon was out enough that he could see across the river to the jungle that was Arlington.

Drew sat down on the floor and looked out at the world that was so changed. DC at night had always been so spectacular. Now it was a strange reminder of everything they had lost. The only consolation was how bright the stars had become with the lack of light pollution.

"I wish I was going with y'all," JP said from behind him.

Drew turned slightly to look at the other man and gave a half-smile. "Would be nice, but someone's gotta keep the fort here. Make sure things don't go all crazy while I'm gone."

"I think you overestimate my ability to keep the crazy at bay," JP retorted with a frown. "This town is full of people who play politics for a living. I'm sure they'll find a way to go crazy regardless of what we do."

"Well, all the more reason to leave someone here who can shoot them if they get out of line," Drew joked.

"I'm gonna tell them you gave me permission." They lapsed into a comfortable silence after that, neither saying anything as they stared over the dark city.

"Well, I'm gonna go to sleep," Drew said with a sigh. "Not sure when my next chance is going to be."

"Well, I hope it's just you and not some alien god asking for a favor."

Drew rolled his eyes in response but didn't feel like pushing his luck by adding to that comment. He was hoping that none of the Protectorate gods would be visiting him too.

Stripping off his armor took a few minutes, but he eventually managed it, leaving it in a heap on the floor as he sank into the bed and closed his eyes. Still, he wasn't quite ready to go to sleep. He'd taken over another node today, his twelfth total. And he had a half dozen skills waiting to be upgraded.

Pulling up his map, he looked at the list of gems that he could upgrade: greater cone of frost, greater fireball, major blink step, major mana sight, major acid arrow, and major lightning bolt were all rare grade and eligible for an upgrade. However, he wasn't really eager to do so since the advanced xatherite had much higher mana requirements.

Alternatively, his two newest xatherite, minor mana tap and solar offering—previously called sacrifice to the sun—were only common grade. He had upgraded both of them since he got them, which earned him his second completed constellation bonus, which was called the Thief's Needle. It was only a four-link with acid arrow and lightning bolt. He pulled up the constellation bonus and xatherite information.

Thief's Needle Constellation: All drain type effects are 1.5x more effective.

Xatherite Crystal Name: Minor Mana Tap
Xatherite Color: Orange
Xatherite Grade: Common
Xatherite Rarity: Uncommon
Type: Magic
Effect: Creates a 2m aura around you that channels mana into you. All mana usage from a source other than the caster in the aura will be less effective, and the charge stat of those who used it will be drained. Caster's charge stat will increase in proportion to the drain. Aura lasts 20 seconds, successful drains last 30 seconds or until the skill has recharged.
Mana recharge time: 3 minutes, 30 seconds.

> *Xatherite Crystal Name: Solar Offering*
> *Xatherite Color: Yellow*
> *Xatherite Grade: Common*
> *Xatherite Rarity: Common*
> *Type: Divine*
> *Effect: Allows you to make a blood sacrifice from one of your slain foes, transferring their vitality into you. Any vitality over your norm will be stored to be used when needed. A larger amount of excess vitality can be stored.*
> *Mana recharge time: 4 days, 14 hours, 24 minutes.*

Which had given him a single linked skill.

> *Linked Skill Name: Noon Mana Sacrifice*
> *Xatherite Color(s): Yellow, Orange*
> *Linked Skill Grade: Common*
> *Type: Divine*
> *Effect: Allows you to make a blood sacrifice from one of your slain foes, transferring a portion of their mana potential into you.*
> *Mana recharge time: 3 days, 7 hours, 19 minutes.*

When he had asked Luke what the skill did, he had had no idea. As far as Drew could tell, it didn't do anything, but he'd still be using it on cooldown. Usually on monsters that had a lot of magical abilities, like the naga water casters. Opening his eyes, he considered his options. The two xatherite were ready to be upgraded again, and they were low enough grade and rarity that he didn't think it would affect his mana fatigue to a large degree.

But the question was, should he upgrade any of the others? Holy shield was another likely upgrade since it was the same grade and rarity as the other two. All the rest would be pushing into the upper tier of xatherite, which would drastically boost the amount of mana fatigue that it would take to sustain a fight. Deciding against upgrading anything but the three common grade xatherite, he queued them up and let the pain of the upgrade take him under.

CHAPTER FIFTEEN – VISIT

The ship was different from before, but there were some similarities. Drew was still looking out of a futuristic viewport at a nebula. This was the sort of visual you'd expect to see in a video game, but which probably wasn't true to life. A portion of the nebula extended away from the central mass of red, looking vaguely like a knight from chess. Which made this the Horsehead Nebula, which Drew had seen a few times in deep space imagery.

"Hello, brother." The voice that spoke to him was both familiar and somehow wrong. Ares' voice, but different. Turning his head, he saw a form that looked remarkably similar to the god. They shared the same close-cropped curly hair and Roman nose. The shape of the face was familiar enough for Drew to assume whoever this was came from the same genetics as Ares. Either a sibling or a variant from a different dimensional slice. His experience talking to Drew-1 had the same feel of similar but other that this man exuded.

"My name is Hades, Knight of the Order of the Dragon." Hades had previously been looking out the window, but he turned to look at Drew, and his black eyes seemed to smolder like cinders. "I believe you have met our brother Ares, so I assume our meeting will be no surprise to you." Unlike Ares, the aura of power around Hades was wild and chaotic, without any of the rigid structure that had made up the other god. It was only by comparison that he could even really notice the differences. They both had a gravity to them, a sense of unbounded power.

"It is a pleasure to meet you, Hades," Drew responded. Unlike on Ares' ship, he had no physical form here, he realized as his voice came out distorted. He existed more as a wisp or ghost. Which was mildly concerning, considering he was talking to the God of Death. Or at least a god of death, Drew corrected, remembering his encounter with Isis.

"So cordial. No wonder that arrogant ass took a fancy to you. But no introduction, which means you might be interesting yet." Hades turned back to the viewport. "Hopefully, the others will be less boring." He paused, considering. "Although perhaps it is more respect, now that you've met your betters." Hades waved a hand through the air as if to dissipate his own musing. "Tell me, what do you plan to do with the sidhe?"

"I figured you already knew who I was." Drew turned his attention away from the god and back toward the viewport. A flash of light had him focus on the cloud more closely, and to his surprise, he realized that countless black dots were moving. Every now and again, one would disappear in a flash of light so minute he hadn't noticed them before.

"What is this?" Drew asked. It couldn't be what he thought it was, could it?

"The sidhe risked much to land a ship near you— millions of dead on both sides. More are dying as we speak, all to create a tiny hole in our defenses long enough for one seed ship to slip in. You have awakened to Retribution. Will you punish them for the deaths their actions have caused?"

"Why don't you help them?" Drew had no limbs, but he bobbed his head forward to indicate the black dots.

"I am Death," Hades said after a moment. "I do not operate on such a small scale. I could purge the sidhe ships, but my own troops would be caught in the act. I have trained and equipped them to the best of my ability. There is no more help I can give them. They will rise or fall on their own strength."

"Why are you even here? I thought Earth was in Ares' territory."

"It is, but your impossible stunt has called many here from across the known. Rarely do we have a chance to fight the fleets of the sidhe in a protracted battle. Whatever it is they want, they are paying for it with blood." Hades paused. "Or sap, I suppose."

"My impossible stunt?" Drew tried to think which of his actions had been impossible.

"Drawing on the power of a divine path xatherite on an integrating planet. Doing so while it was unattuned even." Hades shook his head. "Two impossible actions which have created ripples the likes of which we will be dealing with for millennia."

"I ask again, what will you do with the sidhe?" Hades turned back to look at Drew, who considered his words.

"I guess that depends on what they want. Seems like they've put in a lot of effort to visit. It wouldn't be… cordial to send them away without learning why." It took Drew a moment to remember what Hades had called him. To his surprise, the god chuckled.

"So there is more to you than meets the eye. Retribution is an interesting starting point. It can lead to several dangerous paths." Hades tapped his finger against his chin, considering.

"I thought it was only Justice," Drew said with a frown.

"Well, that's an interesting insight." Hades frowned slightly. "Who told you that? Not Odin's seraph, I assume."

"No, it wasn't Luke." Drew hesitated, trying to decide how much information he should reveal. "Isis told me."

Hades turned to look at him, the easy manner gone and replaced with a demeanor that seemed far more akin to what he would have expected from a death god. "How did you communicate with Isis?"

"She came to me in a dream." Drew tried to control himself, but Hades' full attention was like a weight dragging at him.

"Where was she? Tell me everything." Hades' attention was like a sharp sword, pointed directly at his soul.

"It was a room full of crystals. She just told me I walked a difficult path and that she was hoping I would awake to

Justice," Drew answered before he could control himself, and suddenly the pressure diminished, Hades turning back to the window.

"Interesting. So the cats want an arbiter." Hades tapped a finger against his chin again. "Well, you're certainly nowhere near as boring as I thought you were. Justice is just one of the paths open to you. You are free to choose any of them. But if Isis says you're walking the line of Justice..." He trailed off, considering. "We've never had a Justice. What would that do to the balance?" He paused, laughing at his own words. "Hah, balance." He turned to Drew. "Get it, like Justice. The scales of Justice."

Drew gave a polite laugh to humor the god. "Ahh yes, very funny." He wondered just how important these types that all the gods had were. From his pen and paper roleplaying days, he figured they were a lot like the portfolios of the gods. Did that mean they wanted him to have the Justice domain?

Hades shook his head and turned back to the viewport. "Well, you've given me much to think about. Thank you for telling me the cats are in play." He paused. "Actually, for that little piece of information, I think you deserve a reward." His eyes took on the distant quality of someone looking through his map. "Yes, this should be fun."

> Hades (Cassius Felix-7) would like to trade "desolare" with you. Accept?

Drew mentally commanded the information from the xatherite to appear in front of him.

> *Xatherite Crystal Name: Desolare*
> *Xatherite Color: Red*
> *Xatherite Grade: Common*
> *Xatherite Rarity: Rare*

> *Type: Magic*
> *Effect: Targeting a 6m wide spread, remove all moisture from plant-based lifeforms within the radius. Plants killed by this spell will explode into a cloud of highly absorbent dust.*
> *Mana recharge time: 21 seconds.*

"Take it, no strings attached, as payment for telling me about the cats. You'll find it very useful if you decide the sidhe need to die."

Drew deliberated it. This was a potent ability he could use against any plant-like enemies they encountered. It would have made the Root Horrors and the initial venture into the depths of the stadium much easier. The fact was that he couldn't really afford to leave power like this on the table. He didn't believe for a minute that Hades couldn't twist this to his advantage even then. The whole encounter was strange to Drew. He accepted the trade.

"Thank you. I'm sure this will help save lives."

Hades' lips twitched slightly as if Drew had made a joke. "It's a weapon, Drew, it only takes lives. It doesn't save them. Everything living requires something to die for it to survive. Death is not evil. It is just a part of living." Hades waved again, and Drew felt his consciousness fading away from the god. Returning to his body, he came to, staring up at the ceiling.

"Well, that was... something," Drew said, sitting up and looking out the windows. He wanted to talk about this. He wanted to talk about this with Katie, but that wasn't an option anymore. He realized that she hadn't even said they could still be friends. Like she was cutting him out of her life completely.

Stepping out of his room, he looked around and saw JP sleeping on the couch where Drew and Katie's earlier conversation had taken place. Drew looked at the cop and decided he didn't want to wake someone who slept with a finger on a trigger. He walked back toward his room, the dull echo of his boots on the floor echoing through the mostly empty chamber.

"Something wrong?" JP asked behind him. Drew turned to see the cop half sitting and looking at him with blinking eyes. Turning back, he cast invigorate on JP and watched the sleep immediately flee.

"Had a dream. Wanted to talk to someone about it."

"A dream." JP paused, then looked up. "Like a dream, or a *dream*?"

"I think the second. Come into my room, and we can talk." Drew pointed to the room where Luke usually slept and put a finger to his lips to explain the need to relocate.

"M'kay." JP took a few minutes to pick up several of the guns he had removed to sleep and then followed Drew into his room.

"Who was it this time?" JP asked. He had been told about Isis and Ares.

"Hades." Drew told him everything he remembered from the dream, and they both sat there staring out at the dark.

"Well, shit. What are you gonna do?"

"About what?"

"The sidhe," JP answered, pointing at the barely visible jungle.

"I don't know. I think I need to know why they're here. I guess I'll make a more educated guess when we see what the situation over there is like," Drew said.

"Still, killing millions?" JP shook his head. "What sort of message is worth a million lives?"

"Maybe it's not a message. Maybe they're just here to kill me. Get me while I'm weak. If Hades wasn't lying about how much power he held..." Drew shook his head, the casual way he said he could destroy all those ships. How did you fight something like that?

"What about the Odin's seraph thing?" JP changed the subject.

"Isis said Odin is the head of the Order of Dragons, I think. Maybe the seraph are loyal to him? I'm not really sure." Drew frowned. "Honestly, there is too much politics in all that. Built-up over who knows how many years. Luke said Ares was seven thousand years old."

"Also, the fact that Hades and Ares were the same person originally is super weird to me," JP said with a frown. "I mean, they've had a few thousand years to diverge personalities, but they seemed very different from each other."

"Yeah, they were very different. When I talked to One, he was already different from me in a lot of ways. Harsher. Angrier," Drew said, remembering the scarred face of his alternative dimension persona.

"So, how do souls work across dimensions? Like, do you and One share a soul? Is a new one created when the dimension splits and just given the memories from the body?" JP mused.

"I have no idea. Not even sure if souls exist. I guess this would be one of the better ways to test how that all works. I wonder if there is a xatherite to see souls."

"Well, did Ares and Hades have the same aura?"

"I couldn't use abilities with Hades. It's weird. All three of them had very different communication methods. Isis said my mind protection xatherite made it hard, but it didn't seem like it was difficult with Hades. Also… he was just waiting for me. Isis had to come to me, and I went to Ares."

"Yeah, but that guy on the Olympus told you not to trust Hades and Isis, right?" JP pondered. "Like, you were asleep for a few hours, maybe it took some time for you to get 'caught' or whatever Hades needed, so he knew you were coming."

"Yeah. Themis, I think was his name. He told me not to trust most of them. Added Loki and some other gods, as well. Honestly, I don't remember all of them. Isis, Hades, and Loki stood out to me because they were all different religions. Which seemed odd."

"So, you gonna slot that plant killer xatherite?"

"I dunno, I don't have a good spot to put it in. I could put it in the same constellation as mind shield, but that seems like a waste. Or in with arsenal and mana rampart, but I don't know what kind of links that would make. A dry shield or maybe a dehydrating sword? Nothing great. The other options require waiting for an indigo, yellow, another red, or orange xatherite before I can use them. But it's probably a great ability to put in that top ability, which means I need a yellow or an indigo."

"Well, you're taking over three nodes before you get to the sidhe, right?" JP said, thinking about it. "With only a couple people. You'll probably get xatherite you can put in it. Or at least one no one else wants that you don't mind replacing later."

"Seems like a waste, but yeah, I guess we could probably find something less useful to use as a placeholder." Drew frowned at his map. "Besides, I'm not sure they deserve to die. The human Protectorate and the sidhe are at war. But it sounds like they're taking as many losses as the humans are. Either they really want to kill me and the other red mages, or they really want to talk to me. Either way…" Drew shrugged, unhappy with either choice.

"Could be something else. I mean, you don't have to be the center of the apocalypse," JP said, punching Drew's shoulder lightly.

"You know, that'd actually be nice for once. I don't think it's a coincidence that they landed so close to the shield, though. That's the only thing I've done which would be visible from space."

"I mean, they could be here for the primary nexus and just wanted some breathing room to set up," JP said with a shrug.

"Yes, but then why Earth-3? I get the feeling that there are hundreds, if not thousands, of frontier planets going through Advent right now."

JP had no answer to that, so the two sat in silence for a few moments, each lost in thought. Drew's mind focused back on Katie and those that were staying behind.

"I guess I should probably give you some sort of dad speech about making sure everyone survives while I'm gone." Drew turned his attention to the housing complex area that was some of the only light in the zone.

"Yeah, I'll do what I can." JP scratched his cheek. "But hey, if you and Katie broke up, you wouldn't mind if I made a pass?" It was Drew's turn to punch JP, and their conversation drifted into less serious topics. They were interrupted a few minutes into the random conversation as Daryl showed up in the penthouse. Drew cast invigorate on the scout, and the three of them sat and chatted for the rest of the night. Drew was slightly amused that it took the world ending to meet people like Daryl and JP. People he would gladly have hung out with in his free time.

CHAPTER SIXTEEN – CLIVE

The group got breakfast together, joined by Luke an hour before sunrise. There were clocks and lights now, but everyone had adjusted their schedules to follow the day-night cycle more closely than was typical before. They were early enough to beat most of the crowd, only a few people, mostly wearing armbands, sitting in the cafeteria with them. JP left to drop off the magazines they had refilled overnight, taking advantage of Drew's invigorate.

The other three men headed to the stadium's front gate, which was mostly superfluous now since it was dozens of feet behind the start of the dome. Sarah and Bill were already waiting for them, which was a surprise to Drew. He hadn't been expecting Bill to join them until much closer to their exit time. They climbed to the top of the wall and watched the sunrise over the Anacostia River. Drew was casting refreshing rain on cooldown, and they had a short queue forming up below them as the five waited for Brady to show up.

Gary was the next group member to show up, the shy kid joining them up top with some hesitation. Having found them by whatever means, people discovered where Drew was casting his refreshing rain. Hoeffecker and Brady showed up a few minutes past sunrise proper. Hoeffecker had an aide whose name Drew couldn't recall with her, but Brady had a man dressed in orange camo at his side. He was also one of the few people who Drew had seen with a single shot rifle in his hands.

Drew held up a hand in greeting. Hoeffecker gave a slight wave back. Brady just changed his direction slightly. The man in camo gave an enthusiastic wave back, and Drew frowned. Everything about this guy seemed to scream eccentric.

"Mr. Michalik." Hoeffecker returned his salute as they got closer. "Miss Rothschild," she said, greeting the two officers in the party before nodding to the others. "You all know Mr.

Brady. I'd like to introduce you to Mr. Clive Hensridge." She gestured to the man in orange camo. Drew took a moment to look at his aura. It was a pretty even mix of colors. A little heavier on oranges and greens, perhaps, but like most people, he didn't seem to favor any shade in particular.

The man stuck his hand out to Drew with eagerness. "A pleasure to meet you, Mr. Drew, sir," he said, and Drew frowned as he held the handshake for longer than required to squeeze his hand harder than expected.

"Likewise, Mr. Hensridge," Drew said, pulling his hand away from the man who went on to shake Sarah's hand and give her the same treatment. Drew's estimation of the man dropped a fair amount just from the weird powerplay with the handshake.

"So, Mr. Hensridge," Sarah said, only to be ignored as Clive turned back to Drew. He almost seemed to strike a pose.

"Please, call me Clive. Mr. Hensridge was my father. Real proud of you boys and your work, Mr. Michalik," Clive said, interrupting Sarah, who glared daggers at his back. "Y'all are real American heroes. Thank you for your service."

Drew blinked; he had never liked being thanked for his service. It always felt awkward. "You're welcome." He gave his standard response. "Where are you from, Clive?"

"Originally from the Little Rock area, but came up here for a job a few months before this whole place went to shit. Well, even more to shit than it was before with all the politicians." Clive laughed at his own joke and elbowed Drew in the side like he was in on the joke.

"Why don't you show them what you can do, Clive?" Brady said from the side, clearly reading the frosty glares being sent Clive's way better than the man himself.

"Right, right. You wanna see me shoot first or the stealth?" Clive said, looking at Drew curiously.

"Why don't you shoot first, since we're already up on the wall," Hoeffecker said, and Clive squinted at her for a moment, then shrugged. Pulling out his rifle, he looked around. Drew was glad that at least he had good trigger discipline. His index finger pressed flat rather than on the trigger.

"Whatcha want me to shoot?" Clive turned to Drew, careful to point the gun away from people as he moved.

"Uh…" Drew glanced around then pointed at a car at the edge of the dome. It was about three hundred feet away, and there weren't any people around it. "How about that?" He pointed at a car, and Clive pulled the gun to his shoulder, sighted, and shot in one smooth motion. The round hit the side mirror and broke it off, clearly more powerful than the weapon's stock version. Dropping the gun to his hip, he slid another bullet into the chamber and had it back on his shoulder within a few seconds. The other mirror popped off the car. A third shot impacted the windshield to destroy the third mirror.

"Got a xatherite called penetrating shot. Makes this thing hit like a rhino," Clive said, patting the rifle that was once again resting against his hip.

"Where are you getting your ammo?" Sarah asked. Drew could see Clive's lip pull up slightly as if to sneer at her, but it was controlled enough to be a half-smile.

"Uses a .450 round. I've got a couple magazines modified to use them, I have your guy fill those up, and then strip the rounds out and repeat. Got a couple thousand bullets at this point. Plenty set aside for a rainy day," Clive said, patting one of Pappy's pouches at his side, which was probably how he reloaded so fast.

"What other xatherite do you have?" Hoeffecker asked, and Clive seemed annoyed again at the interruption.

"Well, I got the stealth orange, which is pretty hard to demonstrate for humans because I have to consider you an enemy for it to work. But it gives me and all allies within fifteen feet a camouflaged effect, making it harder to see, smell, or hear what we do. As long as we tiptoe and avoid going right up next to the monsters, we should be fine. I also have an orange that turns any camo gear into armor, and a gun maintenance violet xatherite that makes it so I don't have to clean 'em myself." Clive had turned away from Hoeffecker and was talking directly to Drew.

"Other than that, I have an ability to create whiskey that only works on flasks. Whiskey tastes pretty shit right now, but I'm hoping it gets better as I level it up." Clive nudged Drew in the side again and pulled a flask out for him to try some.

"A bit early for me," Drew said, looking at the just barely rising sun.

"More for me then, sir," Clive said as he took a quick swig. The potent smell of moonshine filled the area almost instantly.

"Ugh, that smells like paint stripper," Sarah said, wrinkling her nose. Clive ignored her, his attention solely focused on Drew.

Drew glanced from Sarah and Hoeffecker to Clive. "Just the five xatherite?" Drew did the math. That was about right for what he would have started with. Sarah had only started with three, after all.

"Yup, my posse has only found one other, and it was a better fit for other people. We've mostly been avoiding fights and collecting supplies," Clive answered, but not before glancing back at Brady for confirmation.

"Alright, let me confer with my team for a bit, and we'll make a decision," Drew said, nodding politely to the Sons and gesturing for his team to follow him a little further down the way. "What do you think?"

"My vote is we don't bring him," Sarah said immediately. "Guy is clearly a sexist prick, barely even acknowledged the colonel or myself. And I just don't trust him to have my back."

"Trust can be earned," Daryl said, glancing at the man. "I followed him around a bit, and he's got a solid stealth skill. If we're looking to make good time and extract civilians, he will be invaluable. I say we bring him. We need his skills. Something about him rubs me the wrong way too, but I'd rather have him somewhere I can watch him than following us."

Luke just shrugged his shoulders. "I have no opinion. I do not think I understand the cultural touchstones you are using to judge him. Earth behavior is…" He paused, searching for the right words. "Still strangely alien to me."

"Alright, Gary?" Drew turned to the teen, who looked like a deer caught in the headlights. He gulped nervously.

"Well, he isn't triggering my sense intent xatherite, so I don't think he intends to do us harm. He does sort of seem like an…" Gary's voice broke as he tried to disguise the curse word. "Asshole to me." Gary added after a few seconds of thought, "So, I guess I'm going to abstain like Luke."

Drew turned to Bill next. The big man frowned in Clive's direction. "I don't know your team dynamics well. But he has some combat capability. I can see some use in creating explosives with that moonshine of his. I'm not a fan of his masochism—"

"Misogyny, I think you mean," Sarah said. "Masochism is where you like pain."

"Right, I'm not a fan of his misogamy." Bill nodded his head in agreement with Sarah. He didn't seem upset by her interrupting him. "But strange times make for strange bedfellows. And we can't change his mind if we don't show him good examples of competent women." Bill half-smiled at Sarah. "I think he will help the team."

"Which leaves me with the tiebreaker," Drew said, frowning between Sarah and Daryl. "I think we follow the old adage, 'keep your friends close, and your enemies closer.' I'm not sure which of those Clive will end up being. I'm not a huge fan of the Sons' political ideas, but I don't think we can afford to turn aside any help we're offered at this point. And Daryl is right; if we need to rescue anyone, he's going to be a godsend evacuating people."

Sarah opened her mouth to object, and Drew raised his hand. "I'll talk to him about the command structure. You're still going to be calling the shots, and if he has a problem with that, we'll send him home. Do you have any other concerns?"

Sarah looked around the room and then sighed and shook her head. "No, the initial vibe just gives me the creeps."

"Understood. Chief, Gary, I think that'll be your job. I think the only concern is if he has other xatherite we don't know about. Speaking of xatherite…" Drew turned to the two of them. "I can see people's maps, Gary. I checked, and I can see yours already. You probably hit level one. I assume that means you hit level one in the human resources building." Gary's map was a star inside of a circle. "Chief, I don't know what other abilities you might have, other than the heal and the blanket fort."

"I have two oranges, a group buff that increases resistance to toxic energy and a personal one that increases my strength value. I also have an indigo that…" Bill paused and seemed to blush slightly. "Well, it keeps my personal appearance at top Navy regulation."

Drew realized that Bill did indeed look in top shape. He even had ironed on creases in his pants, and his hair was all immaculate. "I'm actually a little jealous of that ability. It just sort of… cleans your clothes as you go?"

Bill nodded his head. "Yes, the longer I wear something, the closer to perfect it fits. Any dirt will sort of wear off within a few minutes, and rips and tears will repair within an hour or two. Depends on how bad they are. Not very helpful in combat, but I'll never have to go shopping again."

"Well, alright then. The two of you have pouches of holding? Had Min Sun upgrade your gear?" Both Bill and Gary nodded their heads in agreement. "Alright then." Drew headed back toward Hoeffecker and the Sons, holding his hand out to Clive. "Welcome to the team," he said with the politest smile he could muster. Clive tried to crush his hand again.

"Awesome!" Clive crowed excitedly, drawing some stares from the queue of people waiting for rains.

"We've still got another few hours until the command center is finished." Drew glanced at Hoeffecker. "What can we do to help before we go?"

"Keep up the rain. I'm gonna get JP to come out and fill as many magazines as we can while you're here and have people emptying the bullets out. We can always find someone willing to do risk-free work like that." Hoeffecker paused, looking around. "I'll probably try to drain as much mana out of people as possible while you're here. Actually, if you could head over to the fields, that would be best."

Drew groaned. Hours of casting energizing rain wasn't exactly his favorite way to pass the time. But he understood the need, and he wasn't really looking forward to vast amounts of danger in the near future. Or was he?

Chapter Seventeen – Leaving

The hours before the command center was finished were exactly as boring as Drew assumed they would be. He got a stone that connected him directly to Hoeffecker, they tested it out, and it worked. Brady also gave him one that matched with him. Using the stones was pretty simple. Holding the stone was enough to 'ping' the other stone, causing it to heat up and emit blinks of light. As soon as both stones were touching skin, you could communicate with each other for as long as skin contact was maintained.

The stones could be used for a total of about five minutes of transmissions every two days. They slowly recharged as well, but if you fully drained them, it would take the full twenty four hours before you could use them again. The actual amount varied by the stone. Although Drew couldn't tell the difference, it probably was based on the skill's level when made, but the maker of the stones was kept a secret by the Sons, so there was no way to question him about what the actual differences were. They were waiting in the command center of the new command post, watching as the system ticked down a time to completion.

The room around them shifted. It expanded, and the ceiling rose until it was thirty feet tall, the floor a hundred feet wide and a hundred and fifty feet long. The basic consoles and one table melted into the floor and disappeared. Only the area they were standing on remained unchanged. Consoles sprung up in four orderly rows, two on each side of the central area, where a massive redwood table appeared lined with chairs. One entire wall became a map of the connected node system, with thousands of colored dots representing the denizens. Across from the information wall was a tiered platform with rows of desks.

Drew blinked. Somehow the control room had mimicked the room he had been in when the Advent hit, with noticeable upgrades and shifts to accommodate the slightly different purpose. He wondered how much of that was because he had made the room. Everything was what he considered ideal, even down to the massive slab of wood making up the table. Hoeffecker and Sarah were the only people in the room with him, and he headed toward the desks in the back of the room.

"This is basically a recreation of every watch floor I've ever been on," Drew said, looking around the room, and the other two nodded their heads in agreement. "This should be the Command Duty Officer or CDO spot." He pointed to the lowest table. "And the other two are probably for the colonel and me," Drew said, pointing to the two desks sitting above the CDO desk. Both of which had doors leading into a more private office. Looking around the room, several doors were leading to what looked like conference rooms.

Drew sat down on one of the desks, and immediately a series of holograms lit up across the desk. He started poking around to learn the interface. It was mostly intuitive, but a few of the items took clicking on them to determine their function. "Alright, I found the access control list." The others had come over.

"Oh, neat, I couldn't see any of this from the floor," Sarah said as she came up behind him. "Looks like a little more privacy than I thought there would be."

Drew was adding both of them to the list and giving them admin access. "Alright, I've got you both set up with admin access."

"Alright... let me add JP and Katie to the list, then." Hoeffecker sat at the next desk. Drew pointed out the icon that he had used to get to the list and found them. They already had access, but there was no option to promote them to be admins.

"Hmm, let me see if I can make you a higher tier admin..." Drew said, looking back through the list, but there was no option to allow her to be a tier two admin. "Doesn't look like it. Maybe it needs more nodes or something. Aevis?" He paused, but the AI didn't respond. "Hmm, well, that's a problem. Sarah, grab the CDO spot and poke around a bit." The three of them tried for a few more moments but were unable to find the option to upgrade anything. Drew added the two as admins. "Anyone else you want to have that power while I'm gone?"

Hoeffecker had begun granting people access as they went but turned to him with a pause and then shook her head. "No. I don't think so. If something happens to the three of us, we'll be up a creek anyway, and I don't have anyone I can trust. That reminds me…" She put the communication rock on her desk. "I don't trust this. I don't trust that they don't have a way to listen in on our conversations. If I ever get to the point where the Sons are a threat to the stadium's safety, I'm going to tell you that the dome seems redder than normal. If I say that, head back here as fast as you can, but don't mention it on the comms."

"Do you really think we need that?" Sarah asked from her spot, and Hoeffecker just shrugged slightly.

"Better to have it and not need it, than need it and not have it." Hoeffecker turned to Sarah, "Also, if something happens to Drew, I want you to mention missing pizza. I'm not sure what would happen if Drew is incapacitated, but I don't want them to know before I'm ready to respond."

"Well, that's morbid," Drew muttered. "But I guess that makes sense. Any other messages you think we need to be able to pass?"

"That's the world we live in, sadly. Those are the only two that I'm worried the Sons will overhear. Anything else is less confidential. I'll tell JP in case anything happens to me. I think we should restrict it to just the four of us for now. We can always bring other people in. It's much harder to remove people once they know."

"Alright, anything else you need from me? I'm looking forward to blowing stuff up again, especially after this morning."

"Well, I'd warn you about putting too much trust in Clive, but I don't think I need to," Hoeffecker answered with a shrug. "As far as anything else? We'll keep in touch, check in every twenty-four hours at least. I understand that time can be hard to tell in a dungeon but err on the side of too often. Even if it's just to say you're fine."

"Will do." Drew stood up, and the holo graphics disappeared from over the desk. "Stay safe, colonel."

"You too, Mr. Michalik." The colonel held out her hand for Drew, and he shook it. "You'll be back here in no time," she said with a tight-lipped smile. "Now get out of my hair, I've got a thousand things to do."

"I'll miss you too, ma'am." Drew forced a smile as Hoeffecker sat back down at her desk while he and Sarah walked to the exit spot near the front of the room. The rest of the team was waiting for them outside the pyramid. Luke was coaching Gary through some sword forms, Daryl and Bill stood off to the side with JP. Clive was close enough that he was clearly listening to the three's conversation but not close enough to be included.

"Alright, folks. Let's get this show on the road," Drew said, and they all turned and walked toward the main gate. They couldn't take a direct path, so it took almost fifteen minutes to get there. JP shook everyone's hands as they left. Drew hesitated for a moment, looking around. He hadn't seen Katie since she left his suite the night before. "Take good care of her while I'm gone."

"I'll have her back without a scratch, you'll see," JP responded. The Lando Calrissian quote provoked a smile out of Drew which turned a little grim as he considered the words.

Drew felt odd leaving the stadium, knowing that he wasn't going to be back in the near future. He had bled countless times making this place home, and it felt weird to just… leave it. Still, he glanced south at the violet nodes and knew he had other things that he needed to do. He waved to JP, who had stayed at the gates with the dozens of other people that had shown up to see them off.

"Alright, Clive, activate your aura, and let's get going. How much mana fatigue does it take to use, by the way?" They were heading west along M street, Nat's Park no longer visible to the south. M was a large, divided road. The median had been a ten-foot-wide grass section before the Advent. The grass was waist-high already, with several small trees poking up at fifty-foot intervals. Most of the area had been heavily looted; it was mostly apartment complexes and office buildings.

"Well, I can keep it up for an hour or so, no problem, after that, I start to get headaches, and I can't do much for a few hours," Clive said, scratching his belly in thought.

"Alright, should only take us a little while to get to the first node. It's just up the street a few blocks after it turns into Maine Ave." A few blocks in this instance was closer to twelve or so. The area had been under heavy construction when the Advent hit—a gentrification effort for this part of the District. They ran into several different types of monsters, allowing them to put Clive's aura to the test.

Former scavengers like rats and squirrels didn't seem to notice them at all, the now two or three foot long beasts going about their activities without once looking up. However, a couple of crows took exception to them and took to dropping rocks on the group until Drew managed to kill one with an acid arrow. The rest scattered after that. Large insects and one murderous tree that Gary warned them away from were the rest of their company.

Making their way up Maine Ave, Drew was confused. On the north side of the street was a middle school. A somewhat obvious place for a node to form, but the node was instead on the south side of the street, a nine-story building. Apartments made up the upper floors, but the bottom two floors were a CVS pharmacy. Every previous node had been an important building, federal departments, headquarters, or three-letter agencies. Which made this innocuous CVS all the more bizarre.

"Daryl? Can you look around? I don't see any obvious entrances," Drew asked the scout, who nodded his head before disappearing from sight. Several of the windows had been broken open. A clothing boutique took up a small section of the open block, but the CVS was most of the building.

"There are a couple of other shops on the west side of the block," Daryl's invisible form said. He must be using the bird to scout. "But there isn't anything... important here. Where do you see the node?"

"It's hard to say, but if I had to hazard a guess, I'd say it's almost directly under the CVS," Drew answered.

"There is an alley down the center of the building. If you can give me a better idea of where the node is, we can try to narrow it down."

Drew nodded, and Luke led the way down a cross street until they finally got to the alley, which had a weird glassed-in archway overhead after a ten-meter long tunnel. They made a circuit around the building just to pinpoint the node.

"It's in the CVS," Drew finally said, shaking his head. "I mean, that doesn't make much sense, but that has to be where it is."

"Well, looks like we're raiding a CVS," Sarah announced, and everyone walked toward the front door, which was jammed open by a block of wood. Clearly, there had been some raiding of the building earlier on in the Advent.

"When would someone have raided this place?" Drew wondered.

"The first day, the night of lights," Bill supplied. "I know you guys were in a bunker, but that first night, the sky sort of went crazy. Tons of shooting stars and bright lights and just all sorts of crazy stuff. The power had already gone out, and it was pretty chaotic. Even on the base, we had some looting going on, and that was hours before the monsters started. I would assume the people upstairs probably looted this place for food or something."

"Wait, monsters didn't start spawning until hours later? That doesn't make any sense. I was attacked almost immediately." Drew frowned, remembering the spider that had almost killed him right after leaving the SCIF for the first time.

"You slotted a bunch of xatherite, though, right?" Sarah asked, and when Drew nodded, she continued. "We had been in there for a few days by the time you showed up. You lost consciousness from slotting all your xatherite at once. Still, that would have only had you out for a few hours. Long enough for the spider, but…" She trailed off. He had gone directly from his SCIF to the one Sarah and the others had been in, with only a minor detour to kill the giant spider in the stairwell.

"Can we worry about yer missing days later?" Clive asked. "I see stuff moving around in there, and I don't figure it's gonna be friendly."

Drew glanced toward the CVS entrance but couldn't see far into the darkness of the building. The windows only lit up the place for a few dozen feet. After that, the tall shelves blocked the light.

"Throw some lights in there," Sarah said, pulling out a glowrock and tossing it down the hall. Drew and Luke did the same, spreading globes of light in a couple different directions through the dark space. They each had pockets full of them courtesy of Katie.

Drew saw it then, movement at the far edge of his vision as something low to the ground dashed through the illuminated area.

CHAPTER EIGHTEEN – MATRYOSHKA

As it rolled into view, Drew realized what it was. A three-foot-tall Matryoshka doll, or a nesting doll as most people called them. Drew wasted no time and launched a holy fireball and a frostfireball at the round wood. The spells ripped layers of wood off the doll, but did little to stop its advance. Drew stared transfixed as it twisted oddly to shed the broken layers. Then it rapidly dashed toward the group. Luke stepped forward and spun his ball and chain around and smashed it into the doll, cracking off another few layers.

Gary darted forward and slashed down with his lightsaber, cutting it in half to reveal another ten layers of the doll as it split down the middle. Everyone paused, waiting to see if the doll would keep attacking or if it was over.

"Well, that was a bit like shotgunning a bottle of fireball," Clive said from behind Drew.

Sarah shook her head in disgust, but Drew pushed past it.

"Yeah, not exactly the monster I was expecting from a drugstore," Drew said, glancing down the street.

"I guess they could be a display of those or something," Sarah answered.

"I don't think bullets are gonna hurt that thing," Clive said, and the others murmured in agreement.

"Yeah, it just shrugged off two fireballs and the chain chomp. Shy of Gary's lightsaber, we'd have to put out a lot of damage to take those out," Drew said with a shrug. "Let's hope it's just the one."

It was not just the one. Thankfully, they only came one at a time, so they managed to chip away at the things but not without injury. Both Gary and Clive had taken rolls to the shins and had broken bones. Thankfully, Sarah and Bill had been able to heal them. The entire shop was cleared, and there was no sign of how to get to the node.

"It's… under here somewhere," Drew said.

"You know, I've been thinking about that." Clive held up a part of the doll that had broken his leg. "These things? They're made in Russia, yeah? I bet that this was a secret Russian spy base before the Advent hit, and there is a massive underground tunnel system that they were using to smuggle spies and contraband into the country. Probably comes out somewhere in the river."

"Wouldn't the fact that the water table is so high here basically make tunnels nearly impossible?" Sarah pointed to the west, where the Washington Channel was visible only half a block away.

"I figure if they can build massive underground bomb shelters under the White House and all the Senate buildings, then the Russians can evacuate a few tunnels out here," Clive retorted. "Plus, they could park a ship in the marina and use a diver to go out and get whatever it was, like in that Rock movie."

"Baywatch? You're basing your crazy conspiracy theory around a Baywatch movie?" Sarah's voice was incredulous.

"I mean, it wasn't that bad. Zac Efron is a bit of a pretty boy, but there was plenty of eye candy. Even that Iraqi chick was pretty good looking," Daryl offered.

"First of all, she's Indian, not Iraqi. Secondly, you're disgusting." Sarah growled.

"Now, now, don't be jealous, darling," Clive said, and Drew had to step in.

"Alright, guys, less gabbing and more looking for secret underground Russian spy facilities."

"I could just try to cut through the floor," Gary offered, pointing to his lightsaber.

"If it's a normal dungeon floor, it wouldn't work." Drew had tried to blow up the walls multiple times with his skills. "I guess it wouldn't hurt to try. Worst-case scenario, we know we're in the right spot."

Gary nodded his head apprehensively and tilted the lit blade down into the floor. Sparks flashed, and an acrid smell filled the room, but when he moved the saber away to check, there was no visible sign of damage.

"Well, I guess that confirms that we're in the right spot," Drew said, glancing around. "See if you can cut the walls." Gary went to try and was able to cut through them without a problem.

"Just the floors then," Sarah said next to Drew.

Clive was poking around in the manager's office looking for a secret door entrance while the rest of them sort of milled around. Luke was pushing boxes around and looking for floor hatches. With a shrug, the rest of them got to work, looking for a way down as well.

"I wonder why the trolls could dig through the DTC walls," Daryl said as he and Drew moved a rack to the side so they could check underneath it.

"Not sure. Maybe they had a specific xatherite for it? Or they used the control center to make an opening? We can make some changes like that to our DTCs," Drew answered.

"But they didn't have access to the pyramid, right? It wasn't claimed, like yours or the violets. Just a white node," Daryl asked as they pushed aside the carpeting only to find bare cement underneath.

"Yeah. But maybe the dungeon spawned creatures have some sort of intuitive control over it. The naga could take over nodes without claiming them too," Drew said with a frown. "Maybe it's white because it's a system… assigned node control?" Drew looked around the back room. They had ripped up the carpet and moved everything around, having been at the task for twenty minutes at this point.

"It's kind of fun to just… destroy stuff, but I don't think we're getting anywhere," Drew announced while stretching his arms and back. Then called out loud enough for everyone to hear, "Anyone got anything?" A chorus of no's filtered out from the various rooms they had spread out into. Everyone met back together in a break room. The strange musky smell and mismatched furniture were similar to every employee lounge he'd ever been in. Almost like it had been designed to be uncomfortable for long periods.

"Alright, I'm going to tell Colonel Hoeffecker that we can't find the node entrance," Drew said, pulling out the stone and waiting for it to pulse that she was ready to talk.

"That will mean we're not going to be able to link up the stadium with any other nodes we take over in Arlington," Sarah objected.

"Yeah, it's not ideal." Drew gestured around. "But I also don't want to waste any more time looking for this thing. Maybe Hoeffecker can send some people up here to look for the entrance while we take out the next node. Then we can backtrack a bit to take this one as well."

"What's the next node?" Clive asked. He and Gary were the only members of the group that hadn't seen the node map.

"ICE," Sarah said, and when everyone gave her a weird look, she explained. "The Immigration and Customs Enforcement building. I've been there a few times."

"Well, hopefully it's not a hidden entrance like this one. Luke, any idea what's going on here?" Drew turned to the seraph.

"Hard to say. I think there is probably something to what Clive said. It would make sense for it to be hidden if this was a spy base before. Combining that with the fact that this is probably a puzzle dungeon would make sense that we are unable to find it."

"A puzzle dungeon? Like the water temple was?" Drew asked, remembering how they had to find the specific set of levers and wheels that would slowly drain the dungeon so that they could reach the entrance to the boss room.

"That was more of a hybrid. This one seems like it is more of a straight puzzle. I think your decision to skip it is well warranted. This team is not well equipped to deal with a puzzle dungeon," Luke affirmed. The rock in Drew's hand buzzed, and he lifted it up so that he could speak into it.

"Colonel, we're at the node to the north. It's in a CVS, although we think it was a Russian covert ops station. We cannot find the entrance, and Luke thinks this is probably a puzzle dungeon and recommends we skip it. We're going to move forward to the ICE node. The route here should be moderately safe if you want to send a full group to try to figure out the puzzles while we take out that node." Drew turned to look at Luke. "Do puzzle dungeons normally have monsters in them?"

"No, usually just traps and puzzles. The usual strategy is to send those skilled at disabling locks and traps."

"Not sure if you could hear Luke, but he says it's mostly traps and puzzles and no monsters. Over." Drew spoke and then stopped. The rocks worked a lot like radios, in that only one person could be talking at a time.

"Roger. We don't have many people who are skilled in something like that, but I think we had a locksmith. I'll have to try to track him down. Proceed to the next target, and we'll see what we can do about this puzzle dungeon. Over and out."

Drew put the rock away. Hoeffecker clearly wanted to keep the messages short so as not to eat up too much of the time on the devices. "Alright, we're heading north again. ICE is only a block or two north of us. I think we'll be going through a tunnel." Drew had driven these roads a fair amount on his way to or from work, and he remembered the tiled tunnel in this area. It was long and slightly curved, so you could barely see the other side from the entrance.

Clive's stealth field got them there, but Luke paused near the entrance. The tiles were decorated. The nearest one was a strange cutout with white-barked trees showing through it.

"What is this?" Luke asked.

"I think that's… Vermont?" Drew said, looking at the mosaic. "Yeah, Vermont with some quaking aspens or something."

"What is Vermont?"

"Oh, it's a state, one of the ones to the northeast of us," Sarah answered for Drew.

"And this is supposed to represent Vermont somehow?"

"Yeah, I guess those might be Sugar Maples or something? Vermont is known for its syrup, isn't it?" Drew said, looking at the trees again.

"And what is this one on the other side?" Luke asked, pointing to another state cutout with a scene of a wetlands area.

"I think that's… Alabama? And a swan or a loon? Maybe it's a heron? I'm not really sure what the connection on that one is. I guess they might have a bunch of them down there or something." Drew looked over at Sarah and Daryl, but they both shrugged.

"I think I do not understand Earth artwork," Luke said after a minute of staring between the two images and then looking at several others down the dark tunnel.

"Yeah, art is weird," Drew said with a shrug. He looked through the tunnel and threw a fireball. A nest of spiders built up in the middle began to smolder as the creatures inside burned. A few more followed until the webbing had cleared away, revealing the light on the other side for them. They still waited a few minutes for the acrid smell of burning webbing to clear the air and to make sure none of the creatures were on their way to attack them. Passing through the tunnel, they could see vague images on the side, but none of them resembled anything coherent to Drew.

The other side of the street opened up onto two fifteen-story tall buildings made of white marble on both sides of the road. The ICE building didn't end up being where the node was housed. Instead, it was the building on the west side of the street. Drew looked at it and shook his head. In big block letters across the entryway were the words, "Federal Communications Commission."

"I have no idea what sort of monsters are going to be housed in the FCC, but I have a feeling they're going to be super annoying."

Chapter Nineteen – FCC

Stepping into the FCC building was like stepping into a jungle. The doors opened up into a wide atrium that was completely overgrown. Vines and ferns competed with bamboo to fill the air with greenery, and the buzz of insects filled the space.

"If we have to fight mosquitos, I'm going to scream a lot," Sarah said from behind him, a full-body shudder going through her frame.

"Yeah, those weren't fun." Drew remembered the one swarm of mosquitos he had to fight back at the Coast Guard HQ exchange. Bill had been there with him, and they had been smacking them around with bats while Drew used his cones to kill the group.

"Well, hopefully, they won't notice us," Clive announced from the side. That was when they saw several of the things buzzing through the atrium. Unlike the ones Drew had fought before, which were the size of his hand, these ones were a foot and a half long from head to tail. Their wings were double that size, and the proboscis was at least five inches long.

"Can we just burn the whole thing down?" Sarah's voice was just this side of panic. "I don't mind spiders or giant rats, but I do not like anything that sucks blood."

"It's too green. We'd never burn it down fast enough." Daryl's voice came from nowhere. "I see the pyramid. It's at the end of this atrium. Which is a couple miles long and looks like it's gonna take a while to hack through. There aren't any good paths, although a few hundred feet in, we can kind of follow a river where at least we won't have to cut through the bamboo."

"This sounds every bit as annoying as I would assume a node from the FCC would be," Drew growled. "Alright, I'm going to try to take out a few of those mosquitos next time they come out. Everyone else get ready, in case they swarm us or something. Also, I'm calling them stirges. They're too big to be mosquitos."

"What's a stirge?" Sarah was clearly trying to take her mind off the mosquitos. Her knuckles were white on the grip of her spear. Clive had attached a bayonet to the end of his rifle, although Drew had no idea where he would have gotten one of those. Bill stood behind Drew. He had pulled out an aluminum bat from his pouch and holstered his pistol.

"It's from Dungeons and Dragons, it's… well, exactly how I would describe a foot and a half long mosquito." Drew's eyes were trained on the forest edge, and a flicker of movement was enough for him to launch a gravball. The bamboo compacted down into a small ball, killing the stirge within, but when the spell ended, it exploded out, sending shards of bamboo out like a shrapnel bomb. Drew ducked back, putting his arm up over his face as dozens of sharp bits of bamboo struck his armor.

"Holy fucking shitballs." Clive's curses were more inventive than the rest, but all of them had shards of bamboo sticking out around them.

Drew could tell that a few of the shards had found weak points in his armor and had dug into flesh. He dropped his arm down so that he could watch the aftermath. The gravball had shredded the forest for dozens of feet in every direction. Clumps of bamboo were tilting over and falling down, creating a chain reaction that cleared the immediate area around the entrance. He could see several stirges feebly struggling as their shredded bodies gave up.

A massive rat, easily five feet in length, gulped down several of the twitching stirges before Drew launched a fireball at it. The explosion ripped up more of the bamboo and melted half of the rat, filling the newly made clearing with the smell of burning flesh. Drawn to the smell, several other creatures arrived to take advantage of the carrion. Drew continued to take potshots at the creatures that showed up for nearly thirty minutes.

Sarah and Bill removed the bamboo shrapnel from the party, except for Gary, whose force shield had blocked the splinters. Sarah probably had it the next easiest. She activated her ghost armor, and the shards just fell to the floor under her, and then Bill gave her a hug to heal the damage.

The smell of blood from their wounds and the bodies attracted more stirges. Instead of arriving in a big pack, they came in ones and twos and Drew used his fireball spells to take them out as they appeared. By the time no new creatures showed up to eat the growing pile of corpses, the clearing had expanded a dozen meters on every side.

Drew was the last person to get the shards removed. Most of them had stuck into the underside of his forearm, where he had blocked the shrapnel from hitting his face. The vambrace had a narrow line where the leather didn't overlap, and tiny slivers had worked their way into his flesh through the gap. His passive regeneration had half pushed them out by the time Sarah got to him, the benefit of his vitality reserve from Sacrifice at Noon.

"Well, that actually worked pretty well. I say we just do that." Drew glanced at everyone, "From a safer distance, of course. Now that we have a better sightline, we should be out of the initial gravball's explosion radius."

There were a few grumbles, but no one had a better idea. The sheer quantity of monsters that Drew had killed over the last thirty minutes made everyone less interested in crawling through the jungle. None of the monsters had been particularly durable. There was just a lot of them, to the point that Luke and Gary even had to kill a couple of the faster ones that came from the forest's nearer sections.

"Take cover." Drew gave them a few seconds to hunker down before launching another gravball at the edge of the forest.

Hunkering down was the right choice. Even this far away, a small spattering of wooden slivers hit the group, although they had lost so much force that they didn't hurt. No more monsters were attracted, and Drew figured they had cleared out the nearby area. So he cast another gravball when the cooldown was done.

It took three more castings until they were deep enough into the forest to get another blood frenzy. They were far enough away at this point that none of the monsters attacked them. Clive even managed to snipe one of the biggest stirges out of the air with his rifle. The man clearly wasn't as good a shot as JP. He missed five times before he ended up hitting one. But Drew couldn't blame him. At this distance, his acid arrow spells regularly missed as well—the fast-moving stirges made for excellent target practice.

Unless one could just throw fireballs at the problem. Clive stopped firing after a few dozen rounds, not wanting to use ammo while Drew could kill them easily with his area effect spells. Drew himself threw in the occasional arrow spell, trying to work on his aim with the precision spells. As they slowly progressed through the dungeon, the monsters started getting bigger, tougher, and faster. Just before they got to the river six hours later, the stirges were able to shrug off all but a near-direct hit from a fireball.

There were so many of these bigger creatures that Drew stopped trying to clear out all of them. An injured stirge was easy pickings for the melee combatants. And Luke was using this as a training opportunity with the others. Gary was doing the best of them; his sense intent xatherite allowed him to predict the monsters' trajectories, and his lightsaber was deadly. Sarah's spear and Bill's bat were less effective. The two healers mostly swung their weapons around as a deterrent. Clive managed to pierce a few of the bugs with his bayonet.

Sarah's red xatherite minor pain shell had finally linked up with her green group awareness xatherite after the naga node. The crystals had all upgraded along the way, changing names and linking together. She had actually gotten two linked skills out of it.

Linked Skill Name: Group Pain Shell
Xatherite Color(s): Red, Green
Linked Skill Grade: Intermediate
Type: Magic
Effect: Enshrines all friendly creatures within 7.5m of the target in an aura that reflects a small portion of the damage they receive back at the target. Lasts for 30 seconds.
Mana recharge time: 54.2 seconds.

Linked Skill Name: Linked Damage Reflection
Xatherite Color(s): Red, Green
Linked Skill Grade: Intermediate
Type: Magic
Effect: Enshrines all enemy creatures within 7.5m of the target in an aura that reflects a small portion of the damage they deal back at themselves. Lasts for 30 seconds.
Mana recharge time: 54.2 seconds.

They were basically mirror opposites of each other. One affected friendly targets and one affected hostiles. Which meant she could stack them. The stirges were more precision fighters, relying on their quick speed and small bodies to avoid getting hit. They were made to deal lots of damage without taking any, and Sarah completely negated that. The ability also didn't seem to take armor into effect, and the stirges would basically implode if they managed to actually hit anything. Which was not a super exciting thing for any of them. They all learned to fight with their mouths closed to avoid eating bits of insect goo.

The river changed everything. It had a deep section running through roughly the center of the long chamber, but the entire area had turned into a wetland with minimal dry land. Drew shredded a section of the bamboo, and nothing appeared out of the woods to attack them. He did it again, and still, nothing happened.

"So," Drew said, looking around. "This seems like a bad development."

"Leeches." Sarah was looking into a shallower section of water. Drew looked in, and sure enough, foot long leeches undulated along the bottom of the water.

"Gross," Gary said, sticking his lightsaber into the water and trying to cut one of the beasts. The blade sliced the creature in half, but both sides began thrashing wildly. Almost instantly, dozens of leeches converged on the area. The saber still in the water cut half a dozen more, which only added to the frenzy.

"What is up with this place?" Drew muttered, staring at the blood frenzy. "Everyone, step back. I'm gonna cone of frost them." As everyone took a few steps back, Drew pointed, and the leeches immediately ceased their frenzy as the water turned into a slurry of flesh and ice. The blood in the water brought more of the leeches.

"I say we don't go through the water," Sarah said with a shiver. There were hundreds of giant leeches floating in the water, so many that they weren't sure they were all dead or if they just obstructed the surface enough to block any sight of movement below them.

"Ain't like we got many choices," Clive said. "Guess we could try to monkey through them bamboo? Mayhaps build a raft or something from the bamboo?"

The rest of the group argued about various options they could take to get through the shallow water as Drew looked around. Of the group, he and Sarah were the only ones wearing boots. They were still in their black regulation footwear. They came up to his lower shin, but the rest of his body was tight leather armor or snake scales. He walked away from where the blood frenzy was and unsheathed Robbi's sword. Poking it into the water, he found a spot that was less than a foot deep and took a few steps into the water.

It was relatively clear water at this point. There weren't any leeches near him, so he kept walking. He could see some of their black forms a few dozen paces away, and he slowly waded toward them, testing the depth of the water as he went. It wasn't until he was about a foot away from a leech that it seemed to realize he was there. The thing twisted and made for his leg. Drew gulped and held the sword at the ready. The leech shot toward his foot, clearly trying to attach.

Then it swam away, unable to penetrate the thick leather of his boots. A few others seemed to be attracted to the movement and also approached to nibble at his boots, but were likewise rebuffed by the thick leather. Drew cast a cone with an upward twist so that only the far end would affect the water a dozen feet away from him. Drew watched, and it took almost a minute before they seemed to realize what had happened. The leeches converged on the dead, leaving the area around Drew's feet clear.

"I hate this dungeon," Drew muttered to himself as he trudged back to the group.

Chapter Twenty – Fort

It took them four more hours to go the last mile and a half through the wetlands, Drew causing a feeding frenzy on either side of the group while they walked down the middle. Combined with Clive's stealth ability, the group had been largely ignored. They were all worried that there was something more deadly than the leeches in the water and avoided the deeper and more murky sections. They had been forced to backtrack several times when the water got too deep, but they ended up finding a route where they were never deeper than their knees.

They were sitting on a piece of land that was only an inch underwater; they hadn't seen actual dry land in almost a mile. Until they saw the island the pyramid was on. It was situated in the middle of a large clearing in the bamboo forest, only a foot and a half of dry land surrounding it on the visible sides. The water around it was choked with vegetation that made seeing anything that might be lurking within impossible. The lack of trees meant that the water was deep.

"Something in there is watching us, and it really don't like us." Gary's voice broke the silence as everyone stared at the glade.

"Yeah, I think we all got the 'this is bad' message." Clive snorted from the other side of Drew.

"What do you think? Try to storm it out?" Sarah asked Drew.

"I doubt it would work. This much water just has too much mass for the storm to do much to it." Drew scratched his ear. The one benefit of giant mosquitoes was that at least the swamp wasn't filled with regular-sized ones as well. Some part of him kept expecting to walk through a swarm of them. "Maybe I can throw some fireballs at it if Gary can figure out where it is exactly. The sonic blast from the explosion might work."

"Other choice is what, we swim in there? I dun think my gun's gonna be any good in the water," Clive groused from the side.

"Yeah, none of us have great underwater abilities," Sarah said with a frown. Luke's primary weapon was a ball and chain. It required momentum and freedom of movement, which the water would inhibit. The lightsaber worked as long as the hilt wasn't underwater, which would cause it to short out and need to be resummoned. Her own spear would be as effective as ever, but it was hardly enough to kill a node guardian.

"So we draw it out," Drew announced. "Fighting it on its home turf would be a disaster." Glancing around, he tried to figure where they could make a stand. "Let's back up a bit while we get ready, don't want to tempt fate. Daryl, keep an eye on the lake with your bird. Any information on what the creature is will help."

They retreated a hundred feet or so to another shallow area. Gary and Luke started cutting down bamboo and laying it across the ground. The bamboo here was thick, almost an inch around and plentiful, so they were able to make a reasonably dry spot of wood to stand on.

"We could try making a raft or something." Everyone but Daryl was helping pitch in to make a spot to hold over while trying to think of a plan. None of them were tired or worn out, thanks to Drew's rain spell, but they were all mentally on edge.

"Too flimsy," Drew said; the green wood wasn't easy to break for a human, but he didn't imagine it would be difficult for a guardian monster. Especially if it was something like a giant crocodile or the large nagas. "I mean, realistically, we could probably lure it out with some blood or something, everything here seems to love the stuff. The question is how many leeches are in the water with it and what it… is?"

"Just a bigger leech?" Clive asked. He was the only one of the group that had never fought a node guardian before, but he had asked questions on the way up.

"I mean, maybe. Or a big snake?" Sarah offered. "Swamps have snakes, right?"

"Yeah, but we haven't seen any snakes," Drew said thoughtfully. "Only the rats, stirges, and the leeches. Why rats? They seem… wrong for the dungeon."

"Well, the leeches and stirges need something to drink blood from, right? Maybe the rats were the only options." Sarah was helping Bill prop bamboo sticks around their little area, already several blankets were strung between the bamboo shafts, creating a flimsy wall.

"Do you need a ceiling for your ability?" Drew asked as he sharpened an inch off the bottom of the bamboo shafts so that they could be shoved into the soft ground.

"No, just the walls should be good. It stopped needing a ceiling when it upgraded," Bill answered as he put up the third blanket. They had created a rectangle, for the most part, fifteen feet across and ten feet long. It took them a few more minutes to make the fort, and Drew could actually feel it when the magic went into effect. Warmth and comfort seemed to infuse the place, reminding him of curling up under a blanket over a hot air vent on a cold winter morning as a child.

Looking around, the blankets themselves had changed. Before, they had created a flimsy wall, but now they looked solid. Drew reached out to touch the nearest section and frowned. It was both firm and soft. The edges had the feeling of a blanket, but when he tried to push against it, there wasn't an ounce of give to the structure.

"What exactly are the limitations on this?" Drew asked, turning to Bill.

"Lasts for nine hours or until I disable it. Can't attack out of it, and it takes a significant amount of damage to break into. It also hides itself, we tested it a few times, and even if you know it's there, it's incredibly hard to even realize it's there." Bill answered with a shrug. "Cooldown is ten hours, so I can have one up almost constantly."

"Is that what the sheet says, 'significant'? I have a couple of spells that list that as how much damage they do," Drew asked. The entire group stopped and looked at him. "What?"

"How many spells have significant as a damage modifier?" Sarah's voice was deceptively calm, but everyone was looking at him, making him think something was unusual. He hadn't ever really talked to them about how much damage his spells did.

"Uh, just about everything? Acid arrow and lightning bolt are the only basic spells that aren't significant or higher at this point." Drew glanced at Luke. "But that's nothing compared to Luke's blaster gun thing. My spells weren't hardly doing anything to the fire croc."

"They were ripping off chunks of it, actually," Luke corrected Drew. "My gun does significant damage, for the ten minutes it can be summoned every two months."

"See, highest I can do is… major?" Drew paused midway through his statement to look at Luke confused; his gun had done much more damage than his fireballs had been doing.

"Shit, no wonder he's just ripping stuff apart," Clive muttered.

"Gary's lightsaber does more than that, I bet," Drew said, looking at the teen for assistance.

"It does not, actually. I would guess it is up to small?" Luke asked Gary, who nodded his head in agreement. "But melee weapons are always lower since there are other ways to improve their damage output."

"So…?" Drew trailed off, looking around. "I mean, just because you know the damage attribute doesn't change the spells at all, and they're still clearly not enough for some of these things."

Sarah shook her head, trying to reconcile everything. "I think it has to do with a bad application of damage. Your fireball seems to do less damage toward the outer edge of its explosion. Which is probably why those stirges made it out. Most everyone has minor or small attack skills. A few have moderate."

"That is because few of them have ranged damage spells. They have attack skills." Luke continued when everyone was confused. "An attack skill requires a weapon, and the damage increases based on what weapon you're using. JP has a lot of attack skills. Drew has spells."

"Is my force shield a spell?" Gary questioned from his spot on the rough wooden floor.

"Personal defense skills are a strange one. They are more like temporary summoned equipment than anything else. I would guess it is an orange or a yellow?" Luke responded with a smile.

"Yeah. Yellow."

"These classifications are only for red xatherite. One of the reasons that red mages are so powerful is their ability to attack without a weapon. You will see a few true spells every now and again, but they are not common."

Drew tried to remember if he had seen anyone else casting spells. "Juan had spells."

"Yeah, he could sort of throw fireballs like Drew," Sarah said.

"They were illusionary, right?" Luke said, and they both nodded. "It is not a common set of xatherite, but that does happen. Especially among green xatherite."

Drew and Sarah made eye contact. They were the only ones left of their original group that had met Juan. Drew hadn't known him long, only a few hours, but he gave Sarah a sad smile, which she returned.

"So, bait it out?" Drew finally broke the silence. "We could throw some blood in the water, and that would probably bring it out."

"Where are we going to get blood?"

"We can try a leech or two?" Sarah suggested.

"If there are any other leeches in there, one or two isn't going to cut it. We need to make another feeding frenzy," Drew said after a moment's thought.

"I have a ton of meat," Daryl said, fading into view. "I've been looting stuff as we went. Picked up probably fifty stirges and giant rat's worth of meat."

"That would work," Drew said with a grin. "Did you get anything else?"

"I still hope the xatherite is going to level up and start giving me massive axes out of the bodies, but no—just a lot of proboscises and poor quality rat skin. I figured I would just leave it somewhere the stadium could pick it up. But if we need it to lure the guardian out, we could probably do that."

"Well, I don't think we'll need all of it."

A few tests later and they determined that, unlike the stirges, the leeches required the carrion to be in the water before they would swarm. Which made the whole experience slightly more difficult, since no one wanted to be anywhere near the bait when they triggered the guardian. They ended up making a tiny raft out of bamboo and mud, and then when it was a dozen feet out into the water, Drew hit it with an acid arrow spell.

When that didn't work, he hit it with three more. Which caused the raft to finally capsize, dumping the raw meat into the pool.

Within seconds, a massive rippling announced the presence of the guardian of the node. A thirty-foot-long lamprey. Its black skin was covered in streaks of red, and each tooth in its two-foot-wide ringed mouth was the size of a knife. It almost seemed to suck in the meat, the teeth undulating as it pulled in the flesh. Clive's piercing shot went off to his right, which caused the lamprey to keen as it shifted its attention in the direction of the thing that had hurt it.

Launching half its body out of the pool toward the shooter, Drew flung a gravball behind it even as Luke's ball and chain smashed into the side of the thing's rubbery flesh. The two actions together managed to arrest its forward motion, leaving it half out of the water. Drew concentrated on the back half of the beast, several fireball variants burning the slimy flesh. Still, the front half wriggled and writhed, the brain of the beast unwilling to admit it was dead.

Gary and Luke got tossed to the side in its wild convulsions. Drew cried out in alarm and launched a gravity cone at the beast, which contained its movement enough for the rest of the group to begin peppering it with acid arrows and bullets. Black blood shot into the air, leaving a sizzling behind in its wake and everyone retreated even as they kept shooting. The fifteen seconds before his gravball recharged seemed to last forever, but that was the end of the fish. It shook one last time and then went still, its entire body compressed into rough chunks of flesh that acid burned anything they came into contact with.

"Everyone okay?" Drew asked, and to his relief, he heard five people sound off. Bill and Sarah immediately went to work. Gary had a broken leg, Luke's arm was swelling uncomfortably, and everyone had acid pocks all over their exposed skin. Drew cast a refreshing rain to help clean everyone. The pyramid was still out of reach across the lake. Which forced them to craft a small, two-person raft which they sent across with Luke and Drew. After almost a full day, Drew was able to claim the node.

CHAPTER TWENTY-ONE – HOOK ROLLER

It had been a while since Drew had taken over an unconnected node. He changed the name to FCC Node and installed the remote admin console, but otherwise, they left the node alone. The real benefit was the increased levels to Bill, Clive, and Gary's xatherite. They also managed to harvest two xatherite crystals from the corpse of the guardian. Daryl collected a big, bright indigo while Drew picked up a much smaller and dimmer red.

> *Xatherite Crystal Name: Shadow Silk*
> *Xatherite Color: Indigo*
> *Xatherite Grade: Intermediate*
> *Xatherite Rarity: Uncommon*
> *Type: Physical*
> *Effect: Four tendrils of shadow extend between two designated targets, tethering them together. Deals minor darkness damage to all affected targets as long as they are close together. Any effect which breaks the shadow tendrils causes the portions to explode, dealing significant shadow damage in a 1m radius explosion from the targets.*
> *Mana recharge time: 1 minute, 3 seconds.*

> *Xatherite Crystal Name: Breeze Blade*
> *Xatherite Color: Red*
> *Xatherite Grade: Undeveloped*
> *Xatherite Rarity: Widespread*
> *Type: Magic*
> *Effect: Creates a 1.5m arc that extends up to 10m from the caster, dealing small amounts of wind damage.*
> *Mana recharge time: 14 seconds.*

They were both great finds that Drew would have loved to take for himself. It was strange since the indigo was more like a red than most of the indigos he had seen. The red was also fantastic. Despite its low rarity, Drew assumed it would be one of those abilities that would scale super well with just about any other attacks someone would have, making it a great linked skill option. There was also the matter of desolare, the xatherite Hades had given him.

Shadow silk would allow him to slot desolare in a six-star constellation. But Drew only had two indigo slots, and he was hoping for something more stealth-like to fill those. There was also the fact that blink step and mana sight didn't really seem like they would link well with it. For a six node constellation, having three unlinked seemed like a bad idea. The two in there were already bad enough, since neither of them had linked up already. He could slot desolare in with stricto mentis clypeus, but he wasn't sure that would add a good link either.

In the end, Drew felt like it just wasn't going to link up well, and using it as solely a stepping stone to get to the next constellation seemed like a waste of resources. After some discussion, they decided to give it to Sarah but not have her slot it yet. It would give her another attack power while also playing to her strength as a battlefield controller. She would be able to slot it into a new constellation that also had a blue and her only white. If they got across the river and hadn't found another yellow or indigo for Drew to put desolare where he wanted to, she would trade it back so that they would be ready to fight the sidhe.

Gary ended up getting the red and slotted it into the same linked group as his blue summon lightsaber and an empty green and yellow. They all took a quick meal of jerky and flatbread before heading out the way they came. As they walked back, Drew called in to Hoeffecker.

"Colonel, FCC node is under our control. What is the status on the other node?" Drew kept his message short, not wanting to burn through the charge on the stone.

"Pending still, proceed to next node." Hoeffecker's clipped response sounded tired to Drew, but he put the stone away and nodded to the rest of the group.

"We're gonna keep heading on to the next node," Drew announced to the rest of the group. "I looked at it, and I'm almost positive it's the Jefferson Memorial."

"I always liked the Jefferson," Sarah said. "I used to go there at night to see its lights on the tidal basin."

"Me too. I had a couple friends who proposed there. I hear that's pretty common," Drew said, and Bill nodded his head in agreement.

"That's where I proposed to my wife." Bill's voice was soft, to the point that it actually took Drew a minute to realize what he had said. Sarah was already moving to put an arm around him in a hug despite the rough terrain. As far as he could recall, that was the first time Bill had said anything about his family. To his surprise, Daryl actually appeared next to Bill and laid a hand on his shoulder as well. They stood in silence for a moment before Clive hacked out a loogie.

"Why are we standing in the middle of a swamp?" Clive asked, his voice annoyed, and Drew watched Sarah roll her eyes.

"Shut up, Clive," she said in a growl, which left the man looking between the group members with a confused look.

"M'kay."

The moment was over, though, and they soon moved on, making it to the entrance of the FCC building and making their way along Maine Ave to the set of bridges that would take them across the small channel to Hains Point. The double set of bridges made for a safe crossing. Clive's stealth field prevented them from having to kill a squad of squirrels that had taken over the wooded park around the memorial.

"You know, I half expected this place to be a water purifier filled with mutants," Drew muttered, and Daryl's invisible form laughed beside him. Sarah arched an eyebrow in question and Drew just shook his head. "Don't worry about it. It's from a video game."

The white marble of the rotunda was still gleaming despite the apparent attempts by nature to reclaim her. The grass was growing tall around it, but none was growing within the memorial itself. Inside, the bronze statue of Jefferson could be seen still standing. Slight verdigris showed that it hadn't been polished recently, but otherwise, no monsters seemed to be making the internal area home. Drew glanced over at Gary, who shook his head, indicating that he didn't sense any hostile intent in the area.

Drew climbed up the large marble blocks to enter the rotunda. The white pillars seemed to pick up the sun and reflect it around, illuminating it without the need for artificial lighting. They still had a few hours before sunset, but Drew looked around the space. This had been a solemn place. Jefferson had been one of the most important figures of the American Revolution. Drew had dated a girl who had talked at length about how John Adams and Jefferson died within hours of each other but didn't know it, both saying that the country would be fine as long as the other was still alive. This despite the fact that they had fought for decades over policy.

The others had followed him in, and Drew watched as Luke began to read the script written on the southwest portion of the rotunda. This was the preamble of the Declaration of Independence.

We hold these truths to be self-evident that all men are created equal, that they are endowed by their Creator with certain inalienable rights, among these are life, liberty, and the pursuit of happiness...

"I do not think I understand this," Luke said to Drew. "Who is this 'Creator' the words speak of?"

"The Christian God." Drew paused. "That's what the early founders of America worshiped."

"I never understood that. Who is the Christian god? Most of your Earth religions can be traced back to the pantheons, but…" He waved a hand. "None of the pantheons have just one god."

"That's a good question. I guess you would probably know him under a different name. It's probably the same as the Hebrew god? It's considered bad form to say his name, but I guess you would call him Jehovah?" At Drew's words, Luke spun to glare at him.

"Now I understand why it was taboo to say the name," Luke said with a tight-lipped growl and then strode away, leaving Drew confused as he stared back up at the words cut into the stone. He wondered what could have happened to make the seraph so angry. And for that matter, if the name was taboo, why would his organization be named after Christian angels?

"Would you still think we were all entitled to life, liberty, and the pursuit of happiness these days?" Drew turned and asked the statue. The world was so different now than it had been just a month before. Was that still something that any reasonable person could expect to have? Liberty maybe, they could still allow people the ability to choose their own path. But life? The pursuit of happiness? What did that even look like when monsters existed?

Drew thought back to the kids playing in the maze of furniture they had created. Of anything he had seen since the Advent, that was the closest he had seen to someone pursuing happiness. Maybe that was enough? However, the statue had no wisdom to dispense and Drew turned to look for a way into the DTC. There were stairs leading down into a public restroom, bookshop, and a small museum of Jefferson's life that was the most likely culprit.

Filtering down the stairs behind Luke, they caught their first glimpse of the resident monsters. They resembled spiders in the sense that they had eight legs and were covered in chitin. Each leg was only about a foot and a half long with two segments on it. The main body was oblong in shape, and they were covered in hooked spikes. They moved by rolling, a few of the relevant legs pushing against the floor. Their method of attack was to try to roll you over, the spikes digging into any exposed flesh and then ripping it with the hooks as they continued their roll.

However, they relied heavily on their momentum to do that. The first one made a loud clattering as it charged at Luke. He responded by swinging his leg out, knocking the beast into the wall, bouncing off the concrete, and ricocheting into Gary. He launched a breeze blast at it as he swung his sword; the laser cut through the hard shell and bisected the beast, which scuttled around for a few more seconds before going limp.

"It would appear as though we are fighting hook rollers," Luke said with a frown. "I will be less useful in these fights. Drew's spells, particularly your fire element ones and any piercing weapons, will work best. The chitin shells are very resistant to blunt weapons but are fairly easily penetrated by spears. They usually come in larger numbers, and we should be very cautious in wide-open areas, as they are swarm creatures."

"They really called hook rollers?" Clive asked, poking half of the shell with his bayonet.

"That is a reasonably close approximation of their names. They are not popular enemies to fight, although it will not be bad if it remains closed-off spaces like this," Luke added. They continued down the corridor and fought a few more of them. The distinctive sound they made was loud enough that they knew they were coming well before they were dangerous to the team, and Drew discovered that his disruption links and lightning spells were especially useful.

A stun would cause the things to slide forward on the more flat side of their bodies, breaking off a few of the brittle spike hooks while leaving them open to Gary slicing them apart or Luke, armed with Sarah's spear, pinning them down until Gary was free. After a hundred meters of hallways, they opened up into a wider area. They could see a few dozen of the hook rollers milling about a room that looked like it had once been an expansive ballroom.

"Drew, use a long-range spell to attract some. We'll pull them into the corridor and use it as a chokepoint, so we don't get surrounded," Sarah said while backing away. She was using Robbi's sword since none of them wanted to waste ammunition for the guns.

"Sounds good." Drew waited for everyone to get ready and then launched a barrage of fireball variants at the creatures, managing to catch the nearest half dozen or so within their blasts. Usually, the concussive blast would have killed them, but most of the damage seemed to come from the fire and ice shards in his spells.

Luke and Gary held the front line. Drew stood behind them, having the most ranged attacks by a fair margin. He would back up as the fight moved in closer so the others could use their weapons. Clive stood at the back and shot his rifle, the reverb from the report had the entire group's ears ringing, and Sarah smacked him on the shoulder, shouting words Drew suddenly couldn't hear. With his own growl, he launched acid arrows at the closest hook rollers that were two dozen feet away when he dropped back. His fingers formed the seals needed to cast a storm spell.

The front line clashed with the rollers, Luke's twisted, a low sweeping arc from his ball and chain smashing them back. Ruining their forward momentum as a chain reaction of the light creatures ramming into each other followed. Wind slashes pushed them around further, creating a roadblock for the approaching monsters, causing them to begin piling up a dozen feet away from Luke.

A frostfire storm smashed down right on top of the mass, its circular mass ending eight feet in front of Luke and Gary. The heavy winds pulled at their armor, and the humans backed up a few feet as stray burning-ice would rocket out of the storms and smash into the ground around them. Burning and frozen pieces of hook roller followed shortly after, their entire charge routed. Gary sliced one roller in half that came from the side, just barely managing to escape the deadly vortex.

When the storm died down, none of the rollers were still moving. Drew could feel Sarah's magic sweep over them and the ringing in his ears went away.

"Maybe don't shoot without telling us so we can put in ear protection," Sarah growled at Clive.

CHAPTER TWENTY-TWO – AURAS

The rest of the dungeon followed a similar pattern. The hook rollers ended up being some of the easiest fights they had done in a while. The only time they had any issue was when Gary stumbled and missed his slice on one of the rollers, which then ran into his leg. A second later, the thing rolled off with a significant portion of its hooks still stuck in Gary's leg. Luckily, Sarah's new upgraded ghost armor could be used on others and she was able to pull a dozen hooks out after the combat was over, allowing them to heal the wounds without having to pull them out.

"Definitely going to want to get thicker leg armor," Gary muttered to himself as he rubbed at the holes in the leather, a shudder going through his whole body as he did so. It reminded Drew of people who complained about phantom pain in limbs that had been amputated. The healing magic did more than just close the wounds though, it also removed some of the mental trauma of the injury. Gary was mostly back to normal ten minutes later despite his rather horrific screams after the injury.

Bill's daddy's embrace seemed to work on the mental aspects better even than Sarah's spells. Drew wondered how much of that was a component of the spell and how much of it was just the comfort of having someone hug you. They had taken a short break while Gary was tended to, and they all had a quick meal of dried meat and fruit. That was the only snag they ran into before the node guardian, which was just a bigger hook roller that Drew took out with a gravity storm and a frostfire storm before it even knew they were there.

The whole DTC felt absurdly easy to Drew. When he mentioned this to Luke, the seraph just laughed.

"That is because we have the right tools for the job. Think of how easy that water dungeon back near the stadium would have been if we could breathe underwater. Very few people have a way of dealing with hook rollers from a distance like you do. This means that they have to fight them up close, and you saw how dangerous they can be if they are allowed to swarm. One mistake and people get injured. Tearing out the hooks is worse than the injury itself most of the time. Sarah's phasing skill made that a non-issue.

"Even then, Gary's sword deals heat-related damage, which is the hook roller's natural weakness. Normally, a group would find a dungeon like this and farm it repeatedly for the xatherite."

Drew pondered on Luke's words and realized just how easy it would be for their team specifically to clear out the hook rollers, but he didn't think that any of the rest of the teams would match well. The bullets had barely worked on them. Except for Clive's Penetrating Shot, they all bounced off their tough shells like Luke's ball had. Drew's acid arrows had worked alright, but his fire spells had been the real winner of the day.

Drew quickly claimed the node while the group searched for xatherite.

"Found a yellow," Luke told him as soon as he exited the dimensional space.

"Sarah harvest it?" Drew asked.

"We were waiting to confirm that is what you wanted," Luke responded.

"Why…?" Drew shook his head. He knew the answer to that question. Luke just snorted in laughter. "Sarah, grab it."

The curly-haired ensign reached down to touch the weak-looking xatherite, almost immediately throwing it into a trade window with him.

Xatherite Crystal Name: Shoal Sense
Xatherite Color: Yellow
Xatherite Grade: Primitive
Xatherite Rarity: Common

> *Type: Aura (toggleable)*
> *Effect: User emits aura in 2m, giving friendly targets a weak danger sense.*

"Well, that changes things a little," Drew said, glancing over the yellow. "I think RNGesus just smiled on us." When Sarah raised an eyebrow, he shrugged, not wanting to explain it. "You slot shadow silk, I'll slot this in the link with blink step and mana sight. Maybe I'll be able to bring other people with me or give you all mana sight. Those are probably the best linked options I've seen in a while. That will give me the jump I need to slot desolare in the new constellation."

Sarah nodded her head and glanced around at the others, considering. "I guess that makes sense. You're most likely to be in the middle of danger anyway. What do you think, Luke?" she asked, giving the group a rundown on the skill.

"Drew is often close to the middle of the pack, so giving him an aura will benefit everyone," Luke said after a moment. "Plus, it means you get to keep shadow silk, allowing you more tactical control of a situation. I like it."

Accepting the trade, Drew immediately slotted the low-grade xatherite and began casting refreshing rain as Sarah slotted shadow silk, which would hurt a lot more, being a higher grade and rarity. She closed her eyes as the headache that came with slotting a new xatherite hit her, but that went away after the rain started doing its work and disappeared completely when he cast invigorate on her.

"Alright, one more node down. Anyone else need to upgrade xatherite before we head into Arlington?" Almost everyone said they did, a few having already taken advantage of the rain to do so.

Drew looked at his own list of improved xatherite. Minor mana tap, minor holy shell, and solar offering were ready to upgrade again, and he bumped them up to intermediate. The two minors went away, becoming just mana tap and holy shell.

Solar oblation upgraded to solar offering, and the linked skill had become solar mana offering. None of them changed much, but Drew had stopped hoping for much from upgrades inside the same tier. The headache came back stronger but eased a little as the rain fell over him. The rest were going through similar upgrade-induced headaches.

They trekked back to the entrance of the dungeon and told Hoeffecker that they were done. Unfortunately, there had been no progress made on finding the entrance to the connecting node's DTC.

"I guess we're crossing the bridges then," Drew told the rest of the group. They didn't have anything else that needed to be done on this side of the bridge, and they couldn't delay heading into Arlington until they had found anything.

"Yeah, I think we might have a problem with that." Daryl appeared next to Drew. "I have the bird out... and the bridges look, well, they look bad."

"All of them?" Drew asked; there were six different bridges across the Potomac here. The two railroad bridges, a smaller five-lane bridge, and the two 14th Street bridges, which had ten lanes between them. It was a couple hundred feet walk to where the bridges were, but Drew could see immediately what Daryl had meant. It looked like something had attacked the bridges.

Large chunks of concrete had been ripped off the bridges and were jutting out of the river. Drew could probably have gotten across, using a combination of blink step and gravitas. But none of the others would be able to traverse the nearly destroyed bridges. Looking to the north, the Arlington Memorial Bridge had received similar treatment, although it was in better shape than the 14th Street bridges.

"Daryl, any chance you can check out the northern bridges?" Drew asked as he glanced down at the ley lines under the city. The Jefferson node they had just taken connected to the

Pentagon node across the river. But the node to the north, which looked like it was probably the Lincoln Memorial, didn't connect across the river, only connecting with what Drew assumed had to be the Washington Monument, Kennedy Center, and a third node between the two of them which he wasn't sure of. Probably the Department of State.

"Alright, well, I have good news and bad news," Daryl said after a few minutes of scouting. "Good news is that a turtle the size of… I dunno, a semi-truck… is clearly the culprit destroying the bridges. Bad news is, something killed it, impaled it with a dozen light poles, and I have no idea what."

"Well, that don't sound like something we wanna tango with, you know?" Clive said and then spit on the ground.

"I can't wait for that chew to kill you," Sarah said with disgust.

"Darlin', we got giant turtle killing monsters about, I ain't gonna live long 'nuff to die of cancer. 'Sides, I'm sure yer fancy healing could fix that anyway."

Drew had to give the point to Clive on that one. They didn't exactly have the same life expectancy that they had before Advent.

"Alright, I'll tell Hoeffecker that we'll be using the next set of bridges. Clive, I hope your stealth field got upgraded, because I have a feeling we're going to be putting it through its paces. Anyone else need to upgrade more xatherite? I want us at our best."

"Maybe we should wait then?" Bill spoke up. "It's nearly dark. We can sit tight for tonight, then get a start early tomorrow morning. That gives them more time to find the hidden entrance, and we will have full visibility for crossing the bridge."

Glancing over at the horizon, Drew nodded his head slowly. "Yeah, that makes sense. There aren't a lot of buildings around here. We could set up in the monument, I guess?" Drew glanced back. There was a near-constant movement on the edges of his vision. Clive's stealth field was protecting them from the vast majority of the monsters, but this green area had clearly been home to a lot of small animals and insects that had turned into much larger predators with the Advent. As he watched, a meter-long dragonfly hovering over the field darted off to snatch up a regular-sized squirrel. The squirrel's tail slowly disappeared into its mouth as the mandibles shifted it around in its mouth.

"An enclosed area sounds like a good idea." Gary had followed his eyes and watched the dragonfly consume the small animal. "Nights are always the worst."

"Yeah, we passed by that gift shop earlier. That looked like it was still about the right size for us to be able to use blanket fort in, right?" Sarah asked Bill, who nodded.

"Shouldn't be a problem."

"Well, let's get, before this place becomes busy as a cat on a hot tin roof," Clive said as he turned back to the monument. The rest of the group followed behind him. Gary asked why a cat was on a hot tin roof, but Clive didn't bother to answer the kid. Retracing their steps didn't take long. The stealth aura was very effective.

Drew turned to Luke. "If I activate my aura, will that stop Clive's from working?"

"No. You can only have one aura on at a time, but every person in a party can have an aura. Having an aura up is a constant drain, but you can stack as many of them as you have people. You should not have much trouble with yours until it gets up to advanced grade. You are in your own refreshing rain often enough that it will probably be more like background noise."

Drew decided to test out Luke's advice and mentally toggled shoal sense on. There was a strange immediate sense of the world around him. It was slightly distracting how everything felt more… solid for a moment before it faded into background noise. Luke was the only one close enough to be hit as he did it.

"That is a most peculiar sensation. We should probably get everyone accustomed to it and then test how it will warn you of danger. Once we have set up the fort, that is."

In the end, they didn't set up near the gift shop, but rather just outside of the bathrooms. They did raid the gift shop for as many soft things as they could find, though, since the floor was hard marble. Drew could ensure that none of them needed to sleep, but no one wanted to stand around for the entire night. Most of them had picked up camp chairs during their time at the CVS, one chair would just barely fit through the opening of his pouch of holding at a time, but you could store several of them without eating too much of your space.

"Magic inventories are definitely one of the best parts of the apocalypse," Daryl said as he plopped his chair down next to Drew's. Bill and Sarah were finishing the last corner of the blanket fort. Bill looked around and then moved to stand in the middle of the newly created fort. Drew had been too busy trying to think of a way to kill a giant leech to really watch what Bill was doing last time, but he was curious how his xatherite would turn on.

Bill knelt down on one knee and looked around, then bowed his head and muttered a few words under his breath, and suddenly a sense of warmth and comfort filled the blanket fort. Bill got up but turned away from the rest of the group, a hand reaching up to his face. Drew could tell that he was brushing away a tear, and he wondered what exactly he had to say to make the fort skill active. Then he realized they were going to be stuck in this tunnel doing nothing for a night.

Chapter Twenty-Three – Rules

Drew hadn't quite become accustomed to the weird angle of light from the glow stones. Set around the group in a circle to ward off the darkness, they created some disquieting shadows across the walls. Drew pulled out a light rock from his pouch and then looked up. There were long panels where fluorescent lighting would have illuminated the area before the Advent killed all the electricity.

The ceiling was standard height. Drew jumped, activating gravitas at the height of his jump he floated up to the ceiling. It took him a second or two to figure out how to move the translucent covering on the lights, but once he did, he shoved a light rock in and then pushed the covering back on, allowing gravitas to take him back down to the floor. He landed awkwardly, one foot coming down harder than the other, which left him off balance. Luckily, Luke was there to steady him so that he didn't fall over.

"What are you doing?" the seraph asked, glancing up at the light.

Drew grinned; even with just the one overhead light, the room's weirdly cast shadows had nearly disappeared, leaving it feeling less like a spooky campfire and more like a normal office space.

"Just lightening the mood," Drew answered as he moved around to another light fixture on the opposite side of the fort. Waiting for the cooldown on gravitas, he jumped up and repeated his earlier performance. Although he was more careful with his landing and didn't need to grab onto Luke for support. They had a large supply of glowrocks, saving the ones from Katie during all their delves, so Drew managed to put a half dozen glowrocks in the ceiling. By the end, what had been a gloomy fireside tunnel had become much livelier.

"You know, it's weird to see magical powers being used to change the lights," Sarah said when Drew returned to his camp chair. The others had set up around him near the center of the room where the shadows were the smallest.

"Phenomenal cosmic power, itty bitty living space," Drew said, doing his best Robin Williams impression.

"I miss porn," Clive announced to universal groans. He then pulled out his flask, taking a long swig. "So, we just kicking it 'round here for the night? Not gonna like, go night hunting or whatever?"

"We don't really need additional food," Daryl said, looking around. "Although we're probably stuck with eating cold rations. I don't think we have enough fuel to cook any of the meat I have."

"Not sure I'd want to eat any of it, to be honest," Drew said, trying to think what meat the scout would have been able to harvest during the day. Hook horrors, leeches, mosquitos, and rats?

"Oh come on, rat ain't that bad. 'Specially as big as these'ns get. Normal rats, they is more bone and guts than meat, but these ones give a couple good chunks, I'd bet. Probably tastes like gamey chicken." Clive received disgusted looks from everyone but Luke, who just nodded along in agreement.

"Regardless, we don't have enough fuel for a fire. Actually, come to think of it, how is the stadium cooking things? There aren't anywhere near enough trees to support the level of heat we'd need." Drew had pulled out a bag of the jerky they had taken from the stadium as he pondered.

"There are quite a few people with heating xatherite," Sarah announced. Having pulled an apple out of her pouch, she began cutting it into slices on her lap. "Hard to keep it the right heat levels, which is why they mostly made stews at first. It wasn't until after you made the dome and the housing area that they got facilities built for the purpose, which made everything even easier."

"Huh." Drew had noticed a general improvement in the food quality, but he had assumed that was due to them being able to keep food overnight and increasing the quantity that everyone had. "I didn't notice an individual cooking area, so that's all communal stuff?"

"That is an upgrade you can buy with enough mana now that you have a control center," Luke told him. "Creature comforts are usually far down the list of things node lords buy since defenses are usually more desired."

"I guess I should delve into those menus a little deeper," Drew muttered under his breath. "Just haven't had a lot of time since we made the command center to look through all the options."

"I imagine Hoeffecker has been poring over the options, but she will have limited ability to actually change anything," Luke suggested.

"And I don't suppose I can queue things from here…" Drew asked, having pulled up his remote admin interface and navigating to the control room node. To his surprise, he actually did have some things he could look at from here. There was a list of buildings and a queue of assigned automatic tasks; he could also modify permissions of anyone on the access list. "Where does the power for our interfaces come from?" Drew mused. This was essentially like using a phone app for an MMO.

"It draws on the ambient mana. It is a mostly mental construct, so it does not use up much, but even those functions can disappear if there is not enough mana." Luke had placed his chair on Drew's left. Across from him, Clive had pulled out a deck of cards from somewhere and was shuffling them. Gary, Bill, and Sarah were having a conversation on the other side of Luke while Daryl sat to his right. He had pulled out a book and was reading it.

Drew took a moment to enjoy how bizarre this whole experience was. They were sitting in a blanket fort in the basement of a national monument doing the same things he'd seen people do on every camping trip of his life. Of course, he was also manipulating a mana interface that allowed him almost complete control over thousands of people's lives, and they'd spent the day killing monsters in the same monument they now camped in.

"Alright, I can only see the development queues on most of these nodes," Drew said with a frown.

"There should be a star within a circle to the left of the queue. That is the icon that will show you what you can purchase," Luke answered, and it took Drew a minute to locate the small icon that looked almost like a bulleted list. Mentally focusing on that for the habitat module gave him an extensive list of things he could upgrade, a mana cost, and how long it would take for it to be built. It was grouped up into subsections.

Administrative
Constructs
Defenses
Efficiency
General

Each list was huge. A quick glance at the general one listed everything from additional floodlights in the exterior courtyard to different styles on the toilet faucets. Checking individual nodes, he realized that they each had different lists with hundreds of little things that could be built, most of them costing a few hundred mana or less. Drew collapsed the general tab and opened up the submenu for defenses for the habitat module.

Density - 1,000

| Thickness - 500 |
| Recharge - 750 |
| Opacity - 10,000 |

Each of them had five ticks next to them, allowing him to level up that section for double the mana cost of the previous level. Thickness was the cheapest option, only costing 15,500 mana to fully upgrade. Opacity, on the other hand, would require a whopping 310,000 mana to max out. Clicking over to the main defenses menu, he found a similar list. He could build walls, towers, even automated mana turrets that would unleash a myriad of elemental attacks on any attackers.

All of these were expensive, though. A ten-foot wall around the entire claimed area would cost almost 150,000 mana. Each tower cost 25,000, and adding a turret cost another 25,000 and reduced the mana generation of the node as a whole while it existed. There were even options to create golems that would defend the stadium, but the prices were well outside his price range.

Seeing the reduction in mana generation, Drew clicked over to look at how much each node was actually making. It looked like all the DTCs were making 500 mana a day. Anything that was making a resource, like the biological growth accelerator or the foundry, was putting out 375. The outliers in the pattern were the habitat at 850, command post at 675, and the housing extender at 550. The xatherite concentrator was lower than everything else at 250.

The habitat node having nearly double some of the other ones was convenient since any improvement to the shield or static defenses had to be done with its mana. They could also shift mana between connected nodes, but would lose 30% of the mana he transferred that way. Clicking through the options, it was clear that he could easily spend the mana his nodes had generated with only a small amount of the things he wanted to buy.

Thinking back to his conversation with One, he had said that Drew's nodes were producing more than average amounts of mana. Which meant that it would take even longer to build a stronghold anywhere else. Drew wondered just how much more mana he was getting over the other two splits. A part of him wanted to play this like a strategy game, but something told him that it would take too much time delving through the menus to really get to the meat of this system.

Checking to make sure Hoeffecker was able to spend the mana, he decided to trust her to deal with the stadium's needs while he was off dealing with the sidhe ship. Maybe he could play around with the system once he was back in the command post. The UI there had looked much better, the remote console clearly a barebones version of what he had seen while they were looking for the access control lists. Closing the menu, he stretched.

He had been sitting for almost an hour as he searched through the interface. The others were scattered around the blanket fort. Clive had apparently convinced Daryl, Gary, and Bill to play poker with him. Although Drew couldn't imagine what they were bidding with. Sarah and Luke were sitting in chairs next to him. Sarah had a book out and looked to be heavily focused on its contents. Luke, on the other hand, seemed lost in his own system interface.

Drew stood up and stretched. He could feel pops as he went through his major joints, stretching the muscles as well as he could in his armor.

"Anything good?" Sarah asked, sliding a piece of paper into her book to keep her place as she closed it, giving Drew a view of the cover.

"Are you reading the UCMJ?" Drew asked the ensign, incredulity lacing his voice. The Uniform Code of Military Justice was the legal system that the military operated under.

"Yeah, I am," Sarah said, holding up the handbook for Drew to look at. "You should read it too. I figure this is probably the closest thing we have to a code of laws that are actually relevant."

"All the poor civvies required to follow military law?" Drew shook his head. "I mean, I guess we'd be in a state of martial law if there was enough of a government around to actually declare it. But the UCMJ doesn't have any concessions for civil rights. We can't just force that on people who didn't take the oath."

"I know… but we're at war, Drew. People don't get to be bystanders," Sarah said, pulling the book back and running a hand over the cover. "At least this way, we have a system in place. They may not be willing combatants, but they are combatants now. Aside from the Numb."

Drew hadn't checked in on the Numb much. With the new housing areas, there were floors dedicated to housing the nearly comatose people. Of the forty-five-hundred or so people they had living at the stadium, just over a quarter of them were Numb. Anywhere from six hundred to a thousand worked outside the stadium itself, although only about one-hundred-fifty of those had a combat-capable xatherite. The other twenty-five-hundred odd people were tending to the everyday tasks of the stadium, be that in the fields, kitchens, or taking care of the Numb.

A good chunk of them did nothing at all, just sat in their rooms and did… who knew what. There wasn't enough work to keep everyone busy or enough weapons and ammunition to push outward. So they were just cooling their heels on half rations, unable or unwilling to contribute. Drew had no idea how they could live like that. Hopefully, as the stadium got safer, they would venture out and begin contributing. He had done everything he could to set them up for success, but you couldn't force people to get their acts together. It was up to Gunn and Hoeffecker to keep the peace at the stadium.

"Yeah, I'll read some of it later. Hopefully, I never have to use any of the information in there," Drew said at last. "I think I'm gonna do a workout. Luke, you up for some training?"

The seraph looked up and then nodded his head. "Yes. Of course."

CHAPTER TWENTY-FOUR – METHODS

Drew was sure of one thing: he was a terrible melee combatant. There weren't many options when it would be relevant, since any amount of mana fatigue sufficient to make him unable to cast spells made the sword mostly irrelevant. Which was why he wasn't practicing how to hit. Luke had given him a wooden sword that was about the same size as Robbi's blood sword, and he was using it to block Gary's attacks. Blocking or dodging, although he mostly did the latter.

Mana bulwark made it so that any attack with rotational velocity that wasn't designed to hit him center mass was much easier to evade. The attack slowing down as it came close gave him that extra half a second to not be where Gary's own practice sword was. Luke had tested the real weapon to make sure it would be affected and declared that Drew's shield was fair use. The problem was that Gary could sense Drew's intentions, which made it a deadly game of cat and mouse as Drew had to keep shifting his dodges to prevent Gary's blade from hitting some part of his body.

Drew had started out doing well. The kid used wide sweeping arcs that were probably very useful when you had a laser sword. Against Drew's armor, though, he had taken to wide slashes toward his center mass. It wasn't enough to hit Drew, who had six inches of height on the teen, but as the fight went on, Drew's dodges became slower, the heavy exertion taking its toll on his body.

"Ooof," Drew grunted as Gary managed to land a major blow on his ribs. The first hit of this sortie.

"Dead," Luke declared, and Drew sighed. Allowing his arm to drop, the wooden practice weapon pointed into the ground as he slumped to the floor and splayed out. The pillow fort had enough room for a large practice area.

"Invigorate?" Gary asked. The teen had hit the floor shortly after Drew, clearly exhausted from the exercise. Luke hadn't been letting Drew use his recovery spell, saying that his muscles needed to feel the fatigue or they'd never grow. Which felt like a lie to Drew, but he was pretty sure Luke had never intentionally lied to him before, so he took the statement at face value.

"Give it half an hour or so," Luke said, and the two fighters moaned. "But move over. It is Sarah and Bill's turn." They had been doing this for two hours now, rotating who Luke was putting through the wringer. Drew and Gary had ended up paired together early, both having unfair advantages over anyone but Luke. The seraph could take any three people with relative ease, although he did have to start breaking limbs with his ball and chain if Gary and Drew were both against him.

Glancing over at Gary's prone form, Drew decided that he was too tired to stand up. So he rolled over a few times until he felt a chair against his shoulder. Twisting a bit so that he was lying on his back again, he closed his eyes and focused on his breathing for a minute.

"Come on, Mr. Drew," Gary said, and Drew peeked out to see the teen standing over him with a hand out. "Walk around a bit. You'll get stiff otherwise." Grabbing the hand, Drew grunted.

"Won't matter as soon as I cast refreshing rain," Drew said. "Maybe my body will feel the pain better, and it'll speed the whole thing up." Stretching his sword arm out, he bent down with another grunt to pick up the wooden sword. Placing it on Luke's chair, he slumped down in his own chair, his arms hanging down limply.

Gary sat down next to him, and they both turned their attention to Bill and Sarah's fight. The ensign was using a long stick that was about the same length as her spear. Bill had wrapped a few rags around his bat to soften his blows a bit.

Sarah's speed and reach made it hard for the chief to make any headway, though, and he ended up hitting with his elbow or knees as often as he did with the bat. Luke was coaching Sarah on how to respond when someone smashed her spear aside and then moved in close like Bill was doing.

"You have to maintain the distance. As soon as he gets inside your reach, you are going to be in trouble," Luke reminded as Sarah didn't shift around fast enough and took an elbow to the chin.

Drew glanced over at Gary, who was fiddling with his blade. "So, how does that work exactly?" Drew said, pointing to the hilt. There were enough similarities between Gary's saber and Robbi's that he assumed they were the same type of powers, although he couldn't see Robbi's xatherite anymore. The description on Gary's xatherite was relatively unhelpful. It was a violet xatherite, currently called blade of decision.

> *Create or upgrade a Blade of Decision. Only one blade can exist at any time. Being separated from your blade for more than 24 hours will cause a new blade to be created.*

"You can try it," Gary said, handing the lightsaber over to Drew, who picked it up gingerly, not wanting to make the laser portion appear. "You can't turn it on; it only works for me. I put my finger on that block there, and it turns on." Gary pointed to a pencil sharpener-sized flat section on the side of the hilt. Drew pointed the hilt up and touched his finger to the spot, but nothing happened.

"Robbi's sword was similar. I can use it, but it would shift shapes for him," Drew said, handing the hilt back with a bit of disappointment. He picked up the sword and put it on his lap, pulling it a few inches out of the sheath that Min Sun had made for him. Robbi hadn't needed a sheath, although he wasn't sure where he had kept the blade when he wasn't using it. Drew pushed the blade back in with a sigh. "As much as I'd love a lightsaber, I don't think I'd ever slot a skill like that."

"Well, you don't really need them," Gary said. "I mean, you can run away and deal damage from afar. So it's not like you're dependent on getting close like I used to be. I'm really glad you gave me breeze blade. It's not really… as Jedi-like as a force push or something would be. But I really appreciate you giving it to me, Mr. Drew."

"Oh, man. Mr. Drew? That sounds so strange." Drew shook his head. "You're fine just calling me Drew. I've never much cared for all those honorifics. Never really felt right."

"Uh, that's okay, Mr. Drew. I don't feel right doing that," Gary said as he put the hilt back into his holster. "You from DC, Mr. Drew?" Gary asked as Clive sat down next to him.

"You bin doin' good, kid." Drew winced as he heard the slight slurring in Clive's voice. Clearly, he had been drinking too much of the moonshine from his flask. "Ah hope my daughters are doin' s'good as you."

"I didn't know you had kids." Drew blinked. Something just felt odd when he considered a man like Clive having daughters.

"Yes, sir! Two of 'em, down-home in Nola. I us'ta carry around some pictures, but I didn't grab my wallet during the light show." Nola was what people from New Orleans called their city. He had heard a couple people describe the first night of the Advent as some variant of the light show.

"What was it like? The first night? I was stuck in a bunker the whole time."

"It was… thousands of shooting stars and bright flashes of light, almost like it was daylight, and stars growing bright and dimming and changing color," Gary answered, but Clive nodded his head in agreement. Drew had heard that when a star went nova, it would illuminate the Earth's sky for a minute or two.

"Wish I could have seen that," Drew said, thinking about how cool that would have been.

"It was a sight to see, for sure," Clive said, and Gary nodded his head in agreement.

"So, how old are your daughters?" Gary asked.

"Oldest was a few years older'n you. She was at Perdue. And the other was fixin' to turn seventeen this year. She'd have liked you. She was always messing about with the nerds," Clive said, poking Gary in the shoulder.

"Well, they probably both got maps. So they have a pretty good chance at defending themselves." Drew remembered Hoeffecker saying that almost all the fifteen-year-olds had gotten maps, and everyone older than that had as well.

"Oh, the girls should be fine. I've been teaching them to hunt and shoot since they could hold a gun." Clive leaned back and scratched between his legs. "Their mom's probably dead. Sad I couldn't be there to see the bitch finally kick it."

"I take it you weren't on friendly terms," Drew remarked dryly, causing Clive to laugh.

"Yer could say that. I was a trucker back then, and came home early ta find her in bed with two other guys. Discovered that the bitch were spreading her legs for jus—" Clive shook his head.

"Clive, you're talking to a kid," Bill interrupted. He and Sarah had finished up their spar, and both slumped into chairs in a loose circle. Luke and Daryl followed them.

"If he's grown enough to kill monsters, he's a grown enough to hear about the evils of wimenkind." Clive slapped Gary's back, who gave an audible 'oof.'

"Well, thanks for lumping us all together. Perhaps you can also give him a lesson on the evils of alcohol addiction," Sarah said, wrinkling her nose as the movement caused the scent of Clive's moonshine to waft over her.

"Oh sure, go 'head and shelter him in a safe space. All that does is make him too weak to fight his own battles. This world ain't never been safe, and trying to coddle the kids isn't helping anyone." Clive threw up his arms in disgust.

"We can't just throw them into the deep end and hope they swim," Bill almost growled. "We can give them a place to be safe while also teaching them to deal with the new dangers of our world."

"You ever see a kid learn to swim outside of water?" Clive challenged. "They gotta be thrown in, else they'll never learn."

"That's how you instill a lifelong fear of water into a kid." Bill glared across the circle of chairs.

"Then you keep throwing them in until they get over it."

"That's a good way to make your kids hate you."

"At least they'll be alive to hate me," Clive growled back, and Drew could see that his words hit their mark against Bill.

"Okay, you two. Enough of that," Drew said, standing up. "I'm sure this is mostly stress and fatigue talking. I'm going to cast refreshing rain on everyone. Clive, I don't want you drinking any more of that moonshine tonight. Make some more and store it in extra bottles. That's ammunition, not a beverage. Bill, you should take a round about the fort to see if anything is going on outside." Drew was casting the spell as he talked, and everyone was soon showered in the warm drizzle.

Both men sat and glared daggers at each other, before turning to do as Drew had commanded.

"Well, that was fun," Drew said to Sarah as he slid back into his chair.

"Yeah, got a little tense there," Sarah said, looking between the two men.

"I think Clive is right," Gary said in a voice that didn't carry very far. "I've been feeling so powerless since this whole thing started. It wasn't until you took us into the DTC that I could actually help anyone. All us kids, they've just shoved us into a room and forgotten about us as much as they can. We want to help, and no one will let us. We all feel useless."

"You're not useless, Gary," Sarah said with a frown.

"I know I'm not. I'm not as good as Mr. Drew is, but who cares? No one else is either. I know they just want to protect us, but we can help. We've proven that several times, but no one sees it. We're the ones running messages back and forth for the military, we're carrying stuff between the crafters, and if you would let us, I know we could help fight the monsters."

"I'll talk to Hoeffecker about it when we get back." Drew watched the passion in Gary and realized he might have been discounting the kids more than he should have. He had been one of the ones wanting to keep the kids away from danger. "We'll have to come up with something shy of just throwing you in the deep end. But we can figure something out."

"Thank you, Mr. Drew," Gary said, and the kid seemed to realize that all four of the adults were looking at him, and he sank back into his chair. Drew turned to look at Sarah, who shrugged slightly.

"I think that is a wise course of action," Luke spoke up for the first time in the conversation.

CHAPTER TWENTY-FIVE – STATUES

Outside of the memorial the next morning, they headed northwest. The goal was to cross the small bridge at the front of the tidal basin and then head through western Potomac Park past the baseball fields until they could get to the near side of the Lincoln Memorial and cross the bridge. Thankfully whatever was destroying the bridges across the Potomac had ignored the small two-lane bridge between the two sides of the basin, and they crossed without incident.

Which was when they ran into the goats. Well, they could sort of be called goats. They had the same general shape as a goat... if a goat had an extra pair of legs and two sets of horns. Both the front-facing spikes of a typical goat and then spiraling horns that Drew attributed to bighorn sheep. There was a herd of them grazing on the grass around the baseball fields of the park. They kept the grass to a uniform height of about three feet. The thick grass made it difficult to get a good count of the creatures, but there were several dozen of them.

The nearest was giving them a stink eye with its creepy eyes but didn't seem inclined to stop chewing on the grass to attack them. It was the first clearly system-generated animal that wasn't immediately hostile to them, and the entire group had paused to watch the creatures.

"I think we can probably avoid any conflict with them if we head west along the road. Looks like they are nesting in the woods along the north bank," Daryl announced, having sent his bird ahead to scout out the area. "There are some weird movements in the grass. Can't really tell what they are, but they're clearly not the goats."

"Where did they come from?" Sarah asked with a bit of wonder. "The nearest node is the Lincoln Memorial. These have to be nodeborn, though. Normal goats wouldn't have mutated that much. Would they?" She had turned to Luke, but it was Clive that responded first.

"There wasn't no goats here to mutate, anyways," the man said and then spat on the grass. Drew wondered how long the man had been chewing tobacco for it to develop into this big of a habit. Or if he was just doing it to annoy Sarah, who glared at him every time he did it.

"They are not a mutation," Luke agreed. "As for where they came from… they are most likely a bloom. The system directed free mana here, and these creatures spawned. Think of them as free-roaming, DTC monsters that can reproduce normally but will not be spontaneously generated again."

"Are blooms common?" Sarah asked, watching the goats graze.

"During the Advent? Most likely, they are prevalent. Although I think it would be rare this close to the central nexus. Too many ley lines focus the mana into the DTCs," Luke answered. "We should report they are here, but I doubt Colonel Hoeffecker will do anything about them. They are too far from the stadium to easily herd, and I doubt you would have a spot prepared for manaborn goats."

Nodding his head along with Luke's words, they traveled along the road on the far side of the clearing from where the goats were grazing. The stretch of road curved slightly to the north, and the cherry trees lining the street made it difficult to see more than a couple hundred feet ahead of them. Everyone stayed close to the middle of the road and trusted in Clive and Gary's xatherite for their safety. It was just as they were passing the last baseball field on the right that the situation changed.

A strange white granite statue stood in the middle of a rotunda. A seated man under three angelic visitors in a pillar was odd. But what was even more bizarre were the two stainless steel statues standing guard around it. Draped in a poncho made of the same shining steel as the rest of the statue, both men carried rifles and wore round helmets on their heads.

"Are those the Korean War Monument statues?" Sarah said, her voice cast low so as not to carry.

"Two of them, yeah," Drew said and frowned as the two statues turned to look at him as he spoke. They were pointing their rifles at the group, and their mouths moved, but no sound came out. "Everyone back up…"

"Their guns are not operable," Luke said. "They are part of the original statue and will only be usable as a blunt instrument."

"That isn't going to help us when they swing solid metal clubs at us," Drew groused as he backed up, keeping his eyes on the metallic soldiers.

"So, what're we gonna do?" Clive asked as they backed up enough for the statues to return to a state of attention.

"I'm not sure how well equipped we are to fight steel golems," Drew said with a frown. "If there was just one of them, we could test how durable they are, but with two…" Drew trailed off, glancing to the north where the two steel men were standing.

"Well, we have to get around them. Can we cut through the park?" Sarah turned to look for Daryl. Drew pointed to where the scout was standing, invisible.

"Checking. I think—oh shit." Daryl rarely cursed. "There are a bunch more of them, fanning out around us. I count at least two or three coming in from the north. Their ponchos can bend light or something. They are crawling through the grass."

"Drew, gravball the two by the memorial. We're gonna make a break for the bridge," Sarah whispered.

Drew launched his gravball at the two statues standing guard; they crunched into the cement as they dug their rifles into the terrain. Thin strands of silk connected them as Sarah cast her control spell. One of the two managed to anchor himself, but the other one was flung into the center of the ball, the loud squeal of metal crunching and scraping ringing through the open area as the group ran up Ohio Drive. The clomp of metal on asphalt sounded behind them, but the statues were slower than the humans.

"We need to go up the hill," Clive said, pointing to the arch of the bridge over the road they were currently running down.

"Everyone veer right," Drew called, cutting through the tall grass on the hill. He took a moment to glance behind him, four statues were about fifty feet back, and he launched fireballs at them. Turning back while running, he was lagging a bit behind, but he knew he could blink step forward if he needed to. Luke was keeping pace with him, his head turning to survey for any more threats.

"Hostile intent from the bridge!" Gary shouted. The kid was at the front of the group. Drew glanced back and saw that his spells had indeed slowed down the statues, golems or whatever the Advent had turned the Vietnam Memorial into.

"Coming!" Drew shouted as he blink stepped forward, taking the lead of the group. He could hear Luke curse behind him. As Drew crested the hill, he saw the backside of the Lincoln Memorial in front of him. The pounding of his heartbeat sounded like an earthquake as he twisted to see what Gary had sensed. Four golden or bronze statues—it was hard to tell at first glance—blocked their path onto the bridge. Two men mounted on horses holding a child, while the other two were topless women.

"God damn statues," Drew cursed. He launched a barrage of acid arrows and their variants at them, the shocking and disrupting seemed to lock up three of them.

"Head toward the Lincoln!" Sarah said, arriving next to Drew and seeing the statues for herself.

"My spells aren't doing much to them!" Drew called out as he launched a fireball for good measure at the four golden statues. The backside of the Lincoln wasn't as impressive as the front, the tall white marble of the pillars was still present, but they faced the back wall of the monument. It was surrounded by a ten-foot-tall retaining wall. "But I can slow them down. Let's see if they can climb!" Drew wasn't worried about his own ability to get over the wall. He had gravitas if nothing else. The rest ran toward the wall, Luke throwing Gary and Sarah up with ease as Clive tried to climb the rough rock face.

Daryl went next, turning visible long enough to step on Luke's cupped hands. Clive had made it about two feet up and then lost his footing, falling to the grass. Bill was the next to take Luke's offered boost up, the seraph clearly having to work a lot harder to push the bigger man's weight up over the wall.

"Clive, let Luke help you!" Drew shouted as he turned around to check the location of the statues. They were about sixty feet away from him now, the steel soldiers having joined the golden gate guards. They were lumbering toward him at a slow pace. A line of acid arrows and fireballs carved into the gold and steel golems, knocking them around and slowing them down considerably. Turning back, Luke was helping Clive up, but the man tumbled, his ankle unable to support his weight. Drew ran toward them.

"Sarah, heals? Clive did something to his ankle," Drew shouted, and the brunette looked down the wall and cast her spell. Drew watched Luke pick Clive up by his belt and then toss him up the ten feet into Bill and Daryl's waiting hands. "Go!" Drew shouted to Luke as he activated gravitas to make a thirty-foot jump up the slope. Luke saw his legs pumping and turned, jumping up to catch a hand on the edge of the wall, where Gary helped pull him up.

It became apparent that Drew had misjudged his distances, and he was going to overshoot the wall. He lessened the effect of gravitas, landing on top of the grass with a roll that took the breath from his lungs. He sat there stunned for a moment, wondering why the ground was rumbling. Bill picked him up, giving him a hug as he did, and he could feel the magic of his embrace chasing the fog from his mind. Turning, he saw Gary launch an air slash that washed over the golems without much effect. A shot rang out as Clive fired at one of the golden statues, and its face twisted and crumbled off, leaving a blank head in its wake.

Evidence of Drew's early attacks were visible in the battered statues, clearly now missing a number of less solid parts like hands or clothing that had been blasted off by the magic. They were milling around at the bottom of the terrace but didn't seem able to climb up the walls. Or weren't willing to. Remembering the rumbling, Drew turned toward the building just in time to see a massive white marble form step around the far corner. Lincoln himself, in resplendent white and standing nearly thirty feet tall. In one hand, he held an entire tree that had clearly been ripped out of the ground, and he took one slow step toward them.

"Alright, new plan," Drew said, shooting his full barrage of acid arrows at the golem. "You guys head north and then cut across the bridge. I'll lead the golems away and circle around the monument using blink step and gravitas."

"I will come with you," Luke said, but Drew shook his head.

"No, defend the others. You'll only slow me down." Drew pointed a finger down at the golems and triggered a cone of frost before blink stepping away to the southeast. Holding both hands out toward the golems, he launched another barrage of fireballs. A gravball and a holy gravball both struck Lincoln's left arm, emitting what Drew hoped was the sound of stone cracking. Fireball and frost fireball hit the gold and steel golems while holy frost fireball and holy fireball struck at the gargantuan president, leaving charred black marks on its otherwise white surface.

Drew didn't have time to see if the others were following his commands as he turned and began running around the monument, hoping he hadn't just made one of the worst decisions of his life.

Chapter Twenty-Six – Lincoln

Lincoln was slow. Every step the giant golem took was equivalent to five or six of Drew's steps. The problem lay in just how large it was; it moved twenty feet per step and ignored any terrain changes under four feet tall. Drew managed to keep out of the range of the tree it wielded like a club, but not by much. He felt shoal sense trigger, and he flung himself to the right, rolling twice before pushing himself up and continuing to run as the tree smashed into the ground.

It was briefly tangled in another tree as the giant took a second backswing, and Drew took the chance to blindly cast cone of cold behind him, hoping to slow the creature down. Drew was moving into the front of the memorial now. The iconic steps around him caused his thighs to burn from the effort of running in his boots and armor. He risked a glance back and launched a gravball as a leg drew back to land, hoping to throw the statue off balance and trip it. Drew didn't watch long enough to see if it worked as he was already running again.

In the open, flat area, he pulled enough ahead of the statue that he took a moment to consider his plan. What little of a plan he had, anyway. He needed to build some distance and maybe get up high. But the only thing around here with enough elevation was the memorial itself. To the north, the long black wall of the Vietnam Memorial stretched in a wide V, while to the east was the reflecting pool which framed the Washington Memorial's plinth. Neither of which were going to help him.

From behind, a shot rang out, and Drew cursed. That had to be Clive, which meant the group wasn't running across the bridge like he had told them to. A glance behind him showed Clive, Luke, and Gary rounding the corner. He didn't have enough time to look for them, but he didn't see Sarah, Bill, or Daryl. Then a massive thud sounded out, and the ground shook, causing Drew to stumble slightly. Turning back, he saw Lincoln had slipped and fallen prone, and he launched a barrage of fireballs at it, taking advantage of its temporary immobility to lay in some damage.

Then he started running again. Maybe a gravstorm would be able to do something to the thing? That meant he needed to have five seconds of undistracted spellcasting. He ran down the marble steps toward the reflecting pool. Another rumble told him the golem was getting up again. He could hear more reports from behind him as Clive shot at something. But reaching the lower flat area, he turned and began casting his most devastating spell: gravity squall.

Luke and Gary were fighting two of the soldiers, their stainless steel forms showing obvious signs of conflict. One was missing an arm that looked to have been burned off by Gary's lightsaber, while the other had large chunks broken off as evidence of the chain chomp's higher durability. Drew still couldn't see any evidence of Sarah or Bill, but the two melee combatants were only barely around the corner of the building keeping the soldiers at bay while Clive was firing shots.

The only positive was that they seemed to realize that the stainless steel soldiers were a significant threat and were trying to withdraw back behind the memorial. Drew watched as his fingers interlaced in the symbols needed to cast the spells. Three gold statues came around the corner. But they were heading toward the Lincoln Memorial—and himself—rather than the rest of the team.

The golem of Lincoln was slowly getting to its feet, but Drew was going to be able to get the squall off without a hitch. The only one of the storms that had turned into an advanced grade linked skill meant that it was a tier above the others in potency. As the purple-gray storm took effect, it completely surrounded the statue, even blocking out its head and pulling two silver soldiers into its grasp, the smaller golems having finally caught up to the larger. Drew hoped that they would be able to damage Lincoln, even as he felt a headache forming behind his ears as mana fatigue started to build up inside him.

The statue didn't immediately break out of the squall, but little could be seen beyond the towering mass of clouds. Flashes of purple and blue light illuminated darker shadows within as Drew watched. He was already casting another storm spell, intent on layering it on top of the gravity squall. If his fireball spells couldn't penetrate its white marble exterior, he would need to escalate the situation. Holy frostfire storm dropped next, and the flashes of purple and blue were joined by flashes of brilliant white and red. His headache intensified from a dull ache to a pounding pulse.

Like turning a tornado into a sunset, the layered storm spells glowed in a brilliant array of colors that rivaled the mana storms. Crackles of lightning and miniature explosions of fire and ice swirled around the visible event horizon of the storm. Drew was midway through casting the third storm when Lincoln stepped out of the maelstrom. He could feel his heart beating faster as the massive form seemed to fill his vision. Drew wouldn't have thought the normally placid statue's face could look angry. But it sure looked furious now.

Each lumbering step took the statue closer to Drew by a dozen feet. He ceased the storm casting and peppered it with acid arrows and fireballs. It closed the sixty-foot distance with alarming speed as Drew opened up with a disrupting lightning bolt as it breached the forty-foot mark. The stun took effect, and the statue paused mid-step, the tree in its hands held high as it prepared to smash Drew into pieces. A quick cast of invigorate eliminated the headache even as two of the golden statues rounded the outer edge of the storms.

The Lincoln statue's stun wore off, the left foot beginning to move again. Drew started running toward the statue, the gap between them closing in what felt like an instant. The world seemed to slow down as the tree began to descend toward Drew's head, and his heart fluttered as he pushed himself closer to the statue and sure death. He felt air pressing forward as the statue brought the tree down slightly behind him, the splintering sound as branches broke off upon contact with the hard concrete.

His eyes locked on the white marble of the statue's hand as it came closer to him. One last step, straining against the fear in his chest, Drew activated both force of retribution—for the first time in combat—and cone of gravity. The linked spell's description was unhelpful, just saying it brought down the full weight of retribution in two meters around the caster. He wasn't even sure what it was linked off of; he got it when he upgraded mana tap but there wasn't much else in that constellation that made sense, and Drew assumed whatever it did was powerful.

The sound of cracking marble seemed to confirm that belief. Drew pushed off from the ground with all his adrenaline-filled might and activated gravitas and blink step. An illusionary image appeared where he had jumped off, even as he appeared six meters behind the statue and above it, flying through the air with the aid of gravitas and his own momentum. He hoped the afterimage of his blink step would confuse the statue as he quickly gained height.

Lightning branched out of the storm as he passed over it, striking his foot, and he felt his entire left leg go numb, his armor not seeming to do anything to stop the elemental damage. His goal was to land on the Lincoln Memorial as he left the statue behind on the front steps. Twisting through the air, he turned slightly to see that the closest of Lincoln's arms had broken off while large cracks marred the other. The entire statue was forced to its knees by his gravity spells but still looked like it had a lot of fight left in it.

Looking down, he saw the edge of the white marble of the memorial twenty feet below him, and he dropped gravitas' power to a mere fraction, his stomach lurching uncomfortably as his trajectory suddenly halted and he began free falling. The landing could have gone better. His initial launch had been slightly off-center, and gravitas tended to exaggerate that sort of movement. He had also landed on his numb leg, which crumpled uncomfortably from the contact. Rolling uncontrollably, he pulled hard on gravitas to stop the tumble, and he landed face down on a pane of glass with a thud that knocked the wind out of him.

Gravitas' twenty seconds were up, and he stared down through the tinted glass; Lincoln's seat sat in the middle of the area, oddly empty. Drew's brain finally caught up to him, and he sat up with a groan, rolling a few more times to the side so that he was no longer on the glass. The roof wasn't flat; instead, it housed three sections of glass windows. Luckily, they appeared to have been strengthened by the Advent and had held his weight without complaint. Drew tried to push himself to a crouch with a grunt, but his numb leg refused to accept his weight. Glancing back, there was no sign of the statue. He hoped that meant it hadn't seen where he had gone.

Rolling onto his side, Drew tried to move his leg, but stopped when it sent a thousand pins and needles pulsing through it. He bit his lip against the sensation, forcing himself to flex his foot, pumping blood into the extremity. The gambit seemed to have worked; the statue didn't seem to know where he was. Shuffling slightly, he high crawled along the roof until he could peek over and see what the statues were doing. His storms had died out, leaving his view unobstructed.

Lincoln wasn't nearly as busted as Drew would have liked. Thin black fissures spiderwebbed throughout the statue's form. It didn't seem to be affecting the statue a huge amount, but it was clear Drew was doing at least some damage. Most of it seemed to have been from force of retribution, but the spell only worked within two meters of him, and he didn't want to get that close to it again. The other statues were definitely worse for wear.

Several were pitted and moving slower than they had been before.

Drew did a quick count and realized that they were missing at least one of the golden statues, and he turned and crawled over to the west side, glad that his leg seemed to have woken up again finally. His distraction had allowed them to get down off the ledge they had been on; he could see them already about four hundred feet away, a third of the way across the bridge and being careful to avoid the holes spread around its surface. Luke was carrying Gary, who bounced like he was unconscious. Sarah was running ahead of them, testing the path, while Clive and Bill leaned against each other. There was no sign of Daryl, which was probably a good thing.

Clive's right leg was hanging at the wrong angle, and he was limping to avoid putting weight on it. The broken remains of one of the golden horsemen stood at the foot of the bridge, clearly the source of the injuries the team was sporting. Drew growled again, angry that his distraction had not been enough to pull all of the statues away from the group. The shaking returned, and he turned to see that the Lincoln statue was roaming around the plaza, looking for him. The glint of sun on metal told him the stainless steel soldiers were there as well.

Ducking down behind the short wall around the roof to avoid being seen, Drew felt battered, his body was sore from all the impacts, and he was still breathing hard from his earlier running. He watched two silver statues break away from the main group and begin following after the limping party. A gravball stopped them in their tracks, the screech of twisting metal pulling all attention to their merging forms. It was an eerie counterpoint to the near soundlessness of the rest of the combat.

The crunch of stone compressing sounded behind him as Drew maneuvered so he could do another running jump toward the bridge. Glancing back to the east, he saw the statue's remaining fingers latch onto the side of the roof. Long cracks ran throughout the white marble, even as the statue used them to do a one-armed pull-up and see over the edge of the wall. Shoal sense triggered as the statue focused its attention on him again.

There were still seconds left on gravitas' fifty-nine-second cooldown, and Drew launched a barrage of fireballs at the statue's visible head. The close range of the impacts sent Drew rolling across the roof again, his elbow banging hard against a fixture. Thankfully, the sheer concussive blast had also sent the statue flying. Drew struggled to his feet and then climbed on top of the half-wall along the edge of the roof. Not trusting his balance with his ears ringing, turning so that he could push himself off, he launched away from the building.

A primal part of his mind screamed as he reached the apogee of his jump, and gravity asserted itself on him. For a second, he looked down and realized he was falling sixty feet. Gravitas came off cooldown, and Drew activated it, his momentum pushing himself forward and down. He intended to use the entire twenty seconds of forward movement. And he distracted himself from the sense of falling by counting. Shoal sense was quiet, and he fell far further than he could have run in those same twenty seconds, his arms windmilling wildly as he tried to keep going straight even as he twisted in the air.

Landing on his side, he tried to roll but bashed his hip against the grass with a grunt of pain. Drew groaned as he pushed himself to his feet and glanced behind him. The Lincoln statue, its face blackened, and the fissures covering its body now obvious even from this distance, was making its way around the building, and its long steps were eating up the distance between them. Launching a second full barrage of fireballs at the statue, he activated blink step and appeared twelve meters further ahead. Turning, he hobbled toward the bridge. There wasn't a part of his body that wasn't screaming in pain.

Ahead of him, he could see the others already most of the way across the bridge. Drew stumbled around the prone form of the golden horseman, even as he forced his body to move faster across the open ground of the park and toward the road. He had just made the bridge when shoal sense screamed at him. He threw himself into a side roll as a massive chunk of rock bounced off the asphalt where he had been standing. The wind of its passage was a tangible reminder of how close his death had been. He forced his aching body to move faster as he jumped back to his feet.

A half dozen more stones chased him across the bridge, even as the Lincoln statue stopped at the foot of the bridge. Drew got halfway across before the rocks no longer followed him. He slowed to a sore limp as he moved to join his companions on the far side of the bridge.

"Well, that was a shit show." Daryl appeared next to him when he got close enough, offering a shoulder to help carry him. Drew didn't have the energy to do anything but nod his head in agreement as he slumped down next to Clive and pulled a canteen out of his bag of holding.

"Status report?" Drew asked. Glancing ahead, he could see Gary's unconscious form, red-brown blood streaked down his temple from a head wound. Clive's leg was obviously broken, jutting off to the side just below the knee even as Bill hugged his shaking form. They all looked the worse for wear.

"Not great. Gary's unconscious. Clive shouldn't walk until we heal his leg more and you're barely standing. Luke took some heavy blows, but he's still moving. Bill, Sarah, and myself are uninjured. And Abe is back there tearing up the bridge. Doesn't look like the statues are going to follow us."

Drew nodded, his eyes bleary. "I'll do a refreshing rain as soon as we catch up. What about up ahead?" Drew asked, wincing as he kicked a loose stone on accident.

"That's... a problem. Arlington Cemetery is on the other side there, and it's just crawling with... well, zombies and skeletons," Daryl said, shaking his head.

"You're shitting me?" Drew stopped, looking at the scout in disbelief.

"Nope. There is what looks like some construction headquarters a half block to the south, but I saw at least two roaming groups between here and there."

"Well, fuck."

Chapter Twenty-Seven – Visitor's Center

"We're too exposed." Those were the first words out of Sarah's mouth. They were huddled around Gary's prone form near the end of the bridge and by the railing.

"Agreed," Drew said, looking around, noticing the road that went over the last stretch of the bridge. He turned to Daryl. "Anything in the tunnel under us?"

Daryl held up a finger indicating he was checking and then shook his head.

"Alright, let's move down there until we can get patched up a bit," Drew said, motioning to a set of stairs on the north side of the bridge. The bridge emptied out into a roundabout that led directly into Arlington National Cemetery. A pack of zombies milled about near the entrance to the cemetery, but otherwise, the area was clear. A single line of tall fir trees blocked the river from view, and they quickly descended into the tunnel.

"What happened?" Drew asked Sarah. They were acting as sentinels to make sure nothing approached them for the short distance down into the tunnel.

"When you ran off, we tried to follow, but a couple of statues attacked us. Gary and Luke managed to hold them off while we backed up and headed for the bridge. We were fine until the gold one pincered us. Gary took a bad hit trying to cut off a leg, and then Clive jumped in. Saved his life but took that blow doing it. Luke smashed it pretty quickly after that, but the damage was already done," Sarah said before she glanced at Drew. "Honestly, you don't look like your fights went a whole lot better than ours."

"They didn't. Mostly got battered around a bunch trying to avoid getting hit. I don't think I could have lived through a direct hit from that thing. I managed to do… some damage to it, but not much," Drew said with a frown. "It shrugged off just about everything I had to throw at it."

"Yes, you are a poor match for a golem like that," Luke said from behind him. He set Gary down on a piece of pavement even as Bill and Clive took a rest right next to him. "Your spells are all energy-based. They do not work well against inorganic material with a lot of mass like those statues. Your acid and gravity spells were probably the only ones to do much against it."

"Yeah, gravity squall seemed to slow it down some. But mostly gravball was the big winner in damage," Drew responded as he sat down on the curb in the middle of the tunnel. He turned to Bill. "Any chance we can get a blanket fort up?"

"No, it's still on cooldown." Bill shook his head, glancing around. "I think we need to set Clive's leg before we move him too much." Drew looked at Clive and realized just how pale he was already, clearly in shock. He stood up with a groan.

"How long on your heal, Sarah?" Drew asked as several parts of his body complained at the movement.

"A while yet, I used it on Gary. I think we should avoid moving him until he wakes up," Sarah said with a frown, glancing over at the unconscious teen.

"Alright, Daryl?" Drew asked, and the scout appeared next to him. Drew was casting refreshing rain even as he called out orders. "Make sure we don't have any visitors. We're pretty exposed here, and we need to figure out where we're going next, see if you can't find somewhere safe. Bill and Sarah, get Clive up and moving if you can. Luke, can you keep pushing your healing into Gary?" Drew felt better as his aches and pains smoothed away. "Whenever Sarah's heal is up, we'll group up so we all benefit from it."

Sarah and Bill went to work resetting Clive's leg bone so that it could heal. Drew glanced over at Gary. His rain was clearing away some of the dried blood, and he could see several enormous black and blue bruises forming across the kid's face. Drew could tell he had a few minutes left on invigorate's cooldown and wondered how it could possibly have been less than fifteen minutes since he started running away from the Lincoln statue. Daryl was sitting off to one side, invisible as he sent the bird scouting out for a route forward.

"You alright?" Drew asked Luke, who was hovering over Gary.

"I will be fine. I should have taken out the statue sooner, then Gary would be fine." Luke's hand was on Gary's shoulder, which seemed like the least injured part of the kid. His hand glowed slightly as it transmitted healing energies into it.

"You can't be everywhere," Drew said.

Luke paused, and looked at Drew, then shook his head. "First, you run off without me." Luke held up a hand to forestall Drew's explanation. "I understand why. But that does not change my emotional response. I would very much appreciate it if you did not do that again. I cannot protect you in such situations." The two men lapsed into an uncomfortable silence. "I will redouble my efforts to train both yourself and those around you to ensure that this sort of situation does not repeat."

"I'm sorry, Luke." Drew laid a hand on the seraph's shoulder and received a tight-lipped smile in return. Next, Drew put his hand on Gary's hand and cast invigorate, hoping that the spell's power would increase the kid's recovery.

"Alright, I think I have a spot we can hole up in." Daryl appeared next to Drew. "We're going to have to cross a shallow river and some railroad tracks. But I think I can get us around the main concentrations of undead. We'll be taking a roundabout route, but we're heading for the visitor's center at the front. Hopefully, there aren't any inside. Unfortunately, there are a ton of them patrolling the road and the highway. Cutting across the more wild areas seems like the only viable solution.

Not far if we could go straight, but probably a mile on the route we'll be taking."

"That's a statement I never thought I'd hear in real life," Drew muttered as he glanced over to where Bill and Sarah were tending to Clive. His leg looked to be aligned again, but he was still pale. "How are you feeling, Clive?" Bill was giving him a hug, using his daddy's embrace to heal the downed man.

"I been better." Clive's teeth chattered as he spoke.

"Everyone get close. My healing spell is up," Sarah said, and everyone huddled into the four-meter cylinder around Gary so that they would be included in Sarah's group heal. Drew felt the aches and pains of his earlier fight fading into the background, becoming just a dull memory of what they had been before. Clive's face took on additional color, and Gary seemed to toss fitfully in his sleep.

"Alright, we've got a long way to go. Bill and Sarah, you two grab Gary. He's hopefully light enough that you won't have too much of a problem. Luke, you're in front, Clive you're in the middle. We'll be relying on your stealth aura as much as we can. I'll be holding up the rear. Daryl, you'll be directing us." Drew glanced around to see if anyone had questions, but they all gave him grim looks of confirmation. "Luke, after you," Drew said as he helped Sarah and Bill pick up Gary. Clive hobbled along with them, his leg clearly still bothering him.

They followed a one-lane road for a hundred feet until they got past a line of pine trees. Daryl held up a hand, telling them to wait. And they watched a group of thirty or so skeletons clack past their spot, patrolling the highway. Drew was pretty sure it was in his mind, but they smelled like rotting meat despite wearing the tattered remains of fifty-year-old uniforms. They marched in a haphazard order. Most of them came from injured men.

Skeletons had bullet wounds in the skull or were missing most of their rib cage. A few carried their own dismembered arms in their other hand, the knuckles dragging across the pavement with a dull rasp. Inside the brain cavity of each of the skeletons was a flat, black light that hurt Drew's eyes if he focused on it too long, a mass of energy that was clearly the vitalizing force for the undead. They all advanced across the road with little or no situational awareness, moving ever forward in what felt like a mindless haze.

"This is a good sign," Luke whispered back. "They are unintelligent. They will follow a set patrol. Undead are easy to sneak through unless there is an aware one controlling them. If we avoid the nodes, that should not be a problem."

What followed was nearly an hour of sneaking through ditches and across roads, a shallow river, and train tracks. They had to hop over half a dozen fences which was only possible with Luke's impressive strength and Drew's gravitas ability to move Gary without injuring him further. They were all filthy and tired by the time they sat in the trees around a parking lot looking at what was once the Arlington National Cemetery's Visitor Center.

Patrols of undead walked the roads, but they didn't seem to pay any attention to the parking lot. However, there were guards posted at all of the entrances to the building that Daryl could find.

"I don't see a way to get in without killing at least some guards," Daryl said after ten minutes of scouting. "They look more aware than the wandering packs."

"Does this mean they are under the control of a smart one?" Sarah asked Luke.

The seraph shook his head. "There is almost certainly at least a few higher-level undead controlling the army. There are too many here for that not to be the case. But my guess is that they will be near the nodes, and this is not a node. So their disappearance will probably be noticed, but unless it is a lich, it will take some time for that to happen."

"What's a lich?" Clive asked. He was the only one of the group that looked better now than he had when they first got to the cemetery. His leg seemed to be bothering him much less, and he was barely limping at all. He had also gotten back a lot of the color he had been missing when they started the trip. Several healing spells and hugs had been shunted toward him over the past hour, as often as the patrols and cooldowns would allow.

"An extremely dangerous kind of intelligent undead. They are created by a body that held a position of authority over people in life. Usually, those who die by… unfortunate means and don't have the proper burial services done for them. When they are brought back, they increase in power as more undead join their army," Luke answered without looking at the man. He was still staring toward the building in contemplation.

"So… a president of a country would maybe get that?" Drew asked with a frown.

"Yes, that would be the kind of undead that would become a lich," Luke answered, then turned to Drew with a frown. "Why do you ask?"

"JFK," Sarah answered for him.

"What is a JFK?" Luke looked between them, puzzled.

"Thirty-fifth President of the US, he was assassinated and maybe buried here in Arlington after serving in the Navy during World War II," Sarah answered.

"Maybe buried?" Luke asked, and Sarah nodded her head.

"Yeah, there was a bunch of issues with people trying to steal his body or something. So they had to move it somewhere else. There is a whole conspiracy theory that he was smuggled out and buried in Massachusetts." Sarah looked like she was trying to remember the details for a moment and then shrugged. "I don't remember a ton about it. Mostly just heard it in passing. Not that it really matters; if it isn't JFK, there are a ton of other influential soldiers buried here."

"Well, from the sounds of it, they almost certainly have a lich at the head of the horde. Which will change how we traverse the graveyard. We'll need to avoid any large banks of undead or places of power."

"Like the Tomb of the Unknown Soldier?" Bill said, and after they explained the largely symbolic aspect of the Tomb, Luke agreed. "Yes, anything… memorial-like is going to be extra dangerous with a lich at the head of the horde."

"That still doesn't help us get into the building, and it's getting dark. I have a feeling spending a night outside here is probably a bad idea," Drew said, pulling everyone back to the moment.

"Indeed… we will want to make a quiet entrance. Are you sure this is not a node?" Luke asked Drew for what felt like the hundredth time, and he nodded his head.

"Well, then I suggest we go in through a window. The guards are only at the door entrances. If we sneak in the back window, we should be fine… although it would be nice if we could repair the glass once we're through."

"Alright, Daryl, lead us to a window," Drew commanded.

CHAPTER TWENTY-EIGHT – CHECK

Getting into the visitor's center was easy. So easy that Drew started to think there must be something wrong with their choice. The phrase, 'there is no such thing as a free lunch,' kept running through his mind. He could tell his nerves were affecting the rest of the group, so he took a few seconds to breathe and examine the situation logically. This was essentially a DTC formed around the undead, and there were no dead waiting to be raised as undead in the visitor's center.

So logically, that meant they wouldn't have been created here, and undead would not have felt the need for shelter that a living species would have required. If they hadn't been raised here, then the logical conclusion was that some of these men, who must have been killed while guarding something, were just doing in undeath what they had done in life.

Even to his own brain, the reasoning was suspect, but it was enough to get his mind off the idea that this was clearly a trap set by more of the lotus-eaters. Those monsters had all died when Drew had taken over the stadium node and killed their creche and human hosts. Dozens of people had burned alive when the shield went up, the parasites wiggling out of their brains enough to cause concern even as the shield killed them. At least that's what Drew had been told. He had been healing in the safety of the pyramid from the wounds sustained killing the creche.

Unconsciously, Drew rubbed his hands together. He remembered them being doused in acid, burning and nearly destroyed. They didn't feel any different than they used to, but some part of him knew they should be scared husks, incapable of movement. Shaking against the memory, he looked around the space. Bill had another hour left on his blanket fort skill, the ability required several hours after being torn down to recharge. Which meant that they were reinforcing the small theater they had taken over in a more traditional manner, a barricade of chairs and benches.

"Alright, everyone, gather up," Sarah called, and Drew moved over to stand within the area of effect of her healing spell. The warmth spread over him, and he sighed. It was only mid-afternoon, but he was already mentally exhausted. Having to drag Gary and dodge the undead patrols had taken a lot out of the group. Drew cast refreshing rain and felt some of the tension fade away. Still, there was an expenditure of mental energy that required downtime to get through.

"How is he?" Drew asked Sarah, who was checking on Gary.

"I think he's fine. He had a bunch of broken bones, and the movement hasn't done him any favors," Sarah said with a frown. "I wish I knew more about human anatomy, but that wasn't ever something I was planning on doing before this whole thing happened. I haven't been able to find any books on the subject." She shrugged slightly, and sat back on her heels as she looked at the rest of the party. The others were still stacking stuff in the opening. "I always wanted to help people, just… not like this." She gestured at Gary's unconscious form. "I think he'll wake up in a few hours, and the healing should have him back to one-hundred percent by morning."

"You're doing better than a lot of people. I don't think anyone was ready for this. We just have to, I dunno, roll with the punches?" Drew said with a shrug. "Don't worry too much. I mean, we've just got an army of undead to fight through, and then we need to fight some invading alien elves, and we'll be back at the stadium in no time."

"Except for the part where we have to figure out a way to get past Lincoln and over a bridge he is currently destroying."

"I mean, we could just pull a General Washington and storm the river. I think that was the Potomac?" Drew paused, thinking. "But why would it be in DC? They didn't make the city until he was already president... right?"

"You mean when he crossed the Delaware River... into New Jersey from Pennsylvania?" Sarah asked with a grin.

"Oh, I guess that makes more sense." Drew paused, thinking about it. "Well, it's not really Christmas either, and we aren't eating boot leather." Drew continued to think about the revolutionary war for a moment. "Wait, is Valley Forge in Pennsylvania then?"

"Yes," Sarah said while shaking her head. "Man, if you don't remember any of this stuff, how are we going to teach people like Gary? Or any of the new babies?"

"Huh, I never really considered that we'd have babies soon. Are there many pregnant women at the stadium?" Drew cast an invigorate on Gary while turning a chair so he could lean forward against its back.

"A good amount. A lot of people have been using sex as a stress relief. I think. We've mostly avoided any serious issues with sexual assault, but we had a few women come into the healing center who clearly were selling themselves for food or protection. Mostly they were looking for contraceptives or for help with some bruises. We didn't have much as far as prophylactics are concerned. Only so much supply in the city."

"Damn," Drew said with a frown. "I mean, I guess I knew things were rough for people that didn't want to fight, but I didn't really sit down and think about it." Throwing a glance back toward the stadium and the red ley lines underneath it, he wondered if they were going to be alright.

"Hoeffecker and Gunn are doing a pretty good job of all that," Sarah said with a shrug. "Gunn has a big part to play in keeping everyone feeling safe. I didn't care much for his politics before the Advent... but he's doing pretty well by people now, and I guess that's what is important."

"I guess I should check in with Hoeffecker," Drew said. He hadn't had a chance to report in since they left the Jefferson, and he felt a sudden urge to do so now. He pulled out the communication stone and held it in his hands, waiting for Hoeffecker to pick up the line. He considered what he would say to her.

It took almost ten minutes, during which the rest of the group had finished the barricade. Daryl's bird was stationed outside so that he could watch for any approaching undead, but the rest were taking a much-needed mental break.

Walking over to the side of the room away from everyone else, Drew opened the connection with Hoeffecker. It was a bit of surprise when the voice on the other line wasn't the colonel's.

"JG? Is that you?" Gunnery Sergeant Daniel's voice came from the stone.

"This is IT2… er, Lieutenant Junior Grade Michalik. Is that you, gunny? Where is the colonel?" Drew asked with a frown.

"She finally collapsed an hour or two ago. I don't think the woman has slept since you left. What's your status?"

"We got across the bridge, but I don't think we're going to be able to go back that way. The Lincoln and Korean War Memorials have come alive, and Lincoln got mad we escaped and destroyed the bridge. We're in Arlington Cemetery now… but it's just absolutely crawling with zombies and skeletons."

"Well, shit, the running kind or the shamblers?"

"Shamblers. Thankfully. Lincoln hit us pretty hard, and we're hunkering down in the Visitor's Center here. We'll hopefully be moving out again at first light."

"Alright, I'll tell the colonel when she wakes up."

"What about you guys?" Drew said, glancing back at his group, who were all sitting alone for the most part.

"Not great. Some idiot counted boxes behind the ammo as part of our ammo stockpile. So we're running low, especially without you to juice up JP's ammo creation abilities. We've got him working on that as soon as he comes out of mana fatigue. They also roped in the crayon kid. We've pulled back to patrolling the wall just to conserve ammunition supplies. Hopefully, Dak gets his black powder working soon. It's not a perfect solution but better than nothing. We're okay, the shield isn't in any danger, but morale took a hit."

Drew took a second or two to digest all the information the gunny had told him. Dak was the survivor that Drew had given his only white xatherite to. Metallurgy allowed him to do a lot of amazing things. At least that was the hope. It was more of an infrastructure problem. The crystal had shoved a bunch of information into Dak's head, but building the equipment and facilities needed to take advantage of that information took time and skilled manpower that the stadium just didn't have in large quantities.

"Ouch. Tell JP I'm sorry he's on ammo duty for the next forever."

"Will do, have fun blasting zombies. Daniels out."

With that, the stone sort of buzzed, and Drew realized the longer conversation had put it into cooldown mode, meaning he wouldn't be able to talk to the stadium for twenty-four hours at least. Drew sat down as he thought about what the gunny had just told him. Like always, the stadium was surviving but not thriving. If he was honest with himself, he didn't know what a thriving community would even look like now that the end of the world had come. But the last thing that Daniels had said gave him an idea.

"Daryl?" Drew didn't have mana sight on, but he flashed it for a moment to figure out the scout was standing about five feet away from him. Turning to look at him, he smiled as Daryl faded into view.

"I dislike that you can see me so easily. Makes me worried other monsters will be able to see me as well," Daryl groused as he sat down next to Drew. "I heard most of that… What are you thinking?"

"I need you to see if you can find the tallest thing around, preferably in the direction of the Pentagon," Drew said, and Daryl narrowed his eyes.

"Tallest… You're going to storm-blast the entire cemetery?"

"I'm thinking about it, take out the packs as much as possible. I just don't really want to get stuck between the sidhe and the undead. But unless they have a way of knowing where the storms are coming from, I should be able to just bombard them from afar… as long as I can see what I'm throwing it at."

"Couldn't we have just done that on the sidhe from the stadium?"

"No. I'm not going to bombard the sidhe until I know there aren't any innocent people in there. I'll stick to the open areas for the undead. I doubt there are many living people wandering around the graveyard."

"Alright, I'll send the bird out…" Daryl said as he went invisible again and concentrated. Drew watched as Daryl took a few minutes to get the bird into position, his eyes closed as he focused on the extra senses. "The Air Force Memorial," the scout finally announced. "You could perch on the top of that, but you'll be pretty exposed."

Drew frowned and looked to the south. The memorial wasn't far from his old home. It was built outside of the cemetery, but only just a little bit. Drew felt a sudden need to go there. He could see nodes in that direction, one shining white one before the three violet ones the sidhe had taken over. There were other nodes to the east and west, and he assumed they were controlled by the undead. It was hard to tell exactly since he couldn't see the terrain, just the lines. But his mental map of the area told him the Air Force Memorial was at least close to the node. Situated between the Tomb of the Unknown Soldier and the Pentagon.

"That'll work. If we can take over that node, that'll give us a great staging point for anything else on this side of the river." Drew nodded his head. "We'll stay here until the morning and head to the Air Force Memorial as soon as we can." He cast a last glance over at the still prone form of Gary. Drew hoped the kid woke up soon.

CHAPTER TWENTY-NINE – GRAVEWALK

Gary regained consciousness shortly after midnight. Luke had been putting Drew, Bill, and Sarah through a heavy training regime. Daryl and Clive opted out of training. Daryl because he was the lookout, and Clive because his leg was still bothering him.

"Hey, Mr. Drew," Gary said after Sarah and Bill had looked the kid over and said he just needed more time for the healing to work its magic.

"Hey yourself, Gary. How are you feeling?" Drew sat next to the kid, using one of the camp chairs.

"I'm good now, Mr. Drew." When Drew clearly didn't believe him, he started to shrug but then stopped as a wince went through his body. "I'll be better soon," Gary amended. "It's all my fault. I slipped on the grass and took a hit I was trying to dodge." A glance at his shoes told Drew that the kid was still using the same pair he had on before Advent hit. They probably had been old before this whole mess, and the heightened activity of the post-Advent world hadn't done them any favors.

"We'll have to get you some new shoes. I think there was a shoe store in Pentagon City that we could maybe hit up, would probably be worth grabbing as much as we can."

Gary just laid back down and closed his eyes. Drew could see tears forming in his eyes and tried to think what to say to the kid. After a few moments of awkward silence, he couldn't think of anything, and he got up, murmuring something about hoping Gary felt better, and then went back to his training with Luke. The kid's recovery moved quickly; a few hours after midnight he was up and moving around.

Taking a break from his training with Luke, Drew stopped by to check on Gary, who was sitting near Clive. The smell of alcohol washed over him with a visible wave as he approached the two.

"God damn Clive, how much have you been drinking?" Drew held a hand to his nose. "I feel like I'm getting a contact high just standing here."

"Enough!" Clive said with a hearty laugh, Drew frowned when he realized that Gary was also giggling along with him.

"Did you get Gary drunk?" Drew said, leaning over and grabbing the flask out of Clive's hand.

"Just a little bit," Clive said, holding his fingers together. A quick invigorate on Gary had the teen looking in better shape.

"Bill, can you come cast your toxic resistance on these two?" Drew shook his head. "You two do realize that we're essentially behind enemy lines right? That zombies could come in here and attack us at any moment?" Gary was looking down, clearly ashamed of his actions. Clive, on the other hand, just looked insulted.

"I kin totally kill me some zombies! Let 'em come at me!" The man stood up, pulling out his rifle and waving it around.

"Put that away, you asshole," Sarah growled in a soft voice as she pulled the gun out of Clive's hands, allowing Bill to approach the two of them and cast his spell.

"Hey! That's mine!" Clive shouted.

The sudden noise had clearly drawn some interest from outside the room. And the dull scrape of bone against tile floors was clearly audible on the other side of the barricade. Everyone went silent, as the severity of the situation pierced even Clive's inebriated brain.

"We need to go," Sarah hissed.

"We've still got twenty minutes until dawn," Daryl whispered back.

"Everyone get ready to move. We'll delay if we can, but if they start messing with the barricade, we're going to go out the window," Drew announced, glancing over at Clive who had sobered up quickly after his earlier outbursts. They all quickly gathered up their belongings. Drew kept catching angry glares from Clive from the corner of his eye.

Thankfully, none of the undead seemed intelligent enough to understand what the stack of chairs and tables of their barricade meant. After fifteen tense minutes of pawing at it, two undead stood on either side of it like they were guarding it. The group slipped out through the same window they had come in through five minutes later.

Daryl had been watching since there was enough light, and he had picked out a route for them to take. There was a main road that would take them almost straight to the Air Force Memorial. The problem was that the undead patrolled that area heavily. And the open fields and short headstones of the cemetery made it difficult to hide from any patrols. The saving grace was that the undead were slow and only responded to threats within a specific range of them, so the plan was to cut across the open areas, counting on Clive's aura to keep them safe.

Their first trip through the fringes of the cemetery was in unusual circumstances. Now that they were traveling through the large open areas, Drew had a chance to look around. The grass looked like a battlefield. The ground in front of gravestones had been torn apart by the undead breaking free of their earthly tombs. Most of them made small holes, but every now and again, they came across a coffin that was almost entirely exposed to the air, the dirt from its clearing having rained down around them.

As he was crossing one grave, he felt a thump against the ground. He held up a hand, and the group hunkered down, looking for the threat. Stepping away from the spot where he felt the thump, he watched as the grass and dirt seemed to bubble up and then fall back down. Drew watched it for a few seconds before a thin sliver of white poked its way through the grass. A second later, four other fingers followed, and he watched with fascination as an entire skeletal hand seemed to break through the layer of grass and begin clawing its way free.

Which was when Luke's chained ball landed with the sound of shattering bone on top of the hand.

"The undead are awakening. Careful where you step," the seraph said as he gestured for everyone to keep moving. Drew watched as Luke casually kicked the bone fragments away from the hole and kept moving uphill. They were threading a thin line between a node to the west that Drew was sure was the Tomb of the Unknown Soldier and a node to the east, which was perpetually surrounded by a thick cloud of dust or fog. No one wanted to get close enough to figure out which. They were waiting on the west side of the road for a large patrol to move past when suddenly they stopped. As one, they turned and looked at Drew's group.

With a clatter, they charged toward them. Drew had been on edge, disliking the forced stillness of sneaking through the cemetery. As they charged, a part of him cheered. Standing up to his full height, he pushed his hands out to the charging force and unleashed a holy frostfireball, and a holy fireball at the edges of the group. The two spells tore apart the nearest zombies. The white holy light that permeated them clashed directly with the darkness in their skulls and created an explosion as the undead were destroyed.

That wasn't the point of the attack. The concussive blast from the magics pushed the zombies closer together, bunching them up for a third spell, major holy gravball, which appeared in the center of their ranks. White light ripped the entire detachment apart, even as it pulled them into the center of its destructive magic. A second later, the spell's gravitational pull ended, and the matter exploded out, sending bits of holy magic-infused bone out as shrapnel that decimated the entire patrol.

It felt good to be putting the undead to rest. Swirls of black energy escaped into the air above those undead who didn't have enough holy energy near them when they died, creating a dark haze over the field of slaughter. From the east, a cry shook the air. Black vines of energy twisted in the air, drawing runes that could be seen across all of Arlington.

"We need to go. You just roused the lich," Luke said with a growl, and he took off running to the south and the Air Force Memorial. Drew followed after him, but a rising wind from the east caught his attention. A billowing cloud of ash that vaguely took the shape of a human emerged from the perpetual haze. It moved with the same deceptive slowness that Lincoln had moved with but still was approaching quickly. On the west side, a dozen zombies crested the hill above them.

"Luke, I'm going to take out that big ash thing with a holy storm. Drag me!" Drew shouted as he activated gravitas with enough energy to float himself a few inches above the ground. Luke's arm grabbed his shoulder armor and pulled his weightless form along with him. Drew turned his attention to forming the hand sequences needed to summon a holy frostfire storm. He wasn't taking any chances with not enough firepower. Besides, he hadn't been casting all morning. His mana fatigue hadn't been this low in ages.

Five seconds later, his storm collapsed on the ash cloud, a sound like wailing souls filling the air as the ash giant was subsumed into the holy-infused storm spell. With ten seconds left on gravitas, Drew turned his attention to the zombies charging down the hill at them. His fingers created a holy firestorm to block their approach. The spell went off, and the zombies disappeared inside it, having narrowed their course in their single-minded fury at the sight of the living.

The black energy to the east pulsed harder, but Drew didn't have time to pay attention to it anymore. Returning to full weight, he ran alongside his team, holy variant fireballs blowing apart any groups of zombies that got in their way. Drew wasn't sure how long they ran up the hill on the south side of Arlington, but he was exhausted by the time they crested the rise and saw the fences that had demarcated the border. Not that it was much of a fence. A few feet of stone and a few more feet of iron bars.

Drew turned around and glanced at the graveyard behind them. There weren't any large hills anywhere, but the cemetery was a collection of small hills dotted with lines of white gravestones and trees. It had once been Confederate General Robert E. Lee's plantation, but the Union had seized it after the Civil War to turn it into the nation's war cemetery. Although all the housing was on the northern side, near where JFK had been buried and far from anywhere Drew could physically see.

Except he wasn't limited to just what his eyes could see, not anymore. Aura sight told him something different. On a hill on the far side—at the very edge of his range on acid arrow and his storm spells—stood a figure. To his aura sight, it was darkness incarnate. A man-shaped void that seemed to be staring directly at him, even as he stared back. Drew instinctively knew that this was the lich. The malevolent energy of the undead seemed to seep from it and into the world around it.

Unlike Drew's previous encounters with the wereghouls, who had seemed more animalistic, even the one alpha wereghast he had seen that seemed to retain some level of human intelligence, the lich seemed to embody hatred and destruction.

"Drew?" Sarah tugged on his arm, and he turned away from his inspection of the lich. The undead's attacks had tapered off, either because it became clear that they would have no effect on Drew's party or because they were leaving Arlington. Drew wasn't sure which was the case, but they had not been harassed the last several hundred feet. "Come on. Let's go."

Climbing over the fence was almost laughably easy. There was a small road and then a parking lot, but the Air Force Memorial was nearby. Drew could see the white pulsing energy from the node underneath and added that as another possible reason for the undead to have stopped attacking.

"Any idea what sort of monsters there are here?" Drew asked. Looking around, he didn't see any visible signs of monsters, and the corruption from the cemetery had ended at the wall.

"I'm looking now, but I don't see the pyramid either. Gonna try to find a way down. There must be something here we can use," Daryl answered. There wasn't any cover in the area, so they just stayed in the middle of the road and caught their breath. They had good sightlines, but Drew still felt weird being out in the open without more cover than some parked cars to hide behind.

"Where is Clive?" Gary asked, and Drew looked around. Sure enough, the Sons representative was nowhere to be found.

"When was the last time anyone saw him?" Drew asked. Trying to think back, the mad dash out of the cemetery had been hectic. Had Clive fallen behind? "Daryl, do you see him anywhere?" Drew jumped back up onto the wall and looked through the iron bars. But there was no sign of the other man. None of the others seemed to remember seeing him since midway through the walk.

"I'm checking," Daryl said and Drew watched the aura of the bird swing past overhead. Drew kept scanning with his aura sight, but he wasn't sure if it would see through the other man's stealth field at a distance. "I'm not seeing anything," the scout finally said, causing Drew to frown. Had they been attacked by the undead before or after Clive left? Had the man caused the ambush by removing them from his skill's effect? Or had it really just been a coincidence?

"Maybe Clive's leg was still bothering him?" Gary suggested. "So he couldn't keep up with the run?"

Drew glanced at the kid and nodded his head. "Yeah. I'm sure he'll show up soon. But I don't like this position. I feel... exposed." Scanning the street, he frowned. It was primarily open, with a line of parked cars along the road. "There are some trees we can hide in over there," Drew said, pointing to a thick stand of trees a hundred feet further down the street. "We'll wait there for a bit. If he's coming this way, we'll see him."

CHAPTER THIRTY – DECISIONS

They waited in the trees for what felt like forever, but which Drew was pretty sure was only a few hours. The first two hours, Daryl scanned the cemetery, but it was clear that either Clive was no longer there or he now considered them hostile and his stealth aura made it impossible to see him.

When it became obvious that they wouldn't find Clive, Drew had Daryl focus on the rest of the area. The Pentagon was still whole, which meant that it had been turned into a dungeon. The army of robot dogs patrolling the perimeter made that clear as well. Unlike the dead, the robot dogs moved in an orderly fashion, each patrol evenly spaced and capable of calling for assistance from nearby patrols. There were also strange armored forms at even intervals that Daryl was pretty sure were robot tanks or something. Although they had yet to move, and could have just been some decoration put up by the system.

"How are the robots moving? I thought all electronics were broken in the Advent," Sarah asked. She was looking to the northeast where the Pentagon was with excitement.

"I mean, I don't think it really matters?" Drew answered. "If they are golems, they don't need electronics. And if they aren't, I don't know where we would get the tools to inspect them to figure out why they are working, and everything else isn't. Heck, the only tools I know of that would allow us to even do that require electricity." Sarah's mouth opened a few times as she tried to think of a way around that particular problem.

"Hmm, you're probably right. I guess we can tell Hoeffecker next time you report in, though." They lapsed into silence as they waited for Daryl to finish scouting to the southeast.

"It's too thick," the scout finally said. "I have to keep the bird below the canopy level to see anything. There are still a few visible buildings. You know, stuff that was three or four stories tall before the Advent, and you can kind of see down the streets, but it's like the city was abandoned decades ago rather than a month."

"Any sign of the sidhe?" Luke questioned the scout.

"I mean, other than the forest? I don't know what I'm supposed to be looking for. I catch some movement every now and again, but it's too far away and dark under the tree cover."

"So, we assume they're under the trees somewhere. No sign of any people?" Sarah glanced between Daryl and Drew.

"I mean, I haven't seen any people. But with the trees…" Daryl just shook his head, the frustration clearly evident in his voice.

"We'll have to do it the old-fashioned way. Luke, if we take over this node, what are the odds they'll be able to see it change?" Drew asked. As far as he knew, only his mana sight skill allowed them to see where the ley lines were and if the nodes changed color.

"It depends," Luke said as he considered his following words. "The sidhe are a collection of species that all experience the system in a similar way."

"What do you mean they experience the system in a similar way?" Gary asked, the kid speaking up for the first time in the conversation.

"Humans gather xatherite and can slot it into a map, giving them abilities, but each xatherite has a different power. This makes fighting a human unpredictable. Because you never know what powers they have," Luke answered. "Sidhe growth is less variable. Each species consumes the xatherite crystals to gain a very standard growth progression. Each species is different, but generally consuming a crystal will give a similar result. A red crystal will make an ent stronger, but will expand how much powder a brownie creates every day.

"It comes down to what sort of sidhe they sent. If they have an elf with enough green xatherite, they would be able to see the node change. A zwerg would not."

"What is a zwerg?" Sarah and Gary both asked at the same time.

"A zwerg? They are short fae that usually dwell inside mountains or in mines. They grow long facial hair and are known for being ingenious crafters."

"He means a dwarf," Drew clarified, and the other two nodded their heads in comprehension. "So, if the sidhe are all species that experience the system in a similar way, what does that make the orcs and trolls?"

"They are not part of the sidhe races. I am not entirely sure what the things you called trolls were. I have not seen any Protectorate records of a race like that. The orcs, on the other hand, are known. They are related to the fae, but from a different faction entirely. They are a nomadic tribe hell-bent on finding their lost god. They move like locusts through settled worlds, grabbing all the resources they can acquire in a system before moving on to the next."

"So we hope it's a zwerg they sent and not an elf?" Bill asked.

"There are a half dozen high fae species. I think it is unlikely that they would grow a forest like this unless they had an elf at their helm, though. It could just be a large contingent of dryad and ent troops, but those normally accompany elves as well, so that is most likely what we will find," Luke said.

"So they're likely to know we have the node as soon as we take it," Drew said, glancing back to the memorial to their south, chewing on his lip as he considered their options. "I used to live near here. We'll take over the node and then head to my old apartment, while Daryl watches the node to see what sort of response they have to it being taken over."

"Do you want to clear it out first? We don't know if we'll be injured or not after we take the node." Concern was evident in Sarah's voice as she considered their options. "Without Katie and, as much as I hate to admit it, Clive, we are more likely to take injuries."

Drew considered Sarah's question, feeling somewhat awkward as everyone turned to look at him. "Let's check inside the node, see what we're up against first. If it looks like it's gonna be a rough fight, we'll clear it first. When I said near... it's not really all that close. I think it was a thirty minute walk here before Advent, so... who knows how long that's going to take now."

"We're just gonna leave Clive?" Gary asked, looking to the north and the cemetery.

"Unfortunately. We can't afford to wait for him to show back up. He's got a good shot of surviving on his own, as long as he keeps his aura up and is careful. But that means it's going to be almost impossible to find him..." Drew trailed off, unsure what more he could do for the missing man. Maybe he would show up if they created enough of a disturbance, but he wasn't comfortable doing that until he was more sure of the situation with the sidhe.

There was a large hole in what looked like it had once been a roundabout not far from where they were currently hiding in the trees. A steady wind blew up from the bottom of the shaft leading down, and a spiral staircase looked like it had been cut into the sides of the shaft, which looked like it got wider the further down you descended. There was light from somewhere deeper down below, showing that the stairs ended about two hundred feet down, with a single large opening leading to the east.

"Well, that's a creepy hole," Bill said, as everyone stood around it looking down. "Daryl, send the bird down there?"

"I can try…" Daryl eyed the narrow entrance. "Loons aren't exactly made for navigating narrow passages with a significant updraft."

"But you can just resummon it, right?" Sarah asked. "We could walk down a bit and see if that doesn't help the airflow thing?"

"Well, that would at least give it more space," Daryl said, descending about thirty feet and launching the loon off the side into the center. It wobbled a bunch, trying to descend in the wind without much luck, finally seeming to shoot sideways and crash into the side of the wall and disappearing.

"There are some weird side drafts," Daryl said as he came back up. "They're pretty weak where I was, and they all blew you toward the wall, but…" He shook his head. They weren't going to be able to scout it out much.

"Alright. Luke, lead the way down. You're the least likely to be blown away of all of us," Drew said as he pulled the rope out of his pouch of holding, tying it in a bowline every five feet or so down its length. "Everyone put this around you and move cautiously. This should allow us to catch anyone if the winds pick up."

Everyone stepped into a loop of rope, keeping it around their waist as they descended. Thankfully, the wind never blew them away from the wall, always into it, making it more of a nuisance than a threat to their safety. The two-hundred-foot staircase took half again as long as it should have as people lost their footing when a strong wind would knock them against the wall. Drew was after Luke in the line, so he ran into the big seraph's back when he came to an abrupt halt. Looking up, Drew could see why the man had stopped.

Like a scene from the movie Avatar, they were entering the dungeon on a series of floating rocks connected to each other by pathways of smaller stones and vines. Thousands of birds swirled around the floating islands like schools of fish. In all, there were seventeen islands in a spiral below them, each covered in greenery. Drew watched, enraptured at the sheer scale of the motion below them. Everything was shifting slightly. Rocks drifting on the invisible currents of air.

The sides of the dungeon were a series of jagged rocks where the birds would land to rest, only for another flock to take to the sky to replace them. It created an ever rotating screen of brightly colored bodies that slightly obscured the descent. Not enough for Drew's sharp eyes to miss the pyramid at the bottom of the passage.

"This is the most beautiful death trap I have ever seen," Bill said as the group caught up to Luke and Drew and surveyed the islands below them.

"If you watch the birds, there are some treacherous wind currents," Daryl said, pointing to a flock that shifted to take advantage of the drafts to move through the air at dizzying speeds.

"Yeah. I don't think I can do this," Sarah said, pulling away from the edge of the island and back toward the stairs. "I'm not... afraid of heights. But there are some gaps in those pathways that are going to require jumps I just don't think I'm going to be able to make."

Drew looked again and saw where she was talking about. Parts of the path were rocks floating through the air in a circle pattern that required you to jump from one set to another at the right timing.

"I mean... I could probably just blink step and gravitas through most of this," Drew said, looking down. "I don't see anything that is obviously a guardian, though, but I bet my gravity spells would just absolutely wreck those bird flocks. They don't look like they're much more dangerous than normal birds, but that doesn't mean they are going to be harmless."

"You would have to do it alone," Bill said with a frown, glancing down. "And it would take a long time to get back up."

"Yeah, I might be able to use gravitas to get to the bottom. If I make myself really heavy, the wind shouldn't change things too much, but getting back up would be a problem," Drew said, eyeing the pathways again.

"I can come with you. I can teleport to your location after you blink step," Luke said, glancing down. "And we often trained in environments not unlike this at home. I am not afraid of missing any of the jumps."

"That would leave you lot up here, with a lack of ranged firepower." Drew glanced at Sarah, Bill, Daryl, and Gary.

"We should be pretty safe here," Gary said, glancing around. "We could make a shelter over against the wall with some of these vines. We'd be able to see anything coming from above, and like you said, there aren't a ton of monstrous-looking birds, so we're safe from below."

Drew glanced around and then looked down at the islands below them and breathed out slowly. Trying very hard not to focus on just how far the fall down was. "Well, this is going to suck."

CHAPTER THIRTY-ONE – DESCENT

The first attempt at descent had them swarmed by birds. Drew's cone spells and Sarah's damage reflection ability wreaked havoc on the small creatures, but they still retreated back to the entrance to heal back up and change tactics.

Drew spent almost two hours killing birds. Using his non-attributable spells, namely his storms and gravity point, allowed him to attack from a hidden position without alerting the flocks to where they were. The swarms were clearly agitated, their movements becoming even more erratic. Some of the groups even turned on each other, assaulting in ever-increasing fury as they were unable to find the source of the attacks.

The time wasn't enough to clear the entire dungeon. There were far too many birds for something like that. But it thinned the number down to something manageable. The dungeon floor had become littered with blue and red blood, the bodies of the birds adding even more color to what had previously been a dark stone. Drew wasn't sure where the light for the cavern was coming from. It was well lit and seemed unaffected by the bloody work he had done clearing the birds.

Most of the birds stuck to their own areas, and even with the thinning, they hadn't really expanded their territories. So Drew had cleared away the primary flocks near each of the islands. The plan was to have him float between each island, using blink step to teleport to a safe spot if he was blown off course by the winds, then have Luke use his bonded step to appear next to him, and then leapfrog down the islands using that method.

They figured it would take an hour or so, assuming that none of the islands had additional problems to deal with. Which it didn't look like they did; a few judicious uses of storm had cleared away a lot of the foliage on most of the islands and what was left looked easy enough to navigate. Most of his time had been spent recovering from the mana fatigue caused by casting so many spells back to back. Honestly, Drew was killing more than he felt he really needed to.

Drew had also taken the time to upgrade blink step. It had been sitting at rare and had been ready to upgrade for a long time, but he figured it might give him some extra range that he might need for either the descent or the ascent. Upgrading it knocked him out for a few minutes, but he had learned the strategy for mitigating the risks.

Xatherite Crystal Name: Dimension Door
Xatherite Color: Green
Xatherite Grade: Advanced
Type: Magic
Effect: Move up to 20m without traversing the intervening area. Leaves behind a mental afterimage that lasts 2 seconds. Allows you to bring a willing participant with you.
Mana recharge time: 31.5 seconds.

The extra person was a great addition. It would open up a lot of transportation options for them. He also managed to get an additional eight meters of range on it, which would be nice. The question was how much extra mana fatigue the spell would give him now that it was in the highest tier. The extra person wouldn't help him right now since most of the islands were more than twenty meters apart, although it did cause a debate when Gary said Drew could just ferry the whole group through those particularly tricky portions of the path.

Sarah's fear of heights and the fact that it would extend the time it took to climb back up were the deciding factors. They all wanted to be far enough away from the node when it was conquered to see how the sidhe responded. Which meant Drew was doing most of the delve with just Luke.

The longer he looked down the cone and the hundreds of feet of drop between him and the pyramid, the more he didn't want to do it. He was leaning over the side, psyching himself up for a lot of free-floating, when Bill came up behind him. Turning to look at the chief, he nodded.

"It's not gonna get any easier if you stare at it," Bill said, and Drew couldn't help but agree with the chief.

"Sure, but it's always that first step which is hardest." There were vines directly under Drew. He assumed most parties would be climbing down them to get to the next island. They looked sturdy. Some of them were thicker around than his torso. Those larger vines were woven together with dozens of smaller vines, and they all had a thick quality that spoke of firmness.

"Well, I can always push you," Bill said with a grin and Drew glared at the chief.

"I thought you were supposed to be the nice one."

"There was a phrase my dad used to tell me. I used to tell it to my daughters. They always hated it. But when you lie to someone, you are helping yourself. When you want to help someone, you tell them the truth." Bill shrugged. "This is me helping you," the big chief said as he pushed Drew off the platform. He fell two feet or so but caught himself on the vines. For a moment, he looked down at the vast nothingness that was below him.

"I hate you," Drew growled as he stood up shakily.

"Go get 'em, JG," Bill called from behind him, and Drew muttered a curse under his breath, then pushed himself off the vines. He used gravitas to lighten himself enough that he glided toward the island. Very intentionally focusing on the island he was targeting, and not the drop. When he was close enough for dimension door to take him the rest of the way, he triggered the effect, falling the last six inches to the ground with a heavy thud.

Broken branches and fallen trees made the terrain difficult to maneuver, but Luke appeared next to him a few moments later, and they made their way over to the next edge of the island without any surprises. Drew managed to push himself off the island this time, still careful not to look down as he did. Landing on the second floating mass, he looked back at the start, the light source in the cavern now obvious. Underneath the platform they had been on was a cluster of yellow crystals that emitted a soft light.

The crystals didn't seem all that bright as you could look at them without problems, but they illuminated the area perfectly. Drew chalked the discrepancy up to magic and turned his attention back to the next island. The vines between these two circled almost the entire pit. They went much further than he could get with just his gravitas and dimension door. There were even several large chunks of floating rocks in the middle, acting as resting points for those who made the crossing in the normal way.

Luke followed along behind Drew as he began climbing down the vines, a small part of Drew enjoying the activity. It reminded him of climbing trees or maybe of the Jack in the Beanstalk story. He idly wondered why none of the versions of that story ever talked about how hard it would be to climb a beanstalk for hours on end. Although the nature of the vines actually made the entire process fairly easy.

"You know, this isn't as bad as I was expecting it to be," Drew remarked as he crawled over a section of higher vines to get to the other side.

"As long as you don't look down," Luke muttered.

This, of course, caused Drew to look down, his eyes focusing on the drop between the vines his feet were on. He could feel his stomach clench up. He closed his eyes for a moment to center himself and then ignored that sensation in favor of doing what he needed to.

"Right, don't look down," Drew whispered as he looked over at the next island. Eyeing the distance for a moment, he firmed his resolve. "I'm jumping again," he told Luke before he put action to his words and launched himself off the edge of the vines and toward the next island. He gulped hard as he forced his eyes to stay locked on his target, despite them wanting to look down. A final dimension door, and he was on the next island. A heartbeat later and Luke was beside him, the two men breathing heavily.

"You know, I didn't think I was afraid of heights," Drew said as he sat down for a moment to recover his mental energy.

"I do not think you need to be afraid of heights to have an elevated sense of danger when a misplaced step can kill you," Luke said, looking around the island for any dangers. Something that Drew belatedly realized he should have done as well. Standing up, he looked around. The same post-hurricane look covered the slightly curved surface of the island. Broken and stripped trees littered the ground, making it hard to tell what the island would have originally looked like, but there seemed to be a flat area where pavers had been.

"What is the point of this whole place?" Drew wondered.

"The form dungeons take has been studied by most of the major factions. As far as I know, it has always ended up being somewhat random," Luke answered from behind him.

"This doesn't seem random. All the birds and the floating islands, under the Air Force Memorial?" Drew said, gesturing around them. "This feels like it took a basic theme and went with it."

"Or it could just be a coincidence," Luke responded, and Drew's head wobbled back and forth as he considered it. It seemed like… almost half of the nodes had somehow been related to the thing they were before the integration. The FCC being all bloodsucking monsters, the Navy Archive being paper monsters and printers. There were some exceptions, of course, like those filled with intelligent beings. The naga, trolls, and orcs all seemed pretty random.

"Seems too strong of a coincidence to be entirely without merit, but I guess there hasn't been an overwhelmingly obvious pattern in how it all works," Drew conceded. "Still, it seems like somewhat good odds that if the node had a strong… I guess theme is the word… before the Advent, it'll impart part of that to the DTC that forms around it."

"Yes, I suppose that does seem reasonable. I think you are delaying having to go to the next island."

"Of course I'm delaying," Drew muttered, pushing through the debris to get to the next vine pile. Which was when he realized the fatal flaw in his 'storm them from afar' mentality. The vines here had been shredded by the storm, leaving a meter and a half gap between the island and where the vines drooped under the island. They also looked significantly less viable as a route than the previous ones did. "I'm glad we don't have to use these," Drew said, eyeing the dangling vines.

"Yes, that would have been a problem," Luke said, looking over the edge next to him.

"Alright…" Drew pushed off, and they leapfrogged through the islands until they got to the tenth one. A couple of times they had to fend off a dozen birds or so. Shield of blades and Luke's chain chomp made the small number of birds easy pickings. And as soon as there were less than ten in a flock, they would retreat. Drew paused on the tenth island and cast invigorate on himself.

"So, that was ten gravitas and dimension doors, I think shield of blade's active effect drained some mana too. Any more, and I would have gone into mana fatigue. I think that puts the dimension door at roughly half of what a storm uses. Maybe a little less, with gravitas thrown in." Drew finished off the last of the islands in quick succession, landing at the bottom. The smell of carrion and destruction was evident, if faint. There was a deep pool of water around the island at the bottom, but there were sharp rocks visible at regular intervals. Falling into the water wasn't an option unless you could take a substantial hit.

It hadn't been long enough for the bodies to stink, but the water was littered with bird bodies.

"Might be worth bringing in a net and capturing some of these birds as a food supply," Drew said, glancing at the thick carpet of flesh. "I'll take the node in a bit. I'm gonna cast invigorate on cooldown and then wait until it's off before we take over the node. I want to be able to get up as fast as possible."

Luke nodded, and the two sat down to eat some lunch. They were running low on rations from the stadium, and Drew idly considered bringing some of the plumper-looking birds back to supplement their diets. When he mentioned that to Luke, the seraph agreed, and they spent the rest of their 'downtime' fishing bodies out of the water and storing them in their pouches. When Drew felt his invigorate cooldown finish for the third time since they began their descent, he put his hand on the node to transfer in.

It was only as the door started forming that he got a feeling in his gut telling him something was wrong. The message he got at the end confirmed it. Just like with the stadium node, they hadn't yet killed the guardian.

Chapter Thirty-Two – Kukulkan

Drew not disappearing was enough to clue Luke in, and the seraph immediately went into high alert mode.

"What's wrong?"

"Still a guardian, somewhere," Drew muttered the last under his breath as he scanned the entire pit. Anything could be hiding under the water, but that didn't fit the theme of the dungeon. Everything had been about flight or air in some way. The true island they were standing on was at the bottom of a spiral, which extended to the top of the chasm. They hadn't looked up much. The light from the crystals had gotten brighter as they went, each island adding more and more to the glare as they descended.

Looking up now, Drew could see one island that wasn't like the others. In a sea of light, it was a mote of darkness. Situated almost directly above them was a small floating island, probably only ten meters across and branching off from the main islands in such a way that it hadn't assisted them in their descent at all.

"It's gotta be up there," Drew said, pointing up. Luke's eyes followed him, his hand going up to shade against the glare.

"Well, that is a bitch." Luke's dry delivery of the line couldn't help but draw a laugh from the red mage.

"I think that's the first time I've heard you swear."

"Yes, you are a bad influence on me." Luke's response dripped with sarcasm.

"Wow, that sounded almost human," Drew said with a grin, and Luke nodded.

"Thank you, I am trying to learn to sound more like you. I would like to learn English at some point."

"Wait, you don't speak English?" Drew said, frowning at Luke.

"No, I am speaking Protectorate Military Standard. A language you will also need to learn at some point before you join the fleet. On Earth, the system is converting what I am saying into English for you to understand," Luke answered as the two were making their way over to the vines that would lead them back up. It was hard to see from the bottom how far up they would have to climb to get to wherever the guardian was, but Drew didn't think it was more than a third of the way up.

"Huh." Drew frowned, thinking about the implication of that. "So... is it changing what I'm hearing, or how is that working? I mean, I guess I know that the system can inject information directly into my head, since that's what the system maps are and all, but I don't know if I like the fact that it can change a fundamental sense like that, especially in such a widespread area."

"As far as I know, it is doing a little bit of both? I am not a scholar of the system by any means, so I am not sure how the exact process works. You will notice that anyone who is being translated will sound slightly wooden in tone. That represents itself differently depending on what languages you know," Luke said, jumping over a large root. Drew followed him, considering his words.

"You don't use contractions." They were on the third island when Drew finally realized what the problem was. He had never heard the seraph use a contraction. He had been picking up some idioms, but a lot of the other colloquialisms were missing. "I don't think the orcs or trolls did either. Which makes sense. They probably have their own language they were speaking, and I just sort of heard them in English or whatever it is that the system does.

"I wonder if the system ever just data dumps a language into a monster?" Drew thought back and frowned. "I think the mindworms did... but they probably got it from their hosts. I don't think they could talk without a human, so they just used the human's memories to create speech. I wonder how they communicated with each other in species that cannot speak."

"I am, unfortunately, the wrong person to ask this question of," Luke said with a slight shrug, and they lapsed into silence.

As they got closer to the darkened island, it became evident that the only way to realize this particular section of floating rock was any different from the rest was from below. There was nothing else to mark it as unique. It contained the same willow-like trees that dotted the other islands. Their drooping leaves made it hard to see what was on the island. Stopping on an island about sixty feet across gave Drew an excellent view of the little island, so he cast holy frostfire storm.

The island was consumed in the multicolored energies as a shriek filled the cavern. The sound was overwhelming in its volume, and both men immediately placed their hands on their ears to block out the sound. Drew could feel something in the shriek trying to break through his mental defenses, stricto mentis clypeus's barrier pulsing as it resisted the effect. Luke wasn't as lucky, the seraph falling to his hands and knees as his body lost strength.

The cry ended after a few seconds that seemed to stretch on into eternity, the monster either being dead or unable to continue its screech. The reverberations through the chasm sent lingering pulses against his mind, but they were nowhere near as potent as the initial effect. Luke stayed down, each echo causing his body to shake in pain. The storm over the island raged as Drew prepared for whatever had made that call to come out.

The red, white, and blue energies subsided, allowing him to see the island that had been stripped clear of the leaves that had previously blocked his vision. A single statue sat in the center of the trees, carved to take on the appearance of a snake-like creature. Feathers sprouted from a frill and along its spine. As he watched, the stone regained color, turning from a dark gray to a brilliant array of colors. That was enough for Drew to launch a full complement of fireballs at it, starting with a gravity point and moving on to stagger his attacks at one every second as he worried the snake would just turn back into stone.

That wasn't really a problem, though. As he launched the fourth fireball, the corpse of the feathered serpent went flying. Buffeted by the wind, it eventually fell into the water below. Drew watched with a frown. The snake had looked to be in pretty bad shape. It had managed to survive a storm by turning into stone, and he wasn't going to take any chances with the thing. Beside him, Luke was getting shakily to his feet, twin trails of blood streaming down the sides of his face.

"Well, that was entirely unpleasant. Who would have guessed that a kukulkan would have been in here," Luke said, rubbing his jaws below his ears. "Thankfully, it was just an infant, or that would have been much less ideal."

"That was an infant?" Drew asked incredulously. The kukulkan was at least fifteen feet long, if only a foot or two in girth.

"Yes, the adults are much more aggressive. They are all cunning creatures, but the infants are more ambush predators than the adults. This one was probably waiting for us to be out along one of the vine paths before releasing its sonic attack, and then let gravity and the winds kill us against the rocks."

Drew swallowed loudly as he looked at the sharp rocks that lined the entire cavern. "Do you think I killed it?" Drew asked, looking down. He didn't relish running into the thing again.

"I doubt an infant could turn into stone more than once, and it did not appear to be flying down. I would assume that it is dead, although caution is always wise. They are not venomous, but if you are incapacitated by their sonic blast, they will squeeze you to death."

"Okay. So, back down? The pyramid will tell us if we killed it or not."

It took another fifteen minutes for them to get back down to the pyramid, and Drew put his hand on it. The red door formed, teleporting him into the node.

"Hello, Sub-Lieutenant. Would you like to take over the node?" Aevis had appeared next to him like usual, but Drew shook his head.

"Not just yet, Aevis." Teleporting out, he nodded at Luke. "Shall we find the body? I'll invigorate us again, and then we'll have to wait on the cooldown." The water was cold, even through his boots. It felt like stepping into a glacier-fed lake, but without the summer sun to make the experience more enjoyable.

"Drew, you stay here. I have a xatherite that makes me more resistant to temperature extremes. I'll find the body and bring it back."

It took nearly twenty minutes, but Luke was able to pull the body back to the shore, where he shivered uncontrollably for a few minutes as he got his core body temperature back up. Up close, the snake was gorgeous. The rainbow-colored feathers were razor-sharp, and the scales were iridescent, changing color as he shifted them in the light. Even dead, he had to snap himself out of just staring at the strangely hypnotic creature and Drew assumed a large portion of its attack pattern revolved around putting its prey in a daze.

Glowing right behind its two winged frills were two xatherite crystals, an orange, and an indigo. The orange was small and somewhat dull. Drew assumed it would be a common grade of primitive quality. The indigo was both brighter and significantly larger. Probably uncommon in rarity and common in grade. The snake was heavy enough that neither of them wanted to drag the whole thing up the spiral, but at the same time, it felt like a shame for either of them to harvest the indigo.

"Well, we can't drag that whole snake up to the top for Daryl to gather it… and we can't have him come down because we messed up the roots too much," Drew pondered out loud. "Can we store it in a bag until we get up there? Maybe if we cut off the head?" After using the storage pouches for weeks, Drew had a pretty instinctive sense for what could and could not fit in one, and the snake's head was pushing the limits of what the pouch would store in one go.

"I guess you or me should get the orange anyway," Drew said, glancing at his map. He had five orange slots immediately usable, one in the six-star constellation with dimension door, mana sight, and shoal sense. Two in the nearly empty six-star with stricto mentis clypeus, one in the six-star with arsenal, mana rampart, and aeon. The last in an empty constellation on his virtually untouched left tree. Sarah also had some open oranges that were available.

Drew had to stop himself. No point in counting his eggs before they hatched. He needed to know what the orange did before figuring out who and where it would work best. They didn't have anyone that made particularly good use of oranges. His own harvests had been both good and bad. Mana tap hadn't proven super helpful, primarily due to its limited range and semi-okay links, but invigorate and gravitas were both keystones for his abilities.

"What do you think on the orange?" Drew said, turning to Luke.

"You, of course," Luke answered without thinking about it.

"Alright… let's try to store the orange. It's less valuable, and if I accidentally harvest it, that won't be that bad. Should be fine in the pouches, right?"

"It either will not go in, or it will be fine. No way to know until we try, however."

With Luke's help, Drew used Robbi's blood sword to cut a slice of the skull off. Cutting through the bone was harder than Drew had expected it to be, given how sharp the sword was. They peeled off the scales and then had to step on the blade to get it to cut through the skull, which broke off in a chunk that would have been accidentally harvested for sure if they hadn't wrapped both in cloth before they started.

"Okay, moment of truth," Drew said as he picked up the chunk of skull and crystal and tried to put it into the storage bag. It gave him the same resistance that putting something too big in gave. "No dice," Drew said, glancing around. "Put it in a blanket and just carry the chunk up, maybe." Drew looked up at the spiraling islands above him and frowned. "That should be fine... unless we drop it."

"Then we will not drop it," Luke said as he moved over to cut off the indigo as well. After a few minutes of hacking, they had that piece off as well, and both were tucked into a thick blanket that Luke had been using for his bedding. Drew wrinkled his nose at the blue blood that was staining the bottom before glancing at the rest of the rainbow-scaled serpent.

"We should take as much of this corpse back as we can."

"The meat should be poisonous, but the feathers, scales, and bones would probably be of use," Luke agreed, and they spent another hour and a half butchering the giant snake. Drew had to keep reminding himself that it was just meat as he did so. With Daryl around, they hadn't had to spend a lot of time butchering animals, not since he had made the spider leg spears back in the Coast Guard HQ. That reminded him of Katie, and he felt a heavy weight on his chest.

With a mental effort, he pushed those thoughts aside. Focusing instead on the next step. The sidhe and home, and most importantly: Zoey.

CHAPTER THIRTY-THREE – HOME

Putting his hand on the pyramid for the third time this trip, Drew teleported into the command center.

"Hello, Sub-Lieutenant. Are you ready to take over the node now?" Aevis asked as he appeared in the room, and Drew nodded his head.

"Yes, Aevis, take over the node, install the remote admin console. Rename this Air Force Memorial node." Drew watched as the room shifted to his standard command console configuration, and the name above the link changed from its numeric designator to the more human-sounding name he replaced it with.

"And I'm out. Thanks, Aevis," Drew said with a wave and teleported out of the node again. For a second, he almost thought he saw Aevis smile at him. The trip back to the top of the dungeon took another forty-five minutes, and everyone was ready to go by the time they got up to the top.

"Anything happen up here?" Drew asked, and everyone looked around for a moment as if they didn't want to answer.

"We got hit by that mind scream thing you triggered, but other than that, nothing to report," Sarah said after a moment.

"Ahh, yeah, sorry about that. Did it hit y'all hard?" Drew asked, frowning. There didn't seem to be any lasting damage other than their reticence to talk about what happened.

"Nope, everything was fine here," Sarah answered, but the look she gave him told Drew he should back off from this line of questioning.

"Any activity going on outside?" Drew asked Daryl, who shook his head.

"No, it's hard to see through the trees, but I haven't seen any humans out and about. If they're there, they are well hidden," Daryl answered.

"Alright, let's go home." Drew started taking the stairs up two at a time, but that quickly tired him out, so he shifted to a more normal walking pattern. Everyone but Luke was a bit gassed when they reached the top of the stairs, and Drew gave them a minute break while he cast refreshing rain on everyone. Turning to the south and the street that would take him back to his apartment, Drew could feel himself picking up speed. He was keeping it to a walk but only barely.

The realization that he might be able to see Zoey soon was like a balm on his soul, and it wasn't until Sarah grabbed his shoulder that he realized he'd been walking fast.

"Drew, I know you want to see your house... but we need to do this right. You know the saying, 'slow is smooth, and smooth is fast.'" Sarah's words calmed him down, and he slowed down enough for them to proceed through the drastically different world that his mind told him he recognized, even though it was now covered in green. They passed the Ethiopian bakery that he had meant to try out but had never gotten around to.

They had to detour around the underpass, though, because it was filled with vines covered in thorns, which added another ten minutes to the route. The large walls on the side of the highway were impossible to see, overtaken by ivy and kudzu. Drew wondered what would happen if kudzu got monsterized, and the idea of that much of the strangling, parasitic vine was mildly terrifying. They passed the vine-covered wall and walked down Columbia Pike and the familiar condos that lined the street. Taking the first right, the small offshoot neighborhood that Drew had lived in was barely discernible under the heavy forest that had taken its place.

Cars lined the narrow street, now in perpetual gloom as the trees loomed overhead, the light tinted green and dark by their leaves. The asphalt had split, shoulder height bushes growing in the cracks. The turn-off to Towers Park was even more surreal for Drew. The trees had all grown dozens of feet, and vines had connected the branches above them, leaving the tall grass strangely quiet as the canopy overhead blocked the wind.

There were squirrels, now the size of basketballs, chittering at them from the boughs above, but they seemed unwilling to aggress them. Drew launched an acid arrow at them, and they disappeared into the cover above with angry squeaks.

The red door that marked Drew's house was closed. It was a three-story building, and his and Lincoln's apartment had taken up the northeast corner. Drew wasn't sure if that was a good sign or not, but it was locked when he tried to open it. He had put his keys in the pouch of holding a long time ago, mostly out of habit, but he pulled them out now and unlocked the door. Inside, the air felt stale. The bottom floor had been where he had his room, and a quick check inside told him that it had been untouched.

Going up the stairs to the communal living room, he found some signs of habitation. Clearly, Lincoln had been here since the Advent started. There was a large pile of food boxes and wrappers against the far wall. This had been their shared space, the kitchen and living room. It looked like some effort had been put into blocking the light coming in from the windows. Their dining table was blocking almost all the natural light, and Drew pulled out a glow stone.

"Lincoln?" Drew called out, pausing to listen. The others had filed in behind him but allowed Drew to go first. Climbing the stairs up to the third floor, where Lincoln had his room, was a bit nerve-wracking. There were more signs of having blocked light from exiting the windows. His closet looked ransacked, and there was a crowbar and kitchen knives lying on a table next to the bed that he was convinced weren't there originally. The bathroom didn't smell like it had been used recently, but a bucket and what looked like a makeshift pulley near the window, which was still closed, indicated it had seen use after Advent.

"Nothing here," Drew said, opening the last door into the empty bedroom, left vacant when a roommate had gotten married, and neither Lincoln nor Drew had felt the need to replace him.

"That's… not a bad thing," Sarah said. "At least we didn't find any bodies. They could just be out hunting for food or something."

"Alright, we'll set up here while we watch the node. We'll know by tomorrow morning if they are going to do anything…" Drew said, and everyone started to make themselves at home. Drew wandered downstairs and looked into his room.

Everything was how he had left it, a thin layer of dust proof that no one had come in. All of the things that Drew had considered his own in the room. Looking around, he felt like he should take some of it with him. His computer, his clothes? None of it felt important anymore, not like it had before. He sat down on his bed, running a hand over the spot on the cover where Zoey would sit when he tied his shoes.

"Where are you?" Drew asked the empty room. Standing up, he looked at the pictures of his family on the wall and wondered if they were still alive. He doubted he would ever be able to see them again. Even if they were alive, they were thousands of miles away. His closest sibling was in Boston, an eight-hour drive before the Advent, which would require him to get through Philadelphia and New York City. The rest of them were across the country in the middle of the Rocky Mountains.

They hadn't seemed so far away before the Advent, just a plane ticket. But now, it felt like an unmanageable distance. The pioneers had taken months to get to the west, and that was before there were monsters. But also before there was magic. Maybe magic would help him travel the distance faster. If he could make an ultralight glider? Gravitas would get him into the air easily enough…

Drew realized his thoughts were spiraling, and he grabbed the spare blankets out of his closet. Going back upstairs to the living room, he set them down so everyone would have something comfortable to sit on. The two bachelors had minimal furniture. Everyone was gathered around his coffee table, and he pulled the two crystals out of the bloody blanket and put them down on the center. They were still covered, but the indigo light managed to break through the thin layer of fabric covering it.

"Daryl, you're obviously getting the indigo," Drew said, pointing to the larger crystal. "I think Gary should be the one to grab the little orange. This is just to harvest it, mind you. We'll decide who gets what when we know what the xatherite come out as."

"But why me, Mr. Drew?" Gary asked, staring with wide eyes at the bloodstained rags.

"Because I want to see what sort of buff spell you think a Jedi would get." When everyone looked at him curiously, Drew shrugged. "They can jump incredible distances, control their falls, read minds, predict the future, even see distant things. There is a whole suite of powers that would make us better.

"We need to look at our synergies and figure out how to make optimal builds. If we keep… responding, eventually we're going to get to a point where we can't respond to the monster of the day. Shoal sense was invaluable to me while we were fighting at the memorial. And I think Gary is most likely to get more of those danger sense or physical enhancement type spells. So harvest them and then read the ability to us, and we'll figure out who gets what."

> *Xatherite Crystal Name: Mind Tricks*
> *Xatherite Color: Indigo*
> *Xatherite Grade: Basic*

Xatherite Rarity: Uncommon
Type: Magic
Effect: A targeted creature's (within 15m) ability to sense targets is disrupted. Actively inhibits their senses, making them much more likely to miss their targets.
Mana recharge time: 23 seconds.

Xatherite Crystal Name: Lesser Enhance Body
Xatherite Color: Orange
Xatherite Grade: Primitive
Xatherite Rarity: Common
Type: Magic
Effect: Imbue mana into your body. For 30 seconds, you can increase your physical or speed stats by a minor amount.
Mana recharge time: 1 minute, 13 seconds.

They were both great abilities, but nothing game-changing, at least not for himself. He glanced over everyone's maps but paused when he came to Luke's sheet. He had a single open indigo in an otherwise full grouping. The other abilities were lingua franca, which Drew assumed was his translation ability, shield of faith, and flaming grasp. He hadn't seen the seraph use his flame grasp often, but then very few things lasted long after being hit by the chain chomp.

"Luke, I think you should take mind tricks and fill out that group there," Drew announced. Drew's mind was full of possibilities for linked attacks with those abilities, a ranged fire attack, a language disrupting skill, maybe a confusion shield that made it hard for anyone close to him to target him. There was a lot of potential there, especially since they were going up against the sidhe soon.

"As for the orange…" Drew trailed off. He couldn't see any obvious and significant benefits to any of the slots he could put an orange into on his own map. Sarah had a couple of oranges available, but she didn't really need the buff; maybe if she could use it on other people… Daryl's map was in similar shape. Which left Luke, who he had just given a xatherite to… and Gary. There was an orange in the same four-slot formation as Force Shield.

That opened up another constellation, but Drew also had the feeling that the two abilities would combine into something good. Just because they both came from Gary and were all related to his image of what his powers should be made Drew feel like they had a high synergy.

"Gary, that orange is for you. The force shield constellation." Drew was the only one that could see everyone's maps, but even then, he expected some pushback from the others on his choices. Everyone just nodded and went back to what they were doing before Drew plopped the xatherite down. He cast a refreshing rain when he saw both of the newly enhanced men wince, but otherwise settled down to wait for either Lincoln to come home or to see the sidhe's response to him taking over the Air Force Memorial node.

Drew felt like it was going to be a long night. Going downstairs again, he put his meager shelf of books into his pouch of holding. His time spent in the military had severely diminished the number of physical books that he moved around. Most of the ones that were left, he was keeping for sentimental reasons. Still, that was precisely the kind of book he was looking for at the moment, and he settled in to read about an outcast girl taming fire lizards.

CHAPTER THIRTY-FOUR – DOGS

The sunset, which they only saw because the layer of green light coming in through the leaves above, slowly faded. In its place, a hundred flowers unfolded from the vines that were strung between the trees, each bloom giving off faint bioluminescence. The effect was muted, but still, the night was only half as dark as it should have been, a mixture of red, yellow, blue, and purple lights casting an otherworldly glow on the world outside the windows.

Drew had shifted the table blocking the window over the apartment entrance so that they could watch to see if anything was approaching. As he watched the familiar scene, he realized that the lights were not the only changes. The vines acted as a natural bug repellant.

Not in the sense that the bugs avoided them, but in the sense that they ate all the bugs that came close. Thin tendrils near each flower would snap around any of the supernaturally large bugs the Advent had created, easily holding them in place while other processes ate the body. It was all a silent dance of death that strangely enough made the night almost peaceful. He still remembered his first night topside with Daryl, hiding in a house while an army of bugs waged war outside.

"Sort of crazy, isn't it?" Daryl said from his seat next to him. His bird was perched in the trees near the memorial, not that he could see much in the darkness. "It's like watching two completely different worlds. Out there, it's calm, almost peaceful... well, unless you're near the treetops and those vines. Near the open air of the memorial? It's just like before, tons of movement and fighting."

"It is a defense mechanism the fae developed," Luke said from his spot near the stairs. "The guardian vines eat the small predators, leaving the forest floor safe. The vines feed on the bugs and use that energy to grow even further. They don't damage the trees and only grow on trees, so it makes containing it relatively easy."

"That almost sounds like you admire something the fae did," Sarah accused Luke. They were in the dark since Drew was looking out the window, but he imagined the seraph's face got flustered.

"It is an effective tool that they developed. Nothing more." Luke's tone was harsher than usual. Clearly, Sarah's tease had brushed against something sensitive.

"Pretty and functional," Drew muttered, his thoughts going back to his own attempts at making things. He had always opted for function over form and had been jealous of classmates who could do both easily. The group lapsed into silence after that. Drew faded into a kind of daze as his thoughts wandered while he kept his eyes moving over the view. He immediately snapped out of it when he heard a sound.

"Was that a dog barking?" the red mage questioned softly, his previously limp body going taut as he studied the near darkness outside.

"Yeah, I think so," Gary said, shifting a little so he could get a better look out the window.

A few minutes later, the dog in question came into view. It was hard to see in the darkness, but it was medium-sized and yellow, and perhaps more peculiarly, it was pulling a lanky blonde man wearing a pink vest and a yellow bowtie toward the apartment by his pant cuff. The man in question seemed rather upset at being dragged through the night forest. Drew didn't care. That was Lincoln, and the dog had to be Zoey. Grabbing Gary's shoulder, he cast dimension door, appearing next to Lincoln on the asphalt of their driveway.

The sudden shift caused Gary to lose balance while Drew reached forward to grab Zoey…

Except it wasn't. This dog was clearly a monsterized version of a dog. The teeth were larger, the fur was thicker, more resistant to damage. Looking past the changes, Drew realized he still knew the dog, who wagged her tail and jumped into his arms, licking his face.

"Sadie?" Drew asked, and the dog yipped excitedly in his arms. A moment later, they were joined by a second dog, similar to the first with tawny hair; the medium-sized dogs both did their best to be everywhere around him all at once. "Taco!" Drew exclaimed and did his best to scratch and pet both the dogs as well as he could. It took a few moments for them to calm down, but Drew eventually managed to regain his feet and look at Lincoln, who was standing awkwardly off to one side while Gary had his saber out and pointing at the gangly man.

"It's okay. This is Lincoln, my roommate," Drew said, looking behind him where Luke and the rest were glaring at Drew and the newcomer. "But… we should get inside." Drew gestured back at the house.

Sadie and Taco both went over to sniff the new people, but when Drew pushed the table back against the window to block the light and pulled out a glowstone, the two dogs came back, both jumping up to sit in his lap.

"That dog hates me." It was the first thing Lincoln said, and he was glaring at Sadie. She yipped softly as if in agreement with him before setting her head down on Drew's chest. Taco was staring off into space on the other side of his lap. They were both a little too big for this to be comfortable, strictly speaking. But Drew had missed the two dogs almost as much as he had missed his own. They both belonged to neighbors in the area.

"Where is Zoey? Tony? Mike?" Tony and Mike were the owners of Sadie and Taco, respectively. At the sound of their owner's names, the two dogs whined slightly, and Drew redoubled his efforts to scratch them.

"Tony and Mike didn't make it," Lincoln said after a moment. The kid was in his mid-twenties and had a weird habit of wearing pastels, but Drew enjoyed his company. "Tony made it a week, but some other survivors shot him when he went to go greet them. Mike got attacked by a giant centipede a few nights later. As for Zoey... That's... complicated?"

"What do you mean it's complicated?" Drew pushed past the notice that his two friends had died.

"Well..." Lincoln looked around the room and Drew realized just how out of place he looked. His pink vest and bowtie were a sharp contrast to everyone else's dark blue armor and weapons. In fact, Lincoln didn't have any weapons on him at all. "Okay, this is going to sound weird. But Zoey is the pack leader for all the local dogs around here. Ever since the vines came, she's been spending a lot of time away from the park. She usually takes her pack out hunting at night and checks in on me during the day." There was a lot of information to unpack in that, and Drew was still parsing it when Lincoln continued.

"It all just sort of happened. The first couple of days were normal. But then the dogs started turning into... well..." Lincoln gestured to the two dogs that had previously been a few dozen pounds combined but were now feeling more like they weighed fifty pounds each. "When that started happening, Zoey got... the most of it? I guess that's the way to put it. She is about as big as a... I dunno, a wild pig? Three, maybe four-hundred pounds. Anyway, she was the biggest, and they sort of all just fell back into the pack mentality. I think it made them smarter too. At least Zoey is. Sadie and Taco aren't much smarter."

Sadie turned and growled at Lincoln while Taco stared off into space. Sadie was a basenji before turning into whatever she was now. Taco's origins were more muddled. Taco had been rescued from Puerto Rico and had distemper, resulting in some neurological disorders in the poor puppy. Given what he had seen, Drew was assuming Sadie was more intelligent than Lincoln was giving her credit for.

"I told you she hated me," Lincoln said, pointing at Sadie.

"Where are all the people?" Sarah asked, and Lincoln turned to look at her and then shrugged.

"I don't really know. After Tony died, I sort of retreated to the park, and the dogs have been taking care of me." Lincoln paused for a moment, thinking. "There were a couple of other groups that we used to trade with... but they all disappeared around the time the vines showed up."

"Disappeared or were killed?" Drew questioned.

"Oh, disappeared for sure. They looked like they evacuated. Took most of their stuff and all their food. That's really the only reason I went over there. The puppies are great at getting meat, but not so good at fruit and veggies, so I went to trade some meat for greens, and they all just sort of disappeared. Not even a mysterious Croatoan sign or anything."

"The Roanoke Colony thing?" Sarah looked at the lanky newcomer with a sense of disbelief.

"Yeah, that's right! You know your history." Lincoln stepped forward and held out his hand. "I'm Lincoln, by the way. How did you guys get here?" What followed was a quick introduction of the group and recounting of their trip here from the stadium.

"So, you have a safe area on the other side of the river?" Lincoln looked around the group with a sense of consternation on his face. "And you left? And there is no way to get back?" He slid down the wall and buried his head in his knees while he thought. Drew frowned as he watched his roommate go through what was clearly some sort of emotional breakdown. Bill crouched down next to him and put an arm around him. Drew smiled faintly and pulled the attention away from Lincoln. He turned to the rest of his team.

"Alright, so the odds of the people disappearing right as the sidhe show up seem... slim, to say the least. However, it doesn't seem like they're rounding them up in a violent manner, else they wouldn't have packed up and left." Drew ran a hand through his hair as he considered. "But they could have started treating them differently after they were removed from their fortified position." There were probably plenty of historical accounts of people doing that on Earth.

"We need more intel on where they are and where the people are," Sarah said, glancing over at Daryl.

"Which we won't be getting until morning," Drew said, gesturing outside at the darkness. "Although I wish I would have known they had captives before we announced our presence by taking over the node."

"There is no way you could have known that," Sarah rejoined, and Drew sighed heavily.

"Right, not helpful." Drew nodded his agreement that it wasn't a productive line of thought. His fingers continued to scratch Sadie and Taco's ears as he thought. "Alright, let's go to your spot in the park. There must be a reason you went there instead of staying here. Actually, why did you come here tonight?" Their apartment faced the park; the dog park section was the furthest, on the other side of the tennis courts from the apartment.

"Sadie dragged me here. I assume she must have smelled you or something." Lincoln looked up. He seemed to have regained his emotional balance. However, his long legs betrayed him, and he tripped trying to stand up, face planting into Bill's chest. The healer helped him up, and everyone else started to get ready to leave. After he got to his feet, the lanky man responded, "The dogs moved me out there. I think it's easier for them without the door."

It didn't take long for the rest of the group to be ready to go. Everyone shoved what few personal items they had gotten out into their pouches of holding, much to Lincoln's confusion. Drew just grinned as he kept looking around, trying to figure out where all the items had gone.

The trip under the glowing vines was… magical and surreal. Drew had been throwing spells around for a long time, but this was the first time it felt… real? Like every part of his world had been infused with magic. This was the first time he'd seen something obviously magical that didn't come from a person or a dungeon, he realized. Well, that didn't come from a human or a dungeon. The sidhe were people… probably. Traveling the short distance through Towers Park, they passed the tennis courts, overgrown by the weeds with thick vines blocking sight from either direction.

Behind the courts was the dog park, where Lincoln and the dogs had set up shop. The tall trees kept the vines high off the ground. Tons of scavenged clothing and blankets were scattered around in various spots, marking the dens and sleeping areas, while the fountain in the back still sputtered a weak amount of water into its basin. Trees had grown up all around the former dog park, isolating it from the rest of the forested area.

In the back corner, a still smoking firepit was under a makeshift shelter. Made from what looked like scrap and salvaged wood created to keep them dry during the mana storms, it covered almost a third of the park. Tunnels leading into the ground were visible, but they seemed too small for a human to get into. As they got close, yips from Sadie and Taco caused half a dozen other dogs to come out of the trees and dens. It was clear that these were the ones who had been wounded and were unable to go out hunting as most of them were limping or had large sections of hair ripped out over scabs. Most of them were dogs Drew knew, and he knelt down to greet them all.

"Sarah, Bill? Start healing the dogs, please," Drew said even as he cast refreshing rain over the pack that had congregated around him. The dogs shied away from the water at first, but after Sadie gave a few more commanding barks, they came back into its area of effect. Taco started trying to jump up and bite the drops of water before they got to him.

When all the dogs were mostly healed, the sun had just poked its head over the horizon. Suddenly all of the dogs stood up, their attention focused on the main gateway into the park, where a large golden retriever appeared. Another pack of smaller dogs surrounded her, each carrying haunches of meat in their mouths. Drew looked up, and the world seemed to pause.

"Zoey?" he asked, and the big dog immediately dropped the half a deer-like creature she was carrying and jumped toward him. Bowling him over despite his mana shield's protection, her tail wagging as she licked his face. Drew grunted from the impact but wrapped his hands through her much longer fur, pulling her into a tight hug. "I sure missed you, girl."

CHAPTER THIRTY-FIVE – LUBBERKIN

It took almost ten minutes for Zoey to calm down enough to stop jumping on him. Although she refused to get more than a few feet away from him still, her yellow fur raising slightly if anyone else got too close. In the light of the vines, it had been hard to see what had changed about her, aside from her size, but now he got a good look. It was amazing.

The fur had grown out another couple of inches. Drew was sinking his hands into the coat and amazed at how... kept it was. Either the system had made the hair impossible to mat, or someone had been brushing her. His fingers didn't find any tangles as they worked through her hair. There were clearly several layers to the coat at this point, but Drew wasn't sure what all they did. He had never heard of a dog having more than two layers.

The other changes were easy to see. Zoey was as tall at the shoulder as he was and thicker everywhere. She had hard bumps on her shoulders that Drew had no idea the purpose of. Her snout was longer and more angular, like a wolf's. And her claws and teeth looked quite capable of ripping and shredding. In all, she seemed to be in much better health, especially compared to the smaller dogs around her, which all had minor wounds or patches of missing hair from previous injuries.

"What have you been up to, puppy?" Drew asked the mountain of a dog currently leaning against his side in a slightly uncomfortable way. The fact that she was clean and healthy seemed unusual compared to the rest of the dogs. Drew's inspection of Zoey was cut short as Daryl appeared a few feet away.

"I think they're moving," the scout said. "I can see... what looks like, I don't even know? Walking trees? Treants? There are three of them, and they are all just sort of standing around the entrance to the node."

"Yes, they are called treants. Anything else?" Luke asked. The seraph sat across from Drew on a bench. Zoey had been unwilling to let anyone else close to Drew, her low rumbling growl a clear indicator, so everyone was giving him a bit of space.

"Nothing that's broken the tree line yet. The three treants are just sort of positioning themselves around the entrance in a triangle. Wait... more... things are coming. A couple of massive cats, well, massive for cats, not as big as Zoey. There is something on one of their backs. It looks like a growth or something. No, it's moving now... getting off the cats and walking toward the trees."

"What does it look like?" Luke asked.

"Uh... a furball? Brown and black hair in a ball shape, can't even see any legs or arms," Daryl responded. At his description, Zoey let out a rumbling growl that Drew associated with her not liking something. But it didn't seem like the dog had a particular target for her ire, even as her hackles stood on end. Drew scratched behind her ear to try to comfort the dog, who stopped the growling after a moment and twisted, so he was scratching the other side of her neck.

"A lubberkin then," Luke answered with a frown, a clear look of distaste. "I wouldn't expect one on an elven expedition. Nor would I expect the treants to willingly cooperate with them."

"Why is that?" Drew asked with a frown.

"Just like with the humans, the sidhe are divided into different factions. They have their own names, but most humans just call them the rock and the plant factions. Rock fae like the lubberkin usually operate under the zwerg, whereas the treants and nymphs come under the domain of the elves. For an expedition that is mounted by the plant fae... which we're clearly in," Luke gestured to the verdant plant life all around them. "Having a rock fae is unusual. They are seldom seen on the same planet." Luke's explanation was cut short as Daryl started speaking again.

"The little guy, lubberkin, you called it? It sent a few of its cats down the passage." They waited for a few moments, but there were no further developments until the cats came out of the passage. Daryl started laughing as he described the lubberkin going up to one of the treants and shouting at it. The treants didn't respond to whatever threats the little ball of fur was yelling at them. The argument ended when the lubberkin kicked one of the tree roots, only to be swatted by a branch, rolling ass over teakettle before coming to a stop nearly twenty feet away.

"Okay, the lubberkin is dusting himself off and getting back on one of the cats and heading away. Should I follow him?" Daryl asked, between breaths of laughter.

"No. If you could follow it maybe. But trying to track cats through the forest would be nearly impossible. Especially with those vines preventing you from flying near the canopy," Drew said after a moment of thought. "Stay on the treants, and we'll see what else happens."

Lincoln had gathered all the clumps of meat that the dogs had brought back and was in the process of butchering them. Drew watched with fascination as his roommate rolled up his sleeves to the elbow and then began chopping into the bodies. There was just something… comical about his pastel wardrobe. Somehow he had managed to trade the pink vest in for a powder blue cardigan. His yellow bowtie disappeared as well, replaced by a pale green handkerchief that was poking artfully out of a chest pocket. Completing the attire was a pair of pristine white pants.

"He has to have some sort of xatherite to make his clothes stay clean, right?" Sarah asked from next to Drew. She was staring at Lincoln too. And despite the rather rough living accommodations and current occupation, his clothes were spotless.

"I honestly have no idea with Lincoln. He was a campaign manager before all this, but he always wore those bright colors. He even had a bright red three-piece suit," Drew answered, shaking his head in amazement as Lincoln dropped a bit of meat on his pants before it fell to the dirt. The kid hastily picked the meat up and then blew on it to get the dust off, glancing around to see if anyone had seen him. He saw Sarah and Drew looking at him and awkwardly waved before putting the meat back into the pile.

Drew continued to watch as his roommate butchered all the meat and then put it on a flat stone off to one side of the encampment. Almost immediately, the smell of cooking meat filled the clearing. Nearly a dozen of the pack had shifted to sit in a semi-circle around Lincoln, while a few others were digging into the pile of butchered meat, picking out bones to chew off in a corner. After a few minutes, Lincoln had all the dogs except for Zoey sitting near him, their eyes on the meat and their tails wagging furiously.

"Sadie! No! Leave it!" Lincoln said when Sadie darted over and stole a piece of meat off the stone. Sadie, of course, ignored Lincoln and happily ran off to sit on top of a nearby picnic table and eat her meal. Taco followed her, whining as he leaned against her back. With a long-suffering growl, Sadie tore a section of meat off and moved slightly. Taco jumped on the piece, his tail like a whip behind him.

Time quickly passed as they waited to see what the sidhe's next move was. They had all eaten some food while Luke, Bill, and Gary were all sparring. Drew had tried to join them, but Zoey had made her displeasure at people attacking Drew quite obvious. So he and Sarah were throwing tennis balls at them while they sparred to improve their spatial awareness or something. The park had been right next to a tennis court before, and the dogs had gathered up all the balls for Drew when he started throwing them. Any that missed the combatants were quickly retrieved and put back in Drew's lap.

Daryl was invisible off to one side. Taco had taken to staring at the invisible scout's location, sniffing at the air, and then grumbling to himself. Lincoln was sitting next to Drew, his white pants still immaculate despite sitting in the dirt, proving Sarah's statement that he had some sort of self-cleaning xatherite.

"The lubberkin is back," Daryl announced, and everyone paused to look at him. "He brought back some humans? At least human-sized and shaped, although small for humans. They are wearing some weird armor that looks like bark, though." Daryl described the humans going down into the dungeon and then coming back out a few minutes later. The three treants still hadn't moved from where they had planted themselves around the dungeon, but the lubberkin continued to pace around the entrance with obvious impatience.

"Either nymphs or brownies. Is the bark armor or skin?" Luke said when Daryl described the human-shaped bark creatures.

"Hard to say for sure, but it looks like armor," Daryl said with a shrug.

"Brownies then."

"Brownies are coming back out. They're talking to the lubberkin. One of them is pulling out a horn or something." As he said that, they heard a loud cry from the north of them.

The dogs instantly turned their attention to Zoey, who stood up. For a moment, the dog looked torn, glancing from Drew to the north. When he moved to stand up, she pushed her nose against his chest, pushing him back down.

"I take it you want me to stay," Drew said, and Zoey let loose a deep thrum which he assumed was assent. Then the big dog turned, growling for a few seconds before running to the north and jumping almost ten feet into the air as she cleared the fence. About half the dogs followed her, while Sadie and Taco both shifted, sitting in the spot that Zoey had just left from.

"So… nymphs just called my dog, and she left," Drew said with a frown. Within a minute, Daryl confirmed that the dogs had arrived at the DTC entrance.

"Zoey is going up to the one who blew the horn. It's talking to her… looks like it's asking her to do something. She clearly isn't willing to do whatever it is asking. It almost seems like the thing is confused. Oh wow, she just almost bit the lubberkin in half. Now all the dogs are growling at the cats. Looks like they're about to fight."

"Well, at least the apocalypse hasn't changed the fact that cats and dogs still hate each other," Sarah said under her breath so that only Drew could hear it.

"Zoey never did like cats. Well, she did, but they didn't like the attention she would give them." Drew's attention was on the north and why Zoey would feel the need to respond to the strange figure's requests.

"Okay, the human thing is doing something next to the entrance. It kind of looks like he's growing a tree?" Daryl's voice was full of confusion as the scout tried to describe the alien magic. "Looks like some sort of a sign. He just grew a sign? And now they're all leaving, even the treants. Should I follow them?"

"What does the sign say?" Drew questioned.

"Let me send the bird in closer, didn't want them to sense it, so I'm quite a ways above." They waited a tense couple of seconds as Daryl's bird moved closer to the sign. "It says: Master Red Mage, please attend me at the Army-Navy Country Club. -Lady Noli'ay'niara." The scout had to sound out the name a few times before he got it right.

"How did they know he was a red mage?" Bill said with a frown. For a moment, Drew wondered if his use of aeon had told them what he was, but then he realized there was probably a more straightforward solution.

"Because the node is red. They're just assuming that I'm a red mage based on the color of the node, just like I know that whatever is taking over their nodes is a violet person." Drew's response seemed to satisfy everyone else, but he wondered if there wasn't more to it than that. Hades had told him that his use of aeon had caused the sidhe to respond in the first place. Was there more to it than that? The use of the title master could imply that they didn't know what gender he was, or he could just be reading more into things than was there.

"So the question is, do we visit this Lady Noli or not?" Bill asked, and Drew mentally applauded the rename, which was much easier to say than the entire thing.

"Well, we should at least scout out the country club," Drew said, glancing over at Luke, who nodded his head. "More intelligence isn't going to hurt us."

CHAPTER THIRTY-SIX – SPYING

The country club proved easy enough for the bird to find. It was one of the only areas in Arlington that still had open air. The trees parted to show that the previous golf fairways had been turned into fields. Around the fields were redwood-sized trees, with huts built at the mid-level. Bridges connected the various platforms, and there was a gap between where the huts ended and where the vines began. The tree village was large, made up of hundreds of individual houses, each large enough to accommodate a dozen people with ease.

Which was what they were being used for. The fields were being tended by hundreds of humans, each bent over and involved in back-breaking labor. Around the outside edge of the fields, fae roamed in packs. Ranging from the weird bark creatures that had grown the signs to more lubberkin, each with a handful of monsterized cats following them around, to even more unusual varieties. Glowing balls of light that flitted around the bases of the trees being the most common. Daryl didn't see any treants but wasn't sure if he could distinguish them from the trees unless they were moving.

In total, Daryl counted just under a thousand humans working in the field and nearly a third of that in sidhe forces. That didn't include the lubberkin's cats which it was clear was their primary means of combat. The humans were all dressed in similar attire, loose-fitting yellow shirts, and pants, although it was comforting to see that they at least all looked healthy and clean. Which made it at least a pleasant prison camp… if you could really apply that name to it.

There was no sign of an elf or any larger fortified areas; Daryl assumed that wherever the sidhe commander was would be deeper in the trees, and they had yet to be willing to send the bird under the canopy. Instead, it was flying lazy circles above the fields. Drew would have preferred it land on one of the trees, but the duck-like loon was not made for that, more at home on ponds or lakes. Scouting out the place had taken nearly an hour, at which point they started to discuss how to go about rescuing the humans.

"I still think we should just bombard them from a distance," Luke said with a frown.

"It's too big of a risk. We don't know if they will respond like the trolls did and start killing their captives." Drew shook his head. Luke was perfectly fine with the collateral damage of a thousand humans dying if it meant that they would be able to kill the sidhe from a distance. The rest of the group was unwilling to accept the plan. The problem was that no one else had any better ideas.

"Luke, I know you dislike the sidhe, but I refuse to fire the first shot in this situation. We will not be the aggressors. They have opted for a diplomatic approach. I cannot, in good conscience, respond to that with violence." Drew's gaze was locked on Luke, and he refused to look away until the seraph gave a short nod of acceptance.

"Do they even want to be rescued?" Gary finally asked, and everyone turned to look at him, which caused the kid to blush. "I mean, it looks like they are healthy and safe there. Most of the people at the stadium would be content with that, even if it did mean they had to do manual labor." Gary turned to Daryl. "Are they able to sit down and take breaks? You said there weren't any sidhe in the fields, right?" When Daryl confirmed that, Gary just shrugged.

"Sounds just about like what we are doing, except they're keeping more people busy," Gary said with a shrug. "What they're doing could easily be done by a few of the people with gardening specific xatherite."

"And given that the vines are some form of nature magic, I suppose it would be logical to assume that the sidhe can do that as well," Drew said with a frown. "So why are they having the people work the fields? And where are the humans with those types of xatherite? If we got a bunch of them, it would stand to reason that they aren't all that uncommon."

"Food generating xatherite are indeed quite common. I would expect there to be a dozen or more among that many people," Luke said with a frown.

"So, they must be off doing something else. Maybe growing the vines or whatever it is that the sidhe are doing to make this whole thing into a forest," Sarah said with a frown. "They wouldn't... sacrifice them for more power, would they?"

"The sidhe are many things, but even they would not be able to get xatherite from humans before the system would allow it." Luke's brow creased as he considered his next words. "There should still be several weeks left on the protections of the Advent."

Drew tried to think back to what the messages he had received that night so long ago had said. Had it listed ninety days or one-hundred? Did it have a plus or minus on it? There had definitely been a plus or minus on something, but he couldn't for the life of him remember what it had been. There had been a lot of information, and he hadn't exactly been in the best processing state. How long had it even been since Advent? Two months? Drew shook his head. So much had happened. Spending time in dungeons and not needing to sleep meant that he was well beyond any ordinary reckoning of time.

"Alright, so they aren't going to sacrifice them for power. What is going to happen if Drew storms in there, fireballs blasting every which way?" Sarah asked, and Luke could only shrug in response.

"So, what are we going to do?" Bill asked, looking between Drew and Luke.

"We need more information," Sarah said, her fingers busy rapidly braiding her hair.

"Well, it's not like we can just walk in there and ask them," Drew said, and Sarah turned to look at him, her mouth opening and closing a few times as she parsed what he had just said.

"Why can't we?" Sarah asked, and when everyone looked at her, she shrugged. "I mean, they're gathering captives. We could just get caught and see how they treat us. Worst case scenario, we have to fight our way out… but we're sort of planning on doing that anyway, right?"

Drew scratched his cheek as he considered Sarah's proposal.

"I am afraid they would know I am a seraph," Luke said with a frown. "I have too many xatherite for a native. Drew also should not go."

"We probably shouldn't all go in anyway," Drew said with a frown. "Maybe just send Daryl in? He can figure out what's going on without exposing himself."

"No. Invisibility will not work well on the fae. They do not use their eyes nearly as much as we do," Luke said, shaking his head. "We need a group that looks like it could realistically have survived on its own. If we send everyone but Drew and myself, that should be enough to take you seriously while not being a serious threat. Plus, if it comes to breaking you all out, the two of us have the best shot."

Drew considered Luke's words with a frown; they all made sense, but he didn't like it. He let the idea roll around in his head for a moment while he tried to figure out why it felt so wrong. He realized it was because he was sending people into danger rather than leading them into it. That left an odd taste in his mouth, but once he knew the cause, the rational part of his brain told him that he would have to get used to this. He couldn't do everything himself.

"What about Lincoln? He might know some of the people, and they'll be more likely to talk to him." Drew looked at his former roommate, who looked back, his eyes wide as he smoothed down the front of his powder blue cardigan.

"I… yeah… I can do that." Lincoln almost stuttered the words out. Clearly, the idea of going into the sidhe den made him nervous.

"Alright. Might as well do it now. Circle around to the south, and come at them from the other side of their camp. If you don't come back by tomorrow evening, Luke and I will storm their compound just before sunset. Sarah, will your group sense work that far away?" The xatherite in question was rarely useful, but it allowed Sarah to know the direction of their entire party and roughly how far away they were.

"It should at least tell us when you're getting close," Sarah answered.

"Alright, try to stay close together. You'll probably have to find me, but I imagine it won't be that difficult," Drew said with a nod.

"Why won't it be hard to find you?" Lincoln asked, and everyone laughed.

"Head toward the sound of battle," Bill said with a grin. "That'll be where you find Drew."

Lincoln was clearly having second thoughts on the whole going with them part. He looked between the group and Drew with a bit of confusion.

Lincoln had the hardest time getting ready. He quickly packed a large backpack full of clothes. In doing so, it became evident that the others were traveling light, but they didn't have time to make backpacks that would look authentic, so they just decided to say the pouches were the result of someone who had died before Lincoln joined them.

The dogs were reluctant to let Lincoln go, but Sadie barked twice, and they whined as they went back further into the den. Sadie eyed them all with wariness before turning back to

Drew and giving him a look that seemed to imply she wasn't sure about his sense of judgment.

"How smart have you become exactly?" Drew wondered aloud as he scratched behind Taco's ears. The little dog yipped softly as he curled into a ball on Drew's lap.

Luke had other ideas, and the seraph forced Drew to spar with him. The dogs watched with fascination. They loved the regular refreshing rains that Drew would cast. Luke had decided that Drew needed to practice dodging, which started with teaching him how to fall. Drew wasn't sure how there was so much involved in learning how to fall. The Coast Guard trained him to throw a punch and use pressure points to force compliance while you subdued someone, but most of those techniques were designed to take down humans. They didn't work against things like lubberkin or treants.

The treants, in particular, were what Luke was training him to avoid. The tree-like creatures used their long branches like whips that could be extended at the outside range of Drew's short-distance spells. The seraph had him practice dodging projectiles while shooting lightning bolts at targets around the small grove. Hours later, Drew called the seraph off; the mental energy required of spending hours dodging rocks thrown at him had been exhausting.

There was a strange disconnect between his physical tiredness, almost none, and how tired he felt. Zoey and most of the pack still hadn't returned from wherever they had gone, but there were still more than a dozen dogs around the grove. In a demi haze, he threw tennis balls for them, working off some of his physical energy while he let his mind catch up. Luke cooked them some dinner; there was still plenty of leftover meat from the night's hunt. A pot placed on the large stone slab was used to make a stew, storing the excess in his pouch despite the whining from the dogs.

A storm started brewing as the sun was nearing the horizon. Drew found a series of ladder rungs nailed into the largest of the trees, and climbing up, he watched the black clouds slowly eat away at the golden glow on the horizon. He climbed down far enough to have a clear shot to the ground and then used gravitas to fall to the floor, working on the control needed to land gently without having to tumble, something the earlier descent had told him he hadn't yet perfected.

"Looks like it's going to be pretty bad," Drew told Luke, who nodded.

"Well, the shelter here should keep us mostly dry," Luke said, looking over the wide rooftop area. The nests of bedding leftover from Lincoln and the dogs had a specific scent to them, and the two men didn't particularly need to sleep, so they hung up a few of the larger blankets to block the wind and rain.

The two of them settled into what was one of the worst nights Drew had experienced since the Advent. The shelter didn't even keep them dry. The rain coming down almost horizontally from the biting wind managed to find every hole in their makeshift blanket wall. By the time they realized how cold it would be, all of their firewood was already soaked through. The two men retreated into a large hole in the ground that was mostly dry. The dogs piled in around them kept them moderately warm but filled the space with the scent of wet dog hair.

Chapter Thirty-Seven – Franjean

Just before dawn, Drew had enough of the wet dog smell and he wiggled his way out of the pile. The wind and rain had died down to a calm drizzle an hour earlier. Everything was still muddy and the seats were still soaked from the rain. Sadie and Taco followed him out of the pile, only to lay down in a mostly dry spot between tree roots. The dark reminded him of early mornings taking Zoey here before having to report to watch at 0600. As he sat in the dark, he realized that they should have headed back to the apartment where they would have been out of the weather at least.

Zoey had yet to turn back up from wherever she had gone with the fae. It was clear that they had some power over her; Drew was nervous as to what exactly it was, though. As he paced in the pre-dawn light, he pulled out the communication stone. He could feel it warming up, giving the signal that it was charged and pinging the other stone. Drew kept it in one hand as he struggled to get breakfast ready. Luke saw his efforts and warmed up some more of the stew from the day before using the strange stone that Lincoln was using to cook all the meat.

"What do you think this is?" Drew asked, looking at the stone on the ground.

"Probably something like Katie's glow stones. Although it is an unusual ability, I would be curious to know what sort of person got a xatherite that could create something like this," Luke said, with a shrug. Drew was sometimes amazed at how Luke just accepted all of the strangeness around them, and he wondered if he would ever get to that point.

Eating breakfast with one hand was difficult, but the fact that no one at the stadium had picked up the line for what must have been at least an hour was even more disconcerting. He wished that he had Daryl here so that they could send the bird to check on them. He had been pretty good about not thinking of

Katie since they had left, but last night in the rain had been a constant reminder that she wasn't with them. Drew sat and brooded while Luke trained him to use his shoal sense.

This meant that occasionally Luke would throw something at him, the idea being that shoal sense should tell him if there is danger coming at him and he needed to learn to listen to that just like he did his other senses. It was a mildly annoying experience mostly because as soon as he got invested in the book, a tennis ball would start racing toward his head, a continuation of the dodge training from the night before. Finally having had enough, Drew put the book down and stood up to stretch. Looking around as his limbs creaked, it was a few hours after sunrise.

"I feel like Zoey should be back by now," Drew said, looking around. The dogs were all still here for the most part. One or two were sniffing around the park. "Are we going to have enough food for all if the pack doesn't bring back more meat?" Luke shook his head, having already realized this would be a problem. "Alright, I need to do something more active. Sitting here and waiting is killing me. Can we just go hunt some of the squirrels or something?"

"There should not be much damage in that, a few squirrels should be fine," Luke said and then he grinned. "But no using ranged spells. Squirrels aren't dangerous enough to be a threat to your mana shield. So let us train your weapon summoning skill."

Drew groaned. He remembered how his first encounter with apocalypse squirrels had ended with scrapes and wounds that he had needed Bill to heal. Still, he had grown a lot since then, plus other than acid arrow he probably wouldn't leave much meat if he used his other spells. Which meant that it was a mostly practical restriction. It took a few moments of explaining to the dogs that they were going out to get them food. But Taco seemed to understand and he yipped at Sadie until she seemed to realize it was okay and then she barked at the rest of the dogs and they obeyed.

The squirrels were easy to locate. They were in the same general area they had seen them before. Drew separated from Luke, who had pulled out a spear of his own. That caused Drew to blink, since he'd never seen the other man with it, but he said it would be better for hunting.

Casting arsenal, Drew was surrounded by ghostly red images of weapons in a variety of different shapes and sizes. Picking up a rock, he threw it at one of the squirrels. He grinned as the squirrel dodged and his rock hit the tree behind it. That caused four squirrels to stop chasing each other and focus their attention on him. Another rock followed the first and the squirrels began chittering angrily at him. A third rock was enough to cause them to rush him.

The first squirrel was skewered as it charged head first into the point of a rapier, the thin weapon neatly impaling three fourths of its length into the beast. That was enough to cause the second to skitter to a halt only to have an axe cut its head off in one clean sweep. The third seemed confused by this turn of events, but dodged out of the way as a claymore attacked. Drew had Robbi's blood sword in hand and he swiped at the fourth at the same time as a short spear tried to pierce it. His sword cut slightly into the thick fur around the beast's left shoulder. Drew could tell that he had hurt it, but not much.

The scent of blood pushed the creatures into a frenzy and the uninjured one leapt at Drew. Only to try to twist away as an arming sword slashed toward its body, cutting deeply into the spine. The fourth one jumped forward as well, still not understanding that the arsenal was operating on its own. This time the spear impaled it through the body and pinned it against the ground, where it struggled for a second until Drew lopped its head off with the blood sword. The squelching sound of his sword passing through the muscle and bone of the creature's spine caused him to wince, pulling the blade slightly off and making a jagged cut.

The claymore severed the head off the remaining injured squirrel and Drew looked around in amazement. He was amazed at what an upgrade to a crystal he hardly ever used had done for his combat capabilities. At no point had he even been close to being injured, the spell acting as an impenetrable wall of flashing red light that easily cut through the soft squirrel flesh. He stared at the squirrel he had killed with his own hands and frowned. Suddenly a slight whine from behind him caused him to look up to see Zoey standing off the side, the rest of the dogs surrounding her. What was even more surprising was the bark-skinned little man sitting on her back.

"Quite good-tricksy!" The little man almost giggled. "Good hunter-provider you is!" Drew raised his sword, prepared to defend himself even as Luke walked up next to him. His spear was held at the ready. Seeing their response, the little man barked out a laugh. "Franjean mean you no bad-harm! Franjean am brownie. Pack leader-dog Zoey vouch-nominate you as human-man that raise-guide her. Franjean is come to invite-greet you to safe-happy grove to join-protect other humans!" It took Drew a moment to parse through what the brownie had said with his strange double words.

"Why would we come with you?" Drew asked without hesitation. He glanced back to Luke to make sure he wasn't about to attack despite their earlier conversation. A nod from Luke was enough to satisfy him that he wouldn't attack unless the brownie did first. This seemed to flummox Franjean and he hopped down from Zoey's back and began pacing around a tree.

"They question-ask why they should go-come to the safe-happy grove. The pack-leader spoke-asked for Franjean to travel-visit and speak-talk to them. Franjean saw them kill-slay several monsters without pain-injury. The must-needs be very strong-mighty. None of the native-local humans have questioned-asked why they should venture-sojourn to the safe-happy grove." Franjean turned and marched up to Drew. As he got closer, the weapons of his arsenal shifted, preparing to strike the brownie.

Franjean seemed to realize that venturing forward would be a bad idea, and he paused. Looking from Drew to the floating weapons and then to Luke. Up close, the brownie's form was more obvious, the bark was thick and cracked like a white oak or ponderosa pine. Thick strands of hair curled out of his ears, the only soft looking part of its entire body, and the brownie began stroking them as he considered what to say to Drew. It was somewhat difficult to take him seriously; his face was that of a wrinkled old man, but he was only as tall as Drew's waist.

"Valorous-intrepid you are! Franjean greets you as fellow warriors-soldiers! Franjean requests-implores you to come-follow Franjean to safe-happy grove. So that Franjean can prove-show to the gardener-guide that native-locals are good-worth. Many-some of the dark-shade fae think-speak to the opposite, and your presence-being would go far-long to confirm-verify Franjean's beliefs-hopes." The brownie was almost jumping up and down in his excitement. Although that could just be how they were, given that he hadn't stopped jittering around like a ten-year-old on caffeine since he arrived.

He glanced at Luke, who shrugged slightly to indicate that it was his decision. Drew could read the tension in the seraph, and he was clearly not happy to be so close to the fae and not fighting it. With a sigh, Drew glanced over at Zoey who had kept her distance while the arsenal shifted around him.

"You think we should go to this grove?" Drew asked the dog, who wagged her tail and hopped a little, the sign she used to give him for an affirmation of his question. It had been adorable when she was regular-sized, but in her current car-size the jump actually caused the nearby trees to shake from the kinetic impact of her paws. "Alright. Franjean, we'll go with you. But we need to feed the rest of the dogs before we go." Drew picked up two of the squirrels while Luke bent and picked up the other two. One of the smaller dogs, about the size of a great dane from before the Advent, grabbed the decapitated head.

Drew winced slightly as the dog sent blood spraying around in its enthusiasm. Drew shifted both the squirrels so that he was holding them by their tails and away from him so that the blood and other fluids wouldn't drip onto him. Franjean climbed back on Zoey's back, his short arms grasping the fur and pulling himself up with an ease that Drew was sure he would be unable to match.

"Faster-turbo!" Franjean said as soon as he was perched between her shoulders, his short little fingers pointing forward. Zoey ignored the command and followed along with Drew, staying just behind him as she had been trained to do. They walked in what Drew assumed was silence for the little brownie, who was grumbling under his breath too quietly for Drew to hear.

As soon as they arrived at the camp, Zoey barked twice and all the dogs came to greet her. She then turned around and took a few steps back to the south. Turning slightly to make sure that Drew was following, she led them through vine-covered paths. The pack of dogs around them was more than enough to scare off any predators they might have encountered along the way. They only had to go a few blocks, cutting down past an apartment complex to hit the north side of the country club.

There was evidence of a fence, and what might have once been a tree line blocking the greens, but the rapid growth of the area had turned it into a formidable barrier. As the dogs approached, Franjean hopped off Zoey's back again and raced forward, bowing respectfully to several of the trees and saying something too softly for Drew to catch. Immediately, two treants stepped aside, their branches pulling others with them and revealing an open path through the barrier woods.

The area immediately beyond the trees contained a path of compacted dirt that led through a field of what Drew was pretty sure were potatoes, their leaves and stems turning yellow, unseasonably ready for harvest. There were dozens of humans wandering through the fields, pulling the ripe potatoes from the ground for others to wheel back to a central pavilion. They looked up at Drew and Luke entering with no small amount of interest, their eyes focusing on the armor and weapons in their hands. They didn't seem… afraid, more excited at the idea of new humans. Franjean waved to them all.

"No time-opportunity to talk-chat! Must take-guide these warrior-soldiers to the gardener-guide! They will be at the dwelling-houses later-after! Back to the work-labor of the day-light!" Franjean shout's had the opposite effect, however, and the humans all stood up to get a better look at the two new humans. From the few snatches of conversation he heard, the sticking point was that Franjean had called them warrior-soldiers. The humans didn't stop them and the dogs followed along happily as they wandered through the fairways turned fields.

They passed through what must have been four different holes on the course, travelling the short width until they came to a central area. Here were the massive tree houses that Daryl had described. They were grown several stories above the ground, leaving the area below open for what was clearly the training area for the fae soldiers.

Lubberkin and brownies worked with dogs, cats, and other wild animals. Drew was sure he had seen a pack of badgers in the mix. They all stopped to stare as Franjean proudly paraded them through the training area, shouting for them to make way for the warrior-soldiers who were there to visit the gardener-guide. Glancing behind him, Drew could see that no few of the fae had stopped their training and were following along, minus their animal companions who seemed happy to take a break. Zoey followed along with them, staying at Drew's side but the rest of the dogs peeled off into the rest of the camp, clearly familiar with the place.

They were led to a thick grove of trees, the glowing vines covering them casting the otherwise dimness under the canopy above into a myriad of reds, blues, and violets. Standing near an overgrown entrance of plants were two plant women. They looked somewhat like nymphs; long, smooth skin in a pale shade of green was visible under thick bark armor. Instead of hair, each had a thick patch of violet flowers that started between their eyes and flowed all the way down to their lower back.

"Greetings-welcoming to the guards-protectors of the gardener-guide!" Franjean shouted happily. "Franjean has brought warrior-soldiers of this dirt-source to prove-manifest their strength-vigor!" The brownie's words caused a bit of an uproar among the gathered fae.

Drew and Luke shared a glance that indicated neither were happy about this course of events.

CHAPTER THIRTY-EIGHT – SHANGHAI'D

"Lady Noli'ay'niara is in seclusion, preparing for the arrival of the Harbinger of Blight. She has deferred all non-mission-essential questions about the combat capabilities of the natives to the war council," one of the two dryad's near the entrance said. Her voice had a strange rasp to it that made it sound like leaves being rubbed together to form words. Strange, but not unpleasant. Drew had a feeling that he was the Harbinger of Blight, which was a pretty cool title as far as things went.

At the dryad's words, a large ball of fur stepped forward. Drew knew that this must be a lubberkin. Black and brown fur covered the entire creature in inches of greasy and matted hair, and it carried with it the scent of compost. Drew plugged his nose to keep himself from gagging as the lubberkin inspected him, the coal black eyes hard and inscrutable under fist thick brows.

"You can fight, eh?" The lubberkin's voice reminded Drew of climbing up a shale scree. Although he couldn't quite figure out what about it made him think of that particular experience. The lubberkin snorted. "Come with me." The lubberkin turned away from the gateway guarded by the dryads and walked to the southeast, away from the direction they had come. A glance at Franjean told him that the little brownie was not enthused about the rejection. His rapid muttering took on a sharper tone, although it was at a much quieter volume than before.

"No," Drew said after a moment, and the grove went silent. Even Franjean's muttering stopped and he turned to Drew with a look of shock on his face. Drew dropped the squirrels he was holding in his hands and turned back to look at the dryads. They looked at his bloodstained hands with obvious disdain, but Drew just wanted to make sure that they weren't going to interfere. When they made no movement, Drew turned back to the lubberkin.

"Franjean can lead us to the rest of human fighters. I'll not follow some smelly ball of fur that doesn't even have the sense of decorum to introduce himself to me before ordering me about." Drew's words caused an audible gasp from the assembled faeries.

The lubberkin turned around, his stumpy legs advancing on Drew rapidly. In an instant, Drew had his sword out and pointed at the foul creature. Zoey had advanced as well, a low rumble echoing through her barrel chest. Luke was on his other side, his spear held in a reverse grip that would allow him to swing his ball and chain rapidly.

"No contend-fighting!" Franjean shouted, his tiny hand reaching up and resting on Zoey's nose. Drew wasn't sure how the little brownie had moved so fast, but he was between the humans and the lubberkin in a heartbeat. His other palm held out, horizontally, as if to show that he held nothing in his hands to the lubberkin.

"Fine, let the twig take them. I have better things to do anyway." The lubberkin turned around and the smell of sulfur filled the air. Drew was pretty sure the disgusting thing had just crop dusted them. He fought the urge to complain, not wanting to give the furball more ammunition. Zoey was the only one of their group who did acknowledge the smell, and that seemed involuntary, a sneeze that sent liquid flying at the back of the lubberkin.

"Keep your mutt under control," the lubberkin growled even as it climbed onto the back of a cat that didn't seem quite big enough to carry him. But then again, Drew had no idea how thick his body was under the thick layer of hair. The cat quickly jumped away, leaving the four of them in the middle of the collection of sidhe.

"Come-follow!" Franjean whispered urgently as he jumped onto Zoey's back and then nudged her off to the south. Drew and Luke followed at a quick pace. As they went, it became apparent that there were a number of different sections of the tree city. They had entered through one that was predominantly brownie controlled, passing through a lubberkin one quickly, before arriving at what could only be the human fighter portion.

To Drew's surprise, Sarah and Bill were waiting for them. Sarah's group awareness clearly warning them that they were getting close, Drew shook his head slightly at Sarah's questioning glance. They weren't the only ones waiting for them. A few dozen humans were training with a random collection of weapons and powers. Mostly they used wooden spears and swords, Drew wasn't sure if they were provided by the sidhe as a replacement to metal weapons, or just training weapons. For the most part, they looked to be wearing padded clothing, although it was clearly something the sidhe had given them.

Franjean led them to a central area, where a canvas tent had been set up. A number of desks were set up, but only one of them was manned. An older man, whose left leg ended just above where the knee should have been, with a thick, brown, cocoon-looking bandage around his lower thigh. The man looked up as they entered the tent and gave them an appraising look. His eyes focused on Drew's collar, where the single silver bar of his rank was visible for a moment and then he stood up and gave Drew a salute.

"Good afternoon... Lieutenant?" The lack of identifier on the rest of his equipment made guessing what rank to call him a bit difficult.

"LTJG Michalik, US Coast Guard," Drew responded, returning the salute. "At ease... soldier?" Drew had to guess at the man's service as well, since he wasn't wearing anything

"Ahh, sorry, Sir. I'm Sergeant First Class Reed, US Army. Out of the Pentagon. Or at least I was, back before Advent." The man picked up a crutch, nodding to Franjean. "I've got them, Ranger."

"Good-excellent. Franjean will come-visit soon. Franjean will ask-request audience-meeting with the gardener-guide for warrior-soldiers," the small brownie said, not bothering to dismount from Zoey. He patted her shoulder in an attempt to guide her away. She gave Drew a sidelong look.

"It's okay, Zoey, I'll be here if you need me," Drew said and the dog narrowed her eyes for a moment and then nudged her head against Drew's hand before turning to follow Franjean's orders, bounding off into the rest of the camp.

"Sounds like you've got quite the story," Reed said. "You can drop those kills on the desk there, I'll get some cooks over to add them to chow. Assuming you're fine with that?" Reed pointed to the squirrels both Luke and Drew were still carrying.

"Sure, we were gonna feed the dogs, but I assume they'll be fine here," Drew said, setting the carcasses on the table he designated and then rubbing his hands clean of the blood.

Reed nodded and then motioned for them to follow him as he crutched over to the back of the tent and then kicked it open, revealing a lounge-like area. Several couches filled the room, but there was only one other occupant, a woman who was asleep on one of them. "Take a seat, I can tell you two have got a story and Captain DeVoss over there is bound to want to be the one to hear it."

The sound of Reed's voice was enough to wake the woman up and she sat up with a jolt, looking around with bleary eyes. "I'm awake," she said as she looked around the room in partial confusion. She was wearing the same earth-toned padded clothing that all the humans in the fighting area were using. Two silver bars were sewn into her collar, but it was clear that she was a few years younger than Drew, in her late twenties. "New blood?" she questioned, giving Drew and Luke a once over.

"Yes, ma'am. Lieutenant Michalik, USCG. One of the brownie rangers brought them in just now," Reed said with a grin as he hobbled over to a mess station and poured himself a cup of what looked like coffee. That made Drew smile. Trust the military to figure out how to get coffee in the apocalypse.

"A brownie brought them straight here?" DeVoss said with a frown. "You must have impressed it. There are some jugs behind the mess you can clean up with, and some mud if you're looking for a wakeup," she said, noticing the stains on their hands. Drew took the opportunity to clean his hands more thoroughly, but decided he would be better off without whatever the semi-solid substance in the coffee pot was. Drew could feel the captain's eyes on him as they washed up.

"That's mighty interesting looking armor you have there. Matching stuff too, and post-Advent make if I'm not mistaken. What's odd is we had another couple people come in just yesterday with similar armor." The captain's voice was deceptively calm, but there was an unmistakable undercurrent of violence in her tone. Drew took a moment to process what she was saying and then sighed. "Now, one group of people with similar armor just means they got lucky, but two? Two sounds like an organization. So... how about you tell me who you are?"

"Yes, the people who came in yesterday are part of our team. We sent them in to recon and see what state you guys were in before we went all die hard trying to rescue you." Drew returned the captain's gaze with one of his own. "You don't look like you need rescuing, though. We have a settlement in Nat's Park across the river. We're scouts sent to investigate the jungle, we saw the meteor and assumed the worst."

The captain narrowed her eyes at him for a moment as if considering his words. "That means you're with the Harbinger?

We don't know much about them, just that it has all the faeries in a tizzy. Especially whatever you guys did the day before last."

"Ahh, yes, the Red Mage is there. We've been taking over nodes and created a safe habitat," Drew said with a frown.

"Red Mage, eh?" DeVoss eyed the ruby hilted sword at his side and quirked an eyebrow. "Like the ones that use swords and magic at the same time?" When Drew shook his head, she sighed.

"No, he's all magic. A lot of ranged attack spells." Drew said, trying to give a self-deprecating grin. "Is that why Franjean couldn't get an audience with the gardener?"

"Ahh. Well, yes, although honestly I think that's Grotesque's doing more than anything else. He leads the war council and he'd probably stage a coup d'état if he had any chance of matching Lady Noli in combat." DeVoss got up and fixed a cup for herself. Drew only then realized that Sergeant Ross had vacated the room at some point.

"Who is Grotesque?" Drew asked, slightly confused.

"Oh, he's a lubberkin, short, fuzzy guy with a bad attitude. Real name is something like Gor'ah'tec'ke but we all just call him Grotesque, fits him pretty well. Nasty little fellow, and one hell of an ambusher, little fuzzball rides around on a house cat the size of a cougar. I'm glad he's on our side, but…" DeVoss shuddered, clearly reminded of something unpleasant the lubberkin had done.

"I think we met him. Probably pissed him off too," Drew said with a frown, and DeVoss winced. "Hopefully he isn't the type to hold a grudge."

"I wouldn't count on that." DeVoss sat back down and looked them over. "I'm going to assume that you two know what the hell you're doing. If you can survive getting here from Nat's Park, you're better off than, well… every human we have here." She sighed then glanced around. It didn't escape Drew's attention that had to specify human combatants.

"We're not in Air Force accommodations," DeVoss continued, "but I've lived in on-base housing that is worse. I'll make sure you're bunked in with the rest of your group. I'll have you out on patrols starting tomorrow. You'll be part of Alpha company, they've got the morning patrols."

"Sounds like you've fully cast your lot in with the faeries," Drew accused.

"I'm not going to sugar coat it for you. Most of us would be dead without them, and those of us who were alive would be hungry. Call it desperation or just common sense, but, yes, we've thrown in with the fae." DeVoss locked eyes with Drew and the two stared at each other for a moment before she looked away.

"Look, I'm not saying I wouldn't prefer to stick with human kind, but you dance with the one that brought you. And right now, we wouldn't survive without them." DeVoss looked up long enough to see Drew nod at her words.

"I can understand making sacrifices to survive," Drew said, slightly grudgingly.

"Tell you what, go out with them, get to know them a little bit and you can make your own opinion. We send out half a dozen humans with a group of three-to-four of the faeries. Usually brownies or lubberkin, and their pack of beasts. They're both animal tamers of some variety, dogs and cats mostly. Although they've got some squirrels and even a…" DeVoss shrugged. "Pack? I don't know what you call a group of badgers."

"I think they're called a clan," Drew offered helpfully and DeVoss just shrugged.

"Yeah, a clan of badgers. Anyway, if you impressed Franjean enough that he tried to take you to Lady Noli, I'm sure he'll want to go out with you tomorrow, and you can get a better read on him then. He's the leader of the brownies, as far as we can tell. Their pecking order is dictated by the size of their bound animals. And Zoey is the biggest thing around."

Drew frowned slightly at that. "She was my dog before Advent. Is the bond… reversible?"

"No shit? Badass must run in your family. She's sweet as can be until she's on a hunt, then she's an unholy terror. Hell, Zoey killed a crawler that would have killed me just the other day. As for the reversible thing… you'd have to talk to Franjean." DeVoss rubbed at her wrist absently, probably a reminder of the wound that the crawler had given her.

"Where did you all come from? What were you doing before the asteroid hit? What's a crawler?" Drew asked, trying to steer the conversation away from Zoey. Having just reunited with her, only to realize that she was probably now bound to Franjean… he wasn't entirely prepared to unpack what all that meant to him.

"Crawlers are skeletons or zombies that are missing their legs. Not really a problem, but they tend to play dead until the combat moves past them and then attack from the rear, pretty nasty little ambush predators," DeVoss said while she thought about how to respond to his other question. "Most of us were in… isolated little pockets throughout Arlington. The world went a little crazy for a bit and neighborhoods started banding together into collectives to conserve resources. Most people just hunkered down to try to survive; some of the more aggressive types turned everyone a bit xenophobic.

"I didn't see any of that, me and a few of the others were with a group that were in the Pentagon when it all went down." DeVoss looked down at her mug, turning it around. "There are still a bunch there. The robots that took over the node protected us, but also kept us contained. I was part of a group that was sent to look for a way to escape. That happened right after the seed ship landed. The elves say that they'll help, but they refuse to take action until the Harbinger comes. They say that they don't want to interfere too much with native affairs." Turning to look at Drew, she quirked an eyebrow.

"Where is he, by the way? The elves are… well, it's hard to say if they hate or love him." DeVoss glanced from Luke to Drew. The two of them shared a look as well; Luke inclined his head to Drew, letting him take the lead.

Drew weighed his options. He didn't really know anything about this woman. But at the same time, he didn't want to have to live a life of secrecy, his time working in the secret compartmentalized information facility, the SCIF, at headquarters had proven how little interest he had in not being able to talk about his life.

"He's close. We're here to assess their threat level. Once we know more, he'll make himself known. Why do you think they came here?" Drew asked the young captain and she leaned back, considering him.

"I think Lady Noli wants to form an alliance, the unseelies…" DeVoss trailed off, then gave a hand gesture that Drew interpreted as 'iffy.' "I get the feeling that half of them would be happy to kill him and be done with it. Well, I'm sure you're tired, and I've got a lot of work to do as well, so I'll take you to your people and let you settle in. We'll talk tomorrow." Polishing off the rest of her mug, she guided Drew and Luke to a treehouse that was fifty feet off the ground, accessible via a treant-powered elevator.

"You'll be joining our command cadre, if that's alright with you?" DeVoss said before she left. "We're short on officers, we'll keep your group together. But I'll be sending some of our… greener soldiers out with you."

"Why? You don't know me…" Drew trailed off, looking at DeVoss who just shrugged.

"We need bodies. You guys are capable enough to get here through Arlington Cemetery, that's enough qualification for me." She turned around and walked away, not giving Drew a chance to ask her any further questions.

CHAPTER THIRTY-NINE – TREEHOUSE

Inside the treehouse was set up like a Hogwarts' bedchamber. The trunk of the tree took up a massive section of the interior, but around it was a sort of common area, although it looked pretty sparse. A few tables and some uncomfortable-looking wooden chairs were the only furniture. Spread out on the outside of the common areas were doors leading into what Drew presumed were the bedrooms. Larger spaces on either side looked to be reserved for bathrooms, although Drew wasn't sure how the sidhe got running water in them. Above them, clear veins of what looked like crystalized sap shed light through the area, which was otherwise closed to the outside.

The entire room looked like it had grown up around the tree rather than been built and Drew wondered just how powerful the skills needed to make this must have been. Luke's powers were limited by the mana density of Earth, and they had increased cooldowns. Either whatever they had used to make the entire area was one big skill that would take a long time to recover, or the sidhe had a level of power that far exceeded what Drew was capable of at the current time.

Without the need to sleep, Drew wasn't sure what exactly he was going to be doing in the space, but he imagined it would look weird if he didn't at least spend the night in here. He and Luke had just finished looking around when the others came in.

"Mr. Drew!" Gary shouted to Drew's surprise, even as he ran over and gave him a hug. Drew awkwardly hugged the kid back, patting him uncomfortably on the shoulder a few times.

"What happened?" Sarah asked, after looking around to make sure that Drew and Luke were the only ones present.

"Franjean, one of the brownies, found us as we were hunting for some meat for the dogs. He insisted we come after seeing arsenal at work," Drew answered and Sarah nodded her head, understanding that he hadn't wanted to fight and they didn't have a good reason not to come otherwise. "What about you guys?" They were wearing the same padded clothing that the others were, Drew and Luke definitely standing out in their navy blue leathers.

"They brought us in. We talked to a walking tree lady who called herself a dryad that gave us new clothing, saying that the leather would offend some of the fae. This stuff isn't really as good and they let us keep our armor, but…" Sarah shrugged to indicate that she hadn't wanted to stand out. "Anyway, they asked us a little bit about our powers and stuff, and put us here in what the locals are calling Warrior's Glade.

"This morning we had some more food, and then they had us working with some of the other teams. Everyone is a bit up in arms, because the faeries are all looking forward to some meeting with the Harbinger of Blight." She inclined her head to Drew who nodded, indicating that he assumed that was their title for a Red Mage. "Anyway, we got put on a short patrol out around the perimeter today, nothing serious. Luke's training sessions are more dangerous, really."

"I told the captain that in-processed us that we were in the Harbinger's group, but he was waiting to see what we thought of the camp," Drew said, looking around the group to see everyone nod their heads. Thankfully Gary had released the hug and Drew motioned for them to all take a seat. "How is everyone doing with mana fatigue?" A quick glance told him that he needed to hit them with a refreshing rain, and began casting the spell. When it was done, he looked around. "What do you all think?"

"Everyone seems to be pretty happy to be here," Bill said and Daryl nodded. "I talked to a few people and they've had faeries healing people, giving them food, everything they could ask for, really. You are required to work while you're here, and no one slacks off. They only have a couple dozen Numb so that's… easier to do, I guess."

"Why so few?" Drew asked.

"The few that made it past the first week got killed before the sidhe landed. They're in about the same state as those of us in the DIA building were before you came along," Bill answered, and Drew nodded along with the chief's words. "Honestly, they're only slightly worse off than the stadium is. The undead seem fairly contained, they have plenty of food, and the people are generally pretty safe."

Being reminded of the stadium caused Drew to pull out the communication stone, holding it in his hand to indicate that he wanted to speak to Hoeffecker. A part of him was very concerned that it had been several days since the last time he had been able to talk to the stadium. He could feel the warm pulse that told him the stone had activated.

"I'm fairly sure—" Drew cut off when he saw several people he didn't know enter the treehouse common area.

"You must be this new hotshot," the man at the front of the group said. He was tall, and judging by the visible veins on his arms, had clearly been some sort of lifter before Advent.

"Oh shut up, Marc," the lady behind him said, slapping Marc's shoulder as she stepped past him. They were all wearing the padded jackets that seemed common among the humans at the grove. "Hi, I'm Lisa. Captain DeVoss assigned us to your team. The big lug of a man there is Marc; he was training to be an MMA fighter before this, and still thinks he's tough enough to be our front line fighter. I'm pretty good with a bow, used to do archery as a hobby. Jay throws axes and Esben is the one with the spear."

"Throws axes?" Drew questioned.

"They come back!" Jay announced with a grin, demonstrating by throwing an axe into the air and then having it reappear back in his hand.

"Well, that's… better than just throwing it away," Sarah muttered darkly.

"It would be, if he could hit what he was throwing it at more than half the time," Lisa said with a grin. "But he is getting better."

"So, you guys know what's going on?" Lisa asked. Drew glanced at Sarah, the two sharing a questioning look. "All the rangers have been running around for the last hour. They aren't even talking about the Harbinger anymore. We figure something big is going down."

Drew shook his head.

"We didn't see anything of particular note on our way here," Sarah said. "I mean, other than the massive graveyard full of undead."

"Oh, that's old news." Lisa laughed. That broke the ice and they spent the rest of the evening getting to know the four new additions to the team. None of them were exceptionally skilled, although they were good enough to survive this long into the apocalypse. When Drew asked Esben about their group, he found out that all four of them had lived in a set of condos and were the last survivors from their group. Drew could read between the lines and stopped asking what happened to everyone else.

Drew sat in his bed and tried to sleep. It was the first time he had tried to go to sleep since… he didn't even remember the last time he had intentionally gone to sleep. A week ago? The night that Katie broke up with him? Had he slept then?

Tossing and turning had never been his strong suit, and he got up in frustration after close to an hour. He made his way out of the treehouse. Instead of going down, he opted to continue climbing. Their residence was the lowest on the tree, but there were two more as he climbed further up. On top of the third, he took a moment to look out over the camp. The scent of woodsmoke on the air felt out of place as he looked over the overgrown suburb of Arlington. He listened to the wind for an hour, his thoughts tumbling over and over.

Holding the communication stone, he wondered how bad things must be at the stadium for Hoeffecker to not answer his call. From up here, he could see that there was indeed some commotion at the command tent he had met DeVoss at earlier. A significant number of people came and went as he watched. Shoal sense gave him a slight reverberation, and he turned to see a cloaked figure climbing up the ladder behind him.

"I do not mean to startle thee." The dark hood made it impossible to see the figure's face, but her voice was soft and delicate.

"I'm sorry, just getting some night air," Drew said. "Am I not allowed to be up here?"

"Thou art free to go to any of the public places in the camp," the hooded figure said, and Drew relaxed back against the railing. The figure stood next to him, and they lapsed into companionable silence.

"I hear thou art part of the Harbinger of Blight's inner circle." Drew was almost surprised when she spoke again. Her strangely stilted words reminded him of old scripture.

"Yeah, like I told Captain DeVoss, we're in his party." Drew turned to study the form of the woman next to him, her slim shoulders were about the only thing he could tell about her, everything but her chin in deep shadow.

"What is he like?" It sounded like an innocent question, but he opened up mana sight. Unlike a human's, who had cloud-like auras, all the fae seemed to have veins of mana coursing through their bodies around a central heart or seed.

The hooded figure's core was violet, with veins spreading throughout in a delicate pattern that focused mostly around her stomach before shifting to her hands and feet, and a few stray threads circled around her head like a crown. Most of the mana veins were orange, yellow, or blue. The overlap seemed to only enhance her beauty, lending a sense of power and majesty that was lacking to his unaugmented eyes.

"Uh, you'll just have to meet him. I should probably go back down," Drew said.

The figure nodded as Drew went to the ladder and let himself down.

As he was lowering himself down, Drew heard the woman whisper, "I shall." There was something like a promise in that which sent shivers down his spine. He went straight back to his bedroom and sat in his bed, considering the woman's aura. If the fae had more people like that…

Drew frowned. He could fight them, but what was the point? They seemed to be taking care of humans. They were even training them to be better fighters. The only negative he had was Luke's prejudice. But Earth wasn't part of the Protectorate's war. Not yet, at least. Drew decided that he wasn't interested in joining it without some provocation on the fae's part.

His mind made up, he settled in to reading a book. Just before dawn, he was startled away from his book by the sound of frantic knocking at the entrance to their lounge area. With a confused look, they all stood up. Bill was closest to the door and he opened it, revealing Franjean's overly excited face.

"Greetings-salutations!" the little brownie nearly shouted as Bill opened the door. Looking through the door, Drew could see that there were other people with him, but he wasn't sure who, or even what they were, since there was such a variety of species among the sidhe.

"Unfortunately, we have not the time for your ebullience, Franjean." A dryad stepped forward and past Franjean into the room. She looked around at them and then stomped her foot on the floor. "All now hear the words of the grove tender."

A third figure glided into the room, and overshadowed the group with her almost unnatural beauty. She didn't so much walk as glide into the room. She stood a little over five-foot with a symmetrical and otherworldly beauty that triggered an almost uncanny-valley-like response in him. She looked around the room, leveling her glowing green eyes on each of them, before stopping on Drew.

"I bid you greetings, Drew Michalik. I am Noli'ay'niara, daughter of the first grove." Noli bowed her head slightly. "Forgive me mine trespass upon you at this early hour. I had hoped to give thee more time to accomplish thine desires, but alas, tis not to be. Thy traversal of the graveyard hath stirred up the lich within. An army of his undead minions marches to battle with us now. I regret to so forcefully push thy hand, but the world is not willing to give us the time thy dance requests. Wilt thou stand with my grove and protect thy countrymen?" Noli'ay'niara's voice had a slight reverberation that just added to the surreal nature of everything she did.

Drew pushed his book back into his pouch of holding and looked the group over. That they had known he was the red mage was not unexpected, but it was clear that she knew who he was earlier than they had anticipated her knowing. An army of the undead marching on humans was, of course, something that he would help defend against. To mana sight, it was clear that she was the same as the hooded figure he met the night before.

"I thought the lich couldn't leave the graveyard?" Drew asked, even as the rest of his team started changing out of the padded gear they had been given and into the leather armor.

"Thou speakest true. A lesser undead will be leading the assault. I'm not entirely sure what though," Noli answered.

"Daryl?" Drew said, turning to the scout.

"On it," Daryl said even as Drew turned to Noli, considering her.

There were a dozen questions he wanted to ask the elf, but he couldn't think of what to ask first. He wanted to know why they were here, but that didn't really seem like the kind of conversation you had while preparing for battle. Finally, he decided that he would sit her down for a long conversation later, but he needed to focus on the oncoming horde first. He had seen the innumerable forces that were massing at the graveyard.

"I don't know you, and you don't have my trust yet. But we can discuss why you are here after we defeat this horde. I'm going to need a vantage point to attack from. What should I call you? Because I am not going to be able to repeat your whole name."

"Thou may call me Noli. Follow me," Noli answered then glanced at the others who were still in the middle of changing. "I can lead thee to an observation post, and have Franjean guide the rest of thy team to join us. It would perhaps be expedient to move with utmost haste. My garden is not yet strong enough to repulse such a force."

"Daryl, Luke, with me. The rest of you get geared up and join us as soon as possible," Drew ordered. The scout was halfway changed, but they didn't have time for him to finish.

Noli nodded and the two dryad escorts left the space. She gestured for Drew to follow her as she swept out of the treehouse. The six of them shimmied down the rope ladder that led to their house. An agitated Zoey paced around the area; she bounded up to Drew upon seeing him and butted her head against his chest.

"Hey Zoey, I'm going to go to an observation post with the elf, Franjean will be joining us." Drew said, scratching her thick head with both hands. She whined slightly but stopped when Noli said something in a language that the system did not interpret.

"I have told her that thou wilt be within her sights for the duration of the fight," Noli said and the dog sat down, looking up at the treehouse expectantly.

"We'll be fine, Zoey," Drew said, scratching under her ear for a moment before turning to follow Noli and the dryads. They were led through the camp; humans and fae alike turned to look at them. There was a nervous energy. The fae were moving about with an urgency that the humans were picking up on. To Drew's surprise, DeVoss approached them, giving Noli a salute that she responded to with an incline of her head. The captain was clearly trying to avoid Drew's gaze and he got the sense that she felt slightly guilty.

"We're ready and waiting, just give us the signal, ma'am," DeVoss told Noli.

"Thou hast done well," the elf said, turning to Drew. "I believe thou hast met Sergeant DeVoss; she will be leading the human segment of the defense." Drew nodded his head in understanding. "Sergeant, please come with us. Sub-Lieutenant Michalik will be in charge of the overall defense of the settlement; we are going to the command post now."

Drew frowned. Noli had used his system-assigned rank rather than his American rank, and he assumed she had done the same for DeVoss. Yet another question that he didn't have a proper answer for. DeVoss fell in behind them, staying apace with Luke.

It was apparent that they were heading to the north side of the encampment, particularly a tree that stood twice as tall as those around it, taller even than the ones in the center of the elf camp that had the tree houses built into them. As they got to the bottom, Noli gestured and a collection of vines dropped down from the canopy above.

"Put thy feet in the loops, my vines will carry thee to thy vantage point," Noli said and Drew could see that there were loops at the bottom of the vines that they could step into, as well as loops at about shoulder height to grab on to. Doing as requested, the vines seemed to slither, contracting, and Drew's stomach fell slightly as they accelerated toward the treetop. Slowing down only as they got to a large platform that seemed to have grown out of the tree near the top of the tree's bough.

Only Noli and the humans had made the ascent with him, and Drew looked out to the north, where the setting sun was casting the former town of Arlington in a golden glow. Drew didn't need Daryl to tell him they were in trouble. It was clearly visible from this vantage. A black fog was rolling south from the cemetery, and in the shadow of its passing, a massive army was assembled in ragged rows.

CHAPTER FORTY – BATTLE

There were so many undead that Drew couldn't even begin to try to count their number. Thousands? Hundreds of thousands? They were an unrecognizable mass of bones and decayed flesh. Even from this distance, there was an almost palpable aura of malice that pulsed from the encroaching undead in waves. Each rank of undead was headed by three or four massive, shambling figures. To his mind, these were some sort of amalgamation of smaller forms, and he mentally labeled them as bone golems. Each of the bone golems stood three to five times the height of the skeleton soldiers around them.

Between Drew's position and to the north of Noli's forces were a number of high rise apartment complexes. The streets and parking lots between them were natural choke points for the approaching army. A barrier of thick trees surrounded the sidhe village, a dense wall of foliage thirty feet thick at its narrowest. On the east, it was even thicker, a dense growth that would take considerable effort to bypass. The western side of the village opened up onto a number of single family homes, with yet another thick wall of briars and trees between them and the open fields on the external side of the base.

The human and sidhe forces were already assembling inside the gates, hundreds of fae and humans around each weak point. Roaming bands of lubberkin and brownies were making their way through the thick green walls to the west and east, the trees opening up for them to pass.

"We are sending out skirmishing units to harry them on the flanks," DeVoss said behind him. She was speaking into what looked like an acorn that was clearly directing the troops below. Glancing once more at the undead army to the north, Drew tried to think of a way they could win. The defenders were outnumbered by at least a dozen to one, not even accounting for the bone golems.

"I'm going to try to take out as many of those big bone golems as I can. If they get close to your walls, they might be able to break through. I'll focus on the ones on the outer edges, trying to funnel them in toward the center," Drew said even as his fingers began casting storms. The golems were spread out, though; he would probably only be able to get groups of two at best within the radius of his storm. He took some comfort in knowing that at least the storm would take out a few dozen skeletons as well.

"I don't see any particularly high priority targets other than those golems things," Daryl said beside him, and Drew glanced over at the scout, who had his eyes closed looking through the eyes of the loon. The scout was on Drew's left, Luke was on his right, while DeVoss and Noli stood behind him.

"Do we have an escape plan set up if they break through the barrier hedge?" Drew asked even as a holy storm descended on a set of three bone golems that were standing too close together. The white light of the storm's energies ripped through the ranks of the skeletons around them. Without waiting to see the damage his storm had caused, Drew moved on, not wanting to give the enemy time to realize how bad of an idea clumping up was.

"Nay, losing access to the growth accelerators would be a death sentence for mine people, and the seed cannot be moved until it hath recovered," Noli answered Drew. "Thy support people could retreat to the south, but there is no refuge for them if the grove falls, and removing the troops would spell our doom."

Drew's holy frost storm landed on another pair of the bone golems, their heavy forms disappearing into the thick clouds that appeared.

Glancing to the south, the open fields were obscured by the tall trees at the center of the sidhe camp. His mana sight showed that one of the nodes was directly under the central part of the village, while the second violet node was to the southeast, across the interstate. There would be no easy retreats here, so he glanced back to the north. The advancing army had spread out, large pockets of them hidden behind the skyscrapers.

"We'll just have to stop them, then," Drew said as holy fire storm landed on the street between two tall apartment buildings, killing the skeletons and obscuring the golems that were pushing through the gap there.

"We've got a large group trying to circle around to the east, going under the freeway," Daryl said next to him and Drew nodded his head, his eyes following the scout's pointing arm. A fourth storm, the holy frostfire variant, targeted the group of four golems that had bunched up to get through the tunnel. The attending skeletons were thrown around like rag dolls in the sudden gale, smashing into the concrete around them in a hail of white.

"I am worried that thou will run out of mana at the rate you are casting, Lord Michalak. Mayhap you should pace thyself?" Noli asked, her eyes wide at the sheer amount of mana that Drew was indiscriminately throwing around. Drew could feel the drain on his mental state, and stopped to cast invigorate on himself.

"I'll be fine," the red mage said. "If you can assist, I'll be able to help a fair amount with your mana fatigue." He turned his eyes to the first location that his storm had hit just as the storm ended. The wind dispersed and he could see two heavily corroded and much-diminished bone golems struggling to move. A moment of observation told him that they wouldn't be much of a threat anymore, and he allowed himself a half smile of satisfaction, turning to Daryl. "Let me know if you see any other good shots." The next storm was launched on the west flank, cutting off another street full of approaching undead.

Noli, seeing him continuing to cast his spells, began singing softly under her breath. Drew wasn't sure what she was doing, but tendrils of violet mana were streaming down through the tree underneath them and toward the forest wall on their northern edge. Assuming that the elf knew what she was doing, Drew looked for his next target. A half dozen storms cut off the enemy; each one took out dozens of the undead.

It was not enough. They marched forward in an unending surge of bodies.

A refreshing rain fell around them as Drew took the moment to survey the battlefield once again. The undead were still a block and a half away from the outer wall, and the treants had joined the fight. Thick knots of wood were launched out into the ranks of the undead, landing and exploding in a shrapnel of thorns which shredded the monsters around them, breaking off limbs or shattering skulls. More storms appeared to block their paths; Drew didn't regulate himself as his spells ripped through the ranks of the undead, each claiming dozens of skeletons and more of the bone golems.

Still the undead marched forward.

They had been slowed, and even had their numbers reduced by the thousands. That was just a drop in the bucket. For every skeleton that was killed, a dozen more marched forward. A seemingly unending sea of decay. A hundred meters from the gates, the shambling walk they had adopted turned into a lopsided run. Black light shone from their malicious eye sockets even as the area around the forest sprouted into billions of thick roots that tripped the advance sections of the attacking army.

The charge stalled for a moment, but more undead rushed across the bodies of their fallen comrades. More projectiles flew out from the forest, a painfully small number that did little to deter their enemies. More vines crawled through the spaces between bodies, snagging and tripping the undead and slowly clogging the pathways. Then they hit the outer edge of the screening forest, and were stopped hard, nowhere near the mass needed to push through the heavy undergrowth.

Bone golems made it to the wall, their larger forms ripping trees out by their roots and throwing them away. Treants stepped forward through the wooded growth, their long whip like appendages creating a loud whistling that ended in the loud crack of broken bones. Drew watched as a group of skeletons jumped on top of the many branches, clinging on and trapping the limbs, allowing them to be hacked to pieces. Drew was not sure how a tree screamed, but the sound carried over the wail of battle.

That scene was repeated up and down the line, the fae slowly getting pushed back by sheer numbers. The defenders' only saving grace was the mindlessness of their opponents. They rushed forward without thought and were mowed down in great numbers. Throughout the entire approach, Drew had launched more than two dozen storms, invigorate and renewing rain seeing constant use. Large gaps in the ranks of the undead were a testament to how effective they had been. It was louder than Drew expected; crashes, explosions, and shouts were met by eerie silence from the undead.

Daryl put a hand on his shoulder, and Drew glanced over to the scout. He was pointing down to a section of the forest wall that was right next to a large apartment building. The golems there had been hidden by the building's bulk and were ripping through the trees. A treant slowly retreated, sap-like blood dripping from numerous wounds as other fae and humans were gathering around the area in an attempt to drive the creatures off.

They were close enough for his medium range spells. A gravball struck the middle one, causing it to stutter and compress together before exploding, raining bone shrapnel on the two around it. A holy fireball and a holy frostfireball struck the other two a second later, the other two spells being forced to travel the distance between Drew and the golems. That particular offensive met a short end, but the loss of the treant meant that more skeletons and golems could approach with near impunity. A frost storm filled the area, the most powerful storm spell off cooldown at the moment.

Behind him, Drew could hear DeVoss calling for reinforcements to support the near breach below them. He returned his focus to the battlefield, his eyes scanning for golems that had gotten close. A sudden rush of danger from shoal sense caused him to drop to the floor. Mana rampart slowed the projectile down even as it impacted heavily against the defensive shield itself. An explosion threw him backward and the world went white.

Drew tried to sit up, but something kept him down. There was a horrible ringing sound in his ears, and a pressure on his chest. His eyes were closed. Why were his eyes closed? He tried to open them but it felt like his whole body was moving in slow motion. It took an intense amount of energy, but he managed to flicker his eyes open.

Green.

Above him was a mass of green. An indistinct part of him whispered that it was the leaves. Why were the leaves in front of him? Why was everything so slow? He tried to speak but he felt like he couldn't open his mouth. The ringing wouldn't stop. He tried to move his arm to stop the ringing, but it wouldn't budge. The pressure in his chest suddenly let up, a rush of yellow energy filling his body. Sounds began to trickle into his mind. Those were words, a woman was speaking, Katie? No, she was at the stadium. It must be Sarah.

"All I can… lucky it… his shoulder." There were more words than that, but his mind couldn't quite pick them up. Another voice responded to Sarah, but they were farther away, and harder to hear. There was less pain now, so he tried to sit up; he felt a hand on his shoulder pushing him down.

"Drew?" Sarah's voice cut through the fog surrounding his brain. She was leaning over him. "Stay still. Let me get one more heal off before you get up." It was easier to let it happen, so he laid back down. No, he was doing something. Something important.

A second rush of yellow energy filled him and his mind refocused. He sat up and looked around. They were on the ground, under a tree, but he could tell they were some distance from the forest wall. "How?" Drew's voice croaked, causing him to cough, and Sarah handed him a canteen filled with water that he swallowed with eagerness. "What happened?" Luke was standing beside him, while several other injured were being tended to by fae and human healers alike.

"Someone shot you. A high powered bullet that exploded. Your magic and armor protected you from most of the blast, but you fell out of the tree and hit your head on the way down. Noli caught you before you hit the ground, which saved your life," Sarah answered, looking him over to make sure he wasn't in any additional pain.

"How... army?" Drew managed to croak out and Sarah shook her head.

"We're holding, for now, although I don't know how much longer. We've had two breaches while you were out, but Noli managed to regrow the trees. She's getting close to her limit though..." Sarah trailed off, and Drew looked around. Everyone was tired; they were probably all nearing the limits of their mana fatigue. Which meant that soon the undeads' numbers would win the day for them.

"Where is Daryl?" Drew asked, looking around for the scout, but unsurprisingly not seeing him.

"He is with Noli, helping to coordinate the defense... why?" Luke asked with a frown.

"Because there is only one bastard I know of with a xatherite that can make bullets explode. And I feel like killing Clive," Drew said with a growl.

CHAPTER FORTY-ONE – RETRIBUTION

The memory of Clive's face burned in Drew's core. Deep within him, he felt aeon responding to the anger. It wasn't bursting forth like it had when he fought the trolls after Frank died; it wasn't cold and hot like before. It didn't spike with pain or slow down time. This time it was just the sense of right and wrong, of judgement pending. Without thinking, his feet pulled him closer to the sound of battle in the distance. To where he could mete out Retribution.

"Rekilling him, you mean?" Luke was hurrying to keep up with Drew. Sparing only a single narrow-eyed glance over at the seraph, his expression must have been enough to demand explanation. "It is likely Clive was turned into a graveknight."

"What exactly is a graveknight?" Drew asked, his voice a cold monotone.

"A sapient being, killed through a ritual and directly infused with a part of the lich's power. They keep some of the power they had in life, particularly those gained from xatherite," Luke answered and that caused Drew's steps to falter. Stopping, he turned to look at Luke, even as he rotated his arm trying to shake off the ache of the previous impact. In fact, several of the snake scales that had been sewn into the leather had cracked or were missing chunks that had clearly been broken off from the impact.

"What happens to the person?"

"The graveknight can remember everything, all of the memories are still in there… but Clive is already dead. Just like any of the rest of the undead, they are just puppets for the will of the lich."

Luke's answer caused Drew to nod his head, the sense of retribution inside of him growing more sure. More focused. For the first time, he was able to look around him. There was a constant stream of people bringing nearly unrecognizable wounded humans and fae to Sarah. The other healers and Sarah were categorizing and prioritizing as best they could, but to see some people left to die made Drew's mouth sour.

"We should take the humans and leave, the elf has no choice but to guard our retreat," Luke said from his side. "You know we cannot win this battle."

That caused Drew to pause again, he turned back and looked at Luke, locking eyes with the seraph. Something in that stare froze Luke mid-sentence.

"No. I will not run. I will not give in to fear. You say we cannot win? No, we cannot lose. I don't know what the humans are like where you're from, Luke. But here? We are not creatures you want to corner. These people have given too much, lost too much. Losing would mean all of that effort was in vain. We will not lose, and I will not let others die while I have the power to stop it. I know your opinion on the sidhe, and I don't care for it. I refuse to judge any person because of their heritage. Only their actions matter.

"Look around you. The sidhe have done more to protect these people than the Protectorate has. In my book, that makes them better than Ares, Isis, or Hades. They play games while innocents die. That's not who I am, that's not the kind of man I want to be." Drew was annoyed that he had to look up to meet the seraph's eyes, but he didn't look away. He could feel the presence of aeon slipping out of the shell that he had created for it, it filled the air with an undercurrent of power that made every part of him thrum.

"You are wrong. The Protectorate gave them you." Luke returned the look and then saluted. "Humanity will prevail." Drew nodded, not trusting himself to say anything else as he turned back toward the battle. To his surprise, Gary was standing behind him.

"Mr. Drew! You're awake, Lady Noli'aye…" Gary's voice trailed off as he tried to remember the elf's full name. "The elf queen needs your help." Drew gestured for him to lead and followed after the kid, who scampered through the lines of the defenders with practiced ease. They moved through units of humans and fae alike. All of them had clearly seen combat, bloodied and torn armor reflecting the tired expressions on their faces. A significant number of them had the faraway look on their faces Drew associated with green recruits just out of their first real battle. Drew wondered how they had lasted this long without having experienced one.

The walk caused the feeling in his core to solidify. He could feel it slowly condensing down into something more than it had been before. More than anything, it was the look of hopelessness on their faces. There was nothing they could do to stop what was coming and they knew it.

None of them noticed or even turned to look as Drew and Luke passed them on their way to the north gate where Noli was coordinating the defense. The elf was at the base of the tree they had used as an observation post and was clearly running low on energy. Her vibrant emerald eyes that had seemed to glow before looked dull, her skin and hair had lost their luster. But most telling of all was the band of sweat on her forehead, overshadowing a look of intense concentration on her face as she touched the tree next to her, strands of mana pulsing into the plant life around her.

The dryads that were guarding her allowed them to pass, although they shared mutual glares with Luke as they did so. Drew didn't even bother to greet them, just cast invigorate as he put a hand on her shoulder. The elf gave a visible sign of relief as the spell washed away her mana fatigue. She turned to Drew and gave him a heartrending smile of gratitude.

"Thy return is most welcome, Lord Michalik. I fear that all I can do is delay the inevitable."

"We are losing. I'll head back up and resume bombardment." Drew frowned, glancing up the tree to where he had been shot.

"These undead are controlled. The lich must have sent at least one of his graveknights to lead the assault. Eliminate the knight or knights, and our foe will lose purpose, driven forth not by cruel intent but returning instead to base instinct." Noli's voice was subdued.

"How are we supposed to find a graveknight in the horde? It will surely be protected and hidden. The undead are not prone to exposing their primary weakness." Luke almost scoffed at the idea.

"Thou speakest true, but I see no other hope to ending this siege. We have not the reserves for a protracted conflict. We have been careful not to provoke the lich to prevent just such a response." Noli's words had a bitter taste to them. Drew knew that it was likely his fault that the lich was attacking. They had trespassed on its territory, which triggered this attack.

"I can sense it." Drew turned to look at Gary after the kid made his announcement. He looked uncomfortable as the center of attention. "The graveknights? There are two of them. There is one in charge of the battle who feels kind of like a cold wind, and then there is the one that shot at Mr. Drew, and he feels like... burning slime. The cold one's attention is spread out, but the hot one's focuses in on any spell you cast." Gary gave a nervous smile at the rest.

"Alright." Drew scratched absently at his shoulder, his brain telling him that it should still hurt. Another part of him was spiraling into anger. Retribution was calling.

"I will hide thee within the tree." Drew shot Noli a questioning look and she added, "Twill drain my reserves some, but we need to eliminate those knights."

"Gary?" Drew asked and Noli inclined her head in assent. Drew chewed his lips as he considered the options. Which didn't take long; there weren't really any options. "Alright, let's do it. Luke, join the defenders." The seraph shot him a look of alarm. "The alternative is guarding Noli." The seraph's mouth pressed into a frown. He glanced once at Noli and then saluted Drew.

"May humanity prevail!" Luke nearly shouted before turning to walk toward one of the defensive groups.

"We will," Drew muttered under his breath, before turning to Noli. "Let's do this."

"I will be able to hide thy presence within the tree, but only inasmuch as thou dost not tell the knight where thou art. Thy spells are potent, but refrain from casting any that will draw a line to thee." Noli half smiled at him, and he grunted in annoyance. "Step close to the tree and I will convey thee up." Reminded of a song he listened to often as a child, he began to sing the Red and Black Song under his breath. Gary gave him a weird look, but Drew thought it was appropriate.

"Red, the blood of angry men," Drew chanted, trying to contain aeon within him, even as a vine, similar to the one they ascended with the first time, came down. Drew stepped into the loop and watched as Gary did the same. The teenager put his weapon away so that he could grasp the vine with both hands. When they were both ready, he nodded to Noli and the vine ascended the side of the tree.

"Black, the dark of ages past." He continued the song as they neared a stop about halfway up the tree. Looking around, Drew was confused until he saw that there was a hollow within the tree itself. Pulling himself along the surface of the massive tree, he stepped into the space and was pleasantly surprised. It wasn't large, only about a foot and a half wide, but it encircled almost the entire northern half of the tree, giving Drew plenty of room to slide in and for Gary to follow him.

Illumination in the cavity was courtesy of a layer of transparent brown sap that created a viewing panel, giving Drew a commanding view of the surrounding area. They were well below the platform that they had been on originally and couldn't even see over some of the surrounding buildings. Drew spared a glance over at Gary who was clearly not handling the small space very well.

"I'm fine, Mr. Drew. Just don't like small places." Gary answered Drew's glance.

He absently realized he was probably being reminded of the cages the trolls had kept him in back in the DIA building. In his current state, there wasn't much he could think of to help the kid. Clearing away the attacking undead as fast as possible would let Gary out. Seeing three bone golems approaching a section of the wall that was empty of treants, Drew prepared a holy firestorm, the five seconds it took to cast seeming like an eternity.

"I can sense the commander, but he's… far away. His attention isn't really on this part of the fight," Gary said even as the storm landed, obscuring the undead. "The sniper is looking for us. I can feel him…" Gary closed his eyes then pointed to an apartment complex. "There, he's in that one." That was close enough to be within the range of his gravity point spell and he scanned the building. They were below the level of the roof so he was unable to target that… Worst case, he could just launch a storm on top of it. There were enough broken windows that the knight could easily be hiding inside the building as well.

"Elevation?" Drew asked with a frown; it was impossible to see inside any of the windows.

Gary shook his head. "Because of your spell, he just scanned the tree quickly and then his intent shifted. I'm… not sure," Gary answered, which meant he could continue casting and not draw the knight's attention.

"Well, let's make him keep looking." Drew put action to his words, another storm already ripping apart the outside section of a breach. Gary's face paled as he gave up on controlling Drew.

"Just be careful, Mr. Drew. If he finds us before I find him—you almost died the first time."

The plea from the kid made Drew stutter his rotation of storms and survey the battle. The treants had already dismantled some of the bone golems, the storm landed among the undead soldiers, the living rushing in to fill the gap with their bodies. A few more storms continued raging and Drew noticed an ache behind his eyes. Drew was about to start back into his rotation starting with refreshing rain when he realized the flaw in the plan.

"Damn, I can't cast refreshing rain in here. The sniper will be able to see it." He had invigorate still, but with a nearly fifteen minute cooldown, he would have to limit how many storms he cast. If Gary hadn't stopped him, he might have just rotated through the skills. He took a deep breath and tried to calm the call for immediate retribution from aeon. After a moment, he cast refreshing rain on Noli and the defenders below them so that she could continue to patch up the holes in the barrier. This might be a about patience—

"I think he's on the floor right above us, east corner," Gary said a few moments later, cutting off Drew's attempt at meditative breathing. Drew narrowed his eyes looking at the building.

"The one above the cracked window?" Drew asked and Gary gave several quick nods. Inside the space, he could see the faint outline of a violet mana source surrounding a thick nexus filled with every color of the rainbow.

"Yes," Gary said, and Drew glanced at the lightsaber on Gary's belt.

"Cut the sap, I need direct line of effect," Drew growled, and he could feel aeon churning inside of him, the xatherite crying for retribution.

Gary looked at him; his face was scrunched up as he considered Drew's request and probably weighed it against Lady

Noli's. A grim smile broke onto the kid's face and he pulled out the blade to cut a small hole in the sap.

"Bigger," Drew commanded, and Gary gulped before doing so. When it was big enough for Drew to stick both hands through, he said, "That's enough."

Drew wasn't taking any chances. He stuck his hands through the hole, wincing as a drop of sap, still sizzling from the blade used to cut it, landed on the leather of his gloves. He could feel the heat even through the thick leather. Taking a deep breath, he focused on his spells. First was holy gravity point, followed by the regular version of the gravity spell, the two balls planted on to the left and right of the mana signature inside the building. Following in the wake of the two gravity points were holy fireball, holy frostfireball, frostfire ball and the regular fireball. For good measure, disrupting acid arrow, interrupting arrow, and the normal acid arrow followed after.

The side of the building sagged. The sheer power of Drew's spells dissolved a quarter of the skyrise. Drew watched in slow motion as the section above collapsed, cascading down and demolishing any undead that crowded around the base of the building. Thick clouds of billowing dust expanded, blocking sight of the building. That wasn't enough for Drew, though. Through mana sight, he could tell that the graveknight managed to survive somehow. It was only then that he realized he now had a view unobstructed by sap.

Blood trailed down the side of his head, a gash on his forehead cut by a shard of sap exploding into the chamber around him. With mana bulwark, most of the shrapnel had been pushed away from him. Gary had not been so lucky. The teen was clutching a thick shard of sap that was embedded in his stomach. Visible within the sap was a bullet tip. Dozens of smaller chunks of sap riddled his body, sticking out like a porcupine.

In an instant, he felt the energy from aeon flash through his body. He felt something crack.

A portion of his mind screamed in agony like none he had experienced before. It was ignored. The time for retribution had come, and it would not be stopped by something as simple as torment.

CHAPTER FORTY-TWO – FRACTURED

Now the world slowed to a halt. A portion of him screamed in agony, but it was partitioned off to the side, unable to affect him. Two pressing needs, to get Gary to a healer and to kill Clive, competed in his mind for a split second, and then he reached a hand out, grabbing Gary and activating dimension door. The two of them appeared at the bottom of the tree next to Noli.

"Save him," Drew commanded, handing the bleeding teen to a dryad that stepped forward to help him. His eyes turned to the building he had just partially demolished. The faint image of Clive's aura was gone now, blocked by either debris or distance. There was a solution to that.

Mana sight was upgraded with a thought. More pain joined that partitioned-off portion of his brain in its silent screaming. The world around him exploded into color. Violet energy flowed from Noli into the trees and fae defending the compound. Countless other threads of mana spread throughout the defenders, an interconnected web of magic that Drew didn't have the time to try to figure out. Instead he focused on the undead. Lines of mana, a violet and blue so dark that it looked almost black flowed from all of them back to the north.

Instinctively, Drew knew that this was the connection to the graveknight commander. He made a note of it, but that would come later. First, he had unfinished business. Dimension door was still on cooldown, but retribution would not be held up by something as simple as lack of mana. Drew could feel aeon pull, sucking the mana out of the world around him and filling up the crystalized node within him that was dimension door.

A step later, he was amid the rubble of the crumbling building. Ahead of him, behind a door, was the aura he knew was Clive. Another, much thicker, almost black line flowed from Clive to the lich. Without needing to see him with his normal sight, Drew activated force of retribution. He saw the orange and violet energy of the skill that linked gravitas and aeon settle around the graveknight. The black line immediately shrank to a fine thread. Clive's aura suppressed down to a single flickering candle.

Drawing Robbi's blade, Drew glided across the floor, gravitas activated to stop him from stepping on any part of the crumbling building. The ruby blade flickered in the semi-darkness of the high rise. Drew rounded the corner to see Clive prone on the ground in front of him, the rifle dropped a foot away from his powerless grip. The undead looked back at him with those black void eyes and Drew realized that there was indeed nothing left of Clive.

"This should not be possible." The voice that spoke from Clive was not the one Drew remembered, it spoke of dust and the grave. "How can you wield that power?" For a moment, Drew was confused by what power the undead meant. Could the undead know what force of retribution meant? Drew shook his head; that didn't matter.

Drew considered, for a moment, responding to the undead, to let it bait him into a back and forth discussion. In the end, he just didn't care. This was retribution, nothing more and nothing less. Robbi's blood blade flashed down, the ruby length of the sword cutting through whatever magical protections the lich had put into place that had allowed it to survive his spells. Into the skull, and out again, the black energy that surrounded what remained of the aura around Clive disappeared as he destroyed the head of the graveknight.

Still, there was more to do. Another dimension door, this one straight up, had him hovering over the top of the building. Gravity reasserted itself, slightly, and he landed on what remained of the top of the building. From here, he could see the lines of the undead approaching the sidhe base. Dark clouds hung over the sky above him. If the lich wanted a storm, Drew would give him a storm. Fingers flashed through the signs to summon a squall. He hadn't had a chance to cast the regular version in quite some time, the advanced spell eating up too much mana.

The extra three meters on the radius of the spell nearly doubled the total area of the spell, and that was what he needed right now. When he finished casting, he reached out to the mana around him, pulling it into him again like he had before. The action caused more pain to build up, but like the rest it was partitioned away from the part of him that was making decisions. He cast the squall again.

And again.

And again.

That wasn't all he was doing, though. A constant barrage of fireballs and gravity points issued from his position above the enemy, engulfing every bone golem on the field until there were none left. He could feel that the mana in the area around him was diminished, his efforts at pulling it into him having exhausted the ambient source. So he stepped forward, dimension door taking him to the next high rise, deeper into enemy territory and closer to the graveknight who commanded the army.

A swirling vortex of wind, lightning, and water whipped around the sidhe enclave, creating an impenetrable barrier of destruction. The spells didn't end after their thirty second timer had elapsed. Retribution fed them mana it had gathered from the area around Drew. Looking down, he saw the undead collapsing, the mana that animated their bodies getting pulled into his magic. The black lines of mana pulled up to him and pointed him north.

Another dimension door and he was on another high rise. Drew paused, waiting for the mana to be sucked out of the undead below him, to bring the black lines of mana close enough to him so that he could see where the graveknight was. Another dimension door, another rooftop. He was close enough, he could feel it, the malign mana recoiling from him, but retribution would not be denied, and it pulled again. Hundreds of undead collapsed in the street.

The part of him that was paying for this advance screamed louder, and he could feel the walls of the partition shake as the sheer level of pain threatened to overwhelm even the vastness of whatever power retribution held. Drew understood that time was limited now. Soon he would have to pay the price for this rampage. Another dimension door took him to the last of the high rises. A few of the buildings between him and the cemetery were three stories, but he was close enough.

The graveknight had come close, assured of his own victory. But it was running away now, back to the north and the safety of the lich. The black lines led directly to the knight, encased in a capsule of bone, and being rushed back to the north by several golems. Drew was too far for force of retribution, but another dimension door fixed that. The capsule dropped to the ground, the golems unable to hold it up anymore. A gravity point emerged above their heads, cutting off the top half off all four of the golems.

The blood blade led as Drew walked toward the capsule. When he got closer, a cone of binding ripped out, cracking the graveknight's shell as the bones gave way, snapping them in half and exposing the graveknight. She was young, no older than Gary. Her dirty blonde hair was stained black from caked on dried blood. It was clear that most of the blood had been the girl's. Slashes across her neck where the carotid artery was were the obvious source.

The eyes were the same void black energy that all the undead possessed. The look on her face was not scared, however, more accepting. Drew wondered how much of the girl's memories were retained after the death. But it didn't matter because as soon as the girl locked eyes with him, a thick envelope of mana descended on them both.

"What have you done?" The girl's voice sounded nothing like he expected, instead it reminded him of speeches he had heard from JFK, down to the slight Bostonian lilt. "Am I really so dangerous to you that you would risk this?" There must have been a look of confusion on Drew's face because the girl began to laugh. "You don't even know!"

"This is rich. Bested by a child playing with rules he doesn't even understand. I'll make you a deal: let my armies kill you. I will destroy your body and ensure none have access to the power you are using. That is the only way your people will survive this."

Word of his army was enough to remind Drew that there were more undead about. He swung the sword again, the blood red weapon cutting the skull in half. The dark magic surrounding the graveknight disappeared as he destroyed the node of magic in the head. With the graveknight dead, it was clear that the undead army had significantly reduced capacity. Those near him turned, clearly intent on killing Drew. Retribution pulsed and pulled the mana from their bodies, clearing the area around him in a wide swath.

Looking back to the south, Drew realized that he was stuck in the middle of enemy territory. The undead had ceased their relentless surge forward and were now milling around aimlessly. Dimension door took him back up to the top of the nearest high rise. Here, he surveyed the horde and realized that they were no longer a threat to the sidhe base. He could feel retribution's need diminishing, and with it the partition that was holding back all the pain that had built up from his actions.

Running out of time, he reached out and pulled the mana to him like before, resetting dimension door's cooldown once again. Another hop and he was in the middle of the high rises. He could feel the squalls he set up earlier ending, and he allowed them to. He went to reach out to the mana, in an effort to reset the cooldown again, but it felt like he was ramming into a wall.

Instead, he launched a fireball into the air. His legs felt weak, and he collapsed onto the ground, the partition falling apart as retribution faded completely from him. There was so much pain, and his body refused to acknowledge it for a moment. He struggled to stay awake, knowing how precarious his position was, how exposed he was up on the roof of the high rise.

"Drew?" His mind latched onto the voice. Was he just imagining it? The world was pain, and the voice, he felt arms encircle him and he managed to flutter his eyes open. Six brilliant wings surrounded him. The world around him fell away, and he realized that he was being held by Luke, the seraph having used his wings, which Drew had only seen once before and was in the process of flying them away from the rooftop. "Do not worry, Lord. I will keep you safe."

A part of Drew's mind realized that the seraph still wasn't using contractions. But that was all, as he allowed the pain to overwhelm him and he slipped into blissful darkness. One final thought came to the forefront of his mind; as retribution had activated, he had heard a crack. Something inside him had broken.

EPILOGUE

The foyer Ares waited in was black as the void, its floor surface uneven. It was a show of strength. After all, how many people could claim that the floor of their command deck was built on a dragon's scale? The first red mage had won it after driving the Black Wyrm away from his sector of space long before Ares was born. The Black Wyrm was not the oldest of the dragons, but it was known for its cunning, and it was high on the list of threats. The Hellenic red mage knew he was just distracting himself though.

It wasn't common for him to be called back, even in astral form, to Hlidskjalf. He knew why it was happening, although he wasn't sure exactly what the consequence of this meeting was. The fact that Hades stood beside him was small comfort. Despite being splits of the same person, the millennia since Roma had been settled meant that they had diverged considerably. In fact, of all his siblings, Hades was perhaps the most divergent. The fact that his domain was Death made him another abnormality.

Ares' own domain of War was more in line with the rest of their splitlings.

"How do you think he did it?" Hades whispered next to him as they walked the long hallway.

"I honestly have no idea. You talked to him, how do you think he did it?" Ares' words were exasperated. They had detected Hades' conversation with Drew-3, but he was convinced that was only because Hades had wanted them to know he could.

"You're the one that gave him an aeon." Hades tsked his lips. "I cannot believe the council risked an aeon on a world where we can't even recover it if he dies. It's not like he's at the academy."

"You saw his numbers. They're unprecedented. We couldn't risk him dying," Ares snapped back, then took a moment to collect himself. He couldn't allow Hades to get to him.

"I myself gave the command," Odin's voice thundered, and Ares realized he had been teleported to the very edge of the scale. Odin stood before the void, Hlidskjalf's command deck unlike any other, the podiums that his crew worked on hovered over the scale. Ares knew they were enclosed in a bubble of protective mana, but there was nothing to be seen except the expanse all around. Odin himself stood—Ares had never seen the man sitting—on either side, his faithful aides Huginn and Muninn stood in their raven black uniforms.

"The Terran experiment has been an unprecedented success. Ares, you are to be commended for your shepherding of him. His violation of the Law will need to be remedied. Ironic, given that he is raised to Retribution, but that is why I have called you both here together. We must protect our new brother. Tell me of the sidhe intrusion."

"The sidhe were willing to take unprecedented losses in order to ensure that a single seed ship was able to approach the Sol system on ballistics alone. We were unable to detect them until they passed the dimensional veil. The ship managed to land on Terra and has established a colony-grade grove not far from Subject-3's position. We assume they locked onto the mana signature of his settlement's shield to do so." Ares paused to see if Odin had any questions before continuing.

"Subject-3 established a secure foundation for his habitat before performing a reconnaissance mission to determine the intentions of the invaders. We believe he has entered some sort of alliance with the elf who was on the ship, whom we believe to be the youngest daughter of the Queen. Shortly after his arrival at their colony, they were attacked by a large host of undead. Subject-3 managed to force an attunement on his aeon and began using the full, awakened xatherite in order to enact Retribution on the assault force."

"Do we know which lich launched the attack?" Odin's voice was calm, although Ares could tell that Hades was surprised by the fact that Drew had managed to awaken his aeon as well. Small comforts.

"An analysis of its aura leads us to believe that it is the Forgotten Servant with certain accuracy." Hades breathed in loudly, Ares chalked up another tally, glad to know the Death god hadn't been aware that his ancient enemy was present.

"The Forgotten Servant on a newly Advented world? That is unprecedented." Odin stroked his beard as he considered turning to face the two for the first time.

"Hades, the veil around Terra is weak. Move into position. When our brother dispatches the lich, you will capture and destroy it."

"When? You have such faith in this Sub-Lieutenant?" Hades frowned slightly, it was clear that he wanted nothing more than to attack the Forgotten Servant himself.

"From what I have seen, I have no doubts. Ares, your fleet will be needed to protect our brother until he can atone for his sins. Unfortunately, his awakening has not gone unnoticed, and the Sphinx have demanded they be allowed to officiate. I have no doubt that his transgression will draw many to fight against you. Isis will be joining you to facilitate his atonement. In person. Prepare for a storm, brothers. I feel in my bones that if we emerge on the other side, we will stand supreme."

It was not lost on either of the Hellenic gods that Odin was not nearly as sure of the Protectorate surviving the storm as he was that Drew-3 would kill the lich.

AFTERWORD

We hope you enjoyed Temper! Since reviews are the lifeblood of indie publishing, we'd love it if you could leave a positive review on Amazon! Please use this link to go to the Red Mage: Temper Amazon product page to leave your review: geni.us/RedMage3.

As always, thank you for your support! You are the reason we're able to bring these stories to life.

ABOUT XANDER BOYCE

Xander is a USCG veteran and lifelong sci-fi/fantasy reader. Having begun creating worlds for his pen and paper roleplaying games more than a decade ago, he has always been fascinated by what can be done when people are pushed beyond normal boundaries. He was drawn to science fiction as a way to explore the human condition, and his debut book, *Advent*, is an extension of that desire.

Connect with Xander:
Facebook.com/AuthorXanderBoyce
Facebook.com/groups/AuthorXanderBoyce
Patreon.com/dmxanadu
Discord.gg/h243sg4

ABOUT MOUNTAINDALE PRESS

Dakota and Danielle Krout, a husband and wife team, strive to create as well as publish excellent fantasy and science fiction novels. Self-publishing *The Divine Dungeon: Dungeon Born* in 2016 transformed their careers from Dakota's military and programming background and Danielle's Ph.D. in pharmacology to President and CEO, respectively, of a small press. Their goal is to share their success with other authors and provide captivating fiction to readers with the purpose of solidifying Mountaindale Press as the place 'Where Fantasy Transforms Reality.'

Connect with Mountaindale Press:
MountaindalePress.com
Facebook.com/MountaindalePress
Twitter.com/_Mountaindale
Instagram.com/MountaindalePress

MOUNTAINDALE PRESS TITLES

GAMELIT AND LITRPG

The Completionist Chronicles Series
The Divine Dungeon Series
Full Murderhobo Series
Year of the Sword Series
By: DAKOTA KROUT

Arcana Unlocked Series
By: GREGORY BLACKBURN

A Touch of Power Series
By: JAY BOYCE

Farming Livia Series
Red Mage Series
By: XANDER BOYCE

Space Seasons Series
By: DAWN CHAPMAN

Ether Collapse Series
Ether Flows Series
By: RYAN DEBRUYN

Dr. Druid Series
By: MAXWELL FARMER

Bloodgames Series
By: CHRISTIAN J. GILLILAND

Threads of Fate Series
By: MICHAEL HEAD

Lion's Lineage Series
By: ROHAN HUBLIKAR AND DAKOTA KROUT

Wolfman Warlock Series
By: JAMES HUNTER AND DAKOTA KROUT

Axe Druid Series
High Table Hijinks Series
Mephisto's Magic Online Series
By: CHRISTOPHER JOHNS

Skeleton in Space Series
By: ANDRIES LOUWS

Chronicles of Ethan Series
By: JOHN L. MONK

Necrotic Apocalypse Series
Pixel Dust Series
By: DAVID PETRIE

Viceroy's Pride Series
By: CALE PLAMANN

Henchman Series
By: CARL STUBBLEFIELD

Artorian's Archives Series
By: DENNIS VANDERKERKEN AND DAKOTA KROUT

Made in United States
Troutdale, OR
04/23/2024

19400017R00189